"What the hell do you think you're doing?"

"Quit cursing at me. That's the second time you've done it."

"Fine, then." He shook her again, a little harder this time. "What in blazes do you think you are doing?"

"I was kissing him. That's what I do. I kiss men." Then, acting on instinct alone, she threw her arms around Cole Morgan and proved it.

At the touch of his mouth against hers, lightning struck. The earth quaked. The world as Chrissy knew it shifted on its axis. He tasted of spices and sunshine and fed that cold, empty spot in her soul. The warmth flashed through her, seeping into every hidden place within her. Making her ache with need. Frightening her.

Chrissy wrenched herself away.

For a long moment, they stared at one another, shock a living, breathing entity vibrating between them. *He must have shaken the good sense right out of my head.*

Cole muttered a particularly crude curse. "That's it. You've gone too far. I forbid you to set foot in this plaza again."

Chrissy shrieked as he scooped her up and threw her over his shoulder. She sputtered, "What in the world . . . ?"

The rogue actually swatted her behind, then bit off his words. "Shut your mouth, Bug."

Books by Geralyn Dawson

The Wedding Raffle
The Wedding Ransom
The Bad Luck Wedding Cake
The Kissing Stars
Simmer All Night

Published by POCKET BOOKS

GERALYN DAWSON

Simmer All Night

SONNET BOOKS

New York London Toronto Sydney Singapore

This book is a work of fiction. Names, characters, places and incidents are products of the author's imagination or are used ficti-
tiously. Any resemblance to actual events or locales or persons,
living or dead, is entirely coincidental.

An *Original* Publication of POCKET BOOKS

A Sonnet Book published by
POCKET BOOKS, a division of Simon & Schuster Inc.
1230 Avenue of the Americas, New York, NY 10020

ISBN: 0-671-03410-3

First Sonnet Books printing December 1999

10 9 8 7 6 5 4 3 2 1

SONNET BOOKS and colophon are trademarks of
Simon & Schuster Inc.

Front cover illustration by Ben Perini; tip-in illustration by
Gregg Gulbronson

Printed in the U.S.A.

For Steve

You're always there for me.
Even when we're stuck on a
roundabout in Derby.

Chapter

1

❦

San Antonio, Texas, 1883

I'm going to kill Christina Delaney.

While the bimonthly meeting of the Historical Preservation Society continued without his attention, Cole Morgan reread the note the Delaney family's butler had slipped him moments ago and tried to hide his outrage. The message was from Rand Jenkins, the third partner in the law firm of Morgan, Delaney, and Jenkins. It read:

Thought you and Jake would want to know. Tonight I went down to Military Plaza for supper and discovered a new chili stand serving up spice. Jake's little sister is San Antonio's newest Chili Queen. I may go back for seconds.

Christina a Chili Queen.

His stomach twisted. He could only imagine the scandal this would create. The rebellious daughter of San Antonio's first family had pulled her share of stunts in the past, but this time she had gone too far.

Her behavior wouldn't help Jake professionally. It would upset her mother something fierce.

"I truly am going to kill her."

"What was that, Morgan?" a local businessman asked. "You said you'll go?"

"Go?" He jerked his head up. To Military Plaza? Did they know about Christina already? "Go where?"

"To England, man."

"England? Me?" What the hell had he missed? Cole crushed the note in his fist and quickly shoved it into his pocket. "Why in the world would I want to go to England?"

Elizabeth Delaney sighed as she smoothed a straying strand of graying hair back into her coiffure. "Cole, you haven't been paying attention, have you?"

That quickly, he was thirteen again, mortified at being scolded by the woman he held above all others. "I'm sorry, Miss Elizabeth. I'm afraid I was distracted by a message I just received." *Another sin to lay at Christina's feet.*

Elizabeth's tender smile offered both forgiveness and encouragement. "Word has reached the Historical Society that one of the missing copies of our Declaration of Independence may well be in England. We suspect it was included in papers sent to the Republic of Texas's legation in London some forty-odd years ago. My father, the Earl of Thornbury, has heard a rumor that an Englishman whose family had ties with the Texas embassy in London may have it in his possession. We have unanimously chosen you as our representative to investigate this rumor and, we hope, track the document down and bring it home."

They what? Cole shot an incredulous look around

Elizabeth Delaney's parlor, where the cream of San Antonio society sat smiling at him. "Wouldn't that be a bit like sending a chuck wagon cookie to the ballet?"

"Don't be ridiculous, Cole." Elizabeth Delaney's elegant eyebrows dipped into a frown as she added, "You are every inch the gentleman—when you wish to be, anyway—and I am certain you will hold your own with any peer of the realm."

"She's right," piped up the distinguished owner of a local bank. "You're a home-grown aristocrat, Morgan. You ooze that Texan-born-and-bred pride, but you do it within acceptable bounds for Polite Society. It's a talent, I say. One that will serve you well on this quest."

Aristocrat? His father had been a gardener and his mother a laundry maid in England before emigrating to Texas, for God's sake. Before he could pose another protest, the butler nudged him in the back, reminding Cole of the note. *I need to talk to Jake.*

But first, he needed to get out of going to England.

He shook his head slowly, then motioned toward his best friend, Elizabeth Delaney's son and the new Chili Queen's brother. "Jake should go. The earl is his grandfather, after all, not mine."

"No." Jake folded his arms and leaned back in his seat, eyeing Cole keenly. "Got that new client. Remember? Trial is scheduled to begin in six weeks, but I intend to ask for a delay. This case could drag on for some time. I won't be going anywhere for the foreseeable future."

Cole scowled. He'd forgotten about the murder trial. Maybe it was kismet that he was reminded at this particular moment of the man accused of murdering a family member during a fit of rage. *So I won't kill Christina. I'll just make her wish I had.*

He threw a pleading look to Jake, hoping for help out of this situation. "Maybe this . . . quest . . . could wait until the trial is done? You know I just bought that ranchland west of town, and I'd hoped to spend my extra time during the next few months getting that operation up and running."

Elizabeth Delaney shook her head. "I think a delay is ill-advised. This is the first good lead we've had on any of the missing copies of the Declaration since we started looking two years ago. I strongly feel we dare not waste a moment investigating the matter further."

"You'll do fine, Cole," Jake said, a spark of mischief in his green eyes. "I agree with my mother on this one. You are the perfect choice."

Fine. Thanks for nothing, friend.

As payback, Cole crossed the room and offered a handshake to Jake. "Thanks for the support," he drawled, allowing just a touch of sarcasm to enter his voice as he transferred the crumpled note to the other man's hand. Then, with his back toward the august assembly in the parlor, he gazed out the window toward the rose garden his father had planted for Elizabeth Delaney. England. Hell. His father would turn over in his grave.

Samuel Morgan had cursed his native country for the last six years of his life, ever since a duke's son decided to see what it was like to "swive a breeder" and had raped Sam's pregnant wife. In the attack Rosemary Morgan lost both the child she carried and the promise of having any more. When the young lord was let off with little more than a reprimand, Sam took the question of punishment into his own hands and damn near killed the bastard before gathering his wife and son and running away to Texas.

"Cole?" Elizabeth asked.

England. It was the last place on earth Cole wanted to visit. But Elizabeth wanted him to go. The woman who'd rescued a shattered eight-year-old at the funeral of his parents and taken him to raise as one of her own seldom asked a favor of him. Since he'd gladly lay down his life for the lady, he couldn't refuse this request. "All right," he said with a sigh, turning back to her. "I'll do it."

At least he saw one bright side to the plan. In England, he'd be far away from Christina and her shenanigans.

Elizabeth offered him that certain smile she reserved for special occasions, the one that made Cole feel ten feet tall. "Excellent. I knew we could count on you." She turned to one of the other committee members and asked, "George, do you have the information I requested containing the particulars of this rumor so that Cole may make his plans?"

"I'm still waiting on one name, Elizabeth," the fellow answered. "I hope to have everything ready by the end of the week."

"Very well." To Cole, Elizabeth said, "I'll see you get it as soon as possible, all right?"

He nodded, suddenly looking forward to the trip in spite of himself. He hoped their information was right. It would feel damned good to find one of the missing parchments.

The Republic of Texas's Declaration of Independence was a historically significant document. Unfortunately, when the capitol burned two years earlier, the lone copy the State of Texas had possessed had gone up in smoke. That's when the Historical Preservation Society of San Antonio had decided to instigate a search for the remaining four copies that had disappeared after the Constitutional Convention in 1836. Cole believed the quest a worthy one, and he'd be honored to assist in bringing the document home, though he'd be doing it for Elizabeth as much as for history's sake.

At that point, a choked-off exclamation told Cole his friend had finally read the note. Cole watched as Jake's complexion went red, then white, then red again. Obviously, he liked his sister's new avocation about as much as Cole did.

Watching Jake Delaney's temper build took the fire out of Cole's own anger. She was Jake's sister, after all, not his, despite the fact they'd been raised in each other's pockets. Let Jake take care of the termagant. He'd been happy enough to abandon Cole to an unscheduled sea voyage.

As the meeting's discussion turned to a question of what should be done about the deteriorating condition of the Alamo, Jake rose from his seat and slipped from the parlor and out of the house. Cole ducked out behind him.

This confrontation was one he damn well wanted to witness.

"I can't believe her!" Jake exclaimed when Cole caught up with him halfway along the stone path to the carriage house. "What was she thinking of? How could she do this? She's a Delaney. Delaneys have a reputation to uphold."

"Maybe you need to clarify *what kind* of reputation," Cole suggested.

Jake made a growling noise low in his throat.

All of a sudden, Cole wanted to laugh. With blood-brother Jake taking responsibility for his sister, the burden was off his own shoulders, and he could see past his immediate anger. How typical for Christina to pull a stunt like this. She'd been up to one sort of prank or another all her life. They should have known the last few months of relative peace wouldn't last.

"Look, Jake," Cole said, hoping to ease the tension a bit before they reached the square. If Jake lost control, he'd turn a scandal into a Scandal. "It could be worse. She didn't steal a horse or rob a train. She didn't run off with a patent medicine salesman."

The first two looked to have soothed Jake a bit. The third obviously got his goat. He knifed a glare at Cole. "We don't know that. You know who's in town, hawking his wares on the plaza? Dr. J. L. Lighthall, otherwise known as the Diamond King."

"The Diamond King," Cole repeated. "Isn't he the one who pulls teeth?"

"With lightning dexterity. Women are obsessed with the talent in his hands. He's a handsome scalawag and flashy dresser, and he gives a nightly speech from a gilded chariot that resembles a circus wagon while his minions walk through the crowd selling Lighthall's so-called medicine."

And Chrissy had been spending her evenings listening to this charlatan's drivel? Cole heaved a disgusted sigh. Looked like Christina Elizabeth Delaney had managed to do something exceptionally stupid this time. Considering her vast experience with idiotic acts, surpassing previous efforts took some doing.

The girl had been a pest all her life. She used to drive him and Jake crazy when they were children, trailing at the older boys' heels from the day she learned to walk. By the time she'd turned six, they'd dubbed her "Bug."

Somewhere between the age of nine and twelve her adulation for her brother and his friend had evolved into competition toward them. That's when the more serious trouble started. Dressed as a boy, she once entered a horse race and ran against them both. Beat them, too, dammit. He and Jake had had a hard time living that one down. Then there was the time she played that outhouse prank on the headmaster of Royal Oaks Boys' School and set Cole and her brother up to take the blame. Such incidents went on for months until the night she followed them to the Gentleman's Club and got an eyewitness education of what the world's oldest profession was all about.

One good thing came out of that night, however. The Delaneys sent Christina back east to finishing school, and they'd all enjoyed three years of relative peace prior to her return.

Those Yankees had finished Christina, all right, Cole thought darkly. A tomboy had traveled north. A certified flirt made the trip back south. Over the course of the past five years since coming home to San Antonio, she'd broken seven marriage engagements, innumerable hearts, and now, by the looks of things, the backbone of her brother's patience.

Cole didn't ask whether Jake wanted his help. Instead he climbed into the shotgun seat of the coal-box buggy and waited for his friend to drive them to fetch Chrissy.

After a good five minutes of brooding silence while he drove toward the plaza, Jake started talking. "I can't believe her. Ever since Pa died, she's acted wild as a turpentined cat. Why does she have to be so damned different from other girls? Did my family make it happen? Did the Yankees do it to her? What do you think, Cole?"

What Cole thought was that he should choose his words carefully. Instead, as usual, he was blunt. "She's wild because you've let her get away with it. The girl's played you like a hoedown fiddle since the day we buried your father. You should have taken her in hand years ago, Jake."

"I know," he acknowledged with a sigh. "I just felt so damned guilty."

"You shouldn't. Your father sent her off to school, not you. She shouldn't have followed us to the whore-house."

"You know how close she and Father were. She missed sharing the last three years of his life because of me. I told on her."

"No." Cole resisted the urge to slap some sense into his friend and instead replied in a patient tone. "No, she missed sharing the last years of your father's life due to her own actions. You are not responsible, Jake. She is. Don't forget it."

He shrugged, but sat a little taller in his seat. They rode in silence another few minutes until they passed one of the local Catholic churches. Cole's grin was wry as he cocked his head toward the front doors. "I still say it could be worse. She could be at Frank Simpson's wedding causing a scene."

"Oh, God." Jake shut his eyes and shuddered at the thought.

One of Chrissy's old fiancés was getting married tonight. Cole wouldn't put it past her to waltz into the church and tell ol' Frank she'd changed her mind and wanted him after all. The fool would take her back, Cole knew, even at the altar in front of the priest.

Because Christina Elizabeth Delaney was beautiful. Punch-in-the-gut gorgeous. Cole wasn't exactly certain when the gangly, gawky girl had been transformed into a well-rounded woman with thick, fiery hair, warm malachite eyes trimmed in long, curling lashes, and full, pouty lips that begged a man's kiss. All he knew was that one day he looked up and there she was, breathtaking and alluring.

It had been a damned disconcerting moment for Cole.

Thank God his knowledge of her true nature kept him thinking straight. He'd realized long ago that a good disposition in a woman was much more important to a man's happiness than physical beauty. Ironically, Christina's own mother was responsible for the lesson. To Cole's mind, Elizabeth Delaney was as near to perfection as a woman could be. She was charming, witty, gracious and graceful. Her manners were impeccable, her social skills unsurpassed. She was a Lady with a capital L and Cole had honored and respected her all his life. He hoped when he was ready to marry he could find a woman much like Elizabeth Delaney.

He observed aloud, "Isn't it curious how different your sister is from your mother? One would think two females in the same family would be a good deal more alike."

Jake snorted. "They're as alike as night and day. Of course, Mother was reared in England, so that probably accounts for some of the difference. Remember those stories Pa used to tell about my grandfather? 'Strict disciplinarian' doesn't begin to describe it." After a moment's thought, he added, "You know, I've never looked at it this way before. It truly is amazing to think that Mother and Chrissy belong to the same family. I mean, can you even begin to picture my mother joining the Chili Queens?"

"About as well as I can picture your Christina sitting down to supper with the Queen of England." After a moment's pause, he added, "That word makes me shudder."

"Queen?"

"No. The other one."

"England." Jake considered it a moment, then shrugged. "It'll be fine, Cole. You'll track down our missing Declaration. I have faith in you." Then Jake's mouth settled into a glum smile and he added, "Hell, I think you have the better end of the stick. You get to travel to England and maybe see their queen. I have to stay here and deal with ours."

Cole nodded. Christina Elizabeth Delaney, Chili Queen of San Antonio, Texas. "It's enough to turn a man off beans, isn't it?"

Christina Delaney laughed as she whirled across the plaza to the tune of the Mexican street band.

Wearing a white peasant blouse and a flowing scarlet skirt, she flashed a smile at the handsome vaquero who was her partner and lifted her hands above her head to clap in time to the beat. She loved to dance. She loved to lose herself in music, to feel the rhythm of the song deep within her soul. When she danced, she felt free to be herself.

Chrissy especially loved that feeling.

The yen for freedom had been a part of her since childhood, and she suspected it had its roots in the innumerable times she had watched her brother and Cole go off on an adventure while she was made to stay behind in deference to her gender. For a long, long time she had hated being a girl. She'd tried to deny her femininity, to overcome the liability of being female. Then, in a series of experiences that began with a broken heart and ended with her first severed engagement, she learned the power of being a woman.

After that, Chrissy embraced her womanhood with enthusiasm.

As the song ended, she hugged her dance partner, accepted his kiss on the cheek, then took up with another man for the next dance as the music started anew. She knew she acted recklessly, knew she'd launch San Antonio society tongues wagging with the scandal, but she truly didn't care. The last battle with her mother had driven her to it.

For months she'd tried to conform to Elizabeth's wishes. She'd dressed respectably, acted proper, and tried to get along. She'd even joined the Garden Club despite the fact the flowers they surrounded themselves with invariably made her sneeze. She had felt trapped like a frisky filly in a small corral, but she'd given it her best effort.

Did her mother notice? Hardly. Did she praise Chrissy's efforts? Seldom. Did she ever tell her she loved her? Never. Not ever. Not once in Chrissy's recollection.

However, Elizabeth Delaney sure managed to notice and express her disapproval when Chrissy did something so objectionable as to attend the Garden Club meeting with her hair down. You'd have thought it was the crime of the century, and Chrissy had reached the end of her rope. She quit trying to be what she was not. She might have been born to Society, but she fit in better with those down here in the plaza.

Plaza de Las Armas, or Military Plaza, was an open-air bazaar for hucksters, nighthawks, and peddlers at whose stands might be purchased everything from a pair of spectacles to a serape. But the features which made Military Plaza different from other city squares in the South were the open-air restaurants serving chili con carne and other pungent Mexican dishes to customers seated on small benches around cloth-draped tables. Lanterns and smoldering mesquite fires provided the light. Raven-haired señoritas waited tables and sang out to the cooks: "*Un medio tamales y chili gravey, un plata frijoles, un enchilada y tassa cafe.*"

One stand, however, proved different from the rest. While most of the queens were of Spanish descent, Anglo-Saxon aggressiveness had asserted itself and, this very night, had earned for a certain red-haired, light-eyed woman the acknowledgment of queen of all queens. As announced by the official tabulator a short time ago, on account of her beauty, vivacity, aptitude of repartee, and of course, the superior quality of her chili, Miss Chrissy Delaney had been voted Queen of the Chili Queens of San Antonio, Texas.

Chrissy had started to cry. Acceptance. What a delicious dish.

Then, the band had struck up the music, vaqueros tossed down their sombreros, and Chrissy began to dance. Forty-five minutes later she was still dancing, barefoot now, her eyes alight, her face flushed, her smile as wide as the West Texas plain. She swished her skirt, showed a little ankle, threw a few kisses.

Then she glanced up to see her brother and that starched-shirt, disapproving, hypocritical sidekick of his, Cole I'm-perfect-and-you're-not Morgan.

Chrissy stumbled a step as the night's magic evaporated and frustration took its place. She wanted to scream. She'd known they'd learn of her chili stand eventually. In fact, she'd planned on it.

But she hadn't planned on it being tonight. Her strategy involved sitting down with facts and figures in hand to help her present an unassailable argument why she should be allowed to continue the chili stand. The boys showing up in the midst of a bare-footed hat dance wasn't on her agenda anywhere.

Just my luck. Why did it have to be tonight? Couldn't she have had just this one evening of fun and freedom?

"Apparently not."

"What did you say, sweetheart?" asked the monte dealer with whom she was dancing.

Ignoring the card sharp, she glanced back toward her brother. He had that avenging angel look about him again. The words she'd heard all her life from him and from her parents echoed through her mind. *You're a Delaney, Christina, and Delaneys have a reputation to uphold.*

She turned back to her dance partner, smiled, and said, "I must think of my reputation." Then she grabbed him by the flashy satin lapels, yanked him toward her, and planted a kiss right on his lips.

The sound she heard behind her could have been a volcano blowing its top, but since San Antonio didn't have any volcanoes, she thought it might be her brother. Or maybe Cole.

She ended the scandalous public kiss with a flourish and flashed a saucy smile around the catcalling crowd. Then, adopting a regal mien in keeping with her newly crowned status, she glided over to her chili stand and took up her scepter, otherwise known as a ladle, and prepared to meet the enemy.

She kissed that rogue. In public.

Cole was shocked. Jake was obviously in a similar state because when they reached the chili stand, he simply stood there, his mouth working like a fish out of water. Cole had to take control.

Any tolerance he'd had concerning this situation had evaporated the moment Christina locked her lips on the gambler. He wanted to yell, but thought it best to avoid adding fuel to the gossip fire so he clipped out his words in a low, threatening tone. "What the hell do you think you are doing?"

"Serving up chili con carne, of course," Chrissy replied, accompanying her words with a casual wave of her hand. The one holding the ladle.

A dark, orange-red chili stain blossomed on Cole's favorite white shirt. He rolled his tongue around his mouth to keep from saying something ugly and calmly removed his handkerchief from his jacket pocket, then wiped the spot.

Chrissy picked up a plate, lifted her chin, and said, "Chili, beans, with a tortilla on the side costs a dime. You can pay me later."

"I don't want your chili."

"Then don't stand in my line."

Jake found his voice. "Chrissy, you are supposed to be at the San Antonio Young Ladies' Sewing Circle. This is . . . this is . . . awful."

Anger snapped in her eyes as she looked at her brother. "How can you judge what you haven't tasted? My chili is the best on the plaza. My customers voted it so." She ladled a spoonful of the aromatic mixture onto a plate, added a fork and shoved it at Jake. "Here, see for yourself."

"We've seen all we need to see." Cole swept her with a raking gaze. She looked like a strumpet in her Mexican skirt and blouse, her hair loose and flowing and mussed from the dance. God, surely it was from only the dance. Surely she hadn't taken to serving up more than her chili in Military Plaza.

A sick feeling rolled through his gut at the thought.

Almost against his will, he took a second look, only this time he removed the brotherly blinders he made it his habit to wear and allowed his eyes to feast on the sight of her—the waterfall of burnished copper hair, sparkling green eyes, full red lips. His gaze skimmed her long, graceful neck and the hint of bare shoulder that teased from the edge of her blouse and beckoned a man's kiss. Full breasts, tiny waist, slim, flaring hips draped tonight in scarlet made a man ache to touch.

Cole's mouth went dry. His loins stirred. *Son-ofabitch!* He snapped the blinders back into place, but not before recognizing that every man in the plaza had undoubtedly made a run at her. "How could you do this to your mother?"

The small gasp betrayed her. He'd struck a blow.

He waited for her to strike back.

Cole saw her eye the plate in her hand, and he prepared to duck. But Miss Christina Elizabeth Delaney wouldn't do anything that predictable. No, this woman was much more subtle.

She smiled sweetly. "I don't know about you, but all this dancing has made me hungry. Y'all sit down and have some chili. I'll join you in a moment and we can talk."

"We don't need to talk," Jake interjected. "We need for you to leave the plaza without making a bigger scene than you already have. I'd like to tan your hide right about now, sister. What were you thinking of? You're a Delaney, for God's sake. Delaneys have—"

"A reputation to uphold, I know," she snapped, bristling with defensiveness. "All right. Let's compromise. Sit down with me and as we eat, I'll explain why I joined the Chili Queens rather than the Sewing Circle. I'll answer all your questions." She held out the plate expectantly until her brother took it, then she dished up a second one for Cole.

"Miss Chrissy?" a young man's voice asked. "Would

you like me to give them one of your special pickled peppers to go along with their meal?"

For the first time Cole noticed the pair of youngsters standing behind Christina. The girl looked to be around six; the boy two or three years older. Obviously sister and brother, they watched Cole and Jake closely, the girl's face glowing with interest, the boy's blue eyes narrowed in suspicion as he folded his arms and positioned himself at Chrissy's side.

Another conquest, Cole thought. Poor kid didn't know that particular female didn't need a man's protection. Hell, Chrissy Delaney used a whetstone to file her nails. She could hold her own against damned near anybody.

"Yes, Michael," Chrissy answered after a moment's thought.

"I'll get it," said the girl. She speared an apricot-colored pepper Cole couldn't identify with a fork and added it to his plate before repeating the process with Jake's. Chrissy carried the jar along with a plate of her own to a small, cloth-draped wooden table set to one side of her chili stand. As she took her seat, Jake reached across and yanked her blouse back up over her shoulder. "For God's sake. Can't you at least keep your clothes on?"

The boy and girl took up a position on either side of Chrissy as she gestured for the men to start eating. Warily, Cole tasted the chili. A delicious blend of spices danced across his tongue, and flavor exploded in his mouth. His brows winged up in surprise. "This is good. Really good. Who made it?"

The boy snorted with disgust. "Miss Chrissy made it, of course."

Cole set down his fork abruptly. "And just who are you?"

He straightened his spine, squared his shoulders, and lifted his chin proudly. "Michael Christian Frederick Hans Kleberg." He dipped his head in a brief bow. "This is my sister, Sophia Hannah Mary Gertrude Kleberg. We are Miss Chrissy's friends. And you are . . . ?"

"Mr. Morgan to you."

Young Michael wrinkled his nose while the girl beamed and said, "You can call me Sophie. I know who you are. Miss Chrissy talks to my mama about you. You're the lawyer Cole Morgan who only has two flaws."

Jake and Cole shared a quizzical glance. Chrissy looked down at her lap trying unsuccessfully to hide a smile.

"Everything you say," the girl continued.

"And everything you do," her brother finished. "You don't have to boss around Miss Chrissy anymore, Morgan. She can take care of herself."

Sophie Kleberg nodded. "She's a queen, now. The Queen of the Chili Queens. Mama put her name up for the vote and she won. This very night, she won."

Michael added, "She was proclaimed Queen of the Chili Queens because of *us*." He laid a hand on Chrissy's shoulder. "We will take care of Miss Chrissy."

His fork full of chili extended halfway to his mouth, Jake gawked in shocked surprise over this exchange. Cole pinned Christina with a look. "So, you are giving up the life of a cosseted society daughter to stand over a hot kettle and flirt with blackguards and rogues?"

She bristled. "Flirt?"

Jake glanced from Cole to his sister, then finally tasted the chili. "This *is* good. How did you learn to make it?"

"A blackguard taught me," Chrissy drawled in answer, her angry gaze never leaving Cole. "A rogue gave me the recipe for the pickled peppers. Try one. My chili is delicious, but my peppers are divine." She reached across the table, lifted one of the orange walnut-sized peppers by its stem and leaned forward, holding it out to Cole.

Her movement caused the front of her shirt to gape, and damn him for a blackguard himself, Cole took a peek.

Guiltily, he took a bite of the pepper.

At first he thought the fire in his body resulted from the glimpse of Christina Delaney's unrestrained bosom. Then he realized that the fire was pretty much limited to his mouth. His eyes started watering, his mouth stung like an invasion of stinging scorpions. He tried to talk, but he couldn't work his tongue. *Maybe it burned off.*

He grabbed for the water pitcher sitting on the table and used both hands to tilt it to his mouth where he gulped it, long swallow after long swallow.

The water only made the burning worse. He needed bread to soak up some of the sting, and he'd have yelled for some had his throat not swollen up. As it was, he choked and coughed. Jake started hitting him on the back in a misguided attempt to help.

Tears running down his cheeks, Cole shot a hot-pepper look at Christina. She batted her eyes innocently and said, "Oops, that wasn't one of my pickled peppers. It was a habeñero. I'm always getting those two mixed up."

She stood and carried her plate back to her chili stand. The kids followed, young Romeo shooting a triumphant look over his shoulder.

Cole watched the saucy sway of her scarlet-clad derriere and thought, *I truly am going to kill Christina Delaney.*

Before she kills me.

Chapter

2

Two days after swallowing Christina's pepper, Cole stood at the end of the drive leading up to Delaney house and tested the state of his tongue. Still fuzzy, dammit. He was beginning to worry it might never heal.

Christina had plenty to answer for. It was her fault he hadn't enjoyed what probably was a truly delicious sweet potato pie Miss Mary Ellen Perkins served for dessert last night at the end of their dinner date. His lack of sufficient praise had obviously hurt the woman's feelings and likely cost him a good meal or two in the future. Yes, Cole owed Christina, and somehow he'd see that she paid.

So why then was he so hesitant about attending this morning's get-together? When Elizabeth's request arrived at his boardinghouse rooms late last night he'd expected the note to say she'd finished gathering the information he needed to finalize plans for his trip. Cole had been wrong. Elizabeth had summoned him to a family meeting regarding Christina. Reading the message, Cole's stomach had taken a dive. In fact, the strength of his reaction caused him to seriously consider sending his excuses.

That would have been a first. One of the few constants in his life was that he always did whatever Elizabeth asked of him. But something about this morning's meeting unnerved him. The Delaneys were up to some shenanigans—the expression on Jake's face when Cole spoke to him at the office bright and early this morning clued him into that. Jake mumbled his words and wouldn't meet Cole's eyes, which was totally out of character. No, this soirée might well concern Christina, but the Delaneys had a reason for wanting him there, too.

For the first time Cole was truly glad for his upcoming trip to England. He planned to depart in less than a month. How much trouble could the Delaneys deal out in that short length of time?

Plenty.

Jake sighed heavily and started up the drive. Early summer sunshine beamed through the leaves and dappled his path. The fragrance of roses blooming in Elizabeth's garden smelled so sweet he was tempted to take a detour. But Jake must have been watching for him because he opened the front door and waved Cole forward. "Mother is waiting for you in the library. I'll go get my sister."

He took three steps down the hallway before Cole followed, saying, "Wait. Let me get her. I have something I need to say to her."

"How is your mouth?" Jake inquired, wincing. When Cole simply scowled an answer, he shrugged and added, "She's in the kitchen. Said something about tending her herb garden."

Cole found her sifting flour rather than dirt. Scenting yeast on the air, he deduced she was mixing up bread. "Hello, Christina."

At the sound of his voice her movements froze. Her tone dripped sarcasm as she said, "Morgan. Now my day is truly complete."

"I know just how you feel." He gestured toward the table. "What torture are you cooking up now? Will you add a little rattlesnake milk to your bread to give it a bite?"

She flashed a false smile and batted her lashes. "If I do, rest assured you will receive the first piece."

Cole shot his own insincere grin right back at her. "Lovely. I've been looking for a new bait to use in my mousetraps."

She dumped the measured flour into a bowl, then said, "Go away, Morgan. I find I'm not in the mood to banter this morning, after all."

Neither was Cole, come to think of it. "Do you know what this meeting is about?"

Her gaze grew guarded. "What meeting?"

"This family conclave. Your mother and brother are waiting for us in the library."

Shock ripped across her face. "Us? You'll be there?"

"Your mother sent for me."

"Why?"

He shrugged. "Maybe she thinks a scalded tongue from your habeñero pepper earned me a place at your scolding."

She turned her head and stared out the window toward the garden where a magnolia tree clung to its fading blossoms. Color stained her cheeks, and eyeing her profile, Cole's heart unexpectedly stuttered.

When had she grown into such a staggering beauty? When had she ever looked this pensive, this alone?

Both questions bothered him, so he forced the subject from his mind. "I think your brother and your mother have some scheme up their sleeves. You don't know what it is?"

"No." Sighing, she washed her hands, then removed her apron and looped it over a ladderback chair. "Neither of them have spoken more than a dozen words to me in the past two days. Jake won't look me in the eyes."

Cole frowned. "Me, either."

"I guess we might as well go on in and hear what they have to say." She brushed by him, trailing a lingering scent of onion as she went.

What in the world was that woman putting in her bread? *Might be mouse bait after all.*

Cole followed Chrissy down the hallway toward the library, the click of her heels against the tile floor sounding uncomfortably like the repetitive cock of a gun. Frowning, Cole wondered why he happened to draw that particular analogy.

Just outside the library door, she paused. He watched as she drew a deep breath, straightened her spine, and lifted her chin before walking inside. *The girl always did have pluck.*

Approaching the doorway himself, Cole heard Elizabeth Delaney say, "Christina, please sit down. Is Cole with you?"

"Right here, ma'am," he replied, entering the room.

"Good. Good. Very good." Elizabeth sat regal as a queen behind a broad walnut desk. Jake stood off to one side with his back toward the room as he stared out toward the carriage house, one hand absently playing with the gold tassels on the floral patterned drapery.

He glanced over one shoulder and the look in his eyes as he gazed toward his sister made Cole grimace. *Regret? Why was Jake feeling regret?*

"Please take a seat, Cole." Elizabeth Delaney nodded toward one of the deep leather chairs across the desk from her. "Jake tells me you two are scheduled to meet with a client at eleven, so I'd like to get on with this. We've much to discuss."

Seated in the chair beside him, Christina smoothed her skirt and managed to appear almost prim as she said, "Mother, you've called me here to discuss my chili stand, correct?"

Elizabeth nodded. "Among other things."

"In that case, I don't think we need to keep the boys from their business."

"Men, Chrissy," Jake grumbled. "Not boys."

Shaking her head, Elizabeth replied, "This is a family matter of some importance. Jake and Cole must be part of it."

Christina shot Cole a glare that all but shouted, *You're not family.*

"Cole is family," her mother declared, reading the look as Cole did. Jake nodded in agreement. "In fact, his input into this situation is vital."

"But—"

"Save your breath, Christina," Cole said, trying in his own way to smooth the waters. "I'd just as soon be somewhere else myself, but Miss Elizabeth asked me."

"That's it, then," she muttered just loud enough for

Cole to hear. "If my mother asked you to break both legs, you'd do it just because she asked."

Elizabeth said, "Don't mumble, child."

Christina gave her head a little shake. "Like you said, Mother, let's get on with this, shall we?" Shooting her brother a false smile, she added, "After all, it's not like I've never before been scolded in public."

Jake snorted and turned away from the window. "Our library isn't exactly public, gal. It's nothing like the plaza. You remember the plaza, don't you? The place where you danced like a strumpet and kissed a gambler right on the mouth? Now that's public."

Elizabeth Delaney put a hand to her head, looking tired. "Oh, hush. All of you, quit your bickering." She gestured toward her son. "Jake, I ask you to allow me to do the talking here. This will be difficult enough without your ill-advised comments."

Difficult? The word combined with Elizabeth Delaney's grave tone had Cole's mouth twisting in a frown. He was getting a bad feeling about this.

"Oh, daughter." The heavy sigh blew across the desk like a bitter breeze. Elizabeth's jade-colored eyes shimmered with unshed tears. "It truly breaks my heart that it has come to this. I see so much good in you. You are kind and generous and tender-hearted. You are truly the most compassionate person I know. But in other ways . . . well . . . reckless behavior, poor judgment, ill-considered choices." She ticked off the points on her fingers. "There was the horse race with Scott Jenkins, the gambling incident with Andrew Hobbs, the altercation you inspired between John Halford and Toby Osborne during Sunday services, the late-night fishing excursion with Todd Wright."

"Mother, if you think about it, you'll realize those incidents all happened months ago."

"Well, this . . . this . . . chili kiss in the public square is certainly current. As if that wasn't enough, you attempt to poison our dear Cole—"

"Poison!" Chrissy exclaimed. "I didn't—"

Jake interjected, "That pepper might as well have been poison. Cole was sick as a dog after eating that thing. I was with him. I saw it all. The man lost his supper."

Cole studied his fingernails and observed, "I think we can blame that on the chili, **not** the pepper."

Her glare seared him like her pepper. "The chili! Of all the nerve. Listen, if you're not man enough to handle a little hot pepper, why don't you—"

Elizabeth slapped a hand on the desktop. "Enough. Christina, this is another example of the unladylike behavior that convinced me to make my choice. Daughter, you need structure and discipline in your life."

Chrissy sat back in her chair and folded her arms, her expression mutinous.

Her mother continued, "I've tried. Heaven knows I've tried with you, but obviously I'm lacking in will where you are concerned. I thought long and hard about this, dear, and I see but one solution."

"This is an old conversation, Mother," Chrissy said quickly. "I won't be married off."

Cole's head jerked up in surprise and his gut went tight with tension. Surely Elizabeth didn't . . . certainly she would not . . . was *that* why she'd called him here? Suddenly Cole was damned glad he was already sitting down.

Over the years from time to time people had joked about the possibility of Cole marrying Christina. He'd never taken them seriously. He'd all but grown up with the girl; she was like a sister to him. She was. Honestly.

He shut his eyes, willing away the memories of recent instances when his brotherly blinders had slipped.

A husband for Christina. Cole stifled a shudder at the thought. The man who stood up with Christina Delaney would be tying himself to a tornado of trouble. Hell, with her as a wife, a husband would have to spend half his time chasing off the men who buzzed around her like bees.

Yes, but he'd get to spend the other half in her bed.

He jerked in shock at that thought and shot a guilty glance around the room. No one was paying him any attention, thank God. All eyes were focused on Christina.

Her hands gripped her chair's arms hard, the light in her eyes fierce. "You can't force me to marry. Don't forget your promise."

"No, I won't pressure you to wed," Elizabeth said with a sigh. "My father tried to do that to me, and I swore then I'd never make the same mistake with my children. I won't have you forced into elopement in order to marry the man you love like I was. It caused both me and my father a great deal of pain, and it's only been since your father died that I've felt free to attempt to mend the breach. My father admits he was mistaken in trying to force me to marry the Marquess of Rushton. He's a good man, your grandfather. A fair man. Strict, certainly, and a stickler for maintaining discipline. He provided the balance I needed while I was growing up. That's where your father and I failed you, Christina. We were too lax when it came to discipline."

"Lax?" She leaned forward. "Mother, you sent me away. You made me leave my *home*."

"But look what mischief on your part was required for us to finally act."

Chrissy pushed to her feet, her eyes fierce with anger. "I wasn't the only one up to mischief that night. I followed him," she pointed to her brother, "and him," she gestured toward Cole, "to a bordello. I get shipped off to boarding school, never to see my father again, and what do they get? A slap on the wrists. I'm telling you, Mother, this family exhibits a double standard when it comes to male and female that is downright shameful."

Cole grimaced as Jake protested, "Now, wait a minute."

Elizabeth motioned toward Chrissy's chair. "Please, Christina, resume your seat. I have no intention of revisiting that old argument. We've other, more important items to discuss." She drew a deep breath and said, "I mentioned your grandfather for a reason. The earl is just the person you need right now. I want you to visit him, Christina. I want you to make it an extended visit."

Cole pursed his lips and sucked in a breath. *Not marriage. Elizabeth doesn't want me to marry Christina.* He exhaled, waiting for relief to sweep through him. Instead, the strangest sort of hollow sensation crept over him.

Christina was going away.

He glanced over to gauge her reaction. What he saw caused his gut to twist. Devastation—wrenching and total.

Ah, hell, Christina.

She wilted down into her seat. In a thready voice, she asked, "England? You're sending me away again?"

"I think it's for the best," her mother gently replied. "You need a male influence in your life, and since you've shown no signs of falling in love, a wedding isn't the answer. I know better than to attempt to give your brother authority over you. The ideal solution is for you to spend some time at Hartsworth."

"Sending me away," Christina murmured, her complexion pale, and her gaze fixed and glassy. "Again."

The bewildered hurt in her voice tugged at Cole, made him want to reach out to her in comfort. He didn't disagree with Elizabeth's solution. Christina had brought this on herself. But he hated to see any one in pain, and no one in this room could deny Christina's reaction. She looked battered and beaten.

He threw a half-angry gaze toward Jake. *Do something,* he silently demanded. *Say something.*

Jake wrenched away from his place by the window and began to pace the room. "Don't think of it that way, Chrissy. We're not sending you away. Mother is offering you a wonderful opportunity. Think about it. Travel abroad. You'll get to see sights I've always dreamed of visiting. Do you know how many people would love to be in your shoes?"

Christina extended her feet toward Jake. "Here, you're more than welcome to them."

Elizabeth leaned forward. "You'll love Hartsworth,

Christina. It's a grand manor complete with every luxury imaginable. The gardens are like nothing you've ever seen. I remember house parties Father hosted where merriment filled Hartsworth from wing to wing. And I know how much you love to dance. I'm sure my father will host a ball in your honor during your visit. Oh darling, you'll have the chance to meet a multitude of suitable young gentlemen."

Cole snorted silently. Christina and a stiff-upper-lip Englishman? That would set back relations between the U.S. and Britain a hundred years.

"A gentleman." The corners of Christina's mouth fluttered up, but the smile didn't reach her eyes. She demonstrated that her fighting spirit had returned by straightening in her chair and saying, "Ah, now I see. You want me to marry a foreigner and never come home. From Chili Queen to countess, perhaps? It would be a demotion in my eyes, but I understand why you wouldn't see it that way."

"Dammit, Chrissy, that's not how it is and you know it," Jake said, raking his fingers through his hair.

"Jake, your language," chided Elizabeth.

Chrissy looked at Cole. "Did you know about this?"

"No," he honestly replied. If he had, he'd have shot the idea down. He'd put some thought into this since witnessing her Chili Queen triumph, and he thought he had the problem figured out. Marriage wasn't the answer for Christina. She needed something to exercise her mind. The girl was smart and filled with energy. That's what was getting her in trouble, not the lack of a masculine hand guiding her life. What Christina needed was a project to keep her busy. Something interesting and worthwhile, though. Not some silly little ladies' busy-work.

Then Cole saw the light. The Declaration of Inde-pendence. That's what Elizabeth was about. That's why he'd been made a part of this meeting. He was off the hook; he wouldn't have to make the trip to En-gland, after all. Elizabeth was sending Christina in his place.

Once again Cole waited for the relief to seep through him. Once again he waited in vain.

Apparently, Christina had figured out her mother's plans as well. Rueful amusement shadowed her smile as she spoke to him. "You didn't know either, hmm? Well then, you might want to brace yourself, Cole. I suspect their plot involves you." She looked at her mother. "Am I right?"

"It's not a plot," Elizabeth protested. "Come now, Christina. Be fair."

Cole spied the hesitation in her eyes, however, and he wondered if he'd missed a nuance of this plan. One glance at Jake's apologetic facade made his stomach drop. Whatever he'd missed, he had the feeling he wouldn't like it.

With that, Cole ran out of patience. "Do you need my assistance in some way, Elizabeth?"

She nodded. "It's quite tidy, actually. Your upcom-ing trip to England gave me the idea. In his latest let-ter, Father added two names to the list of those most likely to have the Declaration. Two of the three men own estates near my father's country seat. I've con-cluded it will be well worth your time to expand your visit beyond London."

His search? She still wanted him to go?

"Wait a minute. Why do I still need to make the trip? If Christina is going to England, let her search for the document."

Shock widened Elizabeth's eyes, then she frowned. "Oh, no. That wouldn't do at all."

"Why? She'd be darn good at it. She's almost a professional sneak as it is."

Elizabeth shook her head as Christina glared at him. "My daughter needs structure and guidance, not more practice at subterfuge. No, I'm asking you to personally escort Christina to Hartsworth. Not alone, of course. That wouldn't be at all proper. I've asked Mrs. Cody to accompany her as chaperone. She's such an Anglophile, you know, and she literally jumped at the offer." Then, pinning Cole with that smile he'd never been able to refuse, she added, "Knowing that my daughter is in your care will ease my mind tremendously."

Cole resisted the need to reach up and loosen his necktie. He'd rather escort a nest full of rattlers to England than this particular Chili Queen. He glanced at Christina and her scowl told him she liked the idea about as much as he did. Shifting his gaze toward Jake, he allowed himself to fire off a glare. A good friend would have warned him, at least.

"Will you do it, Cole?" Elizabeth continued.

If anyone other than Elizabeth had asked, he thought with a silent sigh. Hesitating only for a moment, he cleared his throat and gave in gracefully. "Yes, I'll do it."

Relief transformed Elizabeth Delaney's drawn features and she beamed. A thankful grin spread across Jake's face. And Christina, well, Christina looked . . . broken. Damned if he didn't want to go over and give her a hug. A brotherly hug, he assured himself. That's all.

Anything else would be just plain stupid.

Above the rooftops to the west, the setting sun painted deep crimson streaks across a cornflower-blue sky as evening descended on San Antonio. Chrissy had returned to Military Plaza and her chili stand for the supper rush. She knew her mother and brother wouldn't like it, but under the circumstances she honestly didn't care.

After the soirée in the library, she had indulged in a rare bout of self-pity and retreated to her bedroom where she'd cried her eyes dry before falling into an exhausted sleep that lasted most of the afternoon. Upon awakening, she'd felt calm enough and strong enough to think matters through. That's when she'd decided this trip to England might be for the best, after all.

She'd taken an emotional battering this day. No one on earth had the power to hurt her as much as her mother. Her brother came in a close second, though, and when the two of them teamed together and pulled Cole Morgan into the mix, well, they almost always left her feeling bloodied. It had happened too often in the past, and today's business . . . well . . . Chrissy decided she was done with the bleeding. She'd thought about building walls around her heart for some time now. As of this moment, she would start laying brick.

They're sending me away. Again. Throwing me away. Why can't they love me?

As a shudder rolled through her, Chrissy shut her

eyes and willed the self-pity away. She would build those walls. Time and distance from her family would aid in her task. Unlike the years spent away at school, this time she wouldn't grieve for home. This time she'd embrace the new direction her life was taking.

Maybe then all this heartache would go away.

"You should have married Jerry Wharton," Michael Kleberg suggested as he took a sniff of the heady aroma of his mother's baking rolls.

"What?" Chrissy asked, tugged from her reverie by the sound of her young friend's voice. With her chili mixed and simmering over the fire, she had walked the short block to the Kleberg's small house to pick up the cornbread Lana made for her each day.

"You should have married Jerry Wharton. Then your mother couldn't force you to go to England."

"She's not forcing me now." Chrissy stacked muffins into a napkin-draped basket. "I could stay here if I wanted. I am an adult, after all."

From behind her came a woman's voice riddled with amusement. "You have finally figured that out, hmm?"

Chrissy wrinkled her nose at Lana Kleberg, Michael's mother and her very best friend. Widowed a little over a year before, Lana had moved to San Antonio six months ago. She put her talents as a baker to work and was in the process of building a nice little business. Soon she hoped to open a store-front bakery, but for now she sold her wares out of her own tiny kitchen and on the plaza.

"Mama," cried Sophie, lighting up with a smile. "Is your headache gone? Do you feel better?"

"I do."

"I'm so glad," Sophie gave her mother a fierce hug. "I had an idea about your headaches, Mama. Do you think they might be caused by heat? It seems like you're sick more often when it's hot outside."

"No, dummy," said Michael. "It's not the heat. It's what she hears that does it. Mama has headaches when you start talking too much."

"Not so!"

"Is too!

Chrissy wondered if both children might have a point. She, too, had noticed that Lana's spells occurred more frequently on hot days. But she wasn't ready to place all the blame on the weather. Chrissy suspected some of the debilitating headaches were triggered by Lana's children's shenanigans, those of her son in particular. Michael seldom went a day without involving himself in one scrape or another. The ones Lana found out about caused her no little grief and resulted in her doubting her abilities as a mother.

Chrissy thought that was just stupid. Lana was a wonderful mother, loving and caring and sensitive to her children's needs. But apparently, Lana's late husband's mother so often accused Lana of being a terrible mother that at times, Lana believed the lie. The headaches tended to plague her when she was depressed or particularly tense, which is why Chrissy tried to shield her from some of the troubles the children got themselves into.

For instance, Lana still didn't know that Michael had spent two hours locked up in jail earlier this week for picking pockets in the Plaza de Las Armas. Chrissy had paid the boy's bond and made good on his thefts while making a pact with Michael not to tell Lana about the trouble if he didn't repeat the offense.

She had two reasons for holding back the news. First was her concern over Lana's health, but secondly, she did it for the children. Aside from their mother, Chrissy was the only person the Kleberg children knew who they could count on in times of trouble. She didn't want to forfeit their trust. While she didn't approve of Michael's lawlessness, she understood the reason behind it. Family pride made the Klebergs want to support themselves without the benefit of charity, and for the most part they managed.

Lana's pastries sold better than chili down in the plaza, but every now and then unanticipated expenses popped up. In his nine-year-old wisdom, Michael had decided to solve the problem by playing Robin Hood.

I only stole from the rich, Miss Chrissy, he had said to her when she sprung him from the cell. *And I gave it to the poor. Us.*

Chrissy felt somewhat responsible for the boy's actions. After all, she'd been the one to give him the book about the Merry Men of Sherwood Forest.

At that point Sophie interrupted Chrissy's reverie by approaching with a second tray of muffins. The palate-teasing aroma of hot cornbread wafted through the room as the little girl stated, "Michael, I've been thinking."

"Now there's a shock," muttered the boy.

Ignoring that, Sophie continued. "You're wrong. Miss Chrissy couldn't marry Mr. Wharton because she told us she didn't love him, remember?" Sophie moved the muffins from the tray to a basket. "Papa said a person should love who he marries."

Chrissy couldn't help but smile at the girl's earnest expression. Sophie spoke of her father at least a dozen times a day, a way of keeping him close, according to Lana. Both children dealt with their grief over their father's death differently, and Lana somehow managed to give them the support they needed. Chrissy greatly admired the woman's mothering skills. She wished her own mother could take a few lessons from her friend.

Michael answered his sister with a shrug. "Then she should have married George Willard. She loved him a little. I remember her saying she loved the way he kissed."

"Michael," Chrissy protested. "Please."

"What? What did I do now?"

Lana replied. "That was a private conversation, son. You shouldn't have eavesdropped."

"Y'all shouldn't have talked so loud. I am almost ten years old, you know. I'm going to listen about kissing."

"Kissing, ugh," Sophie said with a sniff.

Grinning, Chrissy reached down and tugged gently on the young girl's braid. Somewhere along the course of their friendship, the Klebergs had assumed the role of her romantic advisers. Chrissy honestly didn't mind the interference as it was done out of friendship and caring. Besides, their advice and observations often turned out to be right on the mark. Their comments about Jerry Wharton and George Willard were good examples. "Oh, kissing's not so bad, Sophie. George did have some power to his pucker."

Sophie rolled her eyes. "But you said kisses aren't enough to build a marriage on. Remember, Miss

Chrissy? You said that when you sent George packing."

"Don't you ever forget anything, Sophie?" Chrissy's sigh floated on the air like steam rising from the chili pot.

"Sometimes, but not often. Papa said my memory was extraordinary."

"It's a pain in the neck," Michael observed, folding his arms.

"Michael!" warned his mother.

"Well it is." He turned to Chrissy and said, "I bet you would have tried a little harder to fall in love if you had known about your mama's plan."

Sophie braced her hands on her hips and glared at her brother. "A person can't try to fall in love. It just happens. Papa said so."

Chrissy shook her head and smiled. "You and your father discussed the subject of love quite a bit, didn't you, sweets?"

"I was curious."

"She is always curious," Lana said with a sigh. "She wears out my ears sometimes."

Chrissy silently agreed. In some ways Sophie was six going on sixteen. Her intuition bordered on spooky. She often made observations worthy of someone three times her age, but she would do so while playing with a baby doll. In addition to their conversations about kissing, Chrissy and Lana had also spent a fair amount of time wondering where the child's precociousness came from.

Sophie made a beeline for her mother and threw her arms around her for a hug. "I wear you out but you love me anyway."

"I love you anyway."

When Lana beckoned her son to join them, Chrissy's heart swelled with pleasure and a touch of envy at the show of so much familial affection. The Delaneys certainly never wrapped themselves together in a huge hug.

Suddenly, the group turned on her. "Your turn, Miss Chrissy," said Sophie. "We love you, too, so you don't need a husband."

As the Kleberg children enveloped her, tears stung Chrissy's eyes. This was what had brought her to their home. At the end of this long, stressful day, she'd needed the balm of their friendship, the comfort of their love.

She carried that warm feeling in her heart with her as they toted Lana's baked goods to the plaza a short time later.

While the rest of her family set up their pastry stand next to Chrissy, Lana stirred the chili kettle and brought the conversation back around to Chrissy's troubles. "You know, Chrissy, I find myself wishing we'd never encouraged you to have your own chili stand. I feel like it's my fault that you're in trouble with your family. It's my fault they're sending you to England."

"Don't be ridiculous." Chrissy tossed a chunk of cornbread at Lana. "You are not to blame for anything, and I won't hear otherwise. I like what we've accomplished here. I'm proud of my Chili Queen crown and I wouldn't trade it for anything."

"Is that true?" a deep, masculine voice drawled.

Chrissy froze. *Just what I need to end a perfectly horrible day.* Glancing over her shoulder, she spied Cole

Morgan leaning against a nearby hitching post. Chrissy wanted to groan. Instead, she asked, "What are you doing here?"

Annoyance simmered in his ice-blue eyes. "That's exactly the question I intended to ask you."

"You asked it the other night. Now it's my turn."

Cole gave his broad shoulders a shrug. "Among other things, I thought I should inform you I've made our travel arrangements."

The sinking sensation in her stomach caught her by surprise. "That was quick."

"It was easy. Mrs. Cody apparently entertains herself by planning trips to Great Britain. She had sailing schedules and I telegraphed for tickets. We leave from Galveston three weeks from tomorrow."

"Three weeks," she repeated. Her knees went a little watery at the thought. Maybe she wasn't as ready to throw herself into the new life as she'd tried to tell herself.

Cole nodded. "We could have caught an earlier ship—one sails from New Orleans next week—but I've some loose ends at the office I need to tie up first. Besides, I realize you probably need some time to get used to the notion of making this visit."

"Visit?" She gave her head a toss, sending her hair flying over her shoulder. "This isn't a visit, Morgan. It's a move. I won't be returning to San Antonio."

"Don't say that, Miss Chrissy," Sophie protested, throwing her arms around Chrissy's legs in a hug. "You'll break my heart. Mama, tell her she can't move away."

Lana sighed and said, "Sophie, honey, come here."

At Cole's questioning look, Chrissy introduced

him to Lana. Her friend was gracious, but her children scowled at the man they obviously and correctly perceived as a threat.

"I don't believe you're going away for good," Michael said, folding his arms across his chest. "In fact, I've decided you'll find a wealthy husband over there and you'll sweet talk him into moving you home to Texas."

Chrissy delighted when a muscle twitch betrayed Cole's clenched jaw. If he didn't like that idea, then she loved it. "That's a good idea, Michael. I'll keep it in mind. You know I'll miss you all desperately."

Sophie sniffed. "I'll probably cry my eyes out every single day. You at least have to promise to come back on your wedding trip."

"That's a good idea," agreed Michael. "That way you'll be back in at least six months. It won't take any longer than that for an Englishman to fall in love with you."

"Six months?" Lana shook her head. "Won't take her three."

Michael spoke to Cole. "You'd best arrange for plenty of transportation for Miss Chrissy's things. She'll want to take most of her belongings with her."

"Unless her new husband wants to buy her all new things," Lana mused, tapping a contemplative finger against her lips. "But she'd better take everything with her just in case. In fact, Chrissy, you should really buy an entire new wardrobe in the latest styles so you will dazzle all those Englishmen. You don't want them to think that Texans are backward."

"You have a point," Chrissy said with a grin. "Perhaps I should make a trip up to Fort Worth and visit my favorite dressmaker, Jenny McBride."

Lana smiled. "That's a wonderful idea, Chrissy. She could make you a wedding dress. Aren't her gowns supposed to bring a bride good luck?"

With a winter's chill in his tone, Cole stated flatly, "You'll have room for two trunks and a satchel, Christina. Anything more you'll have to ship under separate arrangements."

"I'll take care of that for you," the boy volunteered. "Don't worry, Miss Chrissy. I'll get everything there in time for your wedding."

Frustration roughened Cole's voice. "She's visiting her grandfather, not getting married."

The Kleberg family shared a look, then shrugged. "You want some chili, Mr. Morgan?" Michael asked. "If not, would you mind moving along? Our hungry customers need a place to line up."

Cole glanced over his shoulder at the near empty square. Chrissy could tell by the set of his jaw that they'd pushed him about far enough. She quickly dished up two bowls of chili and placed them on a tray with a plate of cornbread muffins. "I haven't had supper yet. Will you join me, Cole? No peppers this time."

Grudgingly, he accepted and after excusing herself to the Klebergs, Chrissy led him to a small, out of the way table on the far side of the Plaza de Las Armas.

Taking his seat, Cole glanced back toward where the Kleberg family stood scowling in his direction. "The boy's a cocky little sonofagun, isn't he?"

Chrissy didn't bother with a reply. Having left the comforting and distracting presence of her friends, the energy drained from her body, and she wanted simply to sit down and cry. She'd battled this swing of emotions all day, the high fueled by anger and righteousness, the low a morass of depression, despair, and bone-deep weariness.

"Christina, you can't keep this up."

"Eat your supper, Morgan. Then go away."

"Not until you go home. I swear, woman, your head is harder than Texas red granite. I don't understand what drives you."

"You don't need to understand me. Understanding is not a requirement for the position of delivery boy."

He folded his arms. "Delivery boy?"

She shut her eyes and sighed heavily. "Listen. You and my brother and my mother have nothing to worry about. I've decided not to fight my mother's wishes. I'll go to England. You need not play nanny to me in the meantime."

"Then quit acting like a child!" He gestured across the square. "Close that chili stand and go home where you belong."

"Home?" Her brows winged up. "And where is that, precisely? It starts with a *D*, I remember. Devonshire . . . Dairyshire . . . something like that."

"It's Derbyshire, but I'm talking about Delaney House and you know it. You're only making matters worse by continuing this Chili Queen nonsense. This behavior of yours will destroy what's left of your reputation. Your mother is worried sick about you."

Chrissy's laugh was dry and humorless. "You can come up with something more believable than that."

He waited a beat and said, "I don't know which is more unattractive, self-pity or self-delusion. Be honest, Christina. At least with yourself. In your heart you know it's wrong to doubt your mother's love. It hurts her, and I won't stand for it."

Narrowing her eyes, Chrissy leaned toward him and spoke in a cold, calm voice. "Listen carefully, Cole Morgan. You have no say-so over me. Neither does my brother, nor after this morning, my mother. They washed their hands of me, and they can't have it both ways. They've sent me away for the last time. Delaney House is no longer my home. This town is no longer my home. I don't care what San Antonio society thinks of me, and that includes my family. If I want to be a scandal between now and the moment we board the train to the coast, I will. If I want to have a hot and steamy and very public love affair, I'll do that too. For a little while, until I settle down into my new life in England, I'm free. I'm independent."

"You're crazy!"

The man's tanned complexion had literally turned red. Laughter bubbled up inside Chrissy and she gave it free reign. "Yes, maybe I am. But you know what? Being crazy feels so darn . . . delicious."

As Cole's jaw dropped, another man's voice interrupted the conversation. "Ah, my beautiful sunflower. The minutes have crawled by like days since last we danced. Come to me, *querida*. The music awaits us." Ramon Montoya stood near the middle of the plaza, one arm outstretched.

The flare of anger in Cole's eyes goaded Chrissy into action. Flashing Ramon a winsome smile, she stood and made her way toward the vaquero. She melted into the man's arms, offering up a quick kiss as their feet glided into the music. *Annoying Cole Morgan is so much fun.*

Chrissy expected him to react, but she thought he'd stop short of anything physical. She thought wrong. She heard his growl first, then felt herself being jerked away from Ramon and spun around.

"Hey," protested the vaquero.

"Go away," threatened Cole, his gaze locked on hers.

"Chrissy?"

"It's all right, Ramon. He's family, sort of. Excuse us, please?"

Cole waited until the vaquero had walked away, then he took Chrissy by both shoulders and gave her a little shake. "What the hell do you think you're doing?"

"Quit cursing at me. That's the second time you've done it."

"Fine, then." He shook her again, a little harder this time. "What in blazes do you think you are doing?"

"I was kissing him. That's what I do. I kiss men." Then, acting on instinct alone, she threw her arms around Cole Morgan and proved it.

At the touch of his mouth against hers, lightning struck. The earth quaked. The world as Chrissy knew it shifted on its axis. He tasted of spices and sunshine and fed that cold, empty spot in her soul. The warmth flashed through her, seeping into every hidden place within her. Making her ache with need. Frightening her.

Chrissy wrenched herself away.

For a long moment, they stared at one another, shock a living, breathing entity vibrating between them. *He must have shaken the good sense right out of my head.*

He muttered a particularly crude curse. "That's it. You've gone too far. I forbid you to set foot in this plaza again."

Chrissy sputtered, then shrieked as he scooped her up and threw her over his shoulder. "What in the world . . . ?"

The rogue actually swatted her behind, then bit off his words. "Shut your mouth, Bug."

Bug. He'd called her by her old nickname, something he hadn't done in years. He must really be upset.

As he marched from the plaza she wiggled and kicked and tried to free herself, to no avail. "Put me down, Cole! Don't you dare—"

"I mean it. Shut your mouth or I swear I'll get mean."

"Mean?" She beat on his back. "You cart me off in public like a sack of flour and you say you'll *get* mean? Excuse me, but what's this? What are you going to do that's worse?"

She hit him again for good measure just as he opened his mouth and said, "I'll kiss you."

She froze, going stiff and still in his arms.

I'll kiss you, he'd said.

I wish you would, her heart answered.

Chrissy groaned. What in the world had gotten into her?

She'd never thought about kissing Cole Morgan. Well, almost never. Not for years anyway. She had thought about it when they were children because Cole and Jake used to threaten her with kisses all the time. Back then it had been a way for the boys to exert their will over Chrissy. Childish voices rang in her mind. *Go away, Bug, or we'll kiss you. If you don't climb up in the tree and get our ball down, Cole and I will kiss you. Leave us alone, Bug. Otherwise we'll kiss you.*

It had been a highly effective threat. And an idle one—they never once came near her—but one that worked. For a good many years, Chrissy would rather have eaten rolly-pollies than kissed her brother or his best friend. Nowadays she often gave Jake a peck on the cheek, but the thought of kissing Cole Morgan had never occurred to her.

Well, it sure occurred to you today.

Chrissy grimaced and she argued with herself. *I didn't mean it like a kiss. He goaded me into it. That wasn't really a kiss, it was a fight.*

Uh-huh. And fights like that are what lead a girl into trouble.

Well, I'm not going to get into any trouble. I won't have the chance. I'm going to live with my grandfather, the strict disciplinarian.

Yes, but you are traveling to England with Cole Morgan. He's handsome as sin, tall and dark and a little bit dangerous. Women have swooned over his broad shoulders and muscular form and that fallen angel's face for years. What makes you think you'll be immune?

He's like my brother. I don't think of him that way.

Then why did you kiss him like you did? Face it, Chrissy Delaney, you may be the Chili Queen, but after this kiss it's safe to say that man is the King of Trouble.

Chapter

3

Cole hardly noticed that the spitting hellcat over his shoulder had gone still. He was too busy trying to figure out what had happened back there.

Christina had kissed him. Wrapped her arms around him and laid on a real man-to-woman slobber swap.

And, damn him to the lowest region of hell, he'd gone and gotten a boner out of it.

Which was why he'd thrown her over his shoulder. The last thing he'd needed at that point was for her to notice. And if stirring up his body wasn't bad enough, the woman also scrambled his brain. *Shut your mouth or I swear I'll kiss you.*

Cole winced. Open mouth brought to mind her tongue, which made him think of deep kissing. Deep kissing and Christina Delaney, all in one sentence. Lord, save him.

He cleared his throat. "Kill. I meant kill. Just a slip of the tongue."

In self-defense, he then launched into a harangue

hot enough to scorch her chili, but he could tell she wasn't listening to him. That didn't matter. He wasn't listening either. Instead he was gathering up every last thought about that . . . that . . . exchange and locking it permanently away in what little bit of brain he had left.

Once they were beyond the plaza Cole set her on her feet. He took two deep calming breaths and tried to decide what to say to her.

Before he reached any conclusions, Christina raised her chin regally and said, "I'll be going to my mother's house now. Please find the Klebergs and ask them to tend my chili."

Something in her manner bothered him, caused him to give her a second glance, looking past the queenly facade she presented. She looked almost . . . heartbroken. Cole's stomach dipped. She wasn't all upset because of him and what had happened, surely. No, he knew damned well this sadness now and the recklessness earlier resulted from Elizabeth's decision to send her away. He was less positive about what to say to her about the trip. He fumbled for words. "Christina, I don't . . . I didn't . . . you can't—"

"Never mind. I'll speak with Lana myself. Excuse me, Cole, but it's been a very long day and I'm tired. I'm headed for Delaney House and sleep."

When she turned to leave, he fell into step beside her. "Me, too. Tired, I mean. Both of us. Guess we're not thinking straight, right? Let's get your chili taken care of, then I'll see you home. Do you have a buggy?"

"I walked."

For once she didn't argue with his plan. After a

quick exchange with the Klebergs, they walked the fair distance to Delaney House. Neither spoke until they approached the house, at which point he heard her murmur softly, "Home? Not anymore."

The bleakness in her eyes had Cole wanting to hit something. Instead, he went looking for Jake. He found him at the office studying papers at his desk. "I thought you left for the day," Jake observed.

"I did but now I'm back." Cole sauntered into his partner's office and slumped into a chair. "I want to talk to you."

Jake pushed away the papers and leaned back in his seat. "This is about my sister, isn't it?"

Cole's eyes widened. Who told him about the kiss?

No, that wasn't it. Jake hadn't met him with a right hook, so obviously he didn't know about that bit of foolishness.

Cole dragged a hand down his jaw line, feeling the bristle of an evening beard and searched for the right way to say what was on his mind. "Despite what you and your mother like to say, I'm not a Delaney so I try to keep my mouth shut about family matters as a rule. However . . ."

"This time you're involved."

Cole shot his friend a glare. "Too involved. This entire matter has gotten out of hand. Do you know what idiot idea is roaming around her brain?"

"At least a dozen possibilities pop to mind."

"She says this trip to England won't be just a visit. She intends to go husband hunting over there, to live there permanently."

Following a quick grimace, Jake shook his head. "I find that hard to believe. That marriage talk was all my mother's idea. Chrissy wouldn't agree to it for that reason alone."

Cole brushed his hand at the moth that kept tapping against the lamp. "She is serious, Jake. I saw it in her eyes. She means to make England her home."

Jake set down his pen, and leaning back in his chair, steepled his fingers in front of his blue brocade vest. A series of emotions flickered across his face: surprise, confusion, sorrow, acceptance. "Maybe it's for the best," he finally said, as much to himself as to Cole.

"What?" Cole sat up straight. "How can you say that?"

"We hurt her, my mother and I. We don't mean to. God knows that's the truth. But Chrissy . . . I don't know . . . she wants something . . . needs something . . . from her family that apparently we are incapable of providing. Anything we do try only seems to make it worse. This Chili Queen business? I've figured it out. It's blatant rebellion against our mother for the dressing-down she received for wearing her hair down somewhere she shouldn't have. That and pushing Chrissy to agree to act as co-hostess with her for the Harvest Ball."

"There." Cole slapped the desk. "You've proved my point. Christina dislikes such events. How many times have we heard her complain about her social duties? She may play the game well, but she doesn't enjoy it. If she chafes against the rules here in San Antonio, imagine how she'll feel in England. If her behavior creates scandals in Texas, imagine how it'll be over there. British society must have five rules to every one of ours. She'll be a fish out of water."

Jake waved away his concerns. "She'll do fine. One

thing about my sister, she knows how to make friends, make a place for herself, everywhere she goes. England will be no different. And maybe while she's busy doing that, she'll find the man who will give her the type of family she craves. Heaven knows she hasn't found him here, despite all the looking she's been doing."

"I can't believe I'm hearing this," Cole grumbled, shoving to his feet. "I can't believe you are throwing her away."

Jake stood, his jaw set, his eyes flashing angrily. "Watch your mouth, Morgan, and open up your ears. I love my sister. I want what's best for her, and I don't think she can find that here in San Antonio."

"All right, then. What's wrong with Austin? Aren't ninety miles enough? You have to have thousands?"

The questions hung suspended in the air until Jake blew them away with a heavy sigh and slumped back into his chair. "What I must have is for all this tension in my family to disappear. It's not good for Chrissy, and especially not for our mother. There is something I haven't told you, Cole. About Mother. She's been having spells. With her heart."

"Elizabeth? Ill?" Cole took his seat as anxiety clutched his gut. "But I never . . . she hasn't . . ."

Lines of worry plowed the skin of Jake's brow. In a strained voice, he said, "She hides it, or attempts to, anyway. I only know because I happened to be with her one day when she collapsed."

Cole muttered a epithet. "What does the doctor say?"

"You want the truth?"

Cole's gaze flicked up to meet his partner's grim stare and he nodded.

"He advised a holiday. For my sister. And that was before she took up with the Chili Queens."

The anger rumbled through Cole like a spring thunderstorm. God knows Christina had a lot of faults, but up till now he'd have placed selfishness way down the list. "So she just ignored Elizabeth's illness and continued to cause trouble?"

"Chrissy doesn't know Mother is ill." As Cole shot him an incredulous look Jake hastened to explain. "Mother forbade my telling her and besides, it makes sense to keep quiet. My sister would never leave San Antonio otherwise. You know it's true. But even if she swore to remain on her best behavior, we'd always be waiting for her to stumble. The atmosphere around Delaney House would drip with tension. No, Chrissy needs to go to England. It's better all the way around."

Cole thrummed his fingers against his thigh as he thought about it. Jake's argument made sense—up to a point. "So let her go for a holiday. She doesn't need to plan a permanent move."

Jake shrugged. "No, she doesn't. And as much trouble as she is, I admit I'll miss her something fierce. But since my father died I'm the head of this family, and as such I have to put my mother's needs first. I think a wedding between my sister and a British gentleman might go a long way toward helping my mother recover her health. You haven't heard her talk about it like I have, Cole. She goes on and on and on about this duke's son and that earl's boy. She gets downright giggly at the idea of Chrissy giving her a titled son-in-law."

"Why?" Cole asked, scowling as the news settled in his gut like bad homebrew. "I don't believe it. It makes no sense. For as long as I can remember your mother has denounced the notion of royalty and peerage. She's always talked about how lucky we are to live in America where what a man does counts for more than who his father was."

Jake nodded. "I know. My knuckles still hurt from the rapping she gave them when we were kids and she caught me bragging about how my father was the son of an earl while yours was only a gardener."

"Assistant gardener," Cole absently corrected, his thoughts drifting to the past. He'd grown up thinking a man's family mattered because his gardener father and laundry maid mother had taught him it did. Even after they died the lesson stayed with him. His below-stairs background had planted a chip firmly on his shoulder that he took with him when he moved into Delaney House. Over time, and with a lot of patience and persistence, Elizabeth Delaney convinced him to dislodge that chip. By the time he left Delaney House, an eighteen-year-old man ready to find his place in the world, she had made him believe he was just as good as her blue-blooded son. Was it all a lie?

Cole cleared his throat. "So explain to me why she now thinks Christina should marry a baron."

"No, not a baron. Mother wants at least a viscount for Chrissy." Jake's voice dropped as he added, "She says Chrissy will need the rank to help overcome the disadvantage of being a Texan."

"The hell you say." Cole's mouth dropped open in shock. "That doesn't sound a bit like the Elizabeth Delaney I know. 'Disadvantage of being a Texan.' She really said that?"

"Yep."

"Goddamn, Jake." Cole wrenched from the chair and began to prowl the room. "Something is very, very wrong here."

"That's what I've been trying to tell you." Jake raked his fingers through his hair. "I'm worried half to death about my mother. I've tried to talk with her about it, but she's not having any of that. Just between us, Cole, I wonder if this illness isn't worse than she lets on. Maybe she's afraid for her future, and she's looking to see her baby girl settled as comfortably as possible. The Delaneys have done all right financially, but it's nothing compared to what a man like my grandfather could give Chrissy. I wonder if that's why she has her heart set on a Brit for a son-in-law."

"Do you really think . . . ?" The question faded as Cole was unable to voice his fear aloud.

"I don't know. Maybe. It's why I didn't fight Mother too hard about sending Chrissy away. It's the real reason I agreed that you should go looking for the Declaration of Independence instead of me." He gestured toward the stack of papers on his desk. "This murder case will never go to trial. Our client has an unassailable alibi. I could make the trip, but I'm afraid to leave Mother. I know I can trust you to stand in my place and see to Chrissy's welfare."

Cole exhaled a slow breath as he tried to absorb these new revelations. Elizabeth ill and championing a British lord for a son-in-law. Jake keeping news of his mother's illness to himself.

Then one realization hit Cole like a fist, and he grabbed the back of his chair, leaned on it, and closed his eyes. Speaking softly, he said, "Your father died while Chrissy was away, Jake. Do you know what it would do to her if the same thing happened with your mother?"

In her bedroom at Delaney House, Chrissy abandoned her effort to escape her worries in a book. The story was good, but she couldn't concentrate. Her gaze kept drifting to the framed photograph of her parents that sat on her dressing table.

Banished again. The first time had broken her heart. Facing it again sickened her soul. No matter how hard she tried to build those walls around her emotions, they weren't in place yet. "I'll have to work on that," she murmured, setting down the book and crossing the room to pick up the picture. Tracing the swirls on the carved mahogany frame with a fingertip, she gazed into the past.

Her sentimentality worked against her, she knew. She'd always been one to assign great import to things and events having to do with her family. For instance, she'd been thirteen when her father had Delaney House built, and while she'd been excited to move into the new place, she'd mourned leaving the home where she'd been born. Her brother still teased her about her tears when her parents turned over the keys to the new owners.

Holidays were another opportunity for emotions to cause her trouble. She'd never forget the time her brother skipped Thanksgiving dinner to accompany his current sweetheart's family to the Lake Bliss Spa. Chrissy had salted her cornbread dressing with tears simply because Jake wasn't there to help carve the turkey.

None of the Delaneys understood her reactions;

none of them tried to understand. They dismissed her as being "overly sensitive" and went about their business. It seemed as if she'd spent much of her life apologizing for loving her family too much.

"Well, no more." These feelings were honest emotions and they were her emotions. They deserved at least a little respect. Didn't they?

Chrissy dropped the picture onto her bed. Maybe she had been too sensitive. Maybe she had been foolish. Her mother and brother—and before his death, her father—didn't attach such importance to ties and tradition.

No, that wasn't entirely true. They did place great store upon the family name and social standing. Why, Chrissy wondered, did the Delaney family always count for more in the scheme of things than the individual Delaney?

She pondered the question and had little success arriving at an answer. Eventually, worn by worry and indecision, she fell into sleep.

Hours passed before a sound at her window woke her. *Ping.* A pebble hit the glass. *Ping. Ping. Ping.* She rose from her bed and pushed the window open to hear a fiercely whispered, "Miss Chrissy?"

"Michael?" Moonlight lit Delaney House's back garden as Chrissy gazed down at the boy whose expression radiated fear. "Why are you here? What's the matter?"

"We need you. Please come. My grandparents arrived from New Braunfels. They somehow found out about my picking pockets, and now they're yelling at Mama and saying they're going to take us away from her. I don't know what to do."

"I'll be right down."

Chrissy threw on her clothes and hurried downstairs. Michael met her at the back door and together, they ran through San Antonio's darkened streets toward the Kleberg home. They arrived just as an older couple headed out the front door.

"You'll hear from our attorney tomorrow," said the white-haired man, his accent thick with Bavaria. "Perhaps the marshal, too. My grandchildren need immediate protection."

"You killed my son," added the woman in a scornful tone, her ample bosom heaving. "I'll not let you hurt his babies."

Slamming the door behind them, they conversed in German as they barreled down the front walk, all but knocking Chrissy down in their rush to leave. They didn't see Michael because he'd ducked behind a bush at the sight of them.

Hearing Lana's woeful weeping, Chrissy didn't bother to knock, but stepped right inside. Her heart broke to see her friend standing in the middle of the room, arms wrapped around herself, tears streaming down her face. Sophie stood in the bedroom doorway, her face a picture of fear. Chrissy flashed the girl a reassuring smile, then said, "Lana?"

She turned her head and Chrissy's breath caught. She'd grown accustomed to the expression of grief that sometimes flashed through Lana's eyes, but now . . . oh . . . they were haunting, filled with fear and desperation. "My babies," she said in a desolate tone, all color drained from her face. "My babies."

Then Lana collapsed.

"Mama!" Michael cried, joining Chrissy in the rush

to help the fallen woman. They knelt beside her and Chrissy eased Lana's head into her lap. "Michael, dampen a handkerchief for me, would you please?"

The boy moved fast to do her bidding, and as Chrissy gently wiped her friend's brow, she attempted to reassure them all. "Don't worry. Your mother will be all right. She just had a shock."

Moments later, Lana stirred. "My babies," she said. "I must help . . ."

"Shh . . ." Chrissy soothed. "They're fine. But right now they need to know you're all right."

"All right? Oh. Yes. Of course." Lana sat up and cocked her head as she was wont to do when she concentrated. "Michael? Sophie? Don't be afraid. There is nothing to worry about, except maybe the fact that I'm in sore need of a hug."

Chrissy watched the trio embrace and wondered how anyone could possibly accuse Lana of hurting her children. Why, this woman was the best mother Chrissy had ever known, and she did it without the help of a husband. *It's a crime. That's what it is. The Kleberg grandparents won't get away with it.*

Chrissy intended to make certain of it.

Twenty minutes later Lana had her children settled back into their beds. As she joined Chrissy in the kitchen, she put on a pot of tea and brought the cookie tin to the table. "Oh, Chrissy," she said, rubbing her temple. "At times like this I wish I had something stronger than chocolate in the house."

"Nothing is stronger than chocolate," Chrissy opined as she selected a sweet. "Tell me what happened, Lana. Tell me what those people did to you."

While the women drank their tea, Lana told a story

that had Chrissy so angry she was shaking in her stockings. Lana's husband's parents had never approved of her, which made sharing a home for ten years all the more difficult. That's how long it had taken her husband to save enough money to build them a home of their own. The Klebergs had resisted the move, and they blamed Lana for it.

"But Henry wanted our own house as much as I did, Chrissy. More, even. As long as we were living on the Kleberg dairy farm, his father would never let him be his own man. I know that. He wasn't doing it just for me. If that were true, well, I . . . I couldn't bear it."

Henry had died while using dynamite to help clear the rocky Hill Country site he'd chosen for their home. From the beginning, the Klebergs made it clear they wished their daughter-in-law had been the one to die in the accident. Lost in grief, Lana had shared their opinion. It wasn't until over two months later when she heard her little Sophie repeat her grandmother's lament that she realized what harm the Klebergs were doing to her children.

"I couldn't let them teach such hatred to my babies. They'd already lost their father; they shouldn't lose their mother, too."

"Of course not," Chrissy agreed.

As soon as physically possible, Lana gathered her children and left New Braunfels to settle in San Antonio, where she supported her family with her superior baking. "They were furious when we left," Lana said, sipping her tea. "They promised they would cause me trouble, and now it looks like they're going to keep their word."

Chrissy reached across the small table and took her friend's hand. "How?"

"Somehow the Klebergs found out about Michael's foray into theft. That's all it took for them to contact a lawyer and a judge." She paused and swallowed hard. "They say they're going to take my children away from me, Chrissy. They said I'm unfit to care for them." She sighed long and hard, then added, "Sometimes the headaches leave me incapacitated. Maybe they're right."

Chrissy used one of the pithy epithets she'd learned from her brother and Cole. "Don't be ridiculous. You're a wonderful mother and you're doing a fine job raising your children."

Lana laughed sadly. "So fine that soon I'll be measuring my son's jail cell for curtains."

Chrissy sat back in her chair. "Stop it. Michael is a good boy and you know it. He might be a little misguided at the moment, but he'll get over it. You'll teach him. I'll teach him."

"We won't have the chance," Lana said, tears filling her eyes once more. "They're going to take them away from me. They're wealthy, for one thing. They know I suffer headaches. They'll use them against me, use Michael's troubles. I can't win a fight against them."

Chrissy nibbled at her bottom lip. An idea had been floating through her mind since Lana had started her story and in that instant, Chrissy made up her mind. "You won't have to fight them, Lana."

"What do you mean?"

"I'm leaving town tomorrow, and I find myself in need of a companion. Tell me, Lana, how would you and your family like to go with me to England?"

*　　*　　*

Leaning in for a kiss, Cole gazed into the Widow Larsen's liquid brown eyes and mentally changed them to green. When he realized what he was doing, he scowled and pulled back.

"What is it, darling?" said the wanton widow, pouting prettily. "It is not like you to be so inattentive."

"My apologies, Louise. It's been a frustrating couple of weeks and I'm afraid I'm distracted."

They sat on a couch in her parlor, the scene of a number of romantic trysts between them over the course of the past six months. The encounters remained occasional and strictly physical, which suited them both. Older than Cole by almost a decade, the widow had proposed their arrangement herself, naming as her reasons her need for a man's attentions and her contentment with her current independent lifestyle. As the months passed, she even went out of her way to suggest young ladies about town whom Cole should consider courting when the notion of marriage held some appeal.

He did listen to her. Cole liked both the lady and the sex, and since he'd lost his taste for bordellos following that trouble with Christina, he found his liaison with the widow to be a handy thing. Ordinarily. Tonight it simply didn't feel right.

Wrinkling her dainty nose, Louise said, "Well. Frustration and distraction, hmm? I believe I shall take that as a personal challenge. I am, as you well know, quite talented at dealing with a man's frustrations."

"Why do you think I wanted to see you tonight?" he grumbled.

She laughed, then swooped in for a kiss. Cole responded, trying to lose himself in the moment, but the effort went for naught. The only emotion the delectable widow's kiss aroused in him this evening was indifference. In fact, were he less secure in his masculinity, Cole might have been worried.

Everything was Christina's fault, of course. That kiss he'd sworn to forget never quite left his thoughts. Plus, with only one week to go before their scheduled departure, the worries of traveling with the troublemaker invaded every aspect of his life. For one thing, he couldn't trust her. He couldn't count on her following his instructions, and he couldn't predict her behavior. To Cole's way of thinking, she'd given in much too easily to this plan of her mother's. He wouldn't be at all surprised if on the day of their departure she failed to show up.

"I'll be damned if I'll go after her," he mumbled.

Louise lifted her mouth from his neck and asked, "What?"

Chagrined, Cole paid her lips another visit, determined to get the job done. But despite his best intentions and the skill of Louise Larsen's tongue, his thoughts drifted off once again. He'd known Miss Christina Elizabeth Delaney nearly all her life, and he'd developed a sixth sense where she was concerned. That sense was telling him there was something suspicious about the trip she'd taken to visit a Fort Worth dressmaker. Neither Elizabeth nor Jake agreed with his opinion. They actually believed and were pleased that the minx wanted a new wardrobe to impress potential beaux. Cole didn't buy it for a minute.

"Oh, darling." Louise Larsen sighed. "You do take a woman's breath away. Let's adjourn to my bedroom, shall we?" Standing, she held out her hand toward him. Lamplight reflected off the diamonds in the ring she wore on her left hand, catching Cole's notice. Diamonds alone wouldn't do in a ring for Christina. She should have a fiery ruby or two in her wedding band.

What the hell am I doing thinking about Christina and wedding rings? Determined to find a distraction, he grasped Louise's hand and allowed her to tug him toward the bedroom.

A pounding on the front door stopped him in his tracks. "Morgan! Open up. Sorry to interrupt, but we've got trouble."

"That's Jake Delaney," Louise said with a petulant pout. "What in the world does he want?"

Bang. Bang. Bang. "Cole, you there? Please, I need to talk to you."

Cole shot Louise an apologetic look. She sighed, smiled, and made shooing motions with her hands. "Go on. You weren't up for this tonight anyway."

"I was getting there."

She laughed and leaned over to kiss him on the cheek. "I'd ask who she is, but I think I already know. Go find out from her brother what mischief she's up to this time." Then, framing his face in both hands, she kissed him hard on the mouth. "It's been a pleasure sharing my bed with you, Cole Morgan. I wish you nothing but happiness."

Bang. Bang. Bang. Cole ignored the noise at the door and scowled at his lover. "Now wait just one minute. What do you mean by—"

"Cole!"

"Go."

He glanced from her to the door then back to her again. "All right. But I'll be back."

"No, I don't believe you will," she said softly and a little sadly as he opened the door to a red-faced, wild-eyed Jake Delaney.

"This had better be good," Cole snapped as he lifted his hat from the hall tree and set it on his head.

"Oh, it's not good," Jake replied, sending an "I'm sorry" wave to Louise. "It's bad. Very, very bad."

Cole froze. "Elizabeth?"

"She's fine. It's not her."

"Then what **has** Christina done this time? Burned down Fort Worth? Taken to stage dancing in Hell's Half Acre, perhaps?" Another thought struck him and all amusement in his voice died. "Has she eloped?"

"Not yet, but that may be next." Jake raked his fingers through his hair. He drew a deep breath, then exhaled it in a rush. "She's gone, Cole. One of those Chili Queens delivered a letter."

"From Fort Worth?"

"No. She lied. She didn't go to Fort Worth."

Ah-hah. I was right. "So where did she go? Austin, I bet. She has friends up there."

"Not Austin. England. She went by herself or what might as well be by herself, since those friends of hers the Klebergs went with her and they certainly don't keep her out of trouble."

"You mean England, Texas, up in Red River County?"

"No, and that's English, Texas, not England. I mean England as in London and castles and tea with the queen. Cole, our Chili Queen has gone to England. See?"

He whipped a sheet of paper from his jacket pocket and waved it in front of Cole's face. Cole took it, skimmed it, and his temper built, then exploded. "Dammit, Jake, she went to England!"

"I know."

"By herself!"

"I know. I'd go after her, but I'm afraid to leave Mother."

Cole found it difficult to draw a breath as he attempted to discipline his thoughts and think the matter through. Inside him, fear for Christina raged right alongside his anger at her. Finally, he said, "I'll leave in the morning. With luck I'll find a ship sailing that direction sooner than what's been announced on the schedule."

Jake blew a relieved sigh. "Thank you, Cole. Thank you so damned much. I'll owe you big for this."

Slanting his friend a look, Cole snapped, "You already owe me big for agreeing to take her with me in the first place. Just pray I find her safe and sound. Then I'll be able to take the payment I want."

Jake nodded knowingly. "Out of her hide."

"Does Elizabeth know?"

"No. I won't tell her, not until I can come up with a story that won't worry her, anyway."

Cole stared down at the letter in his hand. "Damn that girl. Running off to England like this. Putting herself in danger. Putting her mother's health at risk." Cole crushed the letter in his fist. "If I've said it once, I've said it a thousand times. When I finally run her to ground, I swear I'm going to kill Christina Delaney."

Chapter

4

Derbyshire, England

As the hired coach rattled through the English countryside toward Hartsworth, the knot in Chrissy's stomach grew to the size of a grapefruit. She'd been running on nerves since leaving San Antonio, and her anxiety level had now reached its peak as they traveled the final few miles toward her grandfather's country estate. "I can't believe I actually did this."

Lana reached out and patted Chrissy's hands as they lay clenched in her lap. "It's all right. We're with you. No need to be worried."

"That's right, Miss Chrissy," Sophie said, mimicking her mother's concerned expression. "We'll take care of you."

Michael turned his attention away from the window just long enough to grin and nod his agreement. The boy had grabbed onto the adventure of an ocean voyage and not let go. For someone who'd caused such trouble of late, he'd been a perfect angel during their trip. If one didn't mind near constant movement, continuous excitement, and unending questions, that is.

For Chrissy, Michael's happiness had been a balm that soothed her own troubled spirit. One particular morning during the trip, Lana and Chrissy had watched the boy question a sailor at length about ship navigation. Lana made the comment that her son and Chrissy shared many similar characteristics, namely his spirit, his curiosity, and his sense of adventure. "It's easier for him, being a boy," she'd added. "The consequences of breaking rules are less serious for males than for females in our society."

Chrissy had mulled that observation over for some time. It was something her own mother had often said during the lectures she'd delivered to her daughter. There aboard the ship taking her away from home, Chrissy had looked at the notion from a mother's point of view, drawing parallels between Michael's behavior and her own. Had she, in her own way, picked pockets in the plaza?

Perhaps. Her actions had certainly hurt her mother at times, and for that, Chrissy did feel a measure of guilt. Had it been selfish of her to rebel against the rules society placed upon females?

Yes, she concluded, in some ways it had.

So why had she done it? She didn't think she was a selfish person by nature. Yet, staring out at the wide, empty ocean, Chrissy had admitted to herself that sometimes she'd intentionally acted up just to get a rise out of her mother. Shame washed through her. *You are twenty going on two, Chrissy Delaney.* How childish could she be?

She'd thought long and hard about her situation before reaching the conclusion that while she was responsible for her own actions, her mother wasn't entirely blameless. Lana's relationship with her son exemplified that point. Where Lana worried about Michael's behavior because of the potential harm to the boy, Elizabeth Delaney's primary concern was how her daughter's actions reflected upon her and upon the exalted Delaney name.

Chrissy finally decided that it came down to a question of degrees of love. Lana loved Michael with her whole heart and soul. Elizabeth loved Chrissy because she was a good woman and it was her duty to love her child. The child in Chrissy yearned for a mother's unfettered love like Lana gave to Michael and Sophie. Elizabeth Delaney's dutiful love left a hollowness inside her daughter that Chrissy had spent years trying to fill in sometimes inappropriate ways.

So what had Chrissy learned from all this pondering? On a bright, golden dawn she'd gazed out over the sapphire sea and swore that when she loved, she would give her heart wholly and unconditionally. If ever there was to be a man in her life, she would demand the same in return. It was, she thought, the only way loving should be done.

With that decided, she had settled back to enjoy the days at sea. The children made the trip a delight, and even their coach trip from Liverpool proved to be a pleasure. Normal sibling squabbles remained at a minimum, and with her children happy and out of reach of her in-laws, Lana relaxed and laughed often, which gladdened Chrissy's heart, as did the fact that her friend suffered not a single headache since leaving Texas.

Now, however, as they traveled the last few miles of their journey, Chrissy suddenly wished she had never left San Antonio. Never before in her life had she been this nervous.

Searching desperately for a distraction, Chrissy followed Michael's lead and turned her attention to the passing countryside. The land here in Derbyshire lived up to her mother's claims of beauty. Fluffy white sheep dotted green rolling hills, and the hedges of holly and hawthorn provided fencing much more pleasing to the eye than the strands of barbed wire now spreading across Texas like a plague.

Momentum shifted her forward in her seat as the coach topped a hill, then she swayed to one side as it made a slow turn. She spied a quaint arched stone bridge and smiled at the ducks perched along one edge. Only after the approaching coach sent the birds flapping toward the water did her gaze lift to the distance and the stately house nestled between lake, hillside, and forest. "Oh my," she breathed, bracing a hand against a cushion to steady herself, as much against the sight before her as the rocking of the coach. Michael whistled softly.

At the sound of her voice, Lana and Sophie joined Michael and Chrissy at the windows. Sophie gasped. "Miss Chrissy, look at that palace! Is that where the Queen lives?"

Chrissy gazed down at the imposing Palladian facade of the great stately home and found it difficult to breathe. "No, the Queen doesn't live here, although according to my mother, she has visited a time or two. That's Hartsworth and it's a country house, not a palace. My mother described the fountain. We've arrived."

"This is it?" The little girl wriggled in her seat. "I get to live there? Just like a princess?"

Lana smoothed her daughter's hair and gently reminded, "Honey, don't forget that here at Hartsworth we work for Miss Chrissy. We're her servants. We are not here to play princess."

Chrissy took the girl's hand in one of her own and squeezed. "You and I will play princess while we're here, I promise. And Lana, we may have to play this servant-mistress nonsense in public, but I'll be hanged if I have to listen to it in private."

The trio fell silent as the coach made its way along the serpentine road toward Hartsworth. Chrissy couldn't take her eyes off the building, shifting windows to keep it in sight as the coach changed direction. A dramatic central portico dominated the main block of the house while curved corridors at each corner linked four pavilions to the center of the house. Three stories tall with a dressed stone facade, it seemed to stretch on forever. Chrissy counted over eighty windows on the front side of the house alone. "No wonder Mother always said Hartsworth was filled with light."

Michael, displaying an unusual measure of insecurity, blew out a heavy breath, then gazed at Chrissy. "Are you certain he'll let us stay here?"

Because Chrissy didn't want to lie, she said, "I'm not completely certain, no. Since we may well have arrived before my mother's letter informing the earl of my impending visit, we might face a few uncomfortable moments, but I doubt he'll turn us away. He and my mother were estranged for many years, and I don't think he'll risk a return to the hostilities."

"What did they fight about?" Sophie asked.

"My father. The earl wanted her to marry someone else, but she eloped with my father."

"Oh."

The coach rattled over another ancient stone bridge and began the final approach to the house. As a footman came out to meet the coach, Michael asked, "What are you going to tell your grandfather? Will you say you ran away?"

"I didn't run away," Chrissy snapped, nervousness adding an edge to her tone. "I left a few days early is all. But I won't tell him that. I'm going to say I've come to England in search of the Declaration of Independence."

"But that is Mr. Morgan's job," Lana protested.

Chrissy made a valiant effort at a smug smile as the coach rolled to a stop. "Yes, it is. And wouldn't it be fun if I found the document before he got here?"

Moments later they passed through the front door into Hartsworth's Great Hall. As a servant went to inform the earl that his granddaughter had arrived from Texas, the newcomers gazed around them in awe. Huge alabaster Corinthian columns rose from a stone floor inlaid with Italian marble to support an arched, painted ceiling, a mythological scene Chrissy couldn't quite place at the moment. Marble statues occupied niches set symmetrically around the room.

"Look, Mama," Sophie called, her voice incredulous. "You can see the boys' talleywhackers on those statues."

Busy gazing above him at the naked breasts on the ceiling, Michael jerked his head down and followed the path of his sister's stare. He muttered something Chrissy couldn't quite catch and clapped a hand over Sophie's eyes. "What kind of house is this? A painted-lady place?"

"It's nothing nasty, Michael," Lana explained, glancing toward Chrissy with a plea in her eyes. "Right?"

"That's right. It's called art. Those sculptures are probably worth more than my mother's entire house."

"No," Michael said.

"Yes."

"Whoa, think of what they'd be worth if they'd finished putting clothes on 'em." Then, shooting Chrissy a look of concern, he added, "I don't think it's good for Sophie to be around such a sight. You and Mama either, for that matter. It's not seemly."

As Chrissy turned away to hide her smile a flash of color in the corridor leading off to her right caught her eyes. Paintings. Then, drawn as if by an invisible string, she moved toward them. "Portraits," she murmured.

The first was of a man of fifty or so wearing some sort of ceremonial robe. Distinguished, she thought. Hard. The next was of a woman with haunting eyes in a sapphire blue dress and triple strand of pearls. A beautiful woman.

Chrissy moved on to the third portrait and mid-step, she froze. Shock washed through her. She knew the face. She knew the locket. But for the dress and the hairstyle, she could have been looking in a mirror.

From behind her, Sophie said, "Miss Chrissy? I think you had better see this."

"Look, honey. Do you know who this is?"

The name came in a man's voice, one brimming with emotion. "Elizabeth? Is it you? Have you finally come home?"

Her heart pounding, Chrissy slowly turned around.

He looked nothing like the grandfather she'd always pictured him to be. He looked exactly like the grandfather she'd always wished she had.

Thirty years or so older than the man in the portrait, the Earl of Thornbury had softened around the edges. His hair and mustache was snow white, his face mapped with lines, his body still tall and straight, but leading with a belly politely termed plump. He'd an air of kindness about him, a gentle mien, despite the disappointment that bloomed in his eyes as he got a good look at her.

"You're not Elizabeth."

"No, I'm her daughter, Christina. I'm your granddaughter."

Then the Earl of Thornbury did the most amazing thing. He threw open his arms, smiled with delight and cried, "Chrissy! My little Texas rose. Come give your granddaddy a hug."

An hour later they sat in a pair of wing chairs before a fire laid in the Italian marble hearth of a cozy room called the little library. It had been love at first sight between the two of them, especially once the earl welcomed Lana and the children as honored guests instead of servants. As her friend settled her children in their rooms in Hartsworth's family wing, Chrissy joined her grandfather for a cup of tea and a bit of get-to-know-you conversation.

They spent some time discussing her mother and brother. Once she'd caught him up on family news and events, talk turned to the reasons behind Chrissy's surprise visit to Hartsworth. His softspoken encouragement and unflinching support opened the floodgates. She rattled on about the Chili Queens and her mother's disapproval. She told him about her aborted trips to the altar and basically filled him in on events all the way back to the brothel incident that got her sent away to school.

"So I'm a harridan and a flirt and an all-around disgrace, Grandfather. Mother sent me to you because according to her you are a strict disciplinarian who will keep me in line."

The earl frowned and turned a contemplative face toward the crackling fire. "I understand why your mother would feel that way. I was a petty tyrant during her formative years, especially after her mother died. But it surprises me that Elizabeth would send you to me." Wry amusement lit his eyes as he said, "After hearing your stories, I must tell you it sounds to me as if you and your mother are very much alike."

"Me like Mama?" She sputtered a laugh. "Not at all, Grandfather. My mother is the perfect lady."

"She was a perfect trial when she was your age, believe me. I was harsh on her, true, but I always acted with the best of intentions. I was right sometimes, wrong others. I did the right thing breaking up her first engagement. I shouldn't have interfered with her romance with your father."

"Mother had a beau before my father?" This was news to Chrissy and it annoyed her in light of all broken-engagement scoldings Elizabeth had delivered.

"She did. Jilted him at the altar. Dealt her reputation a blow, it did. I'd a devil of a time convincing the Marquess of Rushton that Elizabeth would take his suit seriously. Then she made a liar of me. Fell for your father, instead. Younger son, no title. I was furious with the girl."

If she hadn't seen the portrait, Chrissy might wonder if she'd stumbled into the wrong country house. This did not sound like her mother one bit. "Is that what led to your estrangement? You didn't like my father?"

"I liked Delaney well enough. Didn't want him for my Lizzie."

Lizzie? For ultra-proper Elizabeth? Chrissy sat in shock as the earl continued.

"Mainly I resisted their plans to move to Texas. In hindsight, I recognize my efforts to prevent the emigration caused my daughter more than her share of grief, and I don't blame her for holding it against me for so many years. One of my greatest regrets is that we didn't reconcile before your father died. I owed him an apology."

Chrissy's thoughts were in a whirl. "What did you do?"

Her grandfather winced. "I'm ashamed to say, child. Suffice to say your mother was well within her rights when she swore she'd never set foot in England again. She's kept that promise, too, even after all the letters I've sent since our reconciliation begging her to come home." His mouth twisted in a rueful smile as he added, "You inherited your stubbornness from your mother, you know. She gave new meaning to the word."

"I'm not stubborn."

He arched a brow. "Of course you're not. You only crossed an ocean to make a point."

Chrissy scowled at him. "I came to make a new life for myself."

"I see." He folded his hands, steepled two fingers, then thoughtfully tapped his mouth. "So, what kind of 'new life' are you looking for, my dear? What do you want?"

It was Chrissy's turn to stare pensively into the fire as she sipped her tea. Finally, she sighed and said, "I want a home. I want a family."

The earl sat up straight in his chair. "You want to live in England permanently? You want to marry an Englishman?"

She shrugged. "I want children, so yes, I imagine I must have a husband. I don't care what nationality he is."

"What traits do you care about?"

Love without conditions. Acceptance for who I am.

Her teacup rattled the saucer as she set it down. "Oh, I don't know."

"Well let's figure it out, shall we?" The earl pushed to his feet, chortling with delight and rubbing his hands together. "What a glorious, glorious day this is," he said as he gave the bell pull a tug and gave the servant who responded instructions to summon his secretary to the little library. "We've a list to make, my dear. A wish list. Tell me what it is you require in a mate. I'll have a nice selection here within the fortnight."

Chrissy's brows rose at his enthusiasm. Still, she was thrilled with her grandfather's welcome, and since she couldn't see what it would hurt to fall in with the spirit of his game, she settled back in her chair and provided an outline of her version of the perfect man. "Not that such a thing exists," she explained, "but it never hurts to reach for the stars."

Later that night, after Chrissy helped Lana tuck Sophie and Michael into their beds, the two women settled down in Chrissy's elaborately appointed bedroom for a cup of chocolate and a rehash of the day. Chrissy relayed the high points of her conversation with her grandfather, including her list of preferred masculine attributes.

After saying their goodnights, Lana headed for the door connecting Chrissy's bedroom to hers. There, she paused. Glancing back over her shoulder, she presented a picture of perfect innocence as she observed, "Chrissy, about your perfect man list. Tall, strong, handsome, intelligent and the rest. Do you know who those traits you named remind me of? Cole Morgan. Isn't that a coincidence?"

His image flashed in Chrissy's mind as she mentally reviewed her list. *Oh, no.* Somehow, she managed a laugh. "Cole Morgan a perfect man? Lana, my dear friend, you must be dreadfully tired. You're delirious."

"Am I?" she asked with a wise smile. "Or are you denying it just a bit too hard?"

Cole arrived at Hartsworth, appropriately enough, in a driving rainstorm. It was a fitting end to a truly miserable trip. Not a single cloud had shadowed the brilliant blue sky when he'd set out early that morning from the inn. Anxious to see an end to his travels, he'd purchased a horse—which was a polite term for the nag he rode—and made arrangements for his baggage to be sent later. An hour following his departure, clouds began to build, then thirty minutes after that, the sky opened up.

Cole had gone through his entire repertoire of curses a dozen times since. He was angry at England—a Texas sky wouldn't have fooled him—and angry at himself for agreeing to make this trip to begin with. The biggest portion of his temper, however, was reserved for Miss Christina Elizabeth Delaney.

"She'd damn well better be here," he muttered, focusing on the imposing house that loomed before him out of the driving rain. And she'd be well served to have some folks around her when he arrived. Too many times on this godforsaken trip he'd entertained himself by visualizing his hands around that selfish, infuriating woman's neck.

He blamed Christina for the fact that in order to get here sooner, he'd hitched a ride on an inferior freighter rather than the well-equipped passenger ship upon which he'd originally booked tickets. He held her accountable for the fact said freighter had mechanical troubles and limped halfway across the Atlantic. He faulted her for the bad food, the missed trains, the poor beds in inns along the way, and the awful springs on the public coaches that had tortured his behind. Mostly, though, he blamed her for the worry she would cause her ailing mother and the gut-wrenching fear he himself had felt on her behalf. "You'd damn well better be here safe and sound,

Christina. Safe and sound so I can give you what you've got coming."

Of course, Cole's threats against her person were all bluster. He wouldn't physically touch her. Somewhere deep inside him, in a place he didn't particularly want to examine, Cole understood he was better off keeping his hands to himself where Christina was concerned.

As he approached Hartsworth, the size of the place astounded him and stirred up old emotions better left unexplored. His father and mother had worked and lived on a great country estate such as this. Assistant gardener and laundry maid to a duke, his duchess, two daughters and that devil-spawn of a son.

Rain drizzled past Cole's collar, chilling the back of his neck as he vividly remembered the scorn in his father's voice as he spoke of the wealth and excesses of his employer. He recalled marveling over the notion of fifty or more people laboring in a house to make life comfortable for a family of five. And that number didn't include the outside help. The notion continued to boggle the mind today.

Gazing at the house through the splattering rain, he wondered what his father would say if he knew his only son intended to present himself to the lord of this manor as if he were an equal. *He'd be proud as a pup with two tails*, Cole's heart told him.

That's why Samuel Morgan had chosen America as his destination after he'd beat his wife's rapist nearly to death. He had wanted to live in a country that believed all men were created equal. He'd wanted to raise his son to believe it, too.

That much of Samuel's wish for the future had come

true. Cole might be British-born, but he was American-bred. He had an American's awareness that his countrymen had fought a war or two to ensure they wouldn't have to kowtow to a king or queen and lords and ladies. Plus, Cole was Texan to boot. He would consider himself second to no man on the basis of the color of his blood.

"Remember that," he muttered as he reined his sorry-excuse-for-a-horse to a stop at the foot of the gracefully curving stone steps leading up to Hartsworth's front door. Then, as a liveried footman carrying an umbrella splashed toward him, he stared up at the cold stone facade of the Earl of Thornbury's palace and murmured every true Texan's battle cry, "Remember the Alamo."

Dismounting, he reached for his saddlebags as the footman bowed, then offered the umbrella and said, "Welcome to Hartsworth, my lord."

At that, the Texan in him swelled and his voice slipped to a small-town drawl. "I'll take the welcome but give you back the lord business. I'm a plain old mister and proud of it. And you keep the umbrella for those fancy clothes of yours. My hat and duster do the job just as well. I would be grateful if you'd see to the nag for me, though."

The young man's eyes rounded. "Uh, thank you, sir. I'll take good care of your mount, sir, never fear."

"Appreciate it." Cole slung his saddlebags over one shoulder and turned toward the gracefully curved stone steps leading up toward the shelter of the portico.

"Sir?" the footman called after him. "If I may ask, where did you get that hat and coat? I've never seen the likes before."

Cole smiled, the first one all day. "Texas, son. I'm from Texas."

The footman frowned with disappointment. "Oh. I should have known from your voice. That's too bad because my papa needs something like your coat. He works outside all the time—he's the gardener here and his cough, well, it worries me."

Gardner, hmm? "Tell you what. I'll be sending a letter home shortly and I'll order one for him. Just need to know the size."

"Is the price very dear?" the youngster asked hesitantly.

"We'll be able to work something out. Now, why don't you see to that poor horse. I don't know about you, but I'm ready to get out of this weather."

"Yes, sir. Thank you, sir. Thank you indeed."

Cole touched a finger to the brim of his hat and started toward the front steps. Halfway there he paused and turned around to ask the footman what he'd meant with his comment about Cole's voice. Did the boy recognize the drawl because he knew Christina? Was she here safe and sound?

He'd hesitated too long. The rain was falling harder now, and the youngster was hustling the nag away. Cole shrugged, climbed the front steps, and headed for the door, which opened at his approach.

"Welcome to Hartsworth, my lord." A servant snapped his fingers and another man appeared and immediately started to relieve Cole of his saddlebags, coat, and hat. Before he was all that ready to be rid of them, to be honest. After one look at the hall in front of him, he fought the urge to turn around and go back out into the rain. *People actually live in a place this grand?*

"Remember the Alamo," he murmured, retrieving his hat from the servant. At the moment, he felt more comfortable with something in his hands.

"Pardon me, sir?" said the butler or house steward or whatever the hell was the proper title.

"I said I'm no lord."

"I beg your pardon, sir." The fellow actually bowed. "We are expecting Lord Welby this morning. My apologies." Then, his gaze sweeping Cole from head to foot, he scowled suspiciously and asked, "Your card?"

The Texan in Cole once again rumbled to the surface in the face of the butler's snobbishness. "Ace of spades is always my preference," he drawled, slower and thicker than normal. "Hard to go wrong with that one." He reached out and took the servant's hand, giving it a vigorous shake. "Cole Morgan of San Antonio, Texas. I'm here to parley with the earl if you'd be so kind as to holler at him for me."

Horror flashed across the butler's face before being quickly and professionally hidden. Cole wanted to laugh. He'd horrified himself a bit with that exaggeration. If the members of the Historical Society who had labeled him suave and debonair could have seen this, they'd have tripped over themselves looking for someone else to send. *Too bad I didn't know then what I know now.*

The butler replied, "I shall see if the earl is at home."

"You don't know?" Cole called after the departing servant. Then, alone in the great hall, he allowed himself to play tourist and gaze around in wonder. He could as well be in Greece as in England. This was truly the most beautiful room he'd ever seen. The plasterwork adorning the walls and ceiling was artwork in itself. And the murals within those plaster frames—fabulous color and form—the work of a master, obviously.

Cole moved toward the center of the room and stood beneath the domed skylight as he studied the sculptures placed symmetrically around the room. He had the shameful urge to park his hat on top of the fellow with the girlish ringlets whose fig leaves had gone missing. "A well-hung hat rack, that," he mused, suddenly wishing Jake was here to share the joke.

The thought of Jake immediately led to a reminder of his purpose here and he sobered. He should have asked the footman or butler if Christina were here. It wasn't like him to be so hesitant. Why, he wondered, after traveling literally thousands of miles to locate her, was posing the question so damned difficult?

Because if she's not here, your fears for her safety will have come true. Or, because she might be here and already married to that titled Englishman Elizabeth wants her to have.

An explosion of masculine laughter emerging from the corridor leading off the near right corner of the hall distracted him from his bleak musings. Without conscious thought, he moved toward the sound. Just as he prepared to step from the great hall into the window-lined corridor, another voice, another laugh, joined the men's. Cole froze. He knew that laugh, knew that giggle. Relief drenched him.

Christina.

She was safe.

She was laughing.

With a group of men, as usual.

Temper roared through Cole.

"Why the hell am I surprised?" He sucked in a deep breath, gritted his teeth, and slammed his hat atop the nearby marble statue's head. Long, determined steps carried him the length of the corridor past medieval suits of armor, lacquered cabinets, alabaster pedestals crowned with Roman busts, and urns of a dozen different shapes and designs. Cole disregarded the riches, so attuned was he to the song of delight coming from a room ahead.

Another burst of laughter had him halting in the doorway to a billiard room. The scent of tobacco drifted around him as he counted six starched-front gentlemen, two of whom held cue sticks, and one lady attired in bustled blue silk currently bent over the table in the process of lining up her shot, displaying a wealth of decolletage as she did so. He did not, however, see Christina.

The woman took her shot and the balls on the table cracked together. Then Cole heard Christina say in a flirtatious tone, "Oh, Lord Chandler, I'm afraid I sank one of yours."

Cole's gaze jerked around the room, searching out every corner.

"Now, now, Miss Delaney. Thornbury warned us all that you are a fierce competitor."

Miss Delaney? Cole's stare snapped back upon the woman.

"Competitor? Me?" She patted her chest, calling attention to the dip in her neckline. "Oh, la. The earl is such a tease." With a flirtatious wink, she bent forward to take another shot.

Cole was frozen in shock. The lavish gown and hairstyle, the sparkling jewelry around her neck and dangling from her ears. That elaborate bustle. Was that really . . . "Bug"?

She jerked and miscued. The white ball bounced twice on the felt before flying off the table. It hit on the carpet, then rolled onto the tile, the *wrr-wrr-wrr* noise sounding like a wind-up toy in the sudden silence of the room.

Christina, as always, recovered nicely. "Oh, Mr. Morgan. Hello."

"Hello?" he repeated, stalking into the room. "That's all you have to say? Hello and *Mr. Morgan?*" She'd never called him mister in her life.

She glanced at the men around her and shrugged. "Terrible weather we're having, isn't it?"

Cole eyed the graceful curve of her neck as the old fantasy twitched his fingers.

"I say, old man," said a young buck in a precisely tied cravat. "You seem to be dripping all over the Aubusson."

Cole ignored him. "Christina. Shall we have this conversation in front of your . . . friends . . . or would you prefer to conduct it in more private surroundings?"

"I prefer not to have it at all, at the very least not now. I am in the middle of a game here, Mr. Morgan."

She turned her back on him, and whipped that ridiculous bustle around like an exclamation point to an insult.

Mr. Morgan. She played the formal flirt today, he saw. Cole truly teetered on the brink of violence. "Christina Elizabeth Delaney, get your bustle over here or I swear I'll—" He broke off abruptly as something tugged at his sleeve. "Hello, Mr. Morgan."

He glanced down. Blinked. Good Lord, what next? "You're the girl from the plaza. With the Chili Queens."

"Sophie Kleberg." She crooked her index finger, gesturing him closer. Whispering, she added, "I am so glad you finally arrived. My mother and I are very worried about Miss Chrissy and all her gentlemen. Michael would be worried too if he'd stop looking at all the naked ladies on the ceilings."

"Hush your mouth," the boy in question muttered as he took a position on Cole's other side. "I don't do that."

"Do too."

Naked ladies. All her gentlemen. Cole gave his head a shake to clear it, then focused his gaze on the frustrating flirt. Even as he watched she flashed a smile and spoke to a fellow who shot an offended glare in Cole's direction. He heard him say, "Who is that man, my dear? Why does he use that tone with you? What does he want?"

The other men formed ranks around her, a wall of disapproving stares. When she reached out and touched one fellow's sleeve, Cole scowled right back at them. "Her gentlemen?" he asked Michael.

"She already has four beaux and the house party hasn't really started yet."

"So what else is new?"

The boy glanced toward Christina, his tanned brow knitted in a frown. "I'm not certain. Something about her is different now. She's not happy when she bats her lashes."

Cole snorted. "Maybe she's finally figured out it isn't kind of her to lead men around by their . . . noses. Maybe she's finally growing up."

Sophie stomped her foot. Right on top of Cole's. "Miss Chrissy is very kind, and growing up has nothing to do with it. Mama says she's giving up."

"Giving up on what?"

"On love."

Giving up on love? Not hardly. Not by the looks of it. He watched the woman in question giggle and flash a smile at an obviously besotted fool. If anything, she was working at getting it more than ever. That thought made him mad all over again.

The boy said, "C'mon, Sophie. Let's find Mama and tell her Mr. Morgan is here." Glancing at Cole, he added, "She guessed you'd be arriving pretty soon, and she wants to talk to you."

As the children slipped away, Cole thought to himself, *And I want to talk to Christina. Enough of this.* Pasting a smile on his face, he sauntered across the room and eased his way around the protective throng. "My apologies, Christina. I fear I misplaced my manners in my anxiety to see how you were faring." He met each man's gaze before adding a sheepish shrug. "Christina and I grew up together, you see, and I've come to Hartsworth to look after her, standing in for her brother who can't be here. Because of our past, I fear sometimes I treat her with a brother's callous disregard." He extended his hand and gave the tip of her nose a familiar, familial tap. "I guess the news from home can wait. I have a letter for you from your mother. Would you like to introduce me to your friends now? Maybe they'd be interested in tales of your childhood. The mirror story, perhaps?"

It was the Delaney family euphemism for Christina's ill-fated visit to the whorehouse—she'd been discovered when Jake spied her reflection in a mirror. She reacted with a satisfying flash of pique from the brilliant emerald of her eyes.

"A letter from Mother?" she repeated in a falsely sweet tone. "Perhaps I will take a moment now to read it." She batted her eyelashes at the men around her and said, "If you will excuse me?"

"Only if you promise a swift return," piped up a fellow with a bushy mustache.

"Oh, la," she said with a giggle, then swept from the room.

"La?" Cole repeated, following her into the corridor. "What is this 'la' business?"

"We'll talk in the little library," she said over her shoulder, all signs of giggle gone from her voice. "That part of the house will be quiet this time of day."

Her posture remained stiff as a bois d'arc fence post as Cole trailed her back to the Great Hall, then through a few miles of corridors and staircases, pausing once briefly upon meeting two young ladies who requested Christina introduce them to the newcomer. She did so with a studied politeness that added to Cole's scowl. Christina did sass much better than starch. He didn't care for this attitude, not one little bit.

He was pleased to see some other females around this place, however. Considering the scene he'd walked into in the billiard room, Christina could use some competition for the men's attentions. Not that the females he'd just met would do the trick. They appeared to be pleasant enough girls, but they paled in comparison to Christina. Most women did.

Finally, she turned into a room lined with bookshelves filled with leather-bound tomes. Cole was immediately intrigued. His passion for books was part of what had attracted him to law in the first place. "You called this the little library," he said, gazing around him. "Doesn't look very little to me."

"Hartsworth has a larger library a few doors down from the billiard room, but it's more for show. We're now in the family wing and the books here in this room all have to do with gardening. The present earl is avid about his plants." Pausing, she betrayed her first sign of nervousness since his arrival by unconsciously wringing her hands as she asked, "Do you really have a letter from my mother?"

"I have one from your brother. But it's packed in my trunk and that's coming later."

"So you lied. Why am I not surprised."

"Christina?"

"Yes?"

He rounded on her, loomed above her, let the fury loose in his voice as he demanded, "What the hell did you think you were doing running off that way?"

My, my, he looks fierce. Christina glanced around the library looking for a fainting couch. She certainly could use one right about now. Her stomach had an entire flock of butterflies flitting around in it. She'd known this conversation would likely take place someday, but she'd hoped "someday" would arrive much later than today.

"Do you know what concern for you could do to your mother?"

She folded her arms, caught between a smile and a scowl. Elizabeth. Of course. Cole couldn't have picked a better way to chase the butterflies from her stomach. "What," she drawled, "no 'Hello Chrissy, how are you? How was your trip?' Why am I not surprised to hear Mother's name first thing out of your mouth?"

She'd be hanged if she'd tell him she'd sent a letter home at almost every stop along the way, assuring Jake and her mother that the trip was moving along smoothly.

He snorted. "Why waste my breath? Obviously you don't care how your actions affect those who care about you. Obviously you're in fine fettle, considering when I walked in you had your sails hoisted to full flirt."

She sank onto a gold velvet settee with a huff, unwilling to honor that with a response.

"Really, Christina. With this kind of behavior you have proven the validity of the decision to send you here. I've long known you have little regard for your family's feelings, but I never would have guessed you would sink this low. Running off and crossing an ocean without a word, without a man to protect you. I take it Mrs. Kleberg served as your chaperone? You uprooted an entire family on a whim, didn't you?"

She literally bit her tongue to keep from countering that charge. But protesting at this point would be a waste of time. The barrister had arrived, and he'd obviously been sharpening his tongue all the way across the Atlantic. Experience had taught her the quickest way to deal with his harangues was to let him blow until he ran out of breath.

At this rate, it might take till Christmas.

"I want you to think about the people you have hurt with this selfish, stubborn, reckless action of yours. I think you need to . . ."

No wonder the man made such a good lawyer. He could bend a person's ear into a bowknot.

She quit listening and casually crossed her legs. It was easier, and quieter, to tap her foot that way. She did continue to look at him, however. Experience also had taught her that feigning attention tended to nudge him along toward the finish a little quicker.

As Cole paced and moralized, Chrissy couldn't help but compare him to the Englishmen with whom she'd been spending her time. First off, Cole Morgan stood half a head taller than most of the men who'd come courting at Hartsworth. He was taller and broader and, truth be told, more attractive. Oh, Lord Stonebury might be considered more classically handsome, and Lord Warrington was truly a picture of blond perfection, but Chrissy couldn't deny that all in all, when compared to the others, Cole was more . . . masculine. He had a certain roughness about his features that appealed to a woman. He was . . . *How do I describe it?*

". . . appalling decision. Under other circumstances you would . . ."

Chrissy tapped a finger against her lips and considered. What was the word she searched for? Manly? Virile? Strong? Courageous? Yes, Cole was all those things, but so were many of the men here visiting at Hartsworth. Those traits had all been on her list.

What made Cole different from these men? What made him more?

When she heard him mutter, "Doesn't have the sense to spit downwind," she made the connection.

Texan. That's it. Cole Morgan was a blend of valor and swagger that was all Texan.

She thought of the old frontiersmen boasts he and Jake used to repeat when they were little more than boys. Jake would hook his thumbs around his suspenders and say, *I'm the daddy of everything bad that ever crawled out of Buzzard Gap. I was nursed on rotgut and cut my teeth on a saw. Rattlesnakes asked me to come play. Me and those reptiles, we'd sink our teeth into one another to see who was more poisonous. I always won.*

Then it would be Cole's turn to swagger and spout. He, of course, always recited a more long-winded speech than her brother. In a booming voice old for his age, Cole would say, *I was born in an erupting volcano and I was cradled on cholla spines. Wolves and grizzlies and cougars were playmates of mine, and I'm so hard I can kick fire out of flint with my bare toes. I was weaned on rattlesnake milk and even now I put tarantulas and vinegaroons in my whiskey to give it a kick. I'm the death-dealin' demon from San Antone, so hide away, everyone. I'm comin' out to play.*

A man fully grown, Cole still had the attitude, she concluded. Tempered and more subtle, but undeniably there.

". . . need for discipline. You're not fifteen anymore. After the mirror incident, I thought you would learn. But no, you . . ."

Chrissy shifted in her seat, uncrossing her legs when one of her feet started to fall asleep. He was really worked up now. Cole always reacted that way when the subject of her trip to the whorehouse came up. *It's because it embarrasses him*, she thought. He didn't like her, didn't like her *mother*, knowing he'd paid a soiled dove to bed him.

Bet he doesn't have to pay women now. The British ladies who'd stopped them for an introduction on the way to this room weren't unusual. Women threw themselves at Cole all the time. Their behavior made Chrissy sick. So the man was tanned and toned and oozed masculinity. So he had eyes that a woman could drown in and shoulders a woman could cling to. So what if he had a mouth that a woman craved to taste?

Craved to taste? Chrissy snapped to attention at that. Her eyes rounded in horror. Not The Kiss again. She refused to think about it. Swore she'd banish it from her mind. Desperate for a distraction from her thoughts, she interrupted, "I've been searching for the Declaration of Independence."

Cole halted midsentence. "You what?"

"I've begun the search. I'd hoped to get lucky and locate the document before you arrived, but I'm learning that everything takes longer here in England. They've a lot more rules to follow."

His mouth opened and closed repeatedly, and watching him, despite herself, she envisioned those lips moving against hers. *My stars*. Chrissy blinked hard, trying to dispel whatever sickness had come over her. England's mists must be fogging her brain.

"What is the matter with you?" he demanded.

"I don't know," she replied, worriedly. Maybe simple homesickness? An overdose of British men?

"The Historical Society sent *me* to do that job."

She blinked again. Thank God, now they were back on familiar territory—boys are better than girls. Hah. "You yourself said I'd be good at it, Cole Morgan. Don't you remember? You called me a professional sneak."

"Maybe I did. But your mother said it wouldn't do for you to be involved in the search. She said you needed structure and guidance, and she was as right as West Texas rain."

Chrissy pushed to her feet, her blood pumping. "And heaven knows if my mother said it, it is etched in granite and by that I mean your head because there is certainly no difference between the two!"

Cole closed his eyes, his jaw working. Eventually, his voice now controlled and cool, he said, "Christina, please. Our conversation has taken a different turn from what I expected. I think it would behoove us to take a few moments to reassess our situation."

"Oh, I hate it when you talk lawyer-fog." She flounced around the room, frustrated and feeling more alive than she had since first setting foot on British shores. In truth, she enjoyed sparring with this man. Sometimes she won their verbal battles, but not always. It was, she figured, that possibility of defeat that made the duel so stimulating.

Cole took the seat she had vacated and gazed at her expectantly. Finally, she sashayed over to a chair, sank down on to the gold velvet upholstery, and folded her arms. Then, knowing how much Cole hated it, she pursed her lips in a childish pout.

He managed to ignore the gesture. "All right, we'll

table the rest of it for now. I'd like to hear of your efforts in connection to the lost document."

She eyed him thoughtfully. He was ready to listen to her now. *That could be a good thing, or a bad thing.*

Chrissy inhaled a deep breath, then began. "I know you intended to travel to London to speak with Lord Melton because of his family ties to the Republic of Texas. I believe my mother told you Grandfather knows of two other gentlemen who might have information: Viscount Welby and Sir James Parkwood, third Baronet of Craver. Everything fell together tidily when I learned that Sir James has a bachelor son, Mr. John Parkwood, who is a year or two younger than you. The viscount is a widower whose wife died without bearing him an heir."

Cole leaned forward, elbows propped on his knees, head hanging. "Oh, no. I can see where this is going already."

"Actually, it's not going anywhere. They're coming here. Lord Melton, too. My grandfather is hosting a house party that is officially scheduled to begin in two days. You saw some of the early arrivals in the billiard room."

"And Welby and James are on the guest list."

She flashed a brilliant smile. "Lord Welby and Mr. Parkwood. The viscount, Sir James Parkwood, and his daughter are already in residence. Mr. John Parkwood will be joining his family at Hartsworth shortly."

"Meant to become potential suitors, I assume?"

"For all your faults, Morgan, you've never suffered from a lack of intelligence."

"It's a shame I can't say the same about you," he

fired back automatically, in keeping with the familiar pattern between them.

A comfortable quiet settled across the room while he took a moment as if considering her plan. When he shook his head slowly, she knew what was coming. She wrinkled her nose and sniffed in protest.

"You can't do this, Christina. I don't know what lies you told to sneak this past the earl, but I will not allow you to seduce information out of anyone."

"I have no intention of seducing or being seduced," she scoffed. "I intend to do a bit of flirting, that's all. A little innocent flirting."

"Innocent flirting? You?" Cole snorted. "And the Queen invited me for tea at the palace, too."

"But Cole—"

"No but's about it, Bug. The last time you flirted innocently you were five years old. Take it from someone who knows. All you have to do is look at a man to heat his blood. Bat your lashes a time or two and he'll be ready to howl at the moon."

He called me Bug. "Really?" she asked, intrigued.

"Really."

"What if I bat my lashes at you, Cole Morgan? Will you howl at the moon, too?"

That stopped him like a castle wall. Choking, sputtering sounds emerged from his throat.

A stern voice floated from the doorway. "I should like to hear the answer to that question, myself."

Cole came to his feet as Edward Stanton, Earl of Thornbury, roared into the little library like a defending general. "I take it you are the trespasser who went missing from the Great Hall? Who are you and what are you doing alone with my granddaughter?"

A judge would find it difficult to choose a victor in a scowl competition between those two, but Chrissy decided her grandfather's edged out Cole's by a smidgen. However, the Texan won the thundering voice contest when he stormed, "I'm Cole Morgan of San Antonio, Texas, and I'm doing my best not to kill her."

Then Chrissy's grandfather did something so strange that it took an obviously shocked Cole a full ten seconds to respond. The Earl of Thornbury stuck out his hand and said, "Why, you must be Samuel Morgan's boy. It is a pleasure to meet you, son. Your father was one of the finest men I've ever known and by far the greatest gardener. His efforts were wasted over at Dowington Hall. I always said he could grow water lilies in a desert. I certainly hated to hear of the trouble that took him away from England, but I was glad my daughter was able to help your family when they settled in San Antonio. I'd like to hear more about that later, but for now let me welcome you to Hartsworth. Terribly glad to have you here."

Then, he added with a chuckle, "From what I gathered when I walked into this room, I see my granddaughter stirs your blood, too. Best be prepared to stand in line. It's a regular gentlemen's club of Chrissy's conquests here. I can't wait to see who she chooses in the end."

Then, bestowing an indulgent smile on his granddaughter, he added, "Of course, the courting dances themselves are well worth watching. A fine bit of entertainment, that. She's leading half the men in the shire around by the traces already and she's only been here a few weeks."

Chrissy beamed a grin right back at the earl, then swallowed her laughter as Cole gazed at her with panic-glazed eyes. "This is the Earl of Thornbury? This is your grandfather? The man your mother sent you to for discipline?"

"Isn't it delicious?" To add insult to injury, she blew Cole a kiss as she sailed toward the doorway. "Till later, gentlemen. I've an assignation scheduled in the drawing room with Lord Stephen Grayford in ten minutes. I'd best hurry. I would hate to be late for the marquess's second son."

Cole's voice followed her out into the corridor. "It's a nightmare, that's what this is. A waking nightmare. The queen has jumped from the chili pot into the porridge."

Chapter

5

The opulence of the dining room struck Cole as downright shameful. As he took his seat at the table, he felt an uncomfortable urge to squirm. He wasn't exactly a neophyte when it came to fancy meals, either. During the course of his law career, he had dined at the homes of governors, senators, and congressmen both in Texas and in the more formal settings of Washington and New York. He'd partaken of palate-pleasing, seven-course meals served on fine china in extravagantly decorated rooms. He'd shared after-dinner cigars with captains of industry while their elegant wives sipped Lapsang Suchong in the drawing room down the hall. Still, if every one of those elaborate meals served in gilded dining rooms were somehow combined, they would still pale in comparison to dinner at Hartsworth.

California couldn't have had this much gold in 'forty-nine.

Crimson walls and white marble mantels added to the richness of yet another room crowned with a painted ceiling, again a mythological scene filled with naked breasts and cherubs. *Young Michael must have a permanent crick in his neck,* Cole thought, *if not in another part of his anatomy.* Personally, he'd just as soon not eat with all that frolicking taking place above him. Made a fellow feel like a drop of drool might splash into his soup any second.

Fifteen people sat down for dinner—Christina, the earl, Cole, and a dozen early arrivals for the upcoming house party. At Christina's signal, a dizzying array of servants began sweeping in and out of the room, bearing silver salvers laden with dish after dish of aromatic foodstuffs. Despite the superior quality of the offerings, Cole didn't much enjoy his supper. How could he when, at the other end of the table, the Chili Queen was holding court?

Cole had watched this woman practice her wiles upon men innumerable times over the past few years, but never before had her actions bothered him like they did this evening. Tonight her laughter grated like eggshells in the custard. Her flashing smile soured the sweetness of peas. The sparkle in her eyes stuck in his craw like a fish bone, and the dip in her decolletage steamed him like a damned clam.

Because, although he'd seen it all before, this time her flirtation seemed . . . serious.

She shouldn't be here. Christina should be home in Texas bathing babies at St. Mary's orphanage and singing in church. She should be laughing at the supper table with Elizabeth and Jake, not with some hot-eyed, dandified British lords. Hell, better she be in the middle of Military Plaza stirring up chili than this over-decorated dining room stirring up lust.

Because that's exactly what she was doing. Cole saw it in the way the marquess's gaze kept dropping toward her bosom, in how the baron kept licking his lips, and in the heat that flared in the baronet's eyes whenever Christina tilted her head to one side, exposing the length of her neck.

"Woman needs to wear more clothes," he muttered.

"I beg your pardon?" asked Miss Sarah Parkwood. "I'm afraid I didn't hear you clearly."

Good thing. "It was nothing. I'm sorry." Cole offered her an apologetic grin and she smiled in response.

Seated on his right, Miss Parkwood was one of the young ladies Christina had introduced to Cole earlier in the hallway. The woman had been as distracted as he throughout the meal, her romantic hopes obviously pinned on the roving-eyed marquess. Cole considered doing them both a favor by dumping his iced drink into the fellow's lap.

"I said our hostess appears to be attracting quite a bit of attention."

Miss Parkwood sighed wistfully. "I do envy Miss Delaney. She is so very . . . shining."

The girl did sparkle this evening. Dammit all. Her mother would be proud. "You should see her serving up chili. That Christina makes this one look dull as a rusted bucket."

"She's even more beautiful when she is cold?"

Cole's brow creased. Cold? Oh, chili and chilly. "When she's happy, I mean. She's especially beautiful when she is truly happy."

"She appears happy to me," Miss Parkwood observed pointedly when Christina's laughter bubbled into the air.

Studying his long-time friend, Cole could see how Miss Parkwood would think Christina was happy. He knew better, though. He'd missed it at first—the girl could act—but after watching her closely Cole could see the sadness beneath the smiles and sparkle.

It bothered him and he didn't know what to do about it. He couldn't tell Christina why her mother sent her away. Though it might ease her pain in some ways, the facts would certainly hurt her in others. And Jake had been right. The minute Christina heard her mother was ill, she would head for home. That wouldn't be good for Elizabeth.

Unless Christina were married. To a titled lord.

With that, the meal settled in his belly like buttermilk gone bad.

Cole pushed peas around on his museum-quality, hand-painted bone china plate. Maybe he should help Christina find a husband she could tolerate. That way, both hers and her mother's interests would be served. With a husband strong enough to control her and blue-blooded enough to make Elizabeth happy, Christina could return to Texas. She would be home if the worst occurred.

The thought of losing Elizabeth twisted Cole's heart. The thought of it occurring while her estranged daughter batted lashes at a baron thousands of miles away cleaved that heart clean in two. Christina would be destroyed. Cole couldn't let that happen. Yet, he didn't know that he had the stomach to assist in a husband hunt.

Dinner dragged on like a boring Sunday sermon. The lady on his left was an elderly marchioness, and after announcing her disdain for Americans, she ignored Cole completely. That suited him just fine. He used the time to consider what his next move should be.

In all the concern over Christina, he couldn't forget the reason Elizabeth had sent him here. He had a copy of the Declaration of Independence to track down and the sooner done the better.

Thoughtfully, Cole eyed his fellow Texan as she ruled over her grandfather's supper table. So she had this Melton fellow he was supposed to contact and two other potential sources of information on their way to Hartsworth, hmm? Slick work, that. *She'll make some man a damned fine partner.*

Just then she laughed and touched her dinner companion's hand with easy familiarity. Beside him, Miss Parkwood sighed again. "She has such confidence, doesn't she? Are all women in Texas so bold?"

"Let's just say Christina is special." And that, he thought, was the God's honest truth.

Figuring he should do his share in the search for the Declaration, he smiled at Miss Parkwood and observed, "So, I'm told your family holds an interest in the American West?"

They discussed her father's fascination until the sweet course was served. At that point, a newcomer appeared in the dining room to a hail of hearty welcomes. "Who is this?" he inquired of Miss Parkwood.

"He's Bruce Harrington, Viscount Welby."

So this is one of Christina's marks. Cole leaned back in his chair, sipping wine from a crystal goblet, and considered the man. Welby wore his clothes with a high-fashioned casualness that reeked of wealth. He had those blond, pretty features women liked to swoon over and a laugh that had "charming rogue" written all over it. Cole detested him on principle. Welby was the type of fellow who would appeal to Christina.

Cole leaned his head toward Miss Parkwood and confirmed, "He's not married?"

"Oh, no. Welby is one of the most sought-after bachelors in Polite Society. Most ladies think him terribly handsome. He is known for the collection of vests he wears. He has them specially made in Paris."

Cole tried not to scowl as the golden fashion-god viscount strode across the dining room flashing a ready smile and blue satin vest. He paused before the earl and bent his tall, broad-shouldered figure into a respectful bow before voicing an apology for his tardiness that held just the right note of sincerity. Offering the company a sheepish grin, he explained, "I spied an injured dog along the road to Hartsworth, and I stopped to help the poor thing."

"Aww," breathed every last woman at the table.

The viscount proceeded to give a thorough enumeration of the dog's ills and a boring recitation of his efforts to save the animal. Cole watched admiration fill Christina's expression as she made room for the hound's hero at the end of the table beside her. She didn't so much as glance at Cole as a signal or reminder that Welby might be a lead to the missing Declaration.

Because of the viscount, the interminable dinner continued to drag on. Cole sat silently for the most part, listening to the conversation humming at Christina's end of the table as the viscount and the woman from Texas got to know one another. The more he heard, the darker his mood grew. Christina sounded positively . . . English.

She referred to Texas in only the briefest of terms. When Welby spoke of the quality of his horses, she didn't bother to mention how her own father worked as a mustanger upon his immigration to Texas. When he commented on the beauty of the locket she wore around her neck, she failed to mention that the intricate design was the work of a Mexican silversmith who made his living by selling jewelry in the same square where she stirred up her chili. When the viscount mentioned that an acquaintance of his owned a herd of prize-winning longhorn cattle, she didn't bother to mention that Cole and her own brother Jake spent one summer driving cattle north.

Christina's reticence about her home stung like a nettle, and it continued to plague him over the next few days as Hartsworth filled up with guests for the house party. She seldom spoke of life in San Antonio. She rarely spoke of her mother or her brother. It was as if she'd been born anew when she disembarked from the boat in Liverpool. Why, even her speech reflected an attempt to wipe away all trace of a Texas drawl.

As a result, his own words took longer to pronounce, his "e's" took to sounding more like "a's", and his "r's" and "g's" sometimes went missing. The less Texan Christina became, the more layers of sophistication Cole peeled away.

She had not ceased her flirting, but she carried it on in a more subtle manner than he was accustomed to seeing. For instance, Christina took to carrying a fan, something she'd always eschewed in the past. She used the damned prop to say things she used to articulate, and Cole found the affectation even more annoying than her more usual outspokenness.

Still, Cole couldn't deny that as far as the search for the Declaration of Independence was concerned, this division of duty, so to speak, worked well for him and Christina. Though they never actually got together and discussed how they would handle the hunt, a natural division in tasks occurred. A man spoke and acted differently with another man than he did with the woman to whom he paid court. Cole's conversations with Welby, for instance, netted him different information than did Christina's.

This came to light when he came upon Christina sitting by herself in the garden folly following an afternoon stroll with the viscount.

"Sitting all alone?" he drawled as he took a seat beside her. "Must be the first time in days. What happened to Welby? Your grandfather was positively gleeful when he mentioned you were taking a turn through the garden with the most eligible bachelor in England."

His sarcastic tone earned him a nudge with her elbow. "Actually I strolled with Lord Welby *and* Mr. Parkwood, and I learned something important." Her green eyes gleamed with interest as she continued, "Listen, Cole, John mentioned Texas today. I understand you've arranged to meet him at the stables later?"

Cole arched a brow. First names with Parkwood already? That was fast. "Yes, I'm to see him. Apparently he has a passion for horses. He wants my opinion of a hunter your grandfather might sell."

"Good. I want you to ask him about the private club in London that is somehow connected to his family. While the three of us were strolling, Lord

Welby mentioned they have a room decorated with items relating to the American West, and many of them are specific to Texas."

His interest piqued, Cole asked, "What kind of club is this?"

"I'm not certain," she replied. "However, the tone of Lord Welby's voice and the way John reacted to its mention suggested it is something less than proper. I pressed for more information, but he guarded his tongue. He might not be so reticent if you were to ask."

Cole leaned away from her, studied her, read her like a book. "You think it's a bordello."

"The viscount did mention something about costumes," she replied, shrugging.

Cole buried a grin. Chalk up a black mark by Parkwood's name. Ever since the mirror incident, Christina Delaney didn't abide men who frequented houses of ill repute.

Standing, Cole turned his thoughts toward the missing parchment. He paced the confines of the folly, his brow furrowed in thought. Imagine, the Republic of Texas's Declaration of Independence hanging on a whorehouse wall. Half of him bristled with offense at the notion. The other half wanted to laugh. Somehow, it had an appropriate ring. The fathers of the Republic had made four extra copies of the original document and sent them by messenger out around the country in order to spread the word that independence from Mexico had been declared. Considering the business whorehouses did in a country populated mostly by men, chances were good more men would have read the news there than anywhere else.

"I'll see what I can find out about this club," he told her.

"Good." A thoughtful smile curved her lips as she mused, "Since you'll be busy with John, I'll concentrate on Lord Welby."

"Has he provided any information about the quest?"

"Not the Declaration. At this point, my focus with him has to do with my other search."

Other search? Oh. Cole shoved his hands into his pockets as he sneered. "You mean you'll be busy flirting."

"How else am I supposed to find a husband like Mother wants?"

He wanted to ask if she were as free with her kisses over here as she was on the other side of the Atlantic, but he thought twice about bringing that particular subject up.

As she continued rattling about her social life, Cole's mood grew stormy. He wanted to shake some sense into her. She hadn't a clue as to what was truly important here. Of course, that's because she hadn't been told the truth. Cole found the news of Elizabeth's condition hovering on his tongue. Christina had a right to know just why her mother pushed her toward these damned Brits. He'd bet his favorite saddle she'd drop these earls and marquesses like a bad smell and hightail it home to Texas if she knew the facts.

Which was exactly why he couldn't tell her.

He cleared his throat. "If you want to know what I learn from Parkwood, meet me here tomorrow at the same time." He left the folly before she said any more.

He regretted his words the following day when a damp and chilly wind ushered him through the statue garden and past ornate fountains to the wood walk. That in turn led to the folly and his appointed rendezvous with Miss Christina Delaney, Texan spy and husband hunter.

The small stone building was a good ten-minute walk from the house, something he hadn't minded during the recent pleasant weather. Today was a different matter.

"Better we had chosen an indoor spot for this," he muttered. It wasn't like Hartsworth was too small to offer a private corner with its three levels and four wings. Besides, their business wouldn't take a minute. Parkwood had talked freely about his Texas ties, and before their conversation ended, Cole had asked the man outright about the missing Declaration. Parkwood denied ever seeing such a document and Cole believed him. He'd also agreed that such a treasure belonged in Texas, and he volunteered to survey other family members for any information they might possess. The chilly breeze whipped around Cole, and he stuck his hands into his pockets and grumbled, "We're finding a new rendezvous from now on."

Halfway to the folly, he had just rounded a rendition of Zeus when a hissing sound emerging from the marble god's lightning bolt brought him up short.

Hiss-s-s-s. "Mr. Morgan. Wait. Come here." Sophie Kleberg's head popped out from behind Zeus's leg. Her brother waved from over a shoulder, then crooked his fingers at the same time he signaled for quiet. Cole moved toward them.

Michael mouthed the words "Miss Chrissy" while

pointing at the hedge behind him. When Cole was close enough, the boy whispered in his ear. "You've got to stop her, sir. This one worries me."

"This one what?" Cole responded in a normal tone of voice.

"Shush. He waylaid her on the way to your meeting. Said he wanted to talk."

"Who?"

Michael jerked a thumb over his shoulder. "Mr. Welby."

Cole's mouth quirked a grin at the boy's use of the word "mister" instead of "lord" in regard to the viscount. Damned if it didn't please the Texan in him that the boy refused to make any titular distinctions. Because the Kleberg family occupied the space of "dear family friends" rather than servants on the social pecking order at Hartsworth, the boy's insolence was for the most part ignored.

Michael continued, "I think we have a problem with him. I wasn't too worried about any of the others, but Mr. Welby seems dangerous."

"Dangerous? I don't know, Michael. A talk in the garden sounds innocent enough, even if the weather is less than pleasant."

Sophie backed out of the bushes. "Hurry, y'all. They've gone into the maze."

"Come on, Mr. Morgan," the boy responded, tugging on Cole's arm. "What if he wants to do more than talk?"

"He does," warned Sophie, her eyes round with worry. "Earlier when I was spying on Mr. Lord Welby, I heard him tell his valet he has plans for Miss Chrissy. The ladies here say he's the most eligible bachelor in England, and even my Mama thinks he is very nice and she is very, very picky. Miss Chrissy is so beautiful and perfect that of course he'll fall in love with her like everyone else. It could have already happened and he might be ready to propose."

Cole would have replied, but he'd been struck speechless by the idea of Christina cast as perfect.

"We are worried she just might accept," Michael added. "She's been acting even sillier about this wedding stuff than usual. She and Mama talked about what baked goods to have at the wedding supper."

Sophie shook her finger at Cole. "This is your fault, Mr. Morgan. You have to stop her."

"My fault? What did I do?"

"You helped send her away from Texas. Now she's gonna get married and live here forever and that won't make her happy. I think my Mama would be happy living here, but Miss Chrissy won't. She has always said she has Texas in her heart."

"Wait just a minute, there. This wasn't my decision. Elizabeth and Jake had their minds made up when they sprung it on me. And why am I defending myself to a couple of curtain-climbers?" Cole shook his head and firmly pushed aside the doubt that crept into his mind. "Look, as far as Welby goes, I think you are worrying needlessly. She's just flirting."

Surely she wouldn't jump into marriage this fast. Not even impulsive, reckless Christina Delaney.

"Oh, hell," Cole muttered beneath his breath as he started moving toward the maze.

Michael snorted. "Flirting and fluttering. Did you catch a gander at her eyelashes last night during the singing?"

"Liked to have started a windstorm in the music room last night, didn't she?" Cole replied glumly. "But it was that fan, not her eyelashes, that raised the breeze. And she wasn't pointing them at Welby but at some other fellow, so she can't be that serious so fast. She's just doing what she always does. Flirts."

Sophie lifted her chin. "My mama says Miss Chrissy acts well within the bounds of pro . . . prop . . . pro-o-o-"

"Propriety," her brother furnished. "Sophie's right. Mama says Miss Chrissy doesn't act forward because she doesn't need to. Men fall over themselves to be near her no matter what. In fact, I think it's worse here than it was at home because in San Antonio, everybody knew Mr. Jake would kill them if they did wrong by Miss Chrissy. Well, everybody except the vaqueros in the square. I think that's one reason she liked being Chili Queen so much—the men weren't always looking over their shoulder for Jake."

Cole remembered her dancing and kissing that man in the square that night and scowled. Maybe the Kleberg youngsters had a point. Maybe he should have been keeping a closer watch on Christina. He had promised Jake he would. Just because she'd acted within the bounds of acceptable behavior so far while in England didn't mean she couldn't get herself in trouble.

As if she had read his mind, Sophie reached out and tugged on his coat. "I really like Mr. Earl of Thornbury, but he's not much help. He wants her to marry one of these men and stay in England close to him."

"You know better, sir," added Michael. "You know she shouldn't marry one of these Englishmen unless she has fallen in love with them which I promise you she hasn't because that's what she told my mama. You need to fill in for Mr. Jake. You must be her brother."

Be Christina's brother? Cole grimaced. The very idea of it repulsed him, but he wasn't up to digging too deeply for the reason why. "Fine," he said, giving in. He didn't cotton to the idea of Welby for Christina's husband anyway. "Where is she?"

Michael peered through the bushes behind the statue of Zeus, then said dryly, "She's over here. She's letting Mr. Welby look for something in her mouth. With his tongue."

Cole bit off a curse and joined the boy at the bushes. "Dammit," he muttered, staring through the leafy branches toward where the Englishman had Christina wrapped in his arms for a kiss. *Some things never change.* "Children, y'all run along back to the house. I'll take care of this."

Rounding the hedge, he heard the viscount croon, "You take my breath away, my dear. I would be honored if you would consent to being my wife."

Cole didn't give her time to answer as he filled in for Jake. "If you want to keep your tongue, you'll make sure it stays in your own mouth where it belongs."

The couple broke apart. He had the grace to look sheepish. She all but bared her teeth in anger. "Morgan. You need to go away."

He ignored her and turned his fiercest, narrow-eyed glare on the Englishman.

Welby held up his hands, palms out, and offered one of his patent winning smiles. "Now, one moment, Mr. Morgan," he protested. "This is not as unseemly as it appears. I have proposed marriage to her."

"You and the multitude," Cole drawled.

"Cole!"

He continued as though she hadn't spoken. "Listen up and I'll make this simple and sweet. Touch the lady again and I'll take one of those fancy vests you like so much and tie it in a hangman's noose. Around your neck."

"That's enough!" she snapped. "You can't say something like that. You have no hold over me."

"Yes, I do. I promised your brother I'd stand in his stead." With a glance at the Englishman, he added, "You've probably read of his exploits in the newspapers? Killer Jake Delaney?"

The pretty-boy viscount's eyebrows arched above doubting eyes. He met Cole's gaze squarely and his lips twisted in an understated smirk. It was, Cole thought, an English gentleman's way of saying *You're full of bullshit.*

Then Welby offered Christina a gentle smile and said, "Obviously you have family matters to discuss. Christina, you and I shall speak of this again later." With that, he dipped his head in a bow, then turned and retreated toward the house.

Chrissy fumed. "Damn you, Cole Morgan!" Her temper blazing, she barreled up her fist and took a wild swing at him. He dodged that blow easily, but she caught him by surprise with a strong kick to his shin.

Ignoring the pain in her toes, she demanded, "What's the matter with you? Welby proposed marriage, you fool. My first."

"First?" he repeated, rubbing his sore leg. "Fifty-first, maybe."

"My first while in England. From a viscount, no less. Within a month of my arrival. That's why Mother sent me here, Morgan. It's what I'm supposed to do!"

Anger flashed like lightning in his sky blue eyes. He struck like a rattlesnake with the question, "Do you love him?"

That shut her up. While she stood stiff and silent, Cole sent her a smile that was anything but amused. "I guess I have my answer."

Chrissy's defenses rose like a wall. "I like Lord Welby very much. Given time, it could grow into something more. And he professes to admire me for who I am. He doesn't want to change me."

"That's because he hasn't seen the real you," Cole shot back. "You've not been acting like yourself of late, Christina."

"That's not true," she countered, although now that he mentioned it, she suspected he did have a point. In her effort to find love without conditions, had she been placing conditions on herself?

Maybe she had been trying to conform to this society's behavior rules more than she ever had at home. Why? Was she afraid her mother was right after all? Was she afraid no one could love the real Chrissy Delaney?

It was a question she'd have to face another time. Right now she was too busy arguing with Cole.

And feeling more alive than she had in days.

She cleared her throat. "I'm simply trying to make a place for myself in proper society. That's what my family wants for me, what they think I'm too improper to have."

"So you're out to prove them properly wrong, is that it? That's stupid, Christina."

"It's what they want for me," she repeated.

"Since when did you ever do what your family wanted?"

She sucked in a sharp breath. It was a low blow, and ordinarily she'd end the argument by walking off. This time, however, for some reason she couldn't quite comprehend, she felt the need to explain. It was important to her that he understand.

Forcing calm into her voice, she said, "I was born trying to please, Cole Morgan. I was a good girl. I behaved. I did what good little girls were supposed to say and do. So, my mother should have been pleased, right?" When he didn't answer, she said it again, "Right?"

He scowled. "She *was* pleased."

Bitterness spiced her laugh. "Really? And how could you tell? Did she give me hugs and kisses for it? Did she tell me she was proud, that she loved me?"

He remained silent.

"I was very little when your mother died, Cole, but I remember how she used to reach out and hug you every time you walked by. I used to yearn for that."

"Your father used to hug and kiss you. He called you his sweet little love."

"Yes." Chrissy's throat tightened and her eyes stung at the memory. "Yes, he did and for that I am eternally grateful. When I lost him, I lost so very much."

"I know, Christina. He was a damn fine man."

She wrapped her arms around herself, huddling deeper in her cloak. "Both my parents treated Jake differently than they did me. Once you came to live with us, they treated you just like they did Jake."

"But we're boys and you're a girl. Of course they treated us different. And as far as hugging goes, your mother never once hugged me."

"No, but she gave you the smile—you know which one—that special smile she reserves for you when you've pleased her. I don't know, Cole. It's hard to put into words how she made me feel. It wasn't bad, just somehow . . . less. For instance, Mama often boasted about you and Jake to her friends. I never once heard her mention any of my accomplishments."

Cole opened his mouth, then apparently reconsidered and snapped it shut without speaking.

Chrissy continued. "Remember when the three of us played that prank on the smithy?"

"The biggest, meanest man in town," Cole said with a nod.

"Mama chuckled over your bravery. She banished me to my room for a week."

"Well, you did take a risk with that branding iron. We all knew at the time you shouldn't have done that."

"Your action with the tongs wasn't any better." When Cole started to protest, she waved it away and said, "You know what? It didn't bother me too much because at least I got her attention. I was happy to be there because every day she would come by and lecture me about my behavior. I had five uninterrupted minutes of her time."

Exasperation chased across Cole's face. "That was ten years ago, Christina. What does it all matter now? You need to grow up."

She offered a bittersweet smile. "You wouldn't think it should matter now, would you? I did a lot of thinking about this during the voyage to England. Yes, what happened when I was a child shouldn't matter now. I should be able to get beyond those old hurts. It's a childish way to think and I know that, so I'm trying to let it go. Truly, I am. But it's hard, Cole."

"Why?"

"I think it's because no matter how old you are, you never outgrow the need to please your parents. Mama is all I have left."

He raked a hand through his hair. "Let me get this straight. You engage yourself to a platoon of different men, then break it off with each of them. You join the Chili Queens, for God's sake. That's your way of trying to please Elizabeth? Honey, I don't mind telling you, you're going about it all wrong."

"Hardly a platoon, Cole, and it's more complicated than that." Chrissy paced the width of the hedge, then turned around again. Her thoughts and feelings churned in confusion, and she struggled to make sense of them enough to put into words. "Sometimes I feel like I'm a failure at everything I do. Cole, each time I accepted a marriage proposal, I believed my mother would approve of my choice. I was always wrong. I never got the smile, and she always had a snide comment or remark to make."

"And that's why you dumped the fiancés? Because your mama didn't smile? That's a helluva reason to break a man's heart, Christina."

"I didn't break any hearts." She kicked at a small pile of leaves collected in the middle of the path, sending them flying in a spray of yellow, russet and orange. "My beaux played the game well and they fooled me. Every time I said yes, I also believed it to be a love match. So I was willing to bear the burden of her disapproval. But invariably as the wedding date approached, each man proved in one way or another that he didn't love me, not like I deserve to be loved. I won't marry a man I don't love, and I won't marry a man who doesn't love me in return. Love *me*. The real me."

She paused and took a deep breath, smelling rain in the air. "I need that, Cole. I know at times I act rashly, foolishly even, but I'm not a bad person. I don't mean to hurt my family by my actions."

"So why do you do things you know will upset Elizabeth? Why did you become a Chili Queen?"

Sighing, Chrissy allowed her head to drop back, lifting her face toward the sky. She closed her eyes, felt weak sunshine on her skin and smelled the rain on the way. Then she spoke from her heart. "I joined the Chili Queens because the people in the square accept me, Cole. They made me one of them, part of the family." Smiling, she added, "And besides, I make a right fine bowl of Texas Red."

"See, there you go again, acting selfish as sin." Now Cole did the pacing, gesturing wildly as he said, "You already have a family, Christina. And speaking from an orphan's point of view, you're damned lucky to have them. Why do you think you need another one?"

"I don't have to change for the Chili Queens, Cole. I need not pretend to be someone else when I'm with them."

"Honey, you don't have to pretend with me or with Jake. You should know that."

"And if you believe that, you're fooling yourself, Cole Morgan. Let me ask you a question. Why isn't it enough to be loyal and honest and kind? I'm a good person."

"Yes, you are."

"So why do society's rules make me look wicked? Why must I worry about wearing gloves every time I step outside? Why is it such a sin to wear my hair down? Why must I wear a stupid bustle when I'm trying to ride a horse? Do you know how free if feels to wear a Mexican skirt with but a single petticoat beneath it?"

"Can't say I do," he drawled.

"It's wonderful. It's right. It's the way it should be. Why should 'ladies' be forced to wear layer after layer after layer of clothing during a Texas summer when it's hot enough to fry eggs on the back stoop? What purpose do such insane rules serve except to give my mother something to scold me about?"

Cole held up his hands palm out. "All right, Christina, I hear what you're saying."

"Thank you."

"But . . ." he held up a finger. "Having said that, the business you're about here in England doesn't make a lot of sense. Marrying a British lord will only give you more of those kind of rules to live by."

"But it's different over here. I'm different over here. It's easier for me to follow all these silly rules."

"Why?"

She shrugged. "I don't know. Maybe because society as a whole is more proper than it is at home so I'm not constantly faced with temptation. More likely, it's because my mother isn't here to pounce on me every time I slip up. You want to know something funny? I even enjoy parts of life in Polite Society."

"I've noticed you've taken to using a fan."

"Yes I have, and I enjoy it. Mother isn't here to scold me for the way I wield it. You should have seen her the last time I carried one in San Antonio. One little ill-timed flutter during the San Antonio chorale and you'd have thought I shot someone instead of accidentally flirted with him. She doesn't seem to understand that I'm human and humans make mistakes. Does that really mean I don't deserve to be loved?"

Hands braced on his hips, Cole demanded, "Love. That reminds me. This conversation has been quite illuminating, Christina, but you've wandered from the question at hand. Where does all this leave Welby? You weren't going to accept the man, were you? You said you didn't love him."

"Yet," Chrissy corrected. "I said I might be able to fall in love with Lord Welby given time. I think he might fall in love with me."

The two of them had spent a good bit of time together of late. The wishes he'd expressed during their conversations had made quite an impression on her. Welby claimed he was tired of being "the most eligible bachelor in England." He wanted a family. He wanted children. But he wanted a wife who wanted him for more than his wealth and his title. Apparently, such women were difficult to find in English society.

She had felt a twinge of conscience at that because his title made a difference to her. Not because she cared about being a lady. She didn't. She cared about finally proving something to her mother, and maybe to herself.

"Besides," she continued. "What does it matter to

you, Morgan? My marital status has no bearing on the search for the Declaration."

He took a step toward her. "Would you have said yes to him today?"

She closed her eyes and laughed softly, sadly. "You didn't give me the chance to offer Lord Welby my response, and I'm not about to tell you before I tell him. I won't tread on social graces in this."

Sophie Kleberg emerged from behind a bush saying, "Y'all should go inside now. It's starting to rain."

"Sophie!" Christina exclaimed. "Were you spying on us?"

"Of course," replied Michael as he followed his sister into the open.

Sophie nodded briskly. "It's our job. We love you."

Christina dipped her head. Her shoulders started shaking and even she wasn't certain if she were laughing or crying.

The children made a dash for the house. "Better hurry or you'll get wet, Miss Chrissy," the boy called over his shoulder. "You, too, Mr. Morgan."

Christy stared up at the clouds as rain spat from the sky.

Cole looked at her and his mouth twisted in a rueful grin. "We're standing about halfway between Hartsworth and the folly. Which will it be?"

"Which way are you going?"

He shrugged. "I'm cold and your grandfather has brandy in the house. I'm headed for Hartsworth."

Christina, of course, took the folly path.

Chapter

6

❧❧❧

"Contrary woman."

Cole glanced from Christina's departing back to the warm, welcoming, dry facade of Hartsworth. "Just shoot me a-runnin'," he muttered, aiming his feet down the folly path. The woman was headstrong as a mule. He should have figured that whatever he said, she would choose the opposite. She'd been doing that all her life. That was the Christina Delaney he knew.

And, to be honest, the one he'd been missing of late.

He caught up with her just as the sky opened up, drenching them both. Christina let out a squeal and started to run. The rain was cold and wet and miserable.

Damned if Christina didn't start laughing.

Despite himself, a smile lifted the corners of Cole's mouth as he followed her. The girl always had liked playing in the rain. Now she literally skipped her way down the path.

What a mercurial woman she'd grown up to be. A man never knew what he was letting himself in for when he shared time with Christina Delaney. No wonder so many men found her fascinating.

To his credit, she'd never fooled him with the shallow, feather-headed act she sometimes adopted around men. To his shame, he'd never realized how deep her waters ran. Ordinarily, he considered himself an observant man. This time it looked like he'd completely missed the mark.

Take the hug business. He'd never noticed that Elizabeth kept her distance from Christina. Since he, himself, remembered missing his mother's embraces after her death, he could sympathize with Christina a little bit on that one. Still, all she'd had to do was ask. Elizabeth would do anything for her children. Anything for Jake, anyway. *And me.*

But what about Christina? Cold water seeped past his collar as Cole debated the question. He wouldn't accept the notion that Elizabeth mistreated her daughter. But then, Christina hadn't made that claim, had she? She said her mother treated her "less." *What a strange term.*

He ducked into the folly a few steps behind her. The echo of her chuckles brought a full-blown grin to his face. He understood her a little more now, and despite being soaked through to the bone, Cole felt better than he had in weeks. He leaned forward, removed his hat, and gave his head a shake.

"You look just like a dog," she observed with a giggle.

"You're one to talk. Be glad I'm too much a gentlemen to mention you look like a drowned possum."

She stuck out her tongue. He snorted with amusement. Damn, but didn't the day look suddenly brighter, despite the crying gray rain clouds that blocked the sun. Cole realized the run through the rain combined with the preceding conversation had managed to douse the tension that had smoldered between them since Elizabeth first mentioned this trip. Knowing the respite could end at any time, he decided to enjoy it while he could.

Christina must have felt a similar relief. She smiled widely at him as she sat on a stone bench and tugged off her hat, then pulled the pins from her hair. It spilled to her waist in a cascade of red. Next she kicked off her shoes, and yanked off her garters and stockings. Then, she carelessly revealed bare ankles and a good portion of leg while wringing the dampness from her skirt. "Brrr . . . that's cold," she said, shaking with a delicious shiver. "I don't think rain ever gets this cold in Texas."

Cole didn't comment. Upon noting the direction of his gaze, she naturally lifted a leg and teasingly wriggled her toes in his direction.

His breath caught. Tension came roaring back. He was unable to shift his stare from her toes. *This* woman was San Antonio's Christina Delaney. *This* was the Queen of the Chili Queens.

Cole swallowed hard. The proper English lady had taken her fluttering fan and disappeared entirely, leaving a Wild West wanton in her place. God help them all, but it was true. Though British lady she seemed determined to be, in the heart of her, the heat of her, Christina Delaney still bubbled like a pot of hot Texas Red.

Damned if she didn't put him on to simmer himself.

*   *   *

Chrissy shook her hands, flinging water drops from her fingers onto the folly's tile floor. A chill swept over her causing her to shiver, but the warmth within her fended off the cold. Cole didn't know it, and she wouldn't admit it to a soul, but he had saved her. Once she'd managed to put some of her feelings into words, relief had melted through her like warm butter.

She didn't want to marry Lord Welby.

But she might have been reckless enough, impatient enough, to accept him.

"Oh, Cole. Don't you just love the rain?"

The sky had opened up by now with rain falling in torrents, and the temperature had taken a steep drop. Cole shot her a look that questioned her sanity. "Sure I love the rain," he replied. "On a hot summer day, or when it comes to break a drought. That's not the case here though, is it? If it isn't raining already in this godforsaken country, it's about to." He pointed toward Chrissy's bare feet. "I wouldn't be surprised if the people who live around here didn't grow webs between their toes."

Chrissy wiggled hers. "Don't be such a baby, Morgan. You're not sugar. A little rain won't make you melt."

He was staring at her feet when he grumbled, "No, but I'm afraid you could."

"What?"

He closed his eyes and shook his head hard. "Nothing. Never mind. I think all this wet is making my brain misfire." He took a seat on the stone bench opposite her and said, "So, I heard this Melton fellow who I'm supposed to contact isn't going to make it to the house party, after all."

It hurt Chrissy to allow that brain misfire remark to pass without comment, but she felt too mellow to spoil the mood. "A message arrived with word that Lord Melton is ill. Hopefully he'll have a quick recovery and we can speak with him at another time."

Cole told her news about Parkwood, then asked, "What about that fellow Bennet? Did you talk your grandfather into sending an invitation off to him?"

Chrissy nodded. Bennet was a lead Lord Welby had given her, the baron who owned the herd of longhorns. "The note went out this morning. Grandfather expects Lord Bennet to accept. Apparently the fellow has coveted an invitation to Hartsworth for years." She hesitated just a moment, then added, "This is the first thing I have asked of my grandfather that he hasn't been thrilled to do."

Cole pursed his lips. "You know, I've been wondering about that. Your mother always said the earl was a strict disciplinarian. Seems to me you have him wrapped around your finger like a candy bow."

"I can't argue with you."

"Sure you can," he quipped. "You do it all the time."

She sent him a chiding look. "I mean about my grandfather. It's as if he's a different person than the man my mother described."

"Perhaps losing Elizabeth to Texas the way he did taught him something."

Chrissy's mood went as damp as the weather. Glumly, she said, "It's a shame my mother didn't learn the same lesson. She didn't mind 'losing' me to England one little bit."

Cole's sigh rippled across the room. "I was hoping

we were through with that topic for a time, but since you've brought it up again there is something I want to ask. Something I can't figure out. Are you happy living here in England, Christina?"

"You brought her name up, not me." Then, shrugging, she addressed his question. "I find it fascinating to live in a mansion surrounded by treasures and interesting people. Grandfather dotes on me, which I admit is nice, and the gentlemen make it entertaining."

"That part I have picked up on. You're still collecting more than your share of kisses."

For almost a full minute, the only sound to be heard was the splatter of rain against the roof. Chrissy mourned the loss of peace she'd felt moments ago, and she was tempted to make light of the subject he'd introduced. But rather than a quip, when she rose, crossed to the doorway, and stood staring toward Hartsworth's grand southern facade, she wrapped her arms around herself and spoke from her heart. "This is a beautiful place to visit, but it's not home, Cole. It's not home."

He absorbed her statement for a moment before asking, "Will you try to make it one?" She turned as he approached her, and he reached out to tuck a damp strand of fiery hair behind her ear. "Do you believe you are suited to being a lord's lady and living in his castle? Can you be happy doing that?"

"Maybe," she replied, resisting the urge to shiver at his touch. "I'll certainly try. I don't want to fail again, and at least here I'm wanted."

He sighed in exasperation and his voice was tight as he said, "You give new meaning to the word stubborn. It's not that they don't want you, and you know it. Jake and your mother love you. I'm certain they miss you terribly by now."

His words wiped the smile from her face and left her feeling cold for the first time since the rain came. Rubbing her hands up and down her arms, she said, "I seriously doubt that. They were content to have me gone for three years when my father sent me off to school, weren't they? They didn't hesitate to send me away this time, either. No, I'm staying in England. I belong here now. I'll make myself belong. I'll find a lord and become his lady, and I will make England my home."

"Lady Christina," Cole murmured. "Lady Stubborn. Lady Bug."

A grin quirked her lips. Lady Bug. She liked that one.

Fallen leaves skidded into the folly on a cool wind and this time she gave in to the shudder. Cole removed his jacket, then draped it over her shoulders. "You should have picked the house over the folly. You'd be cozy and warm right now inside of Hartsworth." He took a seat on the stone bench out of the wind and gestured for her to sit beside him.

She didn't hesitate. One thing about being big like Cole, he gave off a lot of warmth. She scooted toward him. "It's worth being cold to smell the rain, don't you think? Inside the house, all I smell is women's perfume and furniture wax."

His eyes drifted shut and he drew a deep breath, then held it as if savoring it, before exhaling in a rush. "You need something on your feet," he told her, shifting away.

Chrissy looked at him, her brow furrowed. Why the strange note in the gruffness of his voice? She'd never heard that before. She grabbed his arm and leaned forward, studying him through narrowed eyes. "What's wrong with you?"

"Nothing."

Now he sounded strangled. Nervous, even. Cole Morgan nervous? Imagine that. "Something's wrong."

He scowled at her, but his gaze quickly slid from her eyes down to her lips. In an automatic response, she licked them.

A rumble rose from Cole's throat. A rumble like a groan. Chrissy's eyes widened at the notion and her heartbeat sped up. She'd often heard groans just like that right before a man tried to steal a kiss. Was Cole Morgan finally seeing her as more than his best friend's kid sister?

The notion both shocked and intrigued her, and the last thoughts about the trouble with her mother melted away. Many years ago this had been her fondest dream. Years ago she'd been more than a little in love with Cole, but he never once looked twice at her.

He was looking twice now. He was staring at her ankles, in fact. Maybe overhearing Welby's marriage proposal had finally made him see her in a new light. Was that panic she spied in his eyes?

If this is true . . . well . . . how delicious.

Chrissy decided to test the theory. "You're right, Cole, I do need something on my feet. But my stockings are still soaking wet." Lifting her legs, she twisted around and set her feet in his lap. "Would you rub my toes and warm them up for me?"

She might as well have laid a rattlesnake in his lap. "Christina." He shoved her legs off his and abruptly stood. "You can't ask a man to do that. It's too familiar."

"But you're not a man, you're Cole. You're almost my brother. Jake would rub my feet if he were here and I asked."

The "not a man" part got to him, Chrissy could tell. He set his jaw, jammed his hands into his pockets, and glared at her. "Jake would tell you you're a forward little filly who needs a firm hand—"

"On my feet."

"Against your behind!" He stalked the length of the folly then back again. "Just when I think you've learned something, you up and prove me wrong. What is it with you? Does your mind have some sort of behavior timer that only allows you to act properly for so long before the wanton in you explodes?"

"Wanton?" She straightened. A smile played around her lips. "You think I'm wanton?"

"I do."

"A wanton woman?"

"Yes."

The desire to tease him overwhelmed her good sense. Standing, she said, "Hmm . . . I see. Then maybe I should go back to the house and look for a man who might be wanton, too." Walking toward him, she slightly exaggerated the sway of her hips. Passing by him, she trailed a finger along his arm and added, "Wanton and wanting me."

She took three more steps before he grabbed her wrist and yanked her back. "You've played with fire, Lady Bug. Now it's time you . . ."

As his mouth swooped down on hers, Chrissy mentally finished the sentence on a sigh. *Burned.*

Liquid fire poured from him to her. Heat licked at her, scorched her, consumed her. His mouth was hard against hers, taking, demanding, ravaging. It was everything she'd always dreamed a kiss could be and more. It was nothing like any kiss any man had given her in the past.

Chrissy reveled in it.

She melted against him, offering herself up, welcoming his passion with a wellspring of her own. Her hands crept up around his neck, her fingers sliding into the silky thickness of his hair. His hands impatiently batted at her bustle, then clamped around her waist. He smelled of rain and man and home, and his name beat a pulse through her mind: *Cole, Cole, Cole.* She was burning, soaring, weeping with the dream of it.

There was a wildness about him, something she'd never seen in him before, an air of reckless need that appealed to something basic in Chrissy. When his lips abandoned hers she moaned a protest, until the drag of his tongue down the length of her neck transformed the sound to one of pleasure. She clasped him tighter and felt the unmistakable sign of his arousal pressing hard against her belly. Inwardly, she gasped. *I did that to him. To Cole. I'm the one who's stirring him so.*

Cole's fingers roved and brushed against her breast, once, twice. Then he cupped her, kneaded her, and Chrissy arched her back in offering. And Cole Morgan took.

Soon she felt a draft against her skin as her dress

slipped off her shoulders. His head drifted lower, his mouth trailing wet kisses across the swell of her breasts. With the tug of a ribbon and the scoop of a hand, he bared her completely.

"God, you're beautiful."

Chrissy ached, whimpered, when he deliberately reached out and stroked the rough pad of his thumb across the sensitive flesh of her nipple. Ribbons of pleasure fluttered through her and she gasped. And wanted more.

She wanted his mouth on her.

Cole must have heard her unspoken plea. His lips trailed lower. His tongue dragged once, then twice across her aching peak, sending a fierce stab of longing shooting directly to her woman's core. She clutched his head, urging him on.

He fastened his mouth around her and began to suckle.

Chrissy groaned. Deep inside herself, somewhere apart from this whirlwind of sensation, she was shocked. She hadn't known . . . she hadn't even guessed. Never before had she allowed a man such liberties. Never before had she come close to being tempted. But here, today, in this secluded folly so very far from home, she would willingly, joyfully, give Cole anything he asked. She would yield him anything and everything. Her body. Her innocence. Her heart.

This was Cole Morgan. The man she'd loved half her life.

I'm yours, Cole. Ask me and I'm yours.

But Cole didn't ask.

Cole Morgan let her go.

With a curse, he shoved her away and rolled to his feet. For long, shocking seconds he stood staring at her, his chest rising and falling, his harsh breaths seeming to echo off the folly's stone wall. His gaze lowered to her bosom, the light in his eyes changing, sharpening. Condemning.

And angry hurt washed through Chrissy.

She tugged at her bodice, covering herself, as Cole whirled around and spoke in a tone rough with his own anger now rather than desire. "Dammit. *Dammit*." He thrust his hands through his hair, then clenched them into fists. "What the hell was this? What were we doing?"

"Cole . . ."

"Sonofabitch, Christina." He turned back to glare at her. "Is this the way you act with all your beaux? It's a wonder you haven't presented your poor mother with a bastard grandbaby by now."

Chrissy gasped. Fury knifed her. How dare he! It wasn't the first time Cole had used words to hurt her, but it was certainly the worst. She reacted instinctively, drawing back her arm, and slapping him hard across the cheek. The crack of hand against flesh echoed off the marble walls of the folly.

Head still turned from her blow, he shut his eyes. She blinked back tears. Outside the rain fell in torrents and within Chrissy, a chill seeped into her soul. When Cole finally spoke, he did so in a cold, formal tone. "I apologize. My actions were reprehensible. Rest assured my loss of control will not be repeated."

He left her then, striding outside as though seeking a haven in the storm from the tempest that had wreaked its havoc within. Trembling like a willow in the wind, Chrissy watched him go.

Slowly, she sank to her knees. The marble tile was hard and cold, but the fact barely registered. She didn't weep. She didn't scream. She didn't do much of anything. Chrissy felt distant, deadened, and dazed.

Eventually the sun came out, and she rose, righted herself, then made the trek back to Hartsworth. By the time she reached the house, the numbness had faded and recklessness took its place.

That night at supper, she sat at the opposite end of the table from Cole. Following the sweet course, her grandfather rose from his chair and beamed a smile around the table, asking for his guests' attention. Chrissy watched with dispassionate detachment as he prepared to reveal the decision she'd shared with him a few hours before supper.

The Earl of Thornbury lifted a glass brimming with champagne. "I probably should wait for a formal occasion, but I find I'm too excited to keep quiet. Ladies and gentlemen, it is my great honor to announce the upcoming marriage of the Viscount Welby to my darling granddaughter, Miss Christina Delaney."

Cole had to search to find the woodpile at Hartsworth the following morning, but eventually he located it out behind the brewhouse. Long ago he'd learned that the physically demanding activity of chopping firewood was a great way to work off mental steam.

Cole had a lot of steam that needed working off.

He was angry at Christina, her grandfather, Welby, and the entire British population. He wasn't too happy with Jake and Elizabeth Delaney. Most of all, he was furious with himself. How could he have acted so irresponsibly? How could he have lost control that way? In the space of a few minutes out in that damned, miniature Greek temple, he'd sacrificed every bit of self-discipline and honor and good sense he'd ever possessed to the gods of Stupidity up there on Mount Think-with-Your-Pecker.

And to make it even worse, out of all the women in the world he had to go and act the idiot with Christina Delaney. Elizabeth's daughter. His best friend's sister. A member of a family that had made a place for him.

"I deserve to be horsewhipped," he muttered, giving the ax in his hand another hard swing. He felt the sweat dribble down his back as wood splintered, divided, and fell to each side of the chopping block.

He'd driven her into this betrothal. Cole knew that. It wasn't enough he'd acted like a cad, oh no. Guilt had gotten hold of him and he'd lashed out, using words as a weapon in a manner that was downright cruel. And reckless, reactionary Christina had fought back in the way that nettled him the most.

"Married to that charming, debonair, worried-about-his-vests viscount." Cole set another log on the chopping block. He simply couldn't see it. Of course, he shouldn't have to see it. She shouldn't have agreed to marry the man. She barely knew him. She damn sure couldn't love him. Otherwise that debacle in the folly never would have happened. Christina had a lot of faults, but a lack of loyalty wasn't one of them. If she'd given her heart to one man, she'd never have come so close to giving her body to another.

And damned if it hadn't been close.

Cole swung his ax. Wood split. The physical work helped, but not nearly enough. Tension hummed in him like a hive filled with hornets.

He still couldn't believe it had actually happened. What the hell had gotten into him? Sure it had been a while since he'd had a woman—all right, a long while—but he'd never been a man to let his pecker lead him around. And this was Christina, for God's sake. The girl he should consider his sister. Her brother would kill him.

"Damn straight." If Jake ever found out what mischief Cole had wreaked in the folly—*now there's an appropriate name*—he'd shoot him dead. As well he should. Cole quickly dealt with two more logs and the pile of firewood at his feet continued to grow. Sweat rolled down his face, dripped onto his shoulder. Like rain. Like yesterday.

Memory flashed of a bare-breasted Christina and like lightning, heat filled his loins. "Good God, what have I done?"

Pushed her into a hasty marriage, that's what, came the answer.

Cole sent the ax sailing, twisting round and round like the blades of a windmill. He launched into a string of curses blue enough to make a sapphire sky look pale. What the hell should he do? Chrissy had landed a titled fish—exactly what her mother wanted for her.

While he understood why Elizabeth felt the way she did, he didn't agree with her. Christina shouldn't marry a man she didn't love.

He hated to say it, but this illness had obviously

scrambled Jake's and Elizabeth's thinking. Jake's mistake was understandable. After all, he had no experience with marriage or love. But Elizabeth . . . well . . . under normal circumstances, Cole felt certain she'd know better. After what she'd shared with Christina's father, how could she possibly wish a loveless marriage upon her daughter?

Cole loaded his arms with split logs and carried them to the woodpile. But then, Elizabeth didn't mean for Chrissy to marry without love. She didn't mean for her to accept the first man who'd asked. By accepting Welby's suit, Chrissy was reacting to being sent away from home, reacting to what had transpired between the two of them yesterday in the folly.

Which brought the blame right back around to Cole and the question at hand. "What the hell am I going to do about it?"

"That's almost identical to the question I've been asking."

Cole glanced over his shoulder to see Lana Kleberg standing beside the brewhouse, her two children eyeing the woodpile with interest. He shot the lovely widow a crooked grin, somewhat embarrassed at having been caught talking to himself, until Sophie stepped forward and spoke in a tone filled with awe.

"My goodness, Mr. Morgan. You've cut enough wood to last until Thanksgiving."

Michael folded his arms and snorted with disdain. "All that wouldn't last a winter's morning here at Hartsworth."

"I'm not talking about here. I'm talking about home."

When the bickering continued, Lana Kleberg interrupted. "Enough, children. Run along now while I speak with Mr. Morgan. I'll meet you back at the house in half an hour."

"But Mama," Sophie protested. "You just got over a headache. You might need us to help you back to the house."

"I'll escort your mother," Cole assured the girl.

With that, Michael's obvious disdain notched down into disgust. "We can't count on you. You were supposed to stop Miss Chrissy and you didn't."

Cole had no reply to that. The boy was right, after all.

"Go on children," their mother said sternly.

Throwing Cole a pair of fierce looks, the two obeyed Lana. Cole sauntered over to the tree branch where he'd draped his shirt. Shrugging into it, he asked, "In regard to your question, I take it you were referring to Christina's happy news?"

"Happy news?" Lana wrinkled her nose. "Your sense of humor escapes me, Mr. Morgan."

"Call me Cole, please."

"Please tell me you know how to fix this problem. She simply cannot marry Lord Welby."

"Let's sit down and talk about this, shall we?" Cole gestured toward an iron bench a short distance away. "So," he said, once they were settled, "you are against this marriage? I thought y'all wanted her to marry an Englishman."

"Of course I'm against it. She's not in love with him. That's the kind of marriage she needs, she deserves. To love and be loved in return. She is a very emotional woman. She feels things deeply. It will destroy her spirit to marry without love. You know her,

Cole. You know this won't make her happy. Are you going to stand by and watch her make the biggest mistake of her life?"

Frustration filled him. Lana Kleberg didn't know the whole picture, and he couldn't tell her. "I don't know what to do. What's your idea? What do you think I should do?"

"I don't have an idea, although after watching Chrissy pretend to be happy this morning at breakfast, Michael's solution actually appears worth considering."

Imagining the picture, Cole decided he'd made the right choice in skipping the morning meal. "So what is Michael's solution?"

"He thinks you should go to Welby and threaten to break his legs if he doesn't call the wedding off."

The notion held a note of appeal. Mentally, Cole pictured such a scene. The idea of throwing a few punches at the pretty-faced lord made his fist itch to fly.

He glanced at the boy's mother and observed, "Your boy is a bloodthirsty pup, isn't he?"

She shrugged. "Michael loves Chrissy."

"Well, her family loves her, too. Listen, ma'am, the reality of the situation is that I can't do a blessed thing to Welby. It's not my place to interfere in family matters like this. Her grandfather approves, so our opinions are of no consequence."

"That's a ridiculous objection, Cole," Lana said. "Chrissy and the earl are just getting to know one another. As far as family matters go . . . well . . . it is my place to interfere because she considers me and my children family. She told me so. We talked a lot about family on the voyage over here."

That piqued Cole's interest. "Oh? What did Christina have to say?"

"She said that it takes more than blood relations to make a family, that it takes listening to one another and caring about how a person feels. She said that to be a family, people had to learn to compromise. What I remember most clearly is when she talked about being in love."

"In love? Who the hell was she in love with?"

"My children," Lana replied with a smile. "She asked Michael and Sophie if they'd be her new family. She said she'd always wanted a sister and that she needed a new brother since the one she had didn't want her anymore."

Cole closed his eyes, shaking his head. The part about Jake not wanting her was a clanker. Cole knew his friend loved his sister deeply. Jake honestly believed this trip was the best thing for her. It tore at his heart to think that Christina felt unwanted by her family, even though those feelings were certainly unwarranted. He cleared his throat. "All that is well and good, but I don't see how it has much to bear on what's happening here. As long as Christina is set upon this course of action, like I said before, it doesn't much matter what the rest of us think."

"She does appear to be locked in to the idea," Lana said with a sigh. "The children and I about wore our tongues off last night trying to talk her out of it, and it did us not a whit of good. Why, the girl has enough cotton in her ears to batt a quilt. That leaves us with the wrong bridegroom, which is why we came to see you this morning. This is a man's job. Cole, you need to somehow convince Welby he shouldn't marry Chrissy."

Cole shook his head. "I can't. Word around Hartsworth is that the man is totally besotted. I heard he has already sent for a tailor because he intends to order up a whole new set of vests in order to look his best for his bride-to-be."

Lana snorted with disgust and Cole nodded with agreement at her reaction, then continued, "Besides, from what I'm told of how things are done over here, Welby can't break off the engagement without his honor taking a blow. These Englishmen take honor as seriously as we do at home in Texas."

Lana winced. "Unless something drastic happens Chrissy won't be the one to call the wedding off. Oh, I can't bear it. This has all happened too fast."

Too fast. Hmm. A glimmer of an idea fluttered in Cole's mind. "How fast? When do they plan to do the deed? Is the date set?"

"I asked the viscount that this morning. All he said was 'soon.'" After a moment's pause, she added, "I just don't understand this. I know she's impetuous, but not even Chrissy would jump into an engagement this fast. Something must have happened to push her into making this hasty decision."

Cole winced. Something had happened, all right, and it was his fault. He'd pushed her into acting rashly. He was the reason she was rushing into marriage.

Rushing. Fast. Rash. Hasty. The words bounced around in his brain and finally molded the solution into shape. "Time," he said softly. "That's it. That's what we need."

"Time? What do you mean?"

"A long engagement. It solves both problems.

'Marry in haste, repent at leisure.' I've heard Elizabeth say it. And Chrissy will have time to come to her senses. In fact . . ." his voice trailed off as another flash of inspiration hit him. "Of course. It's perfect."

"What's perfect?" Lana asked, her voice sounding somewhat peeved.

Cole took her hand and lifted it to his mouth for a kiss. "I'll need your help. And the children's. Y'all can concentrate on Welby. I don't think our cause would be served for me to have much to do with him. This plan will take some heavy-duty persuading, but I think I know the arguments we can use. I'll work on Christina, though I'll need to bide my time for a bit, give her a while to cool off. Y'all can start right away, though. Yep, I do think we can pull this off."

"Pull what off!"

He grinned. "Convincing Christina to go home to Texas before she says 'I do.' Don't you see? It's only right that she take her fiancé home to meet her mother."

Chapter

7

The clocks throughout Hartsworth chimed two A.M. as Chrissy hurried down the corridor toward Cole's bedroom. She absolutely, positively didn't want to be doing this, but she had no other choice. She'd never guessed her engagement to Welby would create such trouble, but it had. The viscount was downright possessive of her; he barely let her out of his sight. Every time she ventured from the family quarters at Hartsworth there he'd be, lurking, ready to pounce upon her—in a gentlemanly way, of course. The only time she'd been able to dodge him was when Lana ran interference for her. Thank goodness Lord Welby appeared to have a soft spot for her friend.

Even then, he always found her eventually. Chrissy sometimes wondered if he had a sixth sense that kept him apprised of her location. It was enough to drive her crazy.

It was enough to make her consider calling off the engagement.

Of course, she couldn't do that. Pride, among other

things, wouldn't allow it. Maybe Lana was right and she had acted rashly in accepting the marriage offer, but darned if she'd put up with Cole Morgan ambling around saying "I told you so." And that's exactly what he would do.

In the four days since their . . . meeting . . . in the folly, she and Cole had exchanged exactly two words. They'd passed in a corridor the morning following her betrothal announcement—neither noticed the other in time to alter their direction without being obvious—and he'd said, "Fool," to which she'd replied, "Idiot."

She'd have liked to send Michael on this errand, but the boy and his sister had been pecking at her for days, and she simply couldn't face their unending arguments and Cole Morgan at the same time. The children had made it clear they objected to the betrothal, but what's done was done and they'd simply have to get used to the idea. Time would take care of that situation.

With this other problem, however, time was her enemy.

Which was why she found herself twisting the knob on the door to Cole Morgan's bedroom.

Quickly, she slipped inside and silently shut the door behind her. She waited where she stood for a full minute, working up the nerve to approach the bed.

He slept with both the window drapes and bed curtains open wide. As a result, moonlight spilled through the floor-to-ceiling-length window and cast the room, including his bed, in a silvery glow. Chrissy could easily make out his shape lying there beneath the blankets. Mostly beneath the blankets, that is.

He had one long bare muscular leg flung atop the heap.

Chrissy blinked, then forced her attention to where his head rested on a pillow. He lay on his side, facing her. *He snores. Hah. How uncouth.*

Of course, compared to Jake, who sounded like a sawmill when he slept, Cole's snore passed for mild.

The notion needled her enough to dispel her hesitation and she marched over to the bed, reached for the lump she thought to be his shoulder, and shook. "Wake up, Morgan. I need to talk to you."

His eyes opened. "Gypsy Belle? Is that you?"

Gypsy Belle? That's a soiled dove's name if I've ever heard one. Chrissy made a fist and punched him on the side of his arm. "It's Chrissy, you fool. Wake up. As much as I hate it, I need you."

He sat straight up in bed. "What?"

"Be quiet." She clapped a hand over his mouth. "You'll wake the whole house."

Cole yanked her hand away, then reached out and lit the bedside lamp.

His wavy hair was boyishly rumpled, his eyes still hazy from slumber. Chrissy tried her best to keep her gaze from straying below his neck, but the female in her won out. *Oh my.* A thin dusting of dark hair covered his broad chest and arrowed intriguingly downward to where the covers pooled in his lap.

"What are you doing here?"

She wanted to run her fingers across his chest to see if it was as hard as it looked.

"Bug! What the hell are you doing?"

Nothing. I'm not touching. She didn't intend to, at least, but somehow her hand ended up hovering mere inches above his chest. Thank God he grabbed her around the wrist and pushed her away, snapping her out of her haze. Otherwise, no telling what idiocy she might have attempted.

She pulled back and put some distance between them. "I have to talk to you, and I can't seem to manage it during the daytime."

"That's because Lord Windy stays draped around you like a ratty old coat," Cole grumbled. Then he shook his head. "I can't believe you've done this. What if someone saw you come in here? Don't you have a care for your reputation?"

"Lord *Welby* and no, no one saw me. That's why I waited so late to come. I've been careful."

Cole picked up his gold pocket watch from the table and flipped back the cover. "No, you've been lucky. *If* no one saw you, that is. Christina, since all the guests arrived for the house party, this is one of the busiest times of night."

"What do you mean?"

"Folks are returning to their own rooms following their visits to others."

"At this time of night?" Chrissy scoffed. "That's silly. What could they possibly be . . . oh."

"Yes, oh."

She shrugged. "Well, what's done is done. I'm here now so we might as well not waste the chance."

Warily, Cole replied, "Chance for what?"

"I told you. I need to talk to you."

"No. You told me you need me. It's that kind of talk, Christina, that gets a girl in trouble."

Chrissy blew a frustrated breath. "Pay attention, Morgan. It's about the Declaration."

That got his attention. He made as if to rise from bed, but suddenly he stopped. "Turn around."

"Why?"

"Just do it, please?"

The *please* won her over. She could count on both hands the times he'd said that particular word to her. She did as he asked, then tried not to listen—or not imagine, anyway—as she heard the rustle of clothing.

Finally, he said, "What about the Declaration?"

She turned and tried not to stare at the picture of his long tanned fingers fixing the last button on his pants before reaching for a brilliant white shirt. Somehow, watching him dress seemed more intimate than seeing a good bit of him bare in his bed.

"Christina?"

She cleared her throat. "It's about tomorrow. I don't know if you heard the news, but Lord Bennet arrived at Hartsworth late this evening."

"It's two in the morning. It's tomorrow already."

"Don't be difficult." Chrissy sat on the corner of his bed and ignored the strange look that came over his face. "My grandfather has arranged an entertainment for the afternoon that should appeal to our guests' and Lord Bennet's, in particular, fascination with other lands. However, this plan won't do us one bit of good unless one of us is with Bennet to herd the conversation in the direction we need. I'm afraid that under the circumstances I won't have the opportunity to mine him for information like I did the others."

"Mine, Christina?"

She waved her arm. "A figure of speech."

"And circumstances being the Viscount of Windy."

"That's Viscount *Welby*," she absently corrected. "No 'of.' "

Cole arched a cynical brow. "How interesting that you think it more important to educate me on the nuances of proper address for British aristocracy than to scold me for the slight to your betrothed."

She sighed. "Other than to concede that Welby does like to spend as much time with me as possible, something that's only natural for a fiancé, I might add, I'm not going to waste my breath talking to you about my upcoming marriage." Ignoring his snort, she continued, "I'm here to talk about tomorrow. From gossip I've solicited from other ladies, I believe Lord Bennet may indeed know something about the Declaration. I need you to follow through for me."

Having known him basically all her life, Chrissy knew when she'd managed to trigger his anger. Upon spying the tick in his jaw, she prepared herself for verbal assault.

He began with a lazy drawl. "Correct me if I'm wrong, but isn't *my* job to locate the missing Declaration? I have this vague recollection of being sent here for exactly that reason."

"Now, Cole . . ."

"Don't you 'Now, Cole' me. You risked your reputation by coming to my room tonight to ask me for help for something that is *my* job to do." He braced his hands on his hips and took three steps toward her. Chrissy scooted back just a little bit on his bed. "Do you have any idea how crazy that makes me?"

Pretty crazy, from the looks of it.

"I can't help but wonder just how your brain works, Christina. Maybe while you're here in England we should take you to London and have it studied. Perhaps scientists would discover some peculiarity in your head they could somehow replicate to benefit mankind. I'm sure there must be instances when a recklessness pill might come in handy."

"Aren't you funny."

"No, I'm furious. Do you have no faith at all in my abilities? Do you think I'm so incompetent?" He was right in front of her now, leaning down, his face in hers as he demanded, "Did my lack of control at the folly the other day lead you to conclude I'm as featherheaded as you are?"

"I'm not featherheaded," she protested softly, her throat tight. Pressure built behind her eyes. *I won't cry. I won't.* "And I didn't come to your room because I think you're incompetent."

"Then why, Chrissy? Why?" His breath fogged hotly against her cheeks, and the air between them shimmered with heat.

"I don't know. I don't like how it is between us now. I thought maybe . . . perhaps . . ''

"What!"

A dozen different ideas hovered on her tongue, but the one that slipped out was the last thing she wanted to say. "I thought you found me attractive."

He closed his eyes and shuddered. Long seconds ticked by. "I do," he said finally, his voice a rough croak. "Damn you, Bug, but I do."

His confession was a magnet that pulled her toward him. He smelled of sandalwood and yearning and he was oh, so close.

Chrissy kissed him.

She pressed her lips to his and poured all the feeling, all the confusion, churning inside her into the effort. Cole resisted for only a heartbeat before responding. He muttered something—a curse, she thought—then groaned and took control.

His hands were magic. He knew just where to touch her, just how to stroke her, to feed the spark of her desire. He knelt on the bed, urged her back until she lay sandwiched between the hard length of his body and soft comfort of the mattress. Her head spun, her breasts tingled, and her woman's core ached.

Again, it was happening again. Chrissy knew she should stop it, knew he didn't want this, but she couldn't quite summon the will to say no. In fact, every inch of her body seemed to be screaming *Yes, yes, yes.*

His hands delved beneath her skirt and soon found bare skin. She shivered at his touch, gloried in the scrape of work-roughened skin against her. Passion sang in her blood and lured her toward mindlessness.

But it didn't quite get her there.

Even as his fingers found their goal, worked her, slipped inside her wet heat, sending ribbons of pleasure fluttering through her, Chrissy remembered how he'd reacted the last time in the folly. She recalled the harsh looks. She heard the echo of the words they'd exchanged since.

She didn't want that. This momentary pleasure wasn't worth the heartache that undoubtedly would follow. She only hoped it wasn't already too late to avoid it.

She turned her head, breaking contact, and regretfully pushed against the hardness of his chest. "Cole."

That's all it took. His hand dropped away. Groaning, he rolled off of her and lay on his back, breathing heavily, one arm flung over his eyes. "I wish Jake were here."

"Why?"

"He could just shoot me now and get it over with."

"My brother wouldn't shoot you."

Cole shifted his arm and cocked open one eye. "Quick as a rattler on a rat, he would."

Chrissy didn't argue the point again. Cole seemed so definite and besides, he wouldn't have heard her over the litany of curses he was sputtering. She didn't move or make a sound as he finally wound down and rhetorically observed, "I miss home. I miss the weather and the people and the music and the scent of chili spices hanging on the air. I miss the excitement that arises from San Antonio's mix of cultures. I miss the newness of it all, the sense that I'm living on the edge of civilization. Over here, everything is so . . . settled. So old. Stifling." After a moment's pause, he added, "That must be it."

When seconds ticked by without his elaborating, she prodded, "Must be what?"

"Why I'm all of a sudden losing control around you. You are an exciting woman. I'll give you that. But this . . ." he sat up and made a waving motion with his hand. "This . . ." He stood and paced the room. "This madness. It's got to stop, Chrissy. It's got to stop."

Her heart thumping, Chrissy sat up. She licked her suddenly dry lips, then croaked out the question that had rumbled through her subconscious for hours or days or maybe even years. "Why?"

He stopped short, his head whipping around. "What?"

"I asked why?"

"Why what, Christina?"

She frowned. She'd gone from Christina, to Chrissy, to Bug and now back again. Could there be a better barometer of Cole's frame of mind? Still, she had to ask.

"Why does it need to stop, Cole? I enjoy it and it's obvious you do, too. You know, I've some experience when it comes to kissing, and I honestly don't remember it ever being quite this . . . stimulating before. Maybe we should give it some more time and see where it goes."

He gaped at her. "Forget exciting. You're a menace. *See where it goes?* Didn't you learn anything when you followed me and your brother to the whorehouse? I'll tell you where it goes." He pointed toward the bed. "Are you that reckless, girl?"

She had a sudden vision of her and Cole back in the bed, limbs entwined, their bodies naked. *Yes, I'm that reckless.*

She thought of Lord Welby and her upcoming nuptials and said, "This madness, you call it. It means something, Cole. I think we owe it to ourselves—"

"It means we both have an itch that needs scratching. That's all. It doesn't mean it's right to scratch each other's itches." He stormed around the room, waving his hands as he spoke in a tone no less furious for its quietness. "Damn, I can't believe you are talking this way . . . acting this way . . . with me. No wonder your mother was at her wits' end. You need a keeper."

The words formed on her tongue without conscious thought. "Or a husband."

He froze midpace. His complexion bleached white. The moment spun out like dew on Hartsworth's front lawn and when finally he spoke, Chrissy heard a definite tremor in his tone. "What are you trying to say, Christina?"

Obviously nothing you want to hear. She rose from the bed and smoothed her skirts, pride winging to the rescue. "I'm sure it's not you, Cole. I imagine my feminine juices are simply stirred up in anticipation of my wedding. Welby is such a gentleman, of course, and he wouldn't think of trying to compromise me like this."

"Now wait just one minute," Cole said. "You're the one who—"

She brushed past him, headed for his door. "And I imagine the reason I found it so stimulating is that I allowed you liberties I've never allowed another man. Now that I know, perhaps I'll see what I can do about convincing Welby to act less a gentleman," she opened the door, "and more like you."

"Christina!" He looked red in the face and brought to mind a volcano fixing to blow.

"Don't forget to talk to Lord Bennet tomorrow," she added, peeking out into the hallway to see if the coast was clear. Safer out than in, she slipped into the corridor and started to shut the door. Cole's litany of low-voiced curses had her ducking her head back inside. "You prove my point, Cole Morgan. A gentleman doesn't speak so in front of a lady."

"When I see a lady I'll watch my tongue."

Chrissy yanked the door closed just a little too loudly for after two in the morning. As a result, she picked up her skirts and ran toward her own room, grateful her feet were bare and thus silent against the cold marble tile.

Minutes later, she lay in her own bed, her pulse pounding, her thoughts in a whirl. *What in the world got into me? Cole Morgan a husband? My husband?*

"He's right. It's madness." She wanted a man who would accept the woman she was, who would love her unconditionally. Cole Morgan loving her the way she needed was about as likely as snow in San Antonio's Plaza de Las Armas in August.

Afternoon sunshine beamed down upon the Hartsworth guests who accompanied the Earl of Thornbury on an excursion to the far boundaries of his vast estate for a visit to the medieval castle ruins. In offering the entertainment to his visitors, the earl had explained how he intended to excavate the site for artifacts. He planned to devote an entire room at Hartsworth to display the armor and weapons, pottery and plates, waiting to be found on his estate.

Unknown to the amateur archeologists, the earl had completed a thorough search of the ruins just last year. The artifacts recovered were stored in one of Hartsworth's attic rooms, waiting for the last of the display pieces commissioned by the earl from a local furniture maker whose talent rivaled Chippendale himself. Today, however, a few of the items had been returned to the site where they awaited "discovery" by the house party guests.

Cole had been tipped to the plan by the earl himself, and as he watched the men and women milling around the old stone walls, he agreed that the idea was inspired. What he didn't agree with was Christina's behavior.

"So what else is new?" he muttered, his gaze locked upon his best friend's sister as she walked arm in arm across the park with her betrothed. His best friend's sister—that's how he was determined to think of her—a decision he'd reached sometime during a mostly sleepless night.

Of course, after their most recent encounter, he'd prefer not to think of her at all. Had he been able to forget family connections, he'd have packed his bags that morning and hightailed it for home, abandoning both the search for the Declaration and the woman hellbent on driving him to destruction.

Or, he'd have thrown what little sense he retained to the wind and crawled into her bed to assuage the persistent ache she'd brought to life.

What exactly had happened last night? What was the real reason she'd come to his room? Was it truly this business with Bennet, or something else?

Had she actually broached the notion of marriage between the two of them?

He'd tried to wrap his mind around the questions all night. The various answers he came up with ranged from ridiculous to haunting and left him riddled with self-doubt. If she *had* been talking about hooking up with him, he figured the likeliest reason why was that she wanted to escape this marriage mess she'd gotten herself into with Welby. In a sense, Cole reckoned he owed her his help. He knew as certain as a chicken has feathers that she'd accepted the viscount because of what had happened between the two of them out in the folly.

But what if he'd misunderstood her oblique reference? What if—and he'd had to work himself up to considering this—what if marrying Welby *was* a good move for her? Maybe some of Christina's restlessness resulted from the need to get busy making a home of her own and raising babies of her own instead of playing second-fiddle mother to Lana Kleberg's children. What if with a little time, she could come to love Lord Windy?

Time. It always came back to that. His plan to convince Christina to take Welby home was right on target. So when ten minutes later he spied the earl in conversation with Christina and her betrothed, he chose to saunter over and join in the talk.

"Afternoon, Christina," he said, not quite meeting her emerald gaze. "Thornbury. Welby."

"Good afternoon, Morgan," said the earl. "Glad you decided to join us on our excursion. So, tell me, what do you think of my castle?"

Cole glanced around. From the crumbled walls and heaps of stone, he tried to build a castle which met the image of such fortifications already in his imagination. "It's intriguing, and something I certainly wouldn't see at home. For a man who has lived his life in the New World, the idea of something being so old is definitely a mind teaser."

"I understand the feeling," replied the earl. "My feelings about America are probably quite similar. I'm intrigued by the newness of everything, of unspoiled frontiers. That and the wildlife. I've always had an interest in wildlife."

"I assumed as much from Hartsworth's trophy room. I took a wrong turn in the house one day and for a moment, I thought that lion was going to jump me."

"It is a particularly lifelike display," observed Welby.

While Thornbury and the viscount discussed the talents of various taxidermists, Cole decided now would be a good time to ease the conversation in the direction he wanted. Though he'd have preferred to do this without Christina as witness, the sooner this particular seed was planted, the sooner it would grow, and the sooner this foolish fiancé business could be ended.

"That sounds like you have a fair collection of stuffed animals, Thornbury. Too bad it's limited to African and European critters. I've always said a trophy room isn't complete without an armadillo decorating the mantel."

Christina rolled her gaze toward the sky. "Don't believe him, Grandfather. I don't doubt yours is the first trophy room Cole has ever seen."

Cole studied his fingernails as he casually observed, "Now, I reckon the truth of that depends on what kind of trophies you're talking about. Your brother does have that cigar box full of—"

"Morgan!" she snapped, obviously expecting him to refer to the hair ribbon collection Jake kept as souvenirs of romantic conquests.

"—newspaper clippings about the court cases he has won."

He grinned at the dark look she sent his way, then continued his campaign by addressing the earl. "Something I'd like to hear is a monkey howl, to learn if it resembles a coyote's. I'd like to see what a herd of zebras looks like in comparison to a herd of wild mustangs. I'd like to know how Africa's cougars resemble those that run in Texas. How about you, Thornbury? Any of those questions tickle your fancy?"

He tugged thoughtfully on his snowy mustache. "They all do."

Morgan, you are so good. "Then you should consider a trip to Texas. Think of the creatures you'd get to see in addition to those javelinas. Bobcats. Rattlesnakes. Wild mustangs."

"It does sound tempting," mused the earl. "Mustangs, hmm? The idea of herds of wild horses has always intrigued me. Have you seen them, Morgan?"

"Sure have," he nodded. "Years ago, south Texas was rife with 'em. Nowadays a fella needs to head west to run across them. We have them, though, and I'm telling you, it's a sight to see when a stallion stands atop a rise and trumpets and the mares come a'runnin'."

"Interesting." The earl glanced at his granddaughter. "Have you seen such a sight, my dear?"

Nodding, she looped her hand through her grandfather's arm. "Yes. Not too long ago, actually, while I visited a friend's ranch south of San Antonio. Cole is right. It is something to see. I'll tell you something else you'd find fascinating, Grandfather. With your interest in birdwatching, you'd adore the Gulf Coast. Birds from all over North America fly south to winter in Texas. At times they'll blanket the ground for as far as a person can see."

"Now, Christina, that's a bit of an exaggeration, don't you think?" Cole prodded, knowing the more said about the subject at the moment, the better.

She shrugged. "Not much of one."

Welby hooked his thumbs through the holes in his yellow brocade vest. "What's that animal you mentioned earlier? The one for the mantel?"

"Armadillo. Now you're getting into the smaller animals. We've got your armadillos, possums, jackrabbits. I'm almost tempted to add tarantula spiders to that list as they're just about as big as a possum."

"Now who is exaggerating?" asked Christina.

Cole cut her a grin, then continued. "You've mentioned a curiosity for the West, yourself, Welby. You should consider making the trip, too."

"Actually, I have," the viscount answered. "Mrs. Kleberg raised the question just yesterday and it does offer some appeal."

Morgan, you are so very good.

Cole allowed his gaze to trail across the ruined castle walls and linger on the delighted dowager victoriously displaying the jewel-encrusted sword hilt she'd retrieved from a hidden cache. "Look at that. It gives me a shiver to see a piece of medieval treasure. One thing this trip to England has hammered home for me is the idea of just how big this world of ours is and how many truly fascinating sights it has to offer. It's a shame we such a little of it during our lifetimes."

"That's a good point, Morgan," said the earl.

Cole met first the viscount's gaze, and then the earl's. "If a man has the means and opportunity, why, he almost owes it to himself to get out and travel a bit. Y'all really ought to think about paying Texas a visit. You could see our ocean and forests and mountains. Do some bird watching. Hunt up a herd of mustangs. Thornbury, you could spend some time with your daughter."

Interest fired in the elderly man's eyes at that. "It's quite a long distance."

"It's a lot of miles, yes, but it's not a bad trip. I had a great voyage over," he lied. "In fact, now that I think about it, everything falls into place. You're a wildlife enthusiast. Welby is curious about the American West. Y'all should come home with me when I go. The Delaneys should have the opportunity to meet Christina's intended before the wedding. They could even have the wedding in Texas, for that matter."

"Absolutely not," said Christina, her green eyes snapping.

Welby frowned. "That would be difficult, I'm afraid. The Harrington family has traditions to uphold."

Cole shrugged. "A prenuptial visit then. Elizabeth would love that. Then she and Jake could come back to England with y'all for the wedding."

"Cole!" protested Christina.

"Do you think Elizabeth would actually come home?" asked the earl, hope ringing in his voice. "Do you think she's ready to put aside her vow never to return?"

Christina fumed. "Cole Morgan, hush your mouth."

Ignoring her, he answered the earl's question. "She's never had her only daughter marrying a British viscount before. I think she'd come here if y'all went there first. Think of all you'd see and do. Why," he gestured toward the crumbled castle walls. "We even have a ruin or two ourselves you can gander at—one almost in Christina's backyard. Y'all have heard of the Alamo, I presume?"

Thornbury's brow knitted. "The Alamo. Hmm . . . I don't believe—"

"Pardon me, but did I hear you mention the Alamo?" came a voice from off to Cole's left.

He turned to see a newcomer striding toward them. He was a stocky fellow, a good five inches shorter than Cole with a soft-featured face and gray eyes that struck a discordant note in Cole.

"I'm an expert on the Battle of the Alamo," the newcomer continued. "Do you have questions?"

Yes. Who the hell are you?

The earl cleared his throat. "Bennet. You've arrived."

"That I have, Lord Thornbury. I reached Hartsworth late last evening."

"Lovely," said the earl in a tone of voice that suggested otherwise. "I guess I should introduce you to my visitors. Lord Bennet, my granddaughter, Miss Delaney, and Mr. Morgan of San Antonio, Texas."

Bennet's gasp was audible. "San Antonio! What luck. I'm a Texologist, you see."

"Texologist?" Cole asked.

"A student of all things having to do with Texas, fauna and flora, her people and of course, her history. I have a special interest in Texas history."

Christina's eyes cut toward Cole and she glared her frustration. He knew she must be itching to flay into him about his latest tactic, but she couldn't ignore the opportunity Bennet had handed them on a platter. *Later, Christina,* he silently promised her with his eyes.

Much later, if I have any control over it, he promised himself.

She pasted on a smile and added warmth and encouragement to her voice as she spoke to Bennet. "How interesting, Lord Bennet. What an unusual avocation."

He preened. "Yes, well, I considered becoming an Egyptologist, but I think Texas has more cachet than Egypt. Besides, I like to be a bit different."

"You certainly achieved that goal," observed Welby. To Christina, he added, "This is the baron I mentioned who owns the longhorn cattle."

"Really," Christina said, drawing it out and batting her lashes.

Bennet nodded so fast and furiously he reminded Cole of a hungry puppy begging a treat. "Texas longhorns. A prize-winning herd. I bought the beginnings of the herd on my first trip to Texas ten years ago, and added to it on subsequent visits."

The earl scratched his chin and frowned. "I thought you had Scottish cattle at Harpur Priory."

"No. It's a misconception many people have." Bennet puffed himself up and said, "I raise Texas, not Scottish longhorns."

Cole dragged a hand along his jaw line. "A Texologist, hmm? I know that Egyptologists often create collections of items having to do with Egypt. Do you have a Texas collection?"

"I certainly do. Quite an extensive one, in fact."

"Really? I'd like to see it someday. I own a few items of historical interest concerning Texas, myself. Maybe we could do a little horse trading."

"Horse trading?"

"Swapping stuff out."

"Oh, no. No." Bennet shook his head. "Nothing I own is for sale. I prize all my treasures."

Before Cole could pursue the matter any further, the earl made a *hrrumph* sound low in his throat and said, "Since Bennet is here, Chrissy, why don't you show him around. I'd like to continue the conversation he interrupted."

As protest bloomed in Christina's eyes and her mouth opened to object, Cole moved to interfere. "Careful, Christina. A bee." He moved close to brush away the imaginary insect, then leaned close to whisper in her ear. "Remember the Alamo, Lady Bug."

She shot him a look so proud and fierce and furious that he murmured, "Too bad Davy Crockett didn't have you with him at the charge. The Texans might have won."

Welby scowled as his fiancée departed with another man, then his expression lightened as Lana Kleberg approached. "What did you say, Morgan?" he asked absently.

"Nothing. Just a little memory of Texas. And it puts me in a mind to talk about home. So, gentlemen, what target date shall we set for our departure?"

Christina nursed an anger so hot she thought she just might catch fire. How dare he! What was Cole Morgan thinking? Suggesting she introduce Lord Welby to her family when he knew darned well she had no intentions of ever going home again. Why, the nerve of the man.

Bennet beamed at her. "I must say, Miss Delaney, the sound of your drawl is certain music to my ears."

"What?"

"It's seldom I have the pleasure of hearing those honeyed tones of Texas. When it happens I always harken back to the pleasurable days I have passed in your most fair country."

She blinked twice trying to focus her thoughts on the matter at hand. Curse Cole Morgan for making it so difficult. Curse him for making everything so difficult.

"How many visits did you say you've made to Texas?"

"Three different trips, and one of them was for an extended period of time."

"And did you have a particular reason for choosing Texas as your destination?"

"My maternal great-grandfather made some investments in Texas that my family holds yet today. They require periodic attention, although not as much as I would like. Eight years have passed since I last walked upon those hallowed shores."

Hallowed shores? Chrissy loved Texas herself, but my lands, this man went a bit far.

"Enough about me," he continued. "What of you, Miss Delaney. What part of Texas are you from?"

While they walked and talked, Christina regularly glanced back to where her grandfather and her betrothed conversed with Lana and Cole. She wondered what trouble that traitor Cole Morgan was throwing her way now. When the entire quartet shifted and eyed her with speculation, she was hard-pressed not to stick out her tongue.

She turned her back to them and led Bennet toward the section of the ruins where the dowager had found the sword hilt moments earlier. Smiling brightly at the baron, she asked and answered questions in ways that brought the conversation ever closer to the information she sought. Yet, underneath it all hummed the certain knowledge that the way things had turned out, she could have avoided the humiliating visit to Cole's room entirely.

Feeling the stir of the old recklessness inside her, Chrissy stepped a little closer to Bennet, smiled wider, and batted her lashes even faster. *They can plan all they want. I'll wheedle the information I need from Lord Bennet and if I have any luck at all, he'll be the one who has the Declaration. Cole could be on his way home by the end of the week and I can be done with him.*

If such thoughts created a hollowness in her chest, Chrissy did her level best to ignore it.

Bennet had just begun to speak about his country estate, Harpur Priory, when Michael and Sophie Kleberg scampered up to Chrissy. "Hi, Miss Chrissy," the young girl said. "Whatcha doin'? Where's Mister Welby?"

Michael scowled and grumbled, "I didn't think his leash was this long. I certainly never thought he'd let another man take you walking."

"I'm not a dog, Michael Kleberg," Chrissy scolded, folding her arms and sending him a glower of disapproval.

"There he is," said Sophie, pointing back toward Cole. "Did y'all have a fight, Miss Chrissy? Is that why you're with this stranger and not him?"

"I say," protested Bennet. "Who are you children to criticize such a lovely lady as Miss Delaney?"

"She's not a lady. She's a queen. A Chili Queen. Isn't that right, Miss Chrissy? She's even the Queen of the Chili Queens because all the men and women voted it."

Bennet's eyes widened. "What is a Chili Queen?"

Before Chrissy could form her thoughts, Michael answered in a torrent of words. "Miss Chrissy makes chili and sells it at a chili stand in the plaza at home. Everybody agrees it's the best chili in town and she's the nicest cook so they voted her queen only her family found out and called it a scandal and banished her to England. Now she's decided to marry Mr. Welby who's a nice enough fellow but I'm afraid she'll never be a Chili Queen again."

Chrissy offered a weak smile to the baffled baron whose mouth gaped open in shock. "An earl's granddaughter selling food in public?"

"I'm not an earl's granddaughter at home," she said with quiet pride. "But I am, among other things, an accomplished cook of the most popular dish in the state, oftentimes known as Texas Red."

They were just the right words. "I understand, of course. However, I doubt you'd find your fiancé so accepting. Despite his charming ways, Welby is a stickler for propriety."

"Would he cancel the wedding if he found out?" asked Michael, the very picture of innocence.

He didn't fool Chrissy one little bit. "Michael Kleberg," she warned.

Bennet helped her dodge that particular problem by replying, "No, in this country it is considered the highest breach of honor and breeding for a man to back out once he has offered marriage to a woman.

Were Welby to learn that his intended is known as a Chili Queen in Texas, he'd likely supervise her time more closely."

"He's already stuck to her like a grass burr," Michael said with a snort of disgust. "Why, this is the first chance I've had to talk to Miss Chrissy without him around since she made her great mistake."

"Great mistake?"

"Agreeing to marry him."

"Michael!"

The boy shrugged and Chrissy reached the end of her patience. "I'm not going to stand here and listen to insults from a pair of precocious children. Run along now. I'd like to hear more about Lord Bennet's estate, Harpur Priory."

She ignored the children's frowns of disapproval and turned all her attention toward Bennet, who took her on a imaginary walk-through of his manor house. The fellow was growing on her, Chrissy thought as he described a painted ceiling in minute detail. So what if he was a little pompous? He'd spoken up in her defense and was apparently sincere in his love for Texas. That made up for a lot.

In fact, now that she thought about it, Lord Bennet deserved her esteem much more than Cole Morgan. He certainly never stood up in her defense. Not with anyone who counted, anyway. Not with her mother.

Frustration swamped her like a tidal wave. In that moment, she wanted nothing more than this entire situation to be over with and behind her. So she turned to Bennet and said, "So tell me about your collection, my lord."

"Gladly. I love to talk about my treasures from the Lone Star State."

"Oh." Her stomach sank a little at that. "From statehood. You have nothing a little older? From the time of the Republic, perhaps?"

"I do." His grin was smug. "Actually, the majority of my treasures date back to the Republic of Texas."

"Really? Such as . . . ?"

"Too much to mention, but for example, I have a knife owned by a Texan who died in the Goliad Massacre."

Chrissy literally chewed her tongue to keep from asking about the Declaration outright. After meeting him she doubted Lord Bennet would simply hand over the document if indeed it was in his possession. She would need to play this cautiously. "I'd love to see your collection, Lord Bennet. Perhaps—"

"Sometime in the future," Welby said smoothly as he took possession of her arm and escorted her away from Bennet.

Lana took her other arm and murmured softly, "You need to be more careful, Chrissy. It's one thing to give the man a tour of the ruins, it's another thing to work on ruining yourself."

"I did nothing wrong."

"You needn't actually do something. The appearance of something is enough to set tongues to wagging. You don't want that."

"That's right," agreed Welby. "Your station has changed, my dear. As my viscountess, you'll need to pay close attention to social niceties."

"They don't sound too nice to me," she muttered.

"You're in England, now," Cole said as he sauntered up gently swinging a medieval mace back and forth in his hand. "They don't do nice like we do back home."

Michael Kleberg perched atop a pile of old stone and watched his mother laugh at something Mr. Welby said while holding the visor from a suit of armor up to his eyes. It was good to hear his mother laugh—she didn't do it nearly as often as he thought she should—and he didn't mind that Mr. Welby was the fellow making it happen.

Michael wasn't certain how he knew Mr. Welby was wrong for Miss Chrissy. He just did. It was extra strange because Michael actually liked the man. Mr. Welby didn't ignore him and Sophie like so many adults did. Neither was he like some of these other English folk who treated his mother like they were somehow better than she just because they were peers and she was a farmer's widow. Michael liked that. He liked it a lot.

But he still didn't think Mr. Welby was right for Miss Chrissy. He couldn't say why. Just something in his gut told him so.

The boy's gaze left his mother and trailed across the gaily dressed crowd of treasure-hunters, fifteen or so in number, until he spied Miss Chrissy. "I'm worried about her, Sophie," he said to his little sister, who was seated at his side and busy building a miniature teepee of sticks and grass.

"Who? Mama or Miss Chrissy?"

"Miss Chrissy. She's being stubborn and I'm afraid she'll end up married to Mr. Welby if we don't do something."

"Why would we need to do something? Would it be so awful for Miss Chrissy to marry Mr. Viscount Welby?"

Michael shrugged. "I think it might."

"But why?"

"I don't know why. I just know it."

"All right then." Sophie frowned down at the crowd. "Don't worry, Michael. Mr. Cole has a plan, and we've been doing our part. I already told Miss Chrissy I want to go home to Texas."

"I know." Michael took aim at a stone a few feet away, worked up a spit, and shot. "But I don't like his plan. It's gonna take too long. I think we need to do something right now."

"All right. What do we do?"

Michael took his time, spitting two more times, before he voiced the idea that had been tripping around in his head. "We can be ourselves."

Sophie folded her arms and narrowed her eyes. "Are you being mean, Michael?"

"No, but that's my plan. I think we both should be mean."

"What? I don't understand."

Michael reached into his pocket and removed a pair of peppermint sticks. In a rare display of brotherly love, he offered one to Sophie. "Miss Chrissy says we are all family now, right?"

Sophie nodded. "She loves us."

"So what will happen to us once Miss Chrissy gets married?"

"You know, Michael. Remember? Mama and Miss Chrissy talked about it before she told Mr. Viscount Welby yes. Miss Chrissy promised we'd all live with her and her husband at his castle with the turrets and drawbridge and suits of armor in the hallway."

"I do remember." Michael took a long lick of his candy. "So, what would happen if Welby didn't want us to move to his castle?"

Sophie folded her arms and frowned. "What do you mean, Michael?"

"I think it's time you and me showed these Englishmen the kind of trouble a Texan can do when his dander is up. We need to make Mr. Welby hate us. Then, the minute he tells Miss Chrissy he doesn't want to let us live in his castle . . ."

"The minute Miss Chrissy cancels the wedding!" Sophie clapped her hands together, her eyes sparkling with delight. "Oh, Michael, you're the smartest boy in all of England!"

"I know. I'm a Texan. All the others are English."

When she leaned over and kissed his cheek, he decided he'd been praised enough. He pushed her away. "C'mon, Soph, you're all sticky. Quit kissin' and help me plan."

Slipping off the pile of rocks, he stood with his hands shoved in his pockets while he rolled back and forth on his heels. He stared up above the treeline and whistled softly. Seconds later Sophie joined him, mimicking his actions.

Twenty yards away from the Kleberg children, Cole got disgusted with Welby's flowery wooing of Christina and turned away from the sight. His gaze fell upon Michael and Sophie standing apart from the rest of the picnickers, their heads bent together, their arms gesturing with enthusiasm. Something in their manner caught his interest, and he watched them for a good five minutes.

Mischief seemed to shimmer in the air around them. When they folded their arms and leveled intent gazes upon Welby, Cole suddenly felt better than he had all day. The children were up to no good. Cole knew it as a guaranteed natural fact.

And it had something to do with Welby.

"Well . . . well . . . well, Lord Windy," he murmured. "Something tells me I wouldn't want to be in your shoes for all the tea in England."

Chapter

8

The next-to-last day of the Earl of Thornbury's house party dawned bleak and heavy with rain, a perfect accompaniment to Chrissy's mood. To say the past week had been a challenge to get through was like saying her chili had just a tiny bit of scald.

Her grandfather wanted to go to Texas.

The blame belonged right at Cole Morgan's feet.

"The man is nothing but trouble," she muttered, pushing aside her bedroom window draperies to stare out toward the statue garden where fog swallowed everything but the heads of the marble figures.

How had she lost control of her life? When exactly had it happened? When she accepted Welby's suit? When she led Cole down the folly path? Maybe back before she left Texas, when she allowed pride and hurt feelings to stand in the way of standing up to her mother.

Or maybe she lost control the day she fell in love with Cole.

Chrissy's hand crushed the drapery's hunter green

velvet as her heart skipped a beat. "Love Cole Morgan?" she muttered aloud. "A young girl's love. Familial love, certainly. But not romantic love. Never that."

Sure, Chrissy. Maybe if you say it often enough and fiercely enough you'll begin to believe it.

She groaned and rested her forehead against the windowpane, then lifted it and banged it gently against the cool glass as the bleak truth bubbled up inside her and broke free.

She did love Cole. Romantically. She had loved him for a very long time. How could she have fooled herself into believing otherwise? How could she have been so blind?

Because you knew he didn't love you in return. You knew he wouldn't love a woman like you. Cole wanted someone like Mother, a proper lady. Someone like Miss Parkwood or Lady Sarah Snelling or any of the other young women visiting Hartsworth during the house party. Or Lana. She and Cole had appeared cozy enough together lately. Once Chrissy had interrupted a private tête-à-tête after which Lana wouldn't quite meet her gaze. Who knows, maybe tomorrow night's betrothal ball could celebrate their upcoming nuptials in addition to her own. Chrissy's breath balled in her throat.

"Now you're being silly," she scolded herself. Lana and Cole's relationship was strictly friendship and Chrissy knew it. She was thinking irrationally. "Now that's a shock."

Turning away from the window, she crossed to the fireplace and lifted the brass poker to stir the fire. She tried to tamp down her emotions and think matters through, to decide what if anything she wanted to do with this new truth. Now was no time to follow habit and act rashly. *Such as telling him how I feel.*

After the way their two . . . interludes . . . concluded, she was feeling bruised. A third rejection might well leave her bloody.

Sparks spewed and wood crackled as she rearranged the logs. What a mess. And now she had Welby to deal with. How in the world had she allowed herself to end up engaged to one man while loving another?

Like this is any change? You've been doing the same thing for years now.

She winced at the thought. Was it true? Was that the real reason behind all those broken engagements, not an attempt to please her mother as she'd told herself?

Chrissy pondered the notion for a time until she could no longer deny its truth. All the other beaux, all the fiancés, they had been an attempt to attract Cole's attention. To make him face the prospect of losing her. Well, he faced it just fine both then and now.

How humiliating.

She gave a flaming log a sharp poke. "So what are you going to do this time?" she asked herself softly. "Will you hold to form or will you actually marry Welby?"

If she were to break the engagement, best to do it before the betrothal ball. If she were going to make her home in England, she should probably make an effort to heed their rules of etiquette.

Or maybe I should move to a deserted tropical island where no rules exist but the ones I make up.

That idea had considerable appeal. Chrissy held her chilled hands out toward the fire and observed, "At least on a desert island I'd be warm."

"What's this about a desert island?" asked Lana, standing in the portal of the doorway connecting their two bedrooms. "If you are fleeing to one, then I'm coming with you and I'm leaving my children behind."

For the first time all morning, Chrissy smiled. In the last few days the Kleberg children certainly had taken a turn toward trouble. Chrissy wondered if she was the only person who noticed that most of their pranks had been targeted toward her fiancé. "What mischief has the Terrible Twosome committed this time?"

Lana stepped cautiously across the room and took a seat in the bedside chair. A rosy glow colored her cheeks as she turned and gazed out the window. Not for the first time, Chrissy thought how attractive her best friend was, especially now that the grief had for the most part faded from her Dresden blue eyes. *Maybe it's time we started looking for a husband for her*, she mused.

Sighing, Lana said, "Lord Welby caught them snooping in his bedroom. In his closet. I don't know what to do with them. They've never acted this . . . this . . . rotten before. They've sprinkled itching powder over his underwear, filled his coat pockets with pond slime, and served him a worm sandwich." She closed her eyes and shook her head. "Maybe Mother Kleberg was right. Maybe I am a terrible mother."

"Don't be ridiculous. You're a wonderful mother and you know it. These pranks the children are playing on Welby—they're my fault. It's clear to me what is happening. Michael and Sophie think they're protecting me by striking out at the enemy. They think my marriage to Welby would be a mistake."

Dryly, Lana said, "My children are exceptionally bright."

Chrissy shot Lana a saccharine smile and redirected the conversation. "So, what mischief had they made in Welby's closet?"

"None. He'd caught them before Michael dropped the frog into his boot."

Chrissy's lips twitched. "Hmm. Welby wouldn't have cared for that. He is a fastidious man and he's almost as particular about his footwear as he is about his vests."

"He was very sporting about it, actually. He said no harm was done."

"That was nice. And the children were lucky. I played the same trick on Jake one time, and you should have seen the look on his face when he realized his toes were tickling a toad. I thought he would kill me."

"He probably should have."

After a spell of contemplative silence, both women giggled, then broke into laughter. Chrissy continued laughing long past the time the moment warranted. It was either that or cry. Finally, wiping at her eyes, she said, "Oh, Lana, what am I going to do?"

"I've offered my opinion in the past and it hasn't changed. Don't marry him, Chrissy. You'll regret it if you do."

"Why? Lord Welby is the most eligible bachelor in all of England. He's handsome and intelligent and wealthy and he's been downright patient with Michael's and Sophie's pranks. Even when he took that big bite of worms."

"Yes, he was a good sport about that, too," Lana replied, a hint of wistfulness in her tone.

"And you know what else? I think Welby likes me."

"Of course he likes you. It's only natural. You're the kind of woman every man wants."

Chrissy recalled the look of fury on Cole's face when he stormed from the folly. "No, that's not true. I know that for a fact. Besides, I meant he likes the person I am inside, not this shell that men seem to find attractive. That's nice, Lana. It feels good. I need that right now."

"Oh, honey, being liked for who you are is not what you need in a husband. You need to love and be loved in return. And we both know your feelings don't go that deep with Welby. In fact . . . ," Lana paused and waited until Chrissy met her gaze. ". . . during our weeks here at Hartsworth, I've come to suspect you have deep feelings for another man."

Chrissy didn't respond. She'd barely managed to admit it to herself; she couldn't possibly confirm Lana's suspicions. Instead, she focused her gaze upon her wardrobe and the rainbow of colors its opened doors revealed. "What are you wearing to tomorrow's ball?"

"I swear you're as stubborn as a chili stain. Fine, we won't talk about him. Not now. But I do have more to say to you. Come sit beside me."

Chrissy didn't want to do it, but Lana was using her I'm-the-mother-and-you're-to-do-as-I-say voice. She dragged her feet across the room and sat on the edge of the bed. Lana reached out and took her hand, holding it between both of hers as she earnestly said, "Honey, marriage—a good marriage—is one of the most precious gifts God can give. It's also one of the toughest jobs you'll ever take on. I loved my husband with every fiber of my being, and I know he loved me just as much. Even so, we experienced periods of time when I wondered whether our marriage could survive."

Chrissy didn't want to hear this lecture. "Of course you did. You lived with his parents."

"Haven't I heard that the viscount's mother is alive and living on their estate?"

"Yes, but it's a castle. A big castle."

"And who will be its queen? The dowager or the upstart Texan?" Ignoring Chrissy's petulant pout, Lana continued, "Listen to me. Marriage is tough enough all by itself. Add an interfering mother-in-law to the mix and . . ." Lana shuddered. "I certainly know I would have second thoughts."

"Maybe Welby's mother is nice." Chrissy didn't know why she felt so compelled to argue with her friend. Everything Lana said made sense. All she knew was that the more someone told her not to do something, the more she felt obligated to give it a try. *Maybe I am contrary by nature as Jake so often accused.*

Lana waved her hand. "I've gotten off the subject. A nice mother-in-law is neither here nor there. Please listen to me. I love you like a sister, and I want only the very best for you. If you don't love Lord Welby, don't marry him. Don't condemn yourself to a marriage without love."

"Maybe we'll grow to love one another. It could happen in time. He is a good man."

"Yes, I've spent quite a bit of time with him of late and I've come to realize he is a very good man. And he deserves a good, strong, happy marriage. He deserves a wife who loves him. So give yourself that time, Chrissy. Take that trip to Texas and introduce him to your family. Give yourself the chance to fall in love with him before you say your vows."

"I won't go home."

Lana sighed with frustration. "I've gone about this wrong, haven't I? You'll marry him out of spite. Oh, I've lost patience with you. No wonder you get along so well with my children. The three of you are just alike." Standing, she strode across the bedroom toward the connecting door, bumping into the opened wardrobe door in her haste. "Ouch," she muttered, pushing it aside.

Feeling a pang of conscience, Chrissy said, "Lana, wait."

But her friend didn't pause. Instead she sailed into her own bedroom and slammed the connecting door. Chrissy winced and held her head in her hands. She seriously considered crying.

Door hinges squeaked and Chrissy looked up. Lana stood in the doorway, her color high, her posture proud and righteous. Chrissy felt around two inches tall as her best friend in the world said in a scathing tone of voice, "And Chrissy? Of the pranks being played upon Lord Welby of late? Yours is by far the worst."

Cole stood with a drink in hand, gazing around Hartsworth's saloon and wondering what the hell he was doing there. This saloon was pronounced "salon" and had marble on the floor and Old Master paintings on the walls and Roman busts set on pedestals in niches and alcoves. "Give me a good old Texan saloon any day over this one," he murmured aloud. He preferred sawdust on the floor, tinny piano music to stringed musicians, and sporting girls rather than fan-fluttering ladies. Taking a sip from his crystal glass, Cole relished the smooth bite of whiskey and admitted that the rotgut served in most Texas saloons could use an upgrade. Still, he'd rather be standing in a Hell's Half Acre honky-tonk drinking tonsil paint than this high-falutin' saloon.

Cole tossed back the rest of his drink, then went looking for another. With the poor weather keeping people confined indoors, the saloon was crowded with people. The entire manor house was packed, for that matter, as guests had been arriving all afternoon. Only the Great Hall remained closed to visitors, so special decorations for tomorrow's ball could be put into place. Anticipation sizzled in the air as guests pondered what theme those decorations might present.

According to a gray-haired gossip standing beside him, tomorrow's ball was the first the Earl of Thornbury had hosted in over twenty years. Invitations were difficult to come by and treasured like diamonds. Word had leaked back to London from those fortunate few to be included in his house party that a formal announcement of great import was to be made during the festivities. Rumor had it that Viscount Welby himself had finally found his viscountess in the earl's American granddaughter.

Suddenly, Cole needed some air.

The saloon opened out onto a large portico that overlooked the southern lawn. Cole glanced skyward and was pleased to see blue sky rather than the gray clouds that had blanketed Hartsworth most of the day. He breathed deeply of the fresh, rain-washed air while attempting to tune out the rattle of wheels against cobblestones and the greetings of footmen to an unending procession of guests. Then, having failed to find the haven he sought, he descended the stone steps leading to the lawn and strolled away from the house toward the statue garden.

What he really needed was a ruckus, he thought. A good old barroom brawl to work off some of this uncomfortable edginess plaguing him. Too bad such fracases were difficult to find on an English estate.

He walked briskly along the path, hoping the exercise might rid him of this excess of energy. When he spied others on the path, he veered in another direction. He didn't stop until the scent of cigars and the sound of Welby's laughter reached his ears.

The viscount and what sounded like two other men stood before a fountain depicting Poseidon rising from the sea. Cole halted in the shadows out of sight and unabashedly eavesdropped. They spoke first of horses, and then of the card games due to begin after dinner that evening. Bored, Cole had taken two steps away when Christina's name reached his ears.

"She's a beauty, Welby," said one of the men. "You'll be the envy of London."

"Once you have her tamed," the second man agreed. "She's a bold bit of baggage, I'm afraid. Comes from being reared among barbarians, I imagine."

"That wildness appeals to me," observed the first

sonofabitch. "I hear she's fast, going off with men all by herself, among other things. Have you had her yet, Welby? Is she as delicious as she looks?"

Cole's hand clenched in a fist even as Welby replied, "Enough, Warrington. You'll not dishonor Miss Delaney."

The second bastard chuckled and elbowed the first in the gut. "That's his job."

"Now, chaps, really," Welby protested. "You're not being gentlemen."

"Ah, I know that voice," said the second. "He's going after her tonight. So will you tell us in the morning, Welby? About the wild part? If she's as good as she looks, I might just import a taste of Texas for myself."

Laughter rose in the air and Cole wished for his gun. He tossed back the rest of his whiskey, then let the crystal glass fly. It sailed over the heads of the trio and crashed against Poseidon, splintering into shards. Taking advantage of the distraction, Cole was able to approach the group and land a pair of punches, knocking the bastards to the ground before turning on Welby.

The knife he'd retrieved from the sheath strapped above his ankle gleamed in the moonlight and Welby gasped, partially with fear, but mainly from pain. "Morgan, I didn't . . ."

Cole tightened his already firm grip on the Englishman's balls.

"Got your attention? Good. Listen up, Lord Windy, while I explain a few things about barbarians from Texas. We don't cotton to loud-mouthed, mush-brained fools talking poorly about our women." Cole placed the point of the knife blade against the pulse throbbing at Welby's neck. "We don't hesitate to kill when killing needs doing. And . . ." He tightened his grip on Welby's testicles, ". . . we're expert at making steers out of bulls. We know how to do it quick or . . ." He gave his wrist a twist and spoke above the viscount's yelp, ". . . how to draw it out for as long as the mood suits."

A shove sent the Englishman sprawling. Cole stood over the three men, and spoke in a tone as sharp as the knife in his hand. "Christina Delaney is a lady and you will treat her as such. The first time I get wind of anything otherwise, each one of you boys will get a personal lesson on what gelding is all about."

Cole left them lying on the grass as he marched back toward Hartsworth. He seethed, he steamed, he stewed. *Gentlemen, hell. You'd find more class in a bordello bar.*

How dare they let such filth come out of their mouths? How dare Welby not put a stop to it right away? What kind of man listens to that sort of talk about his woman? Christina didn't know what she was getting herself into.

"Well, she's not going to get into it." He veered off the path, creating a shortcut through the garden as he muttered beneath his breath. "I won't let her."

His overhearing those insults had changed everything. Elizabeth wouldn't want her daughter marrying a man who let other men get by with such obscenity. *Now, chaps.* What sort of objection was that? The man might as well have been wearing a dress.

Such behavior was dishonorable. Welby was dishonorable, and Elizabeth set a high store on honor. No matter what Christina liked to believe, her mother loved her deeply. She wanted the best for her daughter, and the best damn sure wasn't a low-down snake like Welby who let his friends dirty Christina's name. That title might mean a lot to Elizabeth, but it sure as hell didn't mean *that* much. She'd want some nobility in her noble son-in-law. Knowing that, it was Cole's duty as a Delaney family friend to see a halt called to this proposed debacle.

Now all he had to do was convince Christina to see it his way. For a moment, he considered taking news of this incident to the earl, but he quickly reconsidered. Cole liked the old codger, but he didn't trust him. Thornbury approved of the match; he might not see the sin in Welby's namby-pamby defense of his fiancée. Hell, it might be the British male viewpoint, for all Cole knew.

And what about Christina? How would she react to the news? She'd be offended, surely. Wouldn't she? The sonsobitches talked about her as if she were a sporting girl and Welby let them.

A picture of a barefoot Christina dancing in the San Antonio plaza flashed through his mind.

Hell, no telling what that woman might think.

It doesn't matter what she thinks. Not this time, Cole decided as he climbed the stairs to the portico and reentered the saloon. He was putting a stop to this nonsense one way or the other. It was his job. His responsibility. His duty. This time, Chrissy Delaney would by God listen to him and for once in her life, she'd behave.

Purpose roared through Cole's blood as he threaded his way through the throng of people milling in the saloon and headed for the family wing of the house. He wouldn't fail Elizabeth and Jake, not this time. Maybe by stopping this farce of an engagement, he could in part make up for his own deplorable behavior.

Lord, he hoped so. Guilt rode his shoulder every minute of every day when he thought of those wild moments in the folly and then again in his bedroom. A part of him realized those incidents might well be part of the reason why Welby's actions so infuriated Cole. What he'd done was worse. So much worse. His need for redemption went bone deep.

But he wouldn't think about that now. He needed to focus all his energy on convincing Chrissy to do the right thing and call off this marriage. Today, before the damned betrothal was formally announced tomorrow. To hell with his previous plan. He no longer wished this wedding delayed. He wanted it canceled. Now. Tonight. He'd get her back to Texas and reconciled with her family another way.

Maybe. She'd certainly locked up on the idea up till now.

The woman is nothing short of stubborn. She's hard-headed. Willful. Unyielding. Those words and stronger ones punctuated his steps as he climbed the stairs. *She's contrary. Impetuous. Intractable.* He marched down the hall toward her bedroom door. *Ornery. Obstinate.* He rapped on the door. *Bullheaded.* The door cracked open.

Beautiful. So beautiful.

"Cole?" she asked, her jeweled eyes growing wary. "I thought you were my maid. What are you doing here?"

In that moment, he couldn't have told her on a bet.

All memory of what had brought him to her room evaporated from his mind. Only the energy pounding through his blood remained. This Christina Delaney was a far cry from the Chili Queen who danced barefoot in the plaza, her gypsy skirt whirling around trim ankles, her peasant blouse slipping off one shoulder. This Christina was a regal princess, her formal gown a vibrant creation of emerald and gold that paid homage to the perfection of her form. The gown and matching jewels twinkling at her ears and around her neck elevated her above mere mortals, and stood as irrefutable witness to the distance that yawned between an earl's granddaughter and a gardener's grandson.

So damned beautiful. Cole loved the gown. He hated it. "Take it off."

"What?"

He shook his head. *That's not what I . . .* "Call it off."

"What do you mean?" Concern creased her face as she glanced up and down the hallway. "Cole, please. You can't be here. Not now. I'm trying on ball gowns."

"Then let me in."

"I can't. I'm only half-dressed and besides, it's not proper. Go downstairs and I'll—"

"Proper?" he said with a laugh as he pushed past her. "You? Chrissy Delaney? Queen of the Chili Queens?" He stood close to her as he reached around and shoved her bedroom door shut. "When have you ever concerned yourself with 'proper'?"

Her pulse throbbed visibly in her neck. "What is going on here, Cole? What's the matter with you? Have you been drinking?"

His gaze fell to her lips. "Not enough. Not nearly enough."

His blood pounded. Urgency drummed. A haze descended over conscious thought as primal instinct took control. He sensed danger. He recognized a threat. He knew he had to kiss her or die.

With an oath, he dragged her against him and covered her mouth with his. Hard and greedy, his lips took hers. The kiss was savage. Intense. No softness, no gentleness, but an angry display of masculine power.

And, masculine weakness. It was a male's reaction to fear, the aggressive, elemental need to conquer, to control.

To stop her from leaving him.

She struggled in his arms, but he was ruthless in his pursuit. He backed her against the wall, his body pressed tight against hers, breathing her perfume, letting it soak into his senses, the hot, sultry scent of magnolia. Silken strands of fire slid across his skin as his fingers threaded her hair. He gave no quarter, ravaging her mouth with his lips, his tongue, his teeth. Yet with every show of strength, his own weakness grew. He was swamped by a wild, untamed tide of desire that threatened to drown him in tormented pleasure.

He wanted her skin. The damned dress . . .

He moved away just enough to give his hands access to her skirt, only her hand—her fist—found its target first. Breath whooshed from his body as her punch landed just right and she ducked away.

Cole stood with hands braced against the wall, recovering both his breath and his sanity.

"What is wrong with you?" Christina accused.

He couldn't look at her. He couldn't *not* look at her.

Disheveled. Desirable. Devastated. Cole's heart twisted. "I'm sorry. I didn't mean—"

"Stop. Don't say it. You always say it. You never mean it." Long auburn lashes blinked furiously over glistening green eyes. "Why do you do this to me, Cole? Why couldn't you once, just one time, mean it?"

Cole's hackles raised as the threat of danger returned, but an unstoppable force drove him forward and gave voice to the truth that formed on his lips. "Ah, Bug, that's the problem. Don't you know? I mean it every time."

Chrissy froze. For a long moment his ragged breaths were the only sound to be heard in the room. Taking one small step forward, she studied him through narrowed eyes. Cole felt the need to say something, but he didn't know what. The light sparking to life in her eyes confused him. Worried him. It was hope, sweet and sharp, and it cut him like a knife.

"You're angry," she said softly. "Your jaw is set hard as Texas red granite and your spine is as stiff as the statues in the garden."

"I tend to get that way when I'm doing something stupid."

"Are you doing something stupid?"

"Chrissy, I . . ." He blew a frustrated breath. "It's complicated, all right? I want you. I don't *want* to want you, but I do."

She closed her eyes and inhaled deeply, then licked her lips as if savoring the moment. Cole wanted her tongue on him.

Her lashes lifted and she pinned him with her gaze. In a low, challenging voice she said, "Prove it."

Fire shot like lightning through his blood. He didn't move a muscle, not even when she reached up and pulled the pins from her hair. A reckless dare lit her eyes as she shook those long lovely tresses free and Cole couldn't stop the rumble low in his throat.

Throwing her shoulders back, she moved her arms around behind her, freeing the buttons she'd managed to fasten on her own, lifting her bosom high in the process. Cole's mouth went dry at the sight.

He'd taken one inadvertent step forward when a short rap sounded on the door and a ladies' maid hurried inside. "I'm sorry it took me so long, Miss Delaney. I'm new at Thornbury, you know, I couldn't find a soul to—oh." Spying Cole, she stopped in shock.

"That will be all, Susan."

Cole barely recognized the voice as hers, so husky and needy did it sound.

"Yes, miss. Certainly, miss. That's good, miss." She pivoted, but paused at the door. "Are you sure, miss?"

"Very, very sure." As the door shut behind the maid, Chrissy moved to lock it. Then she shrugged and gave a push, and her dress puddled to the floor.

Cole sucked an audible breath past his teeth and tried so hard to fight his way back. "She's wrong. God, Chrissy, this is not good. Nothing good about it."

"That I doubt," she said, tugging the laces of her bustle and shimmying free. "I suspect it will be very, very good." She stepped toward him, offered him her back, lifted her hair and said, "Free me, Cole."

Something inside him snapped.

His surrender was a swift handling of hooks and snaps and strings, and then they were kissing, desperate mouths in a mad battle of teeth and tongue and taste that sucked the strength from Cole's knees. So he dragged her to the floor.

They rolled across the plush carpet. His body burned hot as a paddle-wheeler's furnace, each kiss, every touch, fuel to stoke the fire. His need was a raw, hungry roar that she answered with fevered intensity. Her small teeth nipped at him, tormented him. Her tongue battled his, conquered his. Her hands combed his hair, anchoring him to her greedy mouth as she fed his desire with passion unlike he'd ever known before.

She was the boldest virgin ever born. She was on top of him now, her legs straddling his hips, her weight pressing down on the glorious, tormenting ache of his erection even as her mouth ravished his. Her fingers yanked at his jacket, vest, necktie and shirt, and with every layer of cloth she peeled away, she also took a layer of his civility. When finally her bare fingers brushed his naked chest, he reacted on pure animal instinct.

Linen ripped beneath his fingers as he tore away her last layer of clothing. For a moment, all he did was look at her, drink in the sight of her naked beauty.

Beast that he was, he wanted to howl.

Instead, he rolled her off of him and onto her back. He ravaged her mouth as he learned her with his hands, allowing himself the pleasure he'd wanted, but denied even in his thoughts, for what felt like forever. Smooth lines and silky curves and the softest of skin. Cole wanted to feast upon her.

And so he did. He kissed, licked, and nibbled his way from her mouth, down her neck to those full delicious breasts. There he lingered for a bit until her soft, mewling cries of need and the unconscious roll of her hip spurred him lower. He laved her belly, nipped her hip, then worked his way to that thatch of silken curls he needed to satisfy his craving.

She jumped when his tongue probed the dewy cleft. Gasped aloud at the first languorous stroke. Yelped a meager protest when he settled his thirsty mouth firmly against her and drank of her warm, sweet woman's honey.

Chrissy cried out when she shattered and gave him the gift of her hot, wild climax.

Cole could stand no more. Heart hammering, he lifted her into his arms and stood. Breath raging, he lay her down upon the bed, then quickly tugged off his boots and yanked off his pants. Blood roaring, he spread her legs and knelt between them, positioning himself to take the ultimate prize.

Her wet, narrow passage slipped around him like a glove and slowly, tortuously, he pushed forward until he felt the thin barrier of her innocence. At that point, despite the ferocity of his body's demands, his heart made him pause. He had to say something to her first. Something important. Something . . .

"Chrissy, I . . . I . . ."

She met his gaze and her eyes washed with tears. "Love me, Cole. If just for this one moment, please love me."

She arched her hips and the membrane gave, and Cole found himself buried to the hilt, torn between sighing and screaming as she surrounded his shaft.

Leave it to the Chili Queen to do it herself. Then his mind hazed and instinct again took over, and he moved, slowly out, then in again, stroking, seeking, lost in a paradise of the senses.

Chrissy slid her hands up and down his sweat-slick back in time with the rhythm of his hips. Once she cupped his buttocks and held him against her, grinding, making little kitten noises of need he simply had to taste. Sweet and spicy. So good. So delicious.

With a gasp and a whimper, she dissolved.

The spasms milked him, urged him toward completion, and Cole increased the tempo of his thrusts. The tempest built, a frenzied, violent storm that roared through him, stealing his mind and his will. Cole plunged into her, lost, desperate, but not alone. She was with him. Here. Now. Thrashing beneath him. *Christina. Christina. Christina.*

He threw back his head and ruthlessly, savagely, shot over the top, then fell, plunged, burst into pleasure. With Chrissy flying right there beside him.

Dazed and boneless, Chrissy stared up at the plaster scroll work on the ceiling and tried to catch her breath. Cole lay sprawled beside her, one arm thrown carelessly across her chest, his legs tangled with hers. *Oh my,* she thought. *Oh my.*

She felt so complete. So replete. She knew now that she had waited all her life for this moment with this man. Though her body continued to hum and the heat in her blood had yet to cool, the edge of energy that had plagued her for so long had finally been spent. She snuggled against him, a smug smile pulling at her lips. For the first time in forever,

Chrissy felt like she belonged. She had found a home, here in Cole Morgan's arms. Then he opened his mouth and took that home away.

"I can't believe I did this."

Chrissy braced herself. "What?"

"I can't believe I did this."

Anguish spread outward from her heart as he untangled their legs, slid his arm away, and sat up. "I swore I'd keep my hands off you. I promised myself I'd never lay so much as a finger on you and here I go and lay you, period. I have the self-control of a gnat. I have the honor of a badlands bandit and the morals of a Hell's Half Acre whore."

He looked at her then, his eyes narrowed and hot and condemning. A bullet of pain ripped through her, lodged in her heart as he accused, "Why did I let you seduce me?"

She slapped him.

Cole shut his eyes, the imprint of her hand white against his tan. "Better you had used your fist, Christina. It's no less than I deserve and you always did have a fine right hook."

"Stop it. Just stop it." She blinked furiously, fighting back tears. That edge of energy had returned full force. "Don't you dare ruin this with your mean mouth."

"Seems to me my mouth has already gotten me in plenty of trouble tonight," he responded grimly. "What's a little more?"

Chrissy seriously considered using the right hook, but the opportunity passed when he rose from the bed and grabbed his pants up off the floor. Distracted by the sight of his firmly muscled behind, she missed hearing the first part of his sentence.

". . . can't help but feel lower than a worm in a wagon rut. I tried, truly I tried. But I couldn't find it inside me to do the right thing. I'm as weak-charactered as they come. Even now, bound for hell because of tonight's mischief, I'm fighting myself not to take you again. You are so damned beautiful. So spirited. The most exciting woman I've ever known. You have haunted me for weeks, for months. Hell, for years. I wouldn't admit it, of course. I pretended that I thought of you as a sister. Hell, what a crock. All those fiancés? Every blessed one of them set my gut to churning."

The longer he talked, the better Chrissy felt. She sat up, plumped the pillows, and settled back to watch as he continued to dress and yammer on.

"And this trip to England. I knew from the git-go it was a bad idea. I knew that being around you all the time, far from home and all the reminders of just who you are, I knew in my bones it'd get me in trouble."

By now he had his shirt back on and he tucked its tail into his pants with quick, firm jabs. Chrissy sighed with quiet dismay as he buttoned first his trousers, and then his shirt. Cole's body was truly a thing of beauty to observe.

"I was right. Took little more than two winks and a nod for me to betray my best friend, betray the woman who took me into her home and raised me like her own. It shames me to my soul, it does. Yet, at the same time, I'm itching to crawl back in bed with you and have another go at it. You are truly a pest, Lady Bug, but I've got to tell you, you are my most thrilling fantasy come to life."

A smile bloomed like a rainbow across her face. "Kiss me again, Cole."

"See, there you go again. When it comes to tempting a man, you have Eve beat all to hell."

"Kiss me again, Adam."

For the briefest of seconds, a smile brightened his scowl. "No. I'm not coming near you till you get your clothes back on. In fact, I'm not going to look at you again until that particular task gets accomplished."

"Why?"

"Because you're dangerous, that's why. If I look at you again then I'll want you again and I don't have time for that right now and neither do you. Hurry up and get dressed, Lady Bug. You might recall this house is full of people who've come to hear the announcement of your betrothal."

Actually, Chrissy had forgotten all about the ball and the betrothal. Being reminded of her situation took the smug right out of her smile. "I think I'll just stay in my room."

"No you won't." Cole stood in front of her dresser mirror as he tied his cravat. "You're going to put your dress back on and come with me to find your grandfather. I want to get this problem taken care of today."

The gloomy note in his tone caught her notice as much as the words. Cautiously, she inquired, "What problem?"

He sighed. "Christina, surely you realize you can't marry Welby now."

She studied his reflection in the glass. The hope that had kindled in her heart at his words flickered and died with one look at his sculpted and shadowed face. She'd known Cole Morgan too many years not to recognize when he was angry and trying to hide it.

She licked her lips and said, "This doesn't have to change anything."

He whirled on her then, his eyes blazing. "It damn sure does. If you even begin to think I'll let you go to another man after what just transpired between us in that bed, then you don't know me at all."

"Cole, I—"

"I might have planted my child in your belly. Have you thought about that?"

Chrissy felt the blood drain from her face. *Oh, no.* That possibility had not yet occurred to her.

Cole continued, "Under the circumstances, we've only one solution." He scooped her discarded clothing up off the floor and tossed them to her. "Get dressed and say good-bye to fancy mansions and titled lords, Lady Bug. You've hooked yourself up with a statute wrangler who is happy living in a rooming-house."

"Do you mean . . . ?"

"We have to find your grandfather and tell him there's been a change in groom. You and I are getting married."

Chapter

9

Cole thought it particularly appropriate to be using the underground tunnel leading from the manor house to the orangery in search of the Earl of Thornbury. After all, he certainly felt like a rat.

Not that the tunnel was a dark, dirty haven for rodents. Though it smelled a little musty with all the rain of late, this particular passageway was brick-lined, lantern-lit, broad enough and tall enough to accommodate four men walking abreast. No, the reason Cole felt like a rat was the bait he'd so recently tasted who now scurried beside him and chittered in his ear.

"You can't do this, Cole," Christina insisted yet again. "Would you stop for a moment and listen to me? I said you can't take it upon yourself to break my engagement to Welby and take his place without so much as a by-your-leave to me. I'll make my own decisions, thank you very much. I'm not some weak-willed twittering female who will allow a man to push her around, do you hear?"

Nope, he was the rat. She was a piece of cheese dangled before the rodent, a mouth-watering Chilton, he thought. "Watch your skirt, Christina. There's a puddle of water up ahead. Wouldn't want to ruin your hem."

She made a screeching sound, then lifting her skirt knee-high, took a running jump and sailed over the puddle, placing herself directly in his path. "Stop!"

He stepped around her.

Her squeal was pure frustration. Cole heard the thunk of a rock hitting the tunnel wall and knew she'd kicked it.

"I hate this. I hate being ignored. I hate tunnels. It reminds me of the time we were exploring the caverns up toward New Braunfels and you and Jake hid and made me think you'd left me alone and lost. You were a cruel boy at times, Cole Morgan. The tendency hasn't completely disappeared."

Grimly, Cole pressed on, doing his best not to listen to her harangue. The three hundred yards between the house and the orangery felt more like three hundred miles. Not only did he have guilt dragging him down and Christina wearing out his ears, another problem sunk his stomach to the vicinity of his knees. About halfway between the family wing and the little library where he'd first gone in search of the earl, Cole realized the thought of marrying Christina didn't bother him all that much. In fact, the notion sparked a thrill inside him.

At first he'd tried to tell himself it was just the sex, that for a man so thoroughly reminded of physical pleasure following an extended drought, the idea of regular relations was bound to be a heady one. But by the time a parlor maid told him they'd likely find Christina's grandfather in the orangery, he'd realized that argument didn't hold up. Sex wasn't the reason for his enthusiasm.

So what was? He had the idea the answer was important, but he couldn't think hard enough to figure it out, not with all the yammering Christina was doing in his ear.

"Cole Morgan. You listen to me. I won't be ignored."

"I know. I tried. Didn't get me anywhere."

She ran after him, grabbed hold of his jacket sleeve, planted her feet, and pulled. He dragged her three full steps before Sophie Kleberg's voice stopped him. "Hey, Mr. Cole." The little girl stepped from one of the storage cellars off the main tunnel. "What game are you and Miss Chrissy playing? Can I play, too?"

Christina released Cole's arm immediately and braced her hands on her hips. "Sophie Kleberg. What in heaven's name are you doing down here? Are you by yourself?"

"I'm here, too," said Michael, stepping from the shadows. "We're just playing."

"Does your mother know where you are?" When neither child answered, Christina continued, "I thought not. This tunnel isn't a good place to play."

"Sure it is," said Michael. "We can't break anything down here, and we've been having a little trouble in that area lately. What's a Meissen, anyway? Looked like a plain old bowl to me but the maid brought the roof down with her shriek when we broke it. Really wasn't our fault. Can't hardly run down a hall without tripping over something."

"You shouldn't be running in the hallways at all," Christina scolded.

"But we have to run when we play San Jacinto."

That caught Cole's attention. "San Jacinto?"

Sophie nodded. "It's Michael's turn to win, so we can't play the Alamo. He never lets me be the Texans. I'm always the Mexicans. He just loves to die."

"Well the war is over," Christina declared. "At least for now. You'd best get back to the house. I imagine your mother is looking all over for you."

"Nah, she's not looking for us," Michael said. "She's busy in the kitchen. She said it's been too long since she's done any baking. She's making chocolate cake. In fact, she's making three chocolate cakes and two cherry pies. Is something wrong with our mama, Miss Chrissy? Used to be, the only time she did extra baking was when she was sad. Did something happen?"

"Not that I know of."

Sophie hunkered down and peered intently at a beetle making his way along the brick mortar. Idly, she mentioned, "She's making your favorite spice cake too, Miss Chrissy. Does Mr. Welby like spice cake? I know you love it, Mr. Cole, because I heard you tell Mama so at supper one night. It's a funny thing about favorite foods, isn't it? My papa's favorite food was pork roast. So is Michael's. Mine is mashed potatoes. You know Minnie, the upstairs maid? Her favorite is pickled herring. That stuff makes me want to throw up."

Cole's patience ran out with the notion of up-chucked pickled herring, and he stepped forward to continue down the tunnel toward the orangery.

Christina called, "Wait, Cole." To the children, she said, "Run along now. This place may be safe enough, but I don't like the idea of you down here alone."

"We can't go yet," said Sophie. "We're not finished picking up."

"Sophie!" Michael shot her a "hush up" glare.

"Picking up what?" Christina asked. "What do you have in—oh my heavens! Children, what have you done?"

The alarm in Christina's voice was enough to make Cole stop and backtrack. "What's wrong?"

Christina stood in the storage room surrounded by hat boxes and stacks of cloth, her expression soured as if she'd just tossed back a jigger of unsweetened lemon juice. She replied to his question by reaching down with two fingers and picking up a piece of gold satin embroidered with red and gold thread. Below it was another garment of blue silk shot with gold. Further movement revealed a whole stack of garments. Cole recognized the items at once. "Welby's vests?"

"And hats. Neckties, too."

Cole's mouth twitched with his first urge to smile since leaving Chrissy's bed. This was much worse than a worm sandwich. The viscount would blow like a welding torch. Cole broke into a cheery whistle as he turned to continue toward the orangery.

"Cole, wait!"

"Not my problem, Christina."

"But—"

Cole kept walking and soon the tunnel curved and muted the echo of Christina's voice. Knowing she'd be torn between seeing the Klebergs back to the house and coming with him to face her grandfather, Cole picked up his pace. Now that he'd thought about it, this particular chat between him and the earl would be better made man-to-man.

The heavy citrus scents of lemon and oranges assaulted Cole as he opened the door at the end of the tunnel. He stepped into the building and pulled the door shut behind him. "It's a jungle in here," he muttered, his gaze trailing over tubs of rubber trees and myrtles and pots of pineapples and aloes.

He located the earl in the center of the glass house section of the orangery where hot water assisted intermittent sunshine in keeping the room warm and suitable for exotic, tender plants. Cole tried to blame the humidity for the beads of sweat collecting around his collar as he faced Christina's grandfather. It didn't work.

Wearing canvas gloves and holding a pair of garden shears in his right hand, the elderly gentleman clipped a leaf from an ivy vine and held it up to the light to study. "Morgan," he said, without actually looking at Cole. "I'm surprised to find you among my plants and flowers. The gun room seems more your domain."

With the moment upon him, Cole found words had deserted him. He stared blindly at the yellow center of a white plumeria, breathed deeply the magnolia-like scent, and wished himself to the tropics.

Now the earl scowled at him. "What is it, Morgan? You look as if someone stole that hat you favor."

Cole cleared his throat. "The engagement is off. Christina won't be marrying Welby."

"Hmm . . ." murmured the earl. He set his shears

down beside a clay pot where a green seedling pushed through black soil toward the light. "My granddaughter changed her mind?"

"You could say that."

"Is Welby aware of this development?"

Cole pictured the viscount as he last saw him. "He should be, but I doubt he's that bright."

The earl shuffled down the row, stopping beside a support post where he leaned forward to study a thermometer. He nodded with satisfaction, then asked, "Dare I inquire as to what precipitated my granddaughter's change of heart?"

Damned if Cole didn't feel heat flush his face. Hell, if he felt this way facing Thornbury, imagine how he'd be with Jake and Elizabeth. *Where's your gut, Morgan? Lose the henhouse ways and spit it out.* He squared his shoulders and said, "I have compromised Christina."

"Hmm . . ." The earl frowned down at an aloe plant, plucking an errant myrtle leaf from the pot. "You have been doing that since the day you arrived at Hartsworth, going off alone with her, the daily meetings between the two of you out in the park about this search of yours. I am aware that in Texas social customs are more relaxed than they are here, and for the most part you have been discreet about your assignations. While society would consider my granddaughter's reputation compromised, in view of the circumstances I see no reason why her wedding to Lord Welby should fail to take place."

"That's because you don't know all the circumstances of the assignations," Cole grumbled. Gazing around the hothouse, he spied a hibiscus like Elizabeth grew back home. Familiar with the plant, he recognized the need for water. Lifting the appropriate can from the garden cart, he sprinkled the dirt as he said, "If we were in Texas, you'd be holding a shotgun on me while the preacher spoke the words."

"Are you saying you . . . ?"

"I bedded her." He dropped the can back onto the cart. "I'm going to marry her."

"Hmm . . . I see." The earl tugged off his garden gloves and Cole halfway expected to be slapped with one. But instead, Thornbury dropped the gloves into the tool tin, folded his arms, and smiled. "Well, it is about time."

"What?" Cole blinked and gave his head a shake, certain he'd misheard. "What did you say?"

"I said it's about time. Elizabeth and I were beginning to worry our plan wasn't working."

Every muscle in Cole's body froze. "Plan? What plan?"

"Our plan for the two of you to marry." The Earl of Thornbury reached out and clapped Cole on the shoulders, his green eyes twinkling. "Welcome to the family, son. You may call me Grandfather if you like."

Christina's voice blew through the citrus trees like a winter frost. "Grandfather? Wicked wretch is more like it!"

A strange sort of detachment settled over Cole as he watched Christina bearing down upon the earl. It was as if the heating system had malfunctioned, filling the orangery with a fog that couldn't be seen or felt, but somehow served to insulate him from the action taking place around him.

He observed Christina's rage in the flash of her eyes

and the clench of her fists. He heard it in her tone as she accused, "You planned this? You and my mother?"

He saw the earl's chagrin as he ducked his chin and sheepishly said, "Now, Chrissy . . ."

"Don't 'Now Chrissy' me." She advanced on him, a fiery-haired hellcat spitting her fury. "Tell me how much of it was planned. When it started. Here at Hartsworth? Whose idea was it?"

Cole was two people. One listened to Christina and her grandfather, the other was frozen by a notion he couldn't quite believe.

Elizabeth *wanted* her daughter to marry him?

"It makes no sense," he said as much to himself as to the others. "She went on and on about wanting a titled son-in-law."

The earl nodded. "True. But she thinks nobility is a worthier trait, and using the American definition of the word, she believes you qualify."

"But she never said anything. She never once gave me a hint."

Christina stabbed Cole with a glare. "Are you saying you weren't in on it?"

His own temper flared and helped clear away some of the fog. "If you're going to eavesdrop, do it right," he snapped. "Whose idea was this? This is the first I've heard of any of it." To the earl, he said, "Christina asked whose idea this was. I'd like that answer myself."

The earl shrugged. "My daughter has been writing to me about Christina's marital prospects ever since we healed our estrangement. I don't remember when she first linked your name with hers. Some time ago. She became frustrated when time dragged on and the two of you remained blind to the attraction between you. Then early last summer she told me she was worried you were about to make a commitment to someone else."

Cole assumed the earl referred to Christina. Meeting her gaze, he asked, "Were you engaged early last summer?"

Christina frowned in thought. After a moment, she said, "No, I believe I was between fiancés at that time."

"Not her," said the earl. "You, Morgan. Something about a widow?"

"Elizabeth knew about Louise Larsen?"

Christina asked, "Is that—?"

"No one important," Cole said with a dismissive wave of his hand. His mind spun. He simply couldn't believe this. "Are you trying to tell us that Elizabeth had this marriage notion in her head *before* we came to England?"

"What does it matter? What does any of the whys and wherefores matter? I don't see what has you so upset. All we did was open the door. You two are the ones who waltzed through it." He frowned at the both of them, then added, "And you didn't have to dance all the way to the bed, either, you know. I'm certain that is not what Lady Elizabeth intended. It is within my rights to call you out, Morgan. You compromised my granddaughter."

"I said I'd marry her, didn't I?"

Christina shot a scorching look his way. "Well *she* didn't say she'd marry you."

"You have to marry him, my dear. You have no choice."

"No choice?" she screeched. "I most certainly do have a choice."

Her grandfather chided her with a look. "Now, Christina, it seems to me you made your choice when you fell into bed—"

"Her illness!" Cole interrupted as the preposterous possibility occurred to him. He clutched the old man's arm. "What about her illness?"

"What illness?" Christina asked.

Cole's hand dropped away and he went still as a corpse. An ugly feeling rumbled around his gut. "Thornbury?"

The wealthiest, most powerful man in Derbyshire dipped his chin and shuffled his feet. "Hmm . . ."

Hell. I can't believe it. A sense of betrayal churned his stomach, but on the heels of that, anger began to build. "They lied?" he challenged softly.

Christina slapped his shoulder. "What illness?"

The earl blew out a sigh, then shuffled over to one of the compass-back chairs scattered throughout the orangery. Sinking into the seat, he said, "It was an excuse. Elizabeth is in the peach of health."

Cole slumped back against the wall. Sonofabitch. This was truly unbelievable. That Jake and Elizabeth would pull such a vicious joke on him, why, it was an arrow through the heart.

"Morgan," Christina said in a warning tone.

He looked at her, dumbfounded, and explained. "Jake told me she was ill with a heart condition. Said the doctor prescribed peace and quiet, which is why she was sending you to Hartsworth. I thought she was dying, Chrissy. I thought she might die while we were away. I knew . . . I knew you'd be crushed."

She gasped a breath, then stared at him in disbelief for a long second. "Mama and Jake did that?"

"From what I understand, Jake believes the story of your mother's ill health," the earl interjected. "Elizabeth thought he would be more convincing that way."

Cole didn't know whether that made him feel better or worse. While he was still trying to sort the question out, Christina's temper blew. "How cruel! The nerve of her. The gall. I can't believe she would be so mean to you and Jake."

Despite his emotional confusion, Cole noticed she failed to include herself in that charge against her mother. *Ah, Bug, she has hurt you, hasn't she?*

Energy rolled off Christina in waves as she marched up and down the narrow aisle between pots of pineapple plants and tubs of orange trees. She sputtered and spewed, condemning her mother's insensitivity and interference. She talked with the movement of her hands and head and hips. The woman was in a fury, and Cole was distracted from his troubles by the sheer beauty of the sight.

He loved the fire in her hair and in her heart. He loved her passion. He loved her pride. He loved . . .

Good God, I love her.

The truth of it took his breath away. He reached out for something to hold on to and grabbed the prongs of a garden fork carelessly hung from a support post with the sharp edges out. Metal punctured his skin as Christina wound up her harangue by shaking her finger in her grandfather's face and saying, "Write my mama a letter and tell her this: Her wicked plan failed. She caused no end of grief for nothing. I might have—just possibly, mind you—considered marrying Cole. But now, after what the two of you have done, I'll be going through with my plans as they now stand. You tell my mama that next time she sees me I'll be Lady Welby."

Her words ripped Cole's heart out as she drew herself up regally and added, "Grandfather, you can tell my mother I wouldn't marry Cole Morgan now if he were the last man on earth."

For the next twenty-four hours Chrissy hid from the world in the privacy of her room. She ignored all knocks at her door, even Lana's, and especially the pounding Cole gave it from time to time. When hunger finally caused her to request a tray from her maid, she sent the accompanying notes from Cole and her grandfather back unread, then buried her face in her bed pillow to indulge in yet another bout of crying. She had alternated between tears and temper since storming from the orangery yesterday evening. So far she'd gone through almost a dozen handkerchiefs tending her tears. Indulging her temper had resulted in three broken vases, two cracked decorative plates, and a shattered figurine she regretted throwing the moment it banged against the door. That particular porcelain piece had been among her favorites. She wouldn't have reached for it had Cole not been shouting and pounding on the other side of the locked door.

At some level, Chrissy knew the decisions she'd made yesterday were based on childish emotion rather than adult logic. She'd jumped upon a runaway horse galloping toward disaster, but she couldn't quite manage to summon the strength to holler whoa.

Married to Cole. It was an unacknowledged, but dearly desired dream that had been dangled before her, then snatched away.

From the moment he first mentioned marriage, she'd felt a little thrill even though she'd forced herself to ignore it. Had he allowed them the time to discuss the possibility before rushing off to meet the earl, they might have reached an understanding. She might have abandoned her vow not to marry for anything less than love if he'd even hinted he could grow to love her at least a little in the days to come.

Now, even if he climbed to Hartsworth's rooftop and shouted of his love for her to all of England, she couldn't believe him. One of the constants in Cole Morgan's life was his loyalty to and affection for her mother. For Elizabeth, he would lie. He'd tell Chrissy he loved her, even if he didn't.

She laughed without amusement. Wasn't it just her luck that the one time she and her mother wanted the same thing, Elizabeth managed to make it impossible?

Chrissy swiped at the tears on her cheek. Enough of this. Where was her backbone? Where was her pride? Had she given it away along with her virginity?

No, of course not. She still had her pride, and by God, it would see her through this. It was time to don her armor. The ball would soon begin.

Chrissy's chin came up and her shoulders went back. She dried her tears and rang for her maid.

She was bathed, coiffed, gowned, and selecting her jewelry when the knock sounded at the door connecting her room with Lana's. "Come in," she called.

Lana's expression betrayed her surprise at the easy admittance as she walked into Chrissy's room. Before she could comment on it, Chrissy held an emerald necklace to her neck and asked, "What do you think?"

Lana sighed. "I think you're the most beautiful and foolish woman I've ever seen."

Chrissy wrinkled her nose. "Your compliments leave something to be desired. I meant do you like this necklace with this dress?"

"It's perfect. You are perfectly irrational. Honey, Cole told me what your mother did and while I agree it was awful, you can't marry the viscount out of spite. Not when you are in love with Cole Morgan."

"I never said that. And I'm not marrying Welby out of spite. I like him. He's a nice man and he respects me, Lana, which is more than I can say about my mother and her magic-handed minion."

"Magic hands, Chrissy?" Lana asked wryly. Then, before Chrissy could respond, she added, "Please, honey. Don't make this mistake. At least take some time to reconsider this foolishness."

Emotion churned inside Chrissy. Maybe Lana was right. Maybe she should take some time. She could hide up here in her room until the ball was over, the house party was over. The century was over. Let Mama manipulate someone else for a while. Let her ruin someone else's life. *I can go to London and . . . and . . . open a chili stand in front of Buckingham Palace.* "I wonder if London is ready for a dose of Texas Red."

Lana frowned. "What does chili have to do with this catastrophe of a betrothal ball?" When Chrissy only laughed in response, her friend said, "All right, I give up. I'm obviously wasting my time. Here." She reached into her own gown's bodice and removed a pair of folded slips of paper, and handed them to Chrissy. "Notes from Cole and from your grandfather," she explained as she sailed back into her own room. "Read them if you dare."

"If I dare," Chrissy muttered. Lana knew her well. Now she had to read the messages.

She opened the earl's note first and read it aloud. "I apologize for hurting you, my dear. It was not my intention. Apparently, I haven't learned from the mistakes I made that drove your mother away. Please, I beg of you, do not follow Elizabeth's example. I love you."

Some of the frost melted from her heart. She couldn't stay angry at the man, knowing his motivation was love. She stared at the second note and grimaced. Cole's motivation was something else entirely.

He wrote: *Quit being stubborn and stupid, Lady Bug. Your grandfather's confession changes nothing. You and I are getting married.*

"And you, Cole Morgan, have chili for brains."

Downstairs, Lord Welby waited for her in the saloon, looking quite dashing in a midnight blue vest trimmed in gold. Chrissy's stomach sank. Welby's expression suggested he was as anxious as she to be here.

He bowed and kissed her hand. "Good evening, my dear. You look beautiful as always. Shall we wait by the Marble Hall doorway? The dancing is about to begin."

Chrissy's eyes widened as she spied a pair of cuts along his jaw and discoloration below his eye. "What happened to you, Lord Welby?"

In a blatant attempt to dodge the question, he said,

"I think it is time you called me Bruce, at least when we're having a private conversation."

"Very well. Bruce, what in the world happened to your face?"

He winced. "I see the face powder I borrowed from Mrs. Kleberg doesn't conceal as much as I had hoped. Let's just say your Mr. Morgan and I had a misunderstanding yesterday and leave it at that, all right?"

So that's why Cole was all worked up when he came to me.

She wanted to inquire further, but the viscount continued, "I admit to being eager to see what decorative theme the earl chose for tonight's special event. He's been quite secretive."

"Yes," Chrissy said absently, questions about this misunderstanding still tumbling about her brain. Then, before she could give voice to even one of them, a new sensation captured her attention. She gazed around her. Something was causing her hackles to rise. She felt like a mouse being stalked by . . .

Her gaze lighted on Cole. He stood leaning against the wall. Beside him was an elaborate sconce with ormolu branches above a plaster panel that depicted playful cupids. She thought it strangely appropriate. He was shooting arrows in her direction with his coldly furious blue-eyed gaze, and although he wore finely tailored evening dress, she easily pictured him naked. *Except Cupid is chubby. Cole Morgan is all long, lanky muscle.*

The image disturbed her and Chrissy had to stifle the urge to stick out her tongue at him. She settled for smiling up and batting her lashes at Welby.

From the corner of her eyes she saw Cole unfold

himself from the wall and start toward her. He had the narrow-eyed, lean-hipped swagger of a gunfighter, and she halfway expected him to push aside his jacket and draw from a gunbelt. So when her grandfather stepped up to the double door leading from the saloon into the Marble Hall and called for quiet, she flashed a grin encouraging him to hurry.

The Earl of Thornbury saw her, registered her smile, and beamed. "Ladies and gentlemen, I wish to welcome you all to Hartsworth on this most special occasion. In honor of my darling granddaughter, Miss Christina Delaney of San Antonio, Texas, I invite you all to my portrayal of an authentic Western cowboy dance."

The doors swung open and the earl gestured his guests inside as the music swelled. Christina laughed when a fiddler, a pianist, an accordionist and a banjo player struck up the familiar tune of "Texas Breakdown."

The Great Hall had been transformed. Enormous baskets filled with yellow roses sat in front of each of the marble columns and filled the huge room with the scent of home. Above the far door hung a huge painting depicting crossed flagpoles, one flying the Texas flag, the other the Union Jack. Along each wall were displays of items either from Texas or related to the state.

Christina stood just inside the door in wonder. She found this sight before her as amazing as her first glimpse of Hartsworth and the Marble Hall.

She couldn't believe he had gone to this much trouble. She was touched. She was pleased. She wanted to cry.

Then Welby gasped loudly and she turned to look

at him. His eyes were rounded with shock. "Lord Welby?" she asked. "What's wrong?"

He pointed and croaked out, "Look!"

She followed the path he indicated and her chin dropped. The statues. How could she have missed them before? The giggle started low in her throat and bubbled up. It took all her effort to keep it from bursting free.

Somebody—and she knew without a doubt who those somebodies were—had dressed all the statues in the hall . . . in Viscount Welby's precious vests.

Those scamps. They promised me they'd put them back.

The tittering throughout the hall suggested many of the guests had recognized the vests, as well. Welby's handsome face grew flushed. "Those children!" he exclaimed, obviously reaching the same conclusion as Chrissy. "They've gone too far this time. Mrs. Kleberg is simply too easy on them. They need to be punished and if she won't do it, I will."

Chrissy froze. "Wait a minute, Welby."

"Where are they?" he muttered, seeming to forget Chrissy entirely. He gazed around the hall. "Where is she? This is ridiculous. Doesn't she see she needs help with those two?"

"Welby?"

He patted her hand. "Excuse me, Christina. There is something I must do." Then her fiancé abandoned her on the ballroom floor.

"Well," she said in a feminine huff, her gaze locked on Lord Welby's departing back. "Isn't this a fine how-do-you-do?"

"Not in my eyes, it's not," Cole said, coming up beside her. He gripped her elbow and tugged her toward the center of the hall.

"Cole, what are you—?"

"It's time to do-si-do, sweetheart. Half of England is here watching and waiting for us to show them how it's done. Few folks from Texas, too," he added, nodding toward the musicians.

"Texas?" She jerked her gaze to where he indicated, halfway expecting to see her mother. *Wouldn't that just cap off this day?* Instead she recognized the caller, the fiddler and his pianist, the accordionist and the strummer on the banjo. They were all from San Antonio, the regular players at the Saturday night cowboy dances held in the public assembly hall.

"How did they get here?"

"I doubt they swam," he replied, drawing her toward the center of the hall where three couples waited. "C'mon, we're the fourth two of the opening square."

The fiddler made a fast run-through of his scales and Chrissy quit worrying about Welby. Since her grandfather went to the trouble to make these arrangements, she thought it only right to make the effort to enjoy the results. Besides, she'd always loved square dancing.

She nodded hellos to the three other couples who would participate in this dance, and moments later, the music began and the caller went to work. "Honors right and honors left. All join hands and circle to the left. Break and swing and promenade back."

Chrissy's mind whirled right along with her body as the caller guided them into The Ocean Wave, a dance requiring careful teamwork and timing. It was one of her favorites and though she tried to lose herself in the dance, she found she couldn't.

This particular dance required that Cole rest his hand at her waist. It proved to be a major distraction. Every time he touched her, she burned. Every time he looked at her, his bluebonnet eyes warm and knowing, she sizzled.

Nervously, she cast her gaze around the Great Hall looking for Welby. She needed to see him for a reminder of what she was about. But she didn't spy her fiancé among the crowd, although she did see Lana and both of the children relieving the statues of their wardrobes.

The caller sang out, "Wave to the ocean, wave the sea. Wave that pretty girl back to me."

"Wave, pretty girl," Cole murmured in her ear.

Shivers chased up and down her skin and she yearned to lean against him. The notion brought her to despair. What was she doing? How could she possibly be thinking of marrying Welby when she loved Cole?

The tall, broad Texan swung her around as the dance required, and the dizzying sensation that resulted in her stomach reminded her of the interlude they'd spent in her bed. *How can I go the rest of my life and never know that glory again?*

Maybe lovemaking was always that way. Maybe she'd find the same joy with Welby.

Or maybe not.

The next portion of the dance called for Chrissy to remain in place, clapping to the music while each couple in turn performed their swing. While she did so, her gaze again sought the viscount, and this time she found him. He and Michael Kleberg were busy stripping a blue satin vest off the statue of David. A couple of Welby's gentlemen friends hovered around, apparently offering jibes. The viscount smiled blandly at them, then showed the boy how to properly fold the garment.

Chrissy studied her fiancé, willing herself to feel an allure. It didn't work, so she tried again, mentally enumerating all his attractive features and characteristics. But no, handsome as he was, he didn't make her blood thrum and her heart sing. Almost against her will, she recalled that the single kiss they had shared had raised only mild interest in her.

She lifted her gaze to Cole's mouth. His kiss was different, much different. His hands weren't the only thing that were magic. She wondered if every woman he kissed felt the passion he so easily roused within her.

That thought made her stomach go sour, and she returned her attention to the dance. A few minutes later, the caller began the ending. "Left Allemande, and a right hand grand, Plant your 'taters in a sandy land, And promenade home!"

The ball guests clapped as the music died away. Chrissy pasted on a smile and nodded her acceptance of the accolades. Cole did the same, then lifted her hand to his mouth for a kiss. "A pleasure as always, Lady Bug," he said softly.

The rapid beat of Chrissy's pulse and the shortness of her breath had little to do with the physical exertion of the dance, and everything to do with her partner. As the caller announced a Circle Two-Step, inviting everyone to join in and learn the simple steps, she used the resulting press of dancers to slip away from Cole. Another moment in his presence, of his touch, his kiss, and she might do something even more reckless than her present course of action.

She might agree to marry him.

Chrissy decided she should spend some time with Welby. First, however, she found her grandfather.

"So, do you like my surprise?" the earl asked. "This taste of home?"

"I do," she said smiling. "I'm a little appalled you went to this much trouble, but I do love it. Thank you, Grandfather." She stood on her tiptoes and kissed his cheek.

He beamed and preened. "What's a little trouble when your only granddaughter is getting engaged? Besides, I thought the theme appropriate for you and Morgan."

"Lord Welby and I."

He scowled. "I'm not announcing that betrothal. Never intended to. Want to make it you and that rapscallion Morgan."

"Don't even think about it." Chrissy tensed and scowled right back at him. "Just because I offered my thanks for your efforts, don't think I'm not still furious with you."

"I understand that you are a little upset. Dance some more, child. Activity is good for ridding the body of ill humors." He gave her shoulder an appeasing pat, then called out to an elderly gentleman passing by. After introducing the Marquess of Wirth to Chrissy as an old and dear friend, the trio made small talk for a few minutes.

When the marquess moved on, Chrissy smiled

sweetly up at the earl and returned the conversation to the matter at hand. "Grandfather, try and announce my engagement to Cole Morgan and I will have a case of ill humor the likes of which England has never seen."

"Now, muffin."

"Don't 'muffin' me. I mean it. And while we're discussing this, explain something to me, would you? If you never intended to support my marriage to Welby, why did you go along with the idea?"

The earl frowned down at his fingernails. "Because of Morgan, of course. Your mama told me the man needed encouragement to realize what you mean to him, and after the daggers he shot in Welby's direction the day he arrived, I figured I'd play along and see if the young lord was the push your young man needed."

"He's not my young man," Chrissy insisted.

"If you say so," the earl dryly replied, gazing past her shoulder. "However, you might want to tell him that."

Chrissy didn't have to look to know that Cole was bearing down upon her. Lovely. Just lovely. She couldn't find the fiancé she had, and couldn't get rid of the one she didn't need. Or didn't want to need, anyway.

Sending a groan of frustration skyward, she ducked away from her grandfather, skirted the grand circle forming in the center of the hall and slipped into the hallway leading toward the library and the music room beyond. She'd hide out there for a time and collect herself. And think.

She was beginning to recognize the sensation

creeping over her. She'd felt the same way every time she broke an engagement. *Oh, Chrissy. You're not going through with it, are you? You're going to break it off with Welby.*

Then the sight of the Kleberg children kneeling outside the library door brought her up short. The door was cracked open a little more than an inch and Michael spied inside while Sophie kept her ear pressed toward the opening. Both children's eyes were as round as a Royal Derby plate.

Concerned, Chrissy came up behind them and listened to hear what held them in thrall.

"I will go to her and tell her," came Welby's voice. "For days now my heart has been at odds with my sense of honor. I cannot withdraw my marriage proposal, but neither can I bear to give you up. I have feelings for you, my dear. Deep feelings. It would be wrong for me to say more before I have spoken with Christina."

Deep feelings? Who is in the room with my fiancé?

A feminine, trembling voice spoke. "You mustn't. I won't allow it."

Chrissy's chin dropped in shock.

Chapter

10

"Lana?" Chrissy murmured.

She nudged Michael aside so she could see into the room.

The library's two occupants did not notice her arrival, so intent were they upon each other. Behind a large mahogany library table, Lana stood facing Lord Welby, her expression filled with turmoil. "I spent time with you to help Chrissy, not to win you for myself. I wanted what was best for her."

"You still do. We both know now that I'm not the right man for Miss Delaney. If I were I wouldn't be falling—"

"Don't," she interrupted. "No. You can't. We can't. I forbid it."

"My dear, whether I give voice to it or not does not stop me from feeling it."

"You're mistaken. You hardly know me. Nothing happens this fast." Lana brought her fingers up to her temples and massaged them in small circles.

"It can. It has."

"No. You don't know what you want, Lord Welby. Two weeks ago you wanted Chrissy."

"Two weeks ago I knew I was ready to marry and I methodically went looking for a bride. Yes, Miss Delaney appealed to me. She's a beautiful, fascinating woman." Then his voice deepened, grew husky. "Understand that I never expected to find love in marriage. It's not the way of the Harrington family. I thought with Christina I could find contentment, friendship. I thought I could be happy with that. But then you launched your campaign to convince me to take a trip to Texas and I found out that love can exist. It does exist."

She winced and shut her eyes. "Then it must die."

"Why?"

"Because of Chrissy! You are engaged to marry her. And even if that insurmountable obstacle didn't exist, there is still the problem of who you are and who I am. You are the most eligible bachelor in England. I'm a homespun widow with two hooligan children. You can't . . . be attracted to me."

"Yes, I can, and I am. Very much so." Welby lifted her hand and pressed a kiss against her palm. "I ask you not to speak of yourself and the children in such a deprecatory manner."

"I won't betray my friend."

"Of course you won't. My dear, have you not told me she sets great store in making a love match? Wouldn't it be a greater betrayal of your friendship to allow this farce to go forward knowing love does not exist on either side?"

"But it could, given time," she protested. "You're a wonderful man, and Chrissy could come to see that."

"She loves another," he argued. "Is Cole Morgan the man?"

Lana's head jerked up and her gaze met his, her eyes wide and wary. "I never said that."

Welby gingerly pressed his fingers against the discoloration beneath his eye. "I drew that conclusion on my own."

In the hallway, Michael Kleberg whipped his head around and gaped at Chrissy. He whispered, "You love Mr. Cole?"

"Shush!" she whispered back.

"Mrs. Kleberg," Welby continued. "Lana, I don't wish to hurt Christina either. She is a lovely woman, both inside and out. I recognized that from the beginning. If you recall, I spent a great deal of time with her once she accepted my suit. I kept hoping that as we came to know one another better, something special would bloom between us. It never did. Instead, I began looking forward to the visits of a very beautiful, very special woman who seemed determined to send me to Texas. Did you know I decided to make the trip that very first day?"

Bewilderment colored Lana's voice as she said, "But you argued against it every time."

"Yes. Because I wanted to be with you. I'm afraid my gentlemanly honor is as shallow as a birdbath. However, I am comforted by the knowledge that Christina's affections lie elsewhere. If she's the type of friend you believe her to be, she'll be glad you've found a chance for happiness." He stepped closer, his voice growing intimate. "I won't give you up, my dear. Not when it's taken me so long to find the woman of my dreams. Do not ask me to give you up. Tell me you return my regard."

"I can't," she breathed, pulling away from him. "Even if I did, I can't. Don't you see?" Lana backed away, bumped into the Louis XIV settee, and swayed a bit trying to get her balance. Welby reached for her, steadied her. Their gazes met and held.

Chrissy wouldn't have been surprised to see every lamp wick in the room burst into flame, so heated was the look they shared. A smile began to play about her lips. *Kiss her, Welby. Do it.*

Even as he leaned toward her, Lana wrenched from his arms. "I feel so guilty. I didn't mean for this to happen. I never dreamed a man like you would look twice at me. I never expected to feel like this again."

"Say it, Lana. Say it outright. I need to hear it."

"Oh, Lord Welby." She shut her eyes. "I can't. I can't repay Chrissy's friendship by stealing her fiancé."

Chrissy couldn't bear for Lana to suffer another minute longer. She breezed into the room saying, "Don't be ridiculous. The man is not a piece of jewelry to be filched from a box. Although I will admit he is very pretty."

"Pretty?" Welby repeated, sniffing with disdain as Lana gasped and covered her mouth with her hands. Chrissy saw hope mingled with mortification in her friend's eyes and decided to take the opportunity to cover a little ground with the viscount. Lana deserved the best and Chrissy meant to see that she had it. She had a few questions to ask the man. "Michael, Sophie, you two might as well come in on it. Your knees are probably tired by now. Shut the door behind you."

As the children rushed in and took a bouncing seat on the settee, Chrissy motioned for Welby to sit in one of the desk chairs. Silently, he considered for a moment before tossing her an I'll-indulge-you-just-so-far look and taking the seat. Lana stood behind her children, one trembling hand on each child's shoulder. "Chrissy, I—"

"Be quiet, Lana." Chrissy pursed her lips, folded her arms, and pontificated. "I know it was terribly rude of me to eavesdrop, but it was awfully interesting and let's face it, that's just the sort of scandalous behavior I'm famous for. Now, if I understand this situation correctly, you"— she looked at Welby—"my fiancé, and you"—now to Lana—"my best friend, have fallen in love. Am I right?"

Welby gazed warmly at Lana as he replied, "You are."

"Oh, Chrissy, let me explain," said Lana.

Chrissy held up one finger. "Answer the question, please."

"All right, yes. Yes, I do love him, but I didn't mean to and I wouldn't if he hadn't been so sweet to the children and so nice to me and if I didn't know you didn't love him and I suspected you were in love with Cole."

"Lana dear, let's limit the number of clauses in one sentence here. Otherwise I tend to get lost. Now, where was I? Oh, yes." Chrissy leveled a fierce look at Welby. "Do you have any idea how lucky you are to have earned this woman's love?"

His chin came up. "I am."

"Tell me about it."

"Playing the guardian's role, Christina?" he inquired, arching a brow.

Slyly, she grinned. "Would you rather it be me or Michael?"

He winced. "You have a point. Very well. Allow me to tell you what I see when I look at Mrs. Kleberg." He leveled his gaze upon Lana. "I see a woman of exceptional qualities. I see a woman with a generous spirit, a kind nature, and a gentle patience. I see a strong woman. I see a woman whose subtle sense of humor never fails to bring a smile to my face. I see a woman of quiet beauty who both stirs me and brings me peace. I could go on for hours."

"Oh, Lord Welby," Lana said, her voice trembling on a sigh.

"Darling, don't you think it's time you addressed me by my first name?"

"Oh, Bruce."

Chrissy smothered a smile. "I hope you *will* go on for hours sometime. She obviously loves hearing it. However, I need to know a few things in particular before I countenance this match."

"Match!" Lana protested. "But Chrissy, we haven't . . . he hasn't asked . . . you've made an unwarranted leap—"

"No she hasn't," Welby stated. To Chrissy, he said, "If I were free, my first act would be to ask Lana to become my wife."

Lana squeaked as Chrissy nodded and said, "Consider yourself emancipated as of this moment. However, I get to finish asking my questions before you get around to yours. Now, even though Lana is my dearest friend and I think she is the finest woman in the world, I am not unaware of the potential problems she might bring to a marriage with a British lord. For instance, how do you feel about her lack of pedigree?"

"She's not a horse, Miss Delaney. I'm marrying Lana, not her family tree."

I knew I liked this man, thought Chrissy. "She has no dowry."

He gazed at Lana and his voice gentled. "Her smile, alone, makes her wealthy beyond measure in my eyes."

He is good. "Lord Welby, what are your feelings toward her children?"

"Why, I love them, too, of course."

She cocked her head and studied him carefully. "Even after the pranks? The worm sandwich? The vests on the statues?"

"Especially after all of that. Sophie and Michael have spirit, they have grit. While I won't try to take their father's place, I will be proud to stand in for him and guide them in the years to come."

"But you're supposed to hate us!" Michael exclaimed.

"That's right, Mr. Viscount Welby," Sophie piped up, her brow knotted in confusion. "We did those tricks so you'd be mean back to us and Miss Chrissy wouldn't like you and wouldn't marry you because you aren't the right beau for her and I guess that's because you're supposed to be our mama's beau and I bet our daddy who is an angel up in heaven now picked you out for us." The longer she talked, the more her frown eased. By the time she finished she was beaming. "Isn't that nice of our daddy?"

"Yes," Chrissy said, no longer able to hold back her approving grin. "Yes, it is very nice." To Lana, she added, "I never noticed before that this clause problem runs in the family."

But Lana was obviously hung up on the word "nice." She repeated, "Nice, Chrissy? You think this is nice? Really?"

Smiling gently, she knelt before her friend and took her hands in hers. "Very, very nice."

Tears swam in Lana's eyes. "You understand I didn't set out to undermine your feelings for one another?"

"Honey, Lord Welby and I never had feelings for one another. We pretended to have feelings. We tried to have them. They simply weren't there. You were right, Lana. Whether I like it or not, it seems my heart is given elsewhere. A wedding between myself and your viscount would have been a disaster."

"It is Cole, isn't it? You love him."

Chrissy shrugged. "We're not talking about me. We're talking about you."

"He wants me to marry him, Chrissy."

"I know. It's wonderful."

"But I'm a baker. He's a viscount."

"So he'll gain a little weight around the middle from your kolaches. He can exercise it off by riding his Thoroughbreds."

"He wants a home and a family."

"You can give him that. You're exceptionally good at making a home, and you already have a head start on that family."

A single tear slipped down Lana's cheek. "You really think I should marry him?"

"Yes I do."

Lord Welby sat on the arm of the settee, leaned

over, and pressed a gentle kiss against Lana's hair. "So, Miss Delaney, can I take it that I've passed muster? You sanction a betrothal between me and this lovely woman?"

"Hmm . . ." Chrissy rolled back on her heels. "I have one test left. Lord Welby, are you willing to eat chili once a week?"

He grimaced. "Chili? That is meat and beans and hot spices?"

Chrissy wrinkled her nose. "Only amateurs put beans in their chili."

"Well . . ." The viscount sucked air through his teeth. "I may have to take a stand on this one. I don't believe I desire chili at my table on a weekly basis."

Chrissy sniffed, then gracefully rose to her feet. With a regal tilt of her head, the Chili Queen said, "Good. Because Lana can't make a good chili worth beans. Stick to the kolaches, Welby. And welcome to my family."

She leaned forward to kiss him just as Cole opened the door and looked inside.

"Dammit, woman, don't you ever stop?"

Cole slammed the library door shut behind him and shot Welby a lethal look. "I'd have thought you would have learned after our altercation in the garden. Do you really need another lesson? Are you that anxious to get hurt?"

"Wait one moment, Mr. Morgan."

"No, you hold on. To anything except my . . . except Christina."

The woman, blast her hide, rolled her eyes and said, "Oh, hush, Morgan. You came in late to this party, so shut your mouth and sit down so that Lana can get engaged to Lord Welby."

In the process of crossing the room, Cole pulled up short. "What did you say?"

Christina headed his way, waving a hand. "On second thought, let's give them some privacy. Michael, would you partner me in the next square dance? And Sophie? If you smile pretty and bat your lashes at Mr. Cole, I'll bet you'll get a dance invitation, too."

"I don't want to leave," Michael said. "If he's gonna ask Mama to marry him, then he has to ask me and Sophie, too. We all come together."

"You do at that, Master Michael," Welby said. "And you are right. You and your sister should stay." Then, throwing Cole an icy glare, he added, "Morgan, I prefer you leave immediately."

"You and Lana?" Cole asked, giving his head a little shake as he tried to absorb the news. "But you're betrothed to Christina."

"No he's not," Sophie said. "Miss Chrissy ants-ee-paid him."

Cole's brow furrowed. "She what?"

"I gave him back his betrothal ring."

"But he never gave you a betrothal ring."

"I meant it metaphorically."

Welby fished in his pocket and pulled out the object under discussion. "I was waiting for tonight."

Christina's gaze lighted on the large emerald and half-dozen rubies set in a delicate gold band and she clicked her tongue and teased, "Oh, my. How gorgeous. Maybe I should have fought a little harder to keep you."

"You're too late, Chrissy." Lana gazed dreamily up at the viscount. "He's all mine."

Cole snorted. "Well, I'm lost."

"Of course you are, Morgan." Chrissy took his arm and pulled him along with her toward the door. "Why don't you try telling us something we don't already know?"

For the first time since his arrival at Hartsworth, Cole heard hinges creak as the door swung open. Must have slammed it harder than I thought, he mentally surmised as he gave Lana and the children a wave before following Christina out into the hallway.

She reached around him and pulled the door shut. As soon as the latch clicked she headed away from him.

"Wait a minute. Where do you think you're going?"

"Back to the Great Hall, of course. I need to find my grandfather and tell him so he can make the correct announcement before supper. Then I intend to dance and dance and dance some more. It looks like I'll be reentering the marriage market."

"Over my dead body, you will."

"Whatever it takes, Morgan. Whatever it takes."

Cole caught her by the arm and stopped her in her tracks. "Stop this, Christina. We have to talk. Whether you like it or not, we have a situation here that needs to be resolved, and constantly running away from me won't get the job done."

She shut her eyes and sighed heavily. "I know, Cole. I know we have to talk, that we have some decisions to make, but I honestly don't think I can right now. Today has been quite . . . eventful, to say the least. My mind is spinning like a dust devil. Could we call a truce, please? Just for tonight? No talk of marriage or fiancés or especially my mother. I'd like to dance for a bit, to relax and enjoy this taste of home my grandfather arranged."

"A truce?" Cole allowed his hand to drop away from her. The idea sounded good, real good. It would be nice to spend a few hours without his gut tied up in knots over worrying about what nonsense she'd pull next. He could play it her way—up to a point. He was determined for the earl to announce his and Christina's engagement at supper.

Because he didn't want to lie to her outright, he answered her with carefully chosen words. "I'd like to dance with you, Christina. I'd like that very much. I promise not to bring up the subject of marriage with you."

"Thank you."

Upon reentering the Marble Hall they found the dancing in full swing and laughter ringing throughout the room as couples attempted to do-si-do. When it was over, the caller congratulated the dancers for trying something new, then stated that out of respect to an audience unfamiliar with cowboy dances, he intended to introduce three round dances for every one square. The announcement was met with both applause and a scattering of protest. Some guests obviously enjoyed this departure from the ordinary.

"I should go find my grandfather and tell him about Welby and Lana before he gets it in his mind to announce the wrong engagement," Christina said.

Cole's eyebrows winged upward. "C'mon, Christina. The truce was your idea. You out to break it already?" Then, as the musicians struck up a waltz, Cole took advantage of it by bowing to Christina and asking, "Join me?"

She offered a sheepish smile. "Yes, thank you."

Cole took her in his arms and a sense of rightness stole over him. How had he been so blind to her all this time? How could he have ignored the love that was right in front of his eyes? Though he was still reeling from Elizabeth's interference, he couldn't deny her instincts. If left to his own devices he might never have recognized his feelings for the woman in his arms.

So what did he intend to do about it? As he glanced down at her, the scornful pronouncement she'd made earlier echoed again through his mind. *I wouldn't marry Cole Morgan now if he were the last man on earth.*

"Wrong, Lady Bug," he murmured, as he spun her around.

"Did you say something?" she asked.

"I was trying to remember the last time we waltzed together."

"We've never waltzed together. You've only danced with me once before tonight and it was a square dance."

"Hmm . . . then I reckon today is a day of many firsts."

A blush stained her cheeks pink as she turned her head away from him. *That's right, honey, remember our lovemaking. It'll make it easier for you to accept what happens next.*

Because Cole had decided on his course of action. He wouldn't force her into marriage. He wouldn't bribe her or blackmail her or trick her. Such methods might well be effective, but they weren't right. Not for Christina, and not for him, either.

No, Cole had decided to woo her. He would woo her and he would win her, fair and square. And he knew just how to start.

Cole pulled her toward him, holding her a shade closer than was acceptable in an English ballroom. Tonight she wore an exotic, spicy perfume that seemed to seep through his skin and heat his blood. "I have something I want to say to you, Christina."

She tilted back her head and stared at him suspiciously. "If it has anything to do with weddings, I don't want to hear it."

"You want to hear this. I promise."

She visibly braced herself. "All right."

Cole swallowed a smile and said, "It's a confession, actually. Something I was too proud to say to you, but something I now realize you deserve to know. I'm ashamed I haven't told you before. Christina, I love . . ."

"Don't say it," she interrupted, shutting her eyes. "I won't believe—"

". . . your chili."

She stumbled a step. "My chili? You love my chili?"

"Yes." He offered a solemn nod. "I really love your chili. It's spicy with a brush stroke of sweet. It's bold without being overbearing." He drew a deep breath, then exhaled it on a sigh. "The aroma teases a man's senses, makes his mouth water. One taste makes him burn and leaves him hungry for more."

"Cole," she said suspiciously. "You are talking about my chili, right?"

They danced with right hands clasped, her left resting on his shoulder, his left at her waist. Sneaking his left around to the small of her back, he guided her even closer saying, "Of course I'm talking about your chili. Chrissy, your chili has a flavorful bite to it that's different from any other recipe I've sampled. It heats a man from the inside out. Why, just thinking about it warms my blood. I do believe now that I've had a taste of yours, you've spoiled me for any other woman's fare. After all, you are the Queen of the Chili Queens and I bow to your talent."

Chrissy shifted the position of their clasped hands and gave his index finger a sharp twist.

"Ow," he protested. "What did you do that for?"

"I'm not stupid, Cole Morgan. I recognize innuendo when I hear it."

Damn. So much for suave seduction. Maybe he should rethink his approach. Woo and win. How best to go about it? What method was Christina likely to respond to best? He led her twice around one of the alabaster columns before admitting, "You always have been fun to tease."

She wrinkled her nose. "You and Jake made a career of it."

This was a good approach. She wasn't so defensive. "But you always gave as good as you got. Remember how red in the face Jake got that time you told the Sunday school class that Elizabeth used him as a dressmaker's model whenever she sewed herself a new dress?"

A grin twitched at the corners of her mouth, and Cole literally felt her relax in his arms. She laughed softly before saying, "I worked in front of a mirror for a week to come up with just the right expression and tone of voice to make the lie sound like the truth."

"You were an evil child."

"I did what I had to do to defend myself from older brothers."

Brother? The idea didn't sit well at all, especially not in light of this afternoon's activities. Frowning, he asked, "Is that how you thought of me? Your older brother?"

She shrugged. "You were one of the family."

"You don't think that way now, though, of course. I mean, considering this afternoon and everything. Right?"

Her gaze lifted and locked on his. He tried to read the emotions flitting across her eyes, but she successfully shielded her thoughts. Frustration flickered within him and he repeated his demand. "Right, Chrissy?"

Damn her, all she did was smile.

"Chrissy, how do you feel now?"

"Hot." She slowly circled her lips with her tongue. "Dancing always makes me hot."

Fire shot directly to his loins. He seriously considered throwing her over his shoulder and marching from the room. She held his gaze, watching him knowingly, until the twinkle in her eyes gave her away. "You little tease. This is payback, isn't it?"

She grinned, and as he spun her around to the music, she laughed outright. "You did start it, Morgan, with that talk about my chili. So don't get all huffy on me."

"I'd like to get on you, period," he muttered. "Of course, that's not very *brotherly*."

She had the good sense, then, to end her teasing. "No, Cole, I haven't thought of you as a brother in a very long time. See, you couldn't be both my brother and the beau of my girlish fantasies. Remember, I was infatuated with you for a long time."

Infatuated. That was a good sign, wasn't it? Infatuation could grow into love. Sure would be easier to woo and win her if somewhere along the way she realized her feelings for him had deepened. Hell, now might be as good a time as any to make a stab at finding out just what Christina did feel for him.

Cole eyed the flags hanging above the entry doors and danced her in that direction. The musicians began the last chorus of the waltz as he led her outside onto the Corinthian portico. They joined two other couples who had escaped the crush in the ballroom to stroll outside, and Cole nodded hello to them both while Christina exchanged comments about the ball decorations with one of the women.

Moments later, the caller raised his voice and directed sets to form for the next square dance. The other couples hurried inside to join a square, leaving Cole and Christina alone.

A chilly night breeze swirled around them, and she smiled and said, "This feels good."

Cole agreed. The hand that rested at the small of her back itched to move around to the fullness of her front. "I needed to cool off."

She moved toward the front of the portico and stood at the stone railing, staring out at the wide gravel drive and expanse of lawn that formed the main approach to Hartsworth. Moonbeams spilled upon the fire in her hair, sighed across milky shoulders left bare by her gown's neckline, and bowed to an enticing silhouette of curves.

The idea of carrying her off looked better all the time.

He settled for stepping up behind her and breathing deeply of her scent. "You smell good, Lady Bug," he murmured against her ear. Then, unable to stop himself, he kissed the soft, sensitive skin of her neck, nipped her gently with his teeth, then licked the spot he'd bitten. His voice was rough and raspy as he said, "You taste even better."

"Stop," she protested weakly. "Someone will see."

He turned her around to face him. "Since when do you mind being kissed in public?"

"Since this afternoon. I understand now how quickly physical matters can get out of hand. I'd just as soon not parade around naked on Hartsworth's front steps."

The picture her words conjured up in Cole's mind had him groaning out loud. He needed to woo her and win her, but at the moment all he could think of was wanting her. "Chrissy, walk with me."

"Where?"

"I don't know. Somewhere dark. Somewhere private."

"You're trying to seduce me."

"I reckon I am. I started out wanting to talk, but now it seems the only thing left is the wanting."

"Why?" She ducked away from him. "Is it a plot? Do you have someone standing around ready to discover us? Are you trying to trick me into marrying you?"

Mental frustration combined with his physical frustration and added an edge to his voice. "C'mon, Chrissy. Didn't I promise not to bring up that particular subject?"

"I don't trust you."

Temper flared. "That's a helluva thing to say to the man you're going to marry."

"See!" She pointed an accusing finger his way. "I was right." Whirling away from him, she walked the length of the portico, not stopping until she reached the wing of curved stone steps that descended to the gravel drive.

Cole grimaced and gave his head a shake. What was it with the two of them? One minute they're laughing together, the next they're scrapping like a couple of hungry hounds. Is this what love did to a person? If so, then he'd best get a handle on it right from the start. "No, you're wrong, Bug. You're wrong about just about everything."

He followed her, stopping just an arm's length away from where she stood. "You should trust me. You know why? Because I'm in love with you. I'd cut off my right arm before I'd hurt you. Don't you see that? It doesn't matter what your mother wants or what your brother wants or what your grandfather wants. The only thing that matters is what you and I want. Well, I've figured out my part, honey. I want you. In my life, my house, and my bed. Forever."

His words died away and only silence remained. His pulse pounded and every muscle inside him seemed to clench as he waited for her to speak.

"No," she said finally, her voice sounding wounded and alone. "You don't love me. You're only saying it because of her. Everything you say and do is because of her. Because of my mother."

What? Shocked, Cole reached for her, but she slapped his hand away. Temper rumbled as he flatly said, "That's about the dumbest thing you've ever said."

She gave her head a toss, then turned her back to him.

His temper escalated from a rumble to a roar. "Dammit, Chrissy, I do, too, love you, and it chaps my behind that you're trying to be stubborn about believing me." He braced his hands on his hips and glared at her. "And you know what else? I'm almost certain you love me, too. Otherwise, you never would have given me your innocence. We would never have gone so far. I love you and you love me, and while I won't say that word I promised not to say, we are damn well going to be together from now on. And that is that."

Silence dragged out like a mile of bad road. Then Christina drew herself up, faced him, and said, "Listen, Morgan. In fact, watch my lips form the words while you're listening. I will not marry you."

"Why, dammit?"

She brushed past him, headed for the ballroom where the musicians played "Texas Star." Halfway there she paused and looked over her shoulder. "Because, Cole, I won't marry a man who offers out of guilt. Because I won't settle for a love that is less than it should be. It was wrong of me to consider marriage with Lord Welby, and I've learned something from my mistake. I deserve more than that. I deserve a husband who will love me for the woman I am. That man is not you. I'm not my mother, Cole. She's the kind of lady you admire. She's the kind of lady you want for a wife. I will not marry a man who thinks more of my mother than he does of me." Then

Christina turned her back on him and disappeared inside Hartsworth.

Mouthing a vicious curse, Cole kicked at a loose rock, sending it flying down the steps. It clattered down and down and down until it thwacked against the ground. When the noise finally stopped, a disgusted voice rang out from the shadows beside the doorway.

"Well, my boy," said the Earl of Thornbury. "You certainly bungled that, now, didn't you?"

Cole rounded on the man. "I swear that woman cut her teeth on stubborn. Did you hear all that?"

"I heard enough."

"I told her I loved her. Did you hear that part? I told her I loved her, and she dismissed it out of hand. Woman has more nerve than a toothache. Why, I've had women all but get on their knees and beg me to say those three little words. Never have said it before. Never once."

"You might have been better off had you practiced a time or two before tonight. Your delivery was pitifully poor."

"I don't lie, Thornbury. She knows that."

"Right," said Christina from the doorway. "So all those times you and Jake cut school to go fishing and you sat at the supper table that night and told my father about that day's arithmetic lesson you were telling the truth."

He threw her a blazing look. "I thought you'd left."

"I did. I came back." Christina addressed the earl. "Grandfather, it's almost time for supper to be served, and I believe this is when you intended to formally announce my betrothal to Viscount Welby."

"Now, girl." The old man frowned and pulled on his beard. "I told you I wouldn't make that announcement."

"I'm not asking you to. The situation has changed."

"Darn right it has," Cole interjected.

She shot him a withering glare before continuing, "Grandfather, Lord Welby is to marry my friend, Lana Kleberg."

"What?"

"Yes, it's true." Christina smiled. "We'd like you to announce the happy news tonight."

Cole folded his arms and piped up. "Yes, Thornbury, go ahead and tell your guests about Welby and the widow. But at the same time, you'll need to proclaim your granddaughter's upcoming wedding to me."

"No, he won't," Christina snapped.

"Yes, he will," Cole shot back.

"I won't marry you."

"You damn sure will."

"No."

"Yes."

"No!"

"Yes!"

"Enough!" shouted the earl. "Enough of this bickering. Young Michael and little Sophie act more mature than the pair of you. I am appalled."

Cole faced the earl. "I apologize, sir. However, I must insist you announce my engagement to your granddaughter."

"And I insist you announce Lana's engagement to Lord Welby. Don't attempt to publicly shackle me to this lying snake. I won't hesitate to embarrass us all."

"Now *that* I *do* believe," Cole said. "But you made a mistake warning me, Lady Bug. I won't let it happen."

"You have no choice. I'm the one with the choice, and I say I will not marry you."

"Muleheaded. That's what you are, Chrissy Delaney."

"Well, you're just a big old bully. Just because you're stronger than me doesn't give you the right—"

"That's it," announced the earl. "I've had enough. The two of you are making my head spin, and I am too old for that. I shall take care of this problem here and now."

Thornbury muttered beneath his breath as he walked inside the Great Hall and waved his hands at the caller, signaling the musicians to stop. As the music faded away, the Earl of Thornbury withdrew a handkerchief from his pocket and wiped his brow. "Ladies and gentlemen," he called.

"Grandfather." Chrissy rushed up in front of him and pleaded softly. "Please."

"Do it," demanded Cole.

"Don't," begged Chrissy. "I can't."

"She must."

"Say Welby and Lana."

"Me and your stubborn granddaughter."

Thornbury's gaze stumbled back and forth between the two. He grimaced, looked a little panicked, then proclaimed, "I, Edward Stanton, Earl of Thornbury, do hereby formally announce the betrothal of Bruce Harrington, Viscount Welby, to Mr. Cole Morgan of Texas."

Chapter

11

❧❧❧

The halls of Hartsworth bustled with guests' leave-taking activities as Chrissy made her way downstairs the following morning. The song on her lips and skip to her step were residuals of the mood she'd carried with her to bed last night. She couldn't remember the last time she'd laughed so much.

When the earl made his mixed up announcement, her gaze, like everyone else's in the Great Hall, had turned to Cole and Welby. The horrified shock on both men's faces had started her giggling. When they descended on the earl, full of protest and arm-waving indignation, her giggle had grown to a chortle. Then, as Michael and Sophie joined the jumble, tugging on the earl's coat and beating on Lord Welby's legs, she'd broken out into full laughter.

The shocked and silent guests had looked at her as if she'd lost her mind.

So had her grandfather, Welby, and Cole. In fact, her behavior had given them a bit of a scare and rec-ognizing that, she had pressed her advantage. The

Earl of Thornbury ended up announcing Lord Welby's engagement to Lana Kleberg. He'd said not one word about Chrissy's state of affairs.

Cole had stormed out of the hall in disgust. Chrissy had wanted to do a victory dance. Instead she went in to supper and maneuvered a seat next to Lord Bennet.

It was a relief to have something other than Cole and his marriage demands to think about. In the wake of her recent personal upheaval, Chrissy had neglected the search for the lost Declaration of Independence. Before the soup course ended, she decided to concentrate on that bit of business for the moment, and give all her other concerns—Cole and his lovemaking and his marriage demands, her mother and her interference—time to settle in her head. She had run on emotion all day. It was time to use a little logic for a change.

Midway between the fish and the fowl, she successfully wangled an invitation to Lord Bennet's Harpur Priory to see his Lone Star treasures. She'd gone to bed with a smile on her face and had slept through the night.

Awaking to a sun-kissed morning and feeling refreshed, Chrissy dressed and went downstairs to the drawing room where she bid guest after guest goodbye. Cole remained conspicuously absent, and she told herself she didn't care where he'd gotten off to. She'd almost convinced herself.

By noon, most of the house party guests had departed and Chrissy abandoned her post in the drawing room and made her way to the state anteroom off the saloon where she found Lord Bennet overseeing the packing up of the Western decorations he'd loaned the earl for last night's Texas-theme ball.

The baron stood surrounded by wooden crates spread carelessly across the Devonshire carpet woven in hues of pale pink and blue. "Careful now," he directed a footman. "Use plenty of straw. If anything breaks I'll have your head." Then, upon spying Chrissy, he smiled widely. "Good morning, Miss Delaney. I trust you passed a pleasant night after all the excitement of the ball?"

"Pleasant enough, thank you." She approached him saying, "Oh, what a fine collection of spurs. I didn't see these last night."

Delight sparked his eyes. "Please, please, allow me to show them to you." He launched into a lesson on spurs, showing her gads, gut hooks, and hell-rousers, and pointing out the differences between them and cheaper spurs called tin bellies. "This is only a sampling, of course. I have more at home. I so look forward to your visit, Miss Delaney. I have many, many things to show you."

"I'm sure you do." Chrissy trailed a finger along the contours of a Western saddle. "I can't tell you how much I am looking forward to our trip to Harpur Priory. Last evening's festivities left me feeling homesick, I'm afraid. I look forward to talking with you at length about Texas, Lord Bennet."

"I feel the same."

Chrissy watched as the servants continued to pack up files, boxes, and crates. She oohed over some of the items, aahed over others, and waited for what she judged to be the right moment to ask, "This is all so impressive. Tell me, Lord Bennet, are there many other Englishmen of your acquaintance who share your passion for my home state?"

"Actually, there are a dozen or so men who are interested in the American West—Texas in particular—spread around the country. I exchange letters with them upon occasion."

"Is a Lord Melton among them? I seem to remember my grandfather mentioning his name in connection with Texas."

Bennet frowned. "Melton. Yes. He poses himself as a Texologist, too, although I coined the term. He doesn't collect. His interest in Texas is limited almost exclusively to political topics. He casts himself as a historian, you see, and focuses his studies on Britain's relationship with Texas during the days of the republic. Apparently, Charles Elliott, Britain's chargé d'affaires to Texas, was a cousin or family friend or something, and another family member had something to do with the Texas Legation in London."

"Ah." Chrissy nodded sagely. "So he collects government documents or some such thing?"

"No. He simply studies them. In fact, he's been to Harpur Priory to study my ephemera."

"Oh? What sort of ephemera?" Chrissy pressed.

Bennet shrugged. "Quite a selection of different things. For instance, I have newspapers that date back to the days of the Republic."

Chrissy hoped his assortment of ephemera included more than old newspapers, but she decided to wait until her visit to Harpur Priory to delve further into the matter. If Bennet was in possession of the Declaration, she'd need to step carefully. She couldn't forget how prickly he'd been that day at the ruins when Cole suggested they might do some horse trading with his Texas collection. What would they do if they found out he had the document, but he refused to give it up?

"I would imagine some items in your collection are quite valuable. Has anyone ever stolen anything from you?"

Something ugly flashed in his eyes and he visibly tensed. "Yes. I had supplied items for a museum exhibition and one of my Texas Paterson five-shot revolvers disappeared."

"That's terrible."

"I was quite upset. I no longer display my more valuable items. At times temptation is difficult to deny."

Unbidden, a picture of Cole, naked and kneeling above her flashed through her mind. "Yes, that is so true."

A footman approached Lord Bennet with a question concerning the proper way to pack the barbed wire exhibit. While they conversed, Chrissy did her best to banish Cole Morgan from her thoughts and keep her mind on the business at hand. To that end, when Bennet turned back to her, she said, "Lord Bennet, about those dozen or so men you mentioned who share an interest in Texas. Have you ever considered establishing a formal group where ideas could be shared, papers given, that type of thing?"

Bennet's eyes narrowed as he considered the suggestion. "Hmm . . . an Anglo-Texan Society. No, I haven't, but what an extraordinary idea. I can envision it now. I could give my treatise on the Dauntless Dozen."

"The Dauntless Dozen?" Chrissy asked.

Bennet ticked the names off on his fingers. "William Blazeby, Daniel Bourne, George Brown, Stephen Dennison . . ."

"Heroes of the Alamo," Chrissy said, recognizing the names.

"All of whom were born in England. In researching their backgrounds I have uncovered some very interesting information. In fact, I have considered drafting a letter to Lord Melton in regards to the Dauntless Dozen because I have information he will consider valuable."

"How perfect. You must do this, Lord Bennet. You must organize a society, an Anglo-Texan Society." She beamed a brilliant smile his way, then added, "You'll be its first president, of course."

He drew himself up and his chest puffed with air. "Oh, well. Yes, I suppose I should accept the office if I am the man responsible for creating the organization." He pursed his lips, thought for a moment, then added, "I shall have to consider how best to structure a group such as this. Then perhaps I'll send out invitations to meet at my club in London once the Season starts. I imagine the majority of our potential members will come to town for the festivities."

Chrissy summoned her most disappointed voice to say, "Oh. I had hoped you would organize the association sooner than that. I would love to be a part of it—if you allow women to join, of course. I'm sure my dear friend, Mrs. Kleberg, soon to be Lady Welby, would support the Anglo-Texan Society with her patronage, if females were allowed."

Bennet's eyes brightened. "Of course, of course. I

would not consider having it any other way. And now that I think about it, I don't see why I couldn't host the first meeting at Harpur Priory."

"Wonderful." Chrissy clapped her hands in exaggerated delight. "How soon do you suppose you could arrange the gathering? I shall coordinate my visit with it and—" She broke off abruptly and clapped her hands. Though she'd been steering the conversation this way all along, she made it appear as though the thought had just occurred to her when she said, "Oh, Lord Bennet. I just had the most marvelous idea. Why don't we broaden the scope of the organizational meeting and make it a social event as well as a scholarly meeting."

"A social event?"

"I would imagine that by hosting the organizational meeting at your home, we'll find it more difficult to encourage some of the less enthusiastic potential members to attend. If we make it an event no one would want to miss, it will go a long way toward solving that problem."

"Ah, I see now. An event. I like the idea, but I fear I don't know how such broadening of scope would be accomplished."

"That's easy," Chrissy said, beaming. "We could take my grandfather's idea of the Texas Ball and elaborate on it. We could make it an authentic Texas weekend. We could all pitch in and give demonstrations of our particular talents in addition to the papers. You told me last night you have become quite proficient at lassoing your longhorns. Mr. Morgan does some amazing feats with a gun."

Bennet frowned. "This sounds similar to Buffalo

Bill's Wild West Show. I don't want that. The show portrays the myth of the American West. I have serious, scholarly research to present."

Chrissy waved a hand. "I'm not suggesting a show, but a demonstration, a reenactment. Perhaps Cole's trick shooting is a little too showy, but an exhibition of the proper way to lasso your longhorns would be the perfect complement to a barbecue." She smiled sweetly and added, "I'd be honored to make my chili if you'd like."

"A barbecue," Bennet mused. Then his eyes rounded in horror. "You are not suggesting Mr. Morgan slaughter my longhorns, are you?"

"No, of course not. Any beef cattle will do. Not pork, though. Real Texans eat beef barbecue. We'll have my chili and Lana's cornbread and potato salad and beans. If your guests bring children, we can have a taffy pull. And a dance, of course. No barbecue is complete without a dance. Everyone seemed to enjoy last night's entertainment. Why, the first meeting of the Anglo-Texan Society would make the earl's cowboy ball pale in comparison. Say you intend to make it an annual event and you'll have people clamoring to join."

Bennet folded his arms and gazed into the future. "Yes. The Society will be a scholarly, yet social pursuit."

"Destined to be one of the most prestigious associations in Britain, I imagine. And you, Lord Bennet, will be its founding father."

He hooked his thumbs behind his lapels. "I shall have to get a new portrait painted. Perhaps I'll wear the cowboy hat I purchased in Dallas during my last visit."

"Perfect, Lord Bennet. That sounds just perfect. Now, let's check a calendar and set a date, shall we? And if you'd care to write out the invitations before you leave Hartsworth, I'll make certain they are posted immediately."

"Yes. I'll certainly do that."

Chrissy left the state anteroom a short time later with a spring in her step, appointment book in hand, and Cole Morgan's probable reaction to her news playing like a Shakespearean comedy through her mind. He'd be both impressed and annoyed. He wouldn't be able to deny her plan was a good one, and he wouldn't like it that she'd bested him in the Declaration hunt yet again.

She couldn't wait to tell him.

She tried the library first, but didn't find him there. She checked the billiard room, the gun room, the music room, the state rooms, and all the corridors before trekking out to the orangery where she found the earl once again tending his plants. "Grandfather, have you seen Cole this morning?"

Thornbury glanced up from his seedling and said, "No, he was gone before I awoke."

Chrissy froze. "What do you mean *gone*?"

"It is a simple word, my dear. He has gone. He left. He departed Hartsworth before dawn this morning."

Cole wished for the thousandth time that he'd brought his own horse with him to England. He'd spent too many days traveling on trains, in coaches, and atop rented horses. His rear end would have appreciated the familiar comfort of his own saddle.

Ten days after the cowboy ball, Cole returned to Hartsworth. He arrived with marriage licenses in his pocket and the proverbial burr beneath his rented saddle. In his absence he had discovered that Lady Bug had been stirring up trouble.

"Don't ask me why I'm surprised," he muttered to himself as he swung from his saddle and tossed his reins to a groom. "I should have known Christina wouldn't take my orders lying down."

Using "Christina" and "lying down" in the same sentence had been an unfortunate choice of words. The vision that blew through his mind made him hotter than a San Antonio summer.

This was not the way to deal with the woman. It put him at a disadvantage. Cole would need all his wits about him when he explained what he'd done, and walking around with a poker in his pants tended to drain a man of his brains. To his great dismay, such a condition had become quite common of late. It happened damn near every time he thought about Christina.

He thought of her a lot.

Entering Hartsworth through the servant's door at the back of the house, he wandered into the kitchen where he suspected he might find Lana baking kolaches or her children charming an afternoon snack from the cook. The room was full of people, though empty of Texans, and he had just opened his mouth to ask after Christina when Michael Kleberg came shooting through the doorway, his sister at his heels, and hollering, "It's four o'clock now, Mrs. Peterson. May we please have our cookies and milk? I mean our *biscuits* and milk."

"Me too, Mrs. Peterson?" Cole asked, offering the cook his most roguish smile.

"Mr. Cole!" cried Sophie. "You're back!"

"Thank goodness," Michael said with a grateful sigh.

Cole sat with the children at a table tucked away in a far corner of the kitchen. Thanking the cook, he accepted the plate of shortbread cookies, and took a sip of the glass of milk she handed him. Then he shot the Klebergs a smile and said, "Yes, you scallywags, I'm back. So tell me why you said thank goodness?"

Michael chomped away, swallowed, and answered. "Because Miss Chrissy has gone half crazy since you left. She's running a mile a minute working on Mama's wedding plans and putting together some big barbecue at that church house where Mr. Bennet lives."

Cole frowned into his milk. "Yes, I heard about the Anglo-Texan Society meeting to be held at Harpur Priory."

"That's it. Gonna be school and a barbecue. Miss Chrissy's been making list after list after list."

Sophie's eyes went round and serious. "She's been working on her chili recipe, too. We think she's *changing* it, but we can't hardly believe it because it's already perfect just like it is. Mama says for us not to worry, that the Queen of the Chili Queens won't ruin her recipe. She says with you gone Miss Chrissy doesn't have anyone to tussle with so she's full of pent up energy. Says she's like a pot of chili that has cooked too long without being stirred."

Cole almost spewed his milk. Stirring Chrissy's chili, so to speak, was nearly all he'd thought about of late.

He tossed back the last of his milk, then set the empty glass on the table and rose. "Well, reckon I'd best see to the woman. Do y'all know where I can find her?"

Michael nodded. "She's up at the fishing pavilion on the middle lake. Got a package from Texas yesterday—some new fishing lures she ordered from Castaway Bait Company."

"Really?" The news distracted Cole for a moment. He'd had some mighty good luck on Castaway's bait, himself. "In that case, I reckon I'll go fishing."

Sophie daintily wiped her mouth with a napkin. "Are you going to stir up Miss Chrissy while you're at it?"

"I'll do my best."

"Good." Michael plunked an entire cookie into his mouth, then sputtered crumbs as he said, "Mama told Sophie and me we didn't have to worry, that you'd take care of things once you got back. Mama told us you are just the man for the job."

"I'm the only man for the job," Cole countered.

Leaving the Kleberg children in the kitchen, he strolled outside and started down the path that led to the fishing pavilion. The brisk exercise combined with the anticipation of seeing Christina again invigorated him, and by the time his destination came into view, he was feeling quite the cock-of-the-walk.

"Pent up energy? Needing a stir?" He lengthened his stride. "Reckon it's time, then, that I turn up the heat. Just a little bit, though. Want to take it slower this time." He glanced up at the sky, noted the position of the sun, and smiled. "Don't look now, Lady Bug, but you are going to simmer all night."

Chrissy had always loved to fish. Some of the happiest memories of her childhood were the long summer days spent with Jake and Cole along the banks of the San Antonio River. Back then, using bacon for bait, they'd lure crayfish—or crawdads, as they called them—from their homes along the muddy banks, and name them after the teacher at school or the bad-tempered clerk who manned the mercantile candy counter. They'd bait hooks with breadcrumbs and pull sunfish and perch out of the water by the dozens. When they were in the mood for more serious fishing, they'd dig worms and dangle their hooks for black bass and bluegill.

A few years ago at Christmas, in a rare display of discerning gift-giving, Jake had given Chrissy a tackle box filled with artificial baits made by a Galveston manufacturer called Castaway Bait Company. Even though she still loved to fish, Chrissy had outgrown her willingness to put worms on a hook. The artificial bait not only solved that problem, they added the challenge of accurate casting to the mix and made fishing all the more enjoyable.

Upon learning Hartsworth had a fishing pavilion and visiting it for the first time last week, Chrissy fell in love with the place. Positioned at one end of a small, ornamental lake, and flanked by a pair of boathouses, the stone structure was the size of an average Texan house, but much more richly appointed. From its plasterwork ceiling, to walls hung with gilt-framed oil paintings depicting sea serpents and sirens, to furnishings fine enough to grace a palace and a thick, rich carpet that stretched from wall to wall, the fishing room was a world away from the muddy river bank where Chrissy was accustomed to throwing out her line.

The earl had joined her on her third visit in as

many days, and she had mentioned how much she enjoyed the peaceful privacy of the place. Anxious as always to spoil her, he issued instructions that the building be kept for Chrissy's exclusive use every afternoon. Because safety's sake required she have company whenever she took a boat out onto the lake, most often she contented herself to cast her line from the fishing room's central Venetian window, which extended out over the water.

On those days, an attendant accompanied her to the pavilion, fired up the boilers that supplied hot water to the adjacent plunge bath, lit the fireplace, and then departed, leaving Chrissy to delight in her privacy. Today was one of her solitary days and she reveled in the pleasure of being alone.

I'll catch one more fish, then head for the plunge bath, she thought, casting her line through the window into the water below. *The water should be warm by now.*

The plunge bath had quickly become Chrissy's favorite amenity at Hartsworth. From the fishing room, the bather entered an antechamber with tiled walls and an elaborate mosaic chimneypiece depicting Poseidon's kingdom. From there, double doors led into the skylit plunge pool chamber where a double staircase swept around a central plinth holding a statue of a bathing Diana. Two circular flights of steps with curved ends led from there down to an oval-shaped pool.

It was such a cozy, inviting place that Chrissy contemplated bringing a bed down from Hartsworth and moving in. Here she had the quiet to think and to dream. Here she had no memories of Cole leaning against a fireplace or flipping through a book taken from library walls. Here she could literally let down her hair and don her most comfortable clothes without risking her reputation.

Sunshine beamed through the open window and glinted off the threads of gold woven through the scarlet sash she wore tied around her waist. Setting her fishing pole aside, she lifted one end of the sash and held it up, moving it forward and backward, playing with the sunlight. How good she felt this afternoon, dressed in her Chili Queen clothes without a corset or bustle in sight. She'd slept well last night, too. For the first time in over a week—ten days to be exact—her dreams had been innocent fancies rather than restless, erotic tales with Cole Morgan cast in the starring roll.

"Oh, don't think about him," she grumbled softly. "It's too nice an afternoon to spoil."

Thinking about Cole would definitely spoil the day. She still couldn't believe he'd left without a by-your-leave to her. The shock, the fear, that gripped her when her grandfather announced his departure had shaken her very foundation. Thank goodness Welby knew of his plans and had been able to assure Chrissy that he'd left only on some mysterious errand and had promised to return to Hartsworth as quickly as possible. The scope of her relief had appalled her and sparked an anger that had brewed ever since. When she wasn't dreaming about him, that is.

Searching for a distraction, she rearranged her chair until it sat scandalously in the sun. "You wicked woman," she said with a grin, kicking off her shoes and pulling off her stockings. One of the main purposes of the fishing pavilion was to allow ladies to dabble a hook without subjecting them to sunshine.

Happy to risk the scandal of a few freckles, she propped her bare feet up on the window sill, the fishing line threaded between two of her toes, and tipped her chair back so that it rested on only two legs.

Warm rays of sunlight kissed her skin, soaked into her bones. "Hmm . . ." she murmured, stretching languidly. Confident of her privacy, she tugged up the hem of her scarlet-colored skirt and the white petticoat beneath, baring her legs to the sun's heat. From the fireplace behind her drifted the pleasing aroma of chili as it cooked in the Dutch oven she'd appropriated from the kitchen at Hartsworth.

Shutting her eyes, she allowed her mind to wander and soon found herself at home in Texas. She was reclining along the bank of the San Antonio River on a beautiful autumn afternoon. Floating along on the soft, gentle breeze came the scents and sounds of the Plaza de Las Armas a short distance away. Chili con queso and patent medicine hawkers and music—bold, soul-stirring notes that seeped into a woman's blood and made her feet want to dance. And Cole, the man she loved, talking to her. Scolding her. Whipping her skirt down over her legs as he said, "Dammit, Chrissy. Anyone could come walking by and get a right fine eyeful. Don't you have any sense?"

Everything happened at once. She jerked open her eyes, a fish yanked on her line, and she lost her balance and tumbled to the floor, landing hard on her behind. "Cole!" she exclaimed, staring up in astonishment.

His gaze shifted from her bare legs to her naked shoulders then back to her legs. "Oh, God."

Tension flared like a match flame between them. A

part of Chrissy wanted to cover herself and demand to know where he'd been. For ten long days now her anger had simmered. He'd left without a word, without so much as a note, and she'd be hanged if she'd allow a man to treat her so rudely.

Yet for those same ten days, another newly awakened side of her had done its share of simmering. That Chrissy wanted to lie back and beckon him to follow, to use her mouth for things other than talking.

"Oh, God," he breathed again.

Time hung suspended, finally broken by the clatter of her fishing pole falling to the ground. Cole jerked as if he'd been hooked himself. "You have a catch, Christina. Do something with it."

Oh, don't I want to.

When she didn't move, he gave an exasperated snort and reached for the pole himself, grumbling beneath his breath all the while. "Fool woman. Won't pay attention. Waste a good bait." He reeled in the fish, a nice two-pound trout, then removed the hook and tossed the fish out the window and into the stream as he continued his complaints. "Doesn't have the sense God gave a goat. Brand new Castaway Musky Minnow. Makes it all the way across the Atlantic then dang near gets lost in a Derbyshire stream. No business fishing if you can't pay attention."

He propped the pole against the wall, washed his hands in the nearby marble sink provided for that purpose, then grabbed a towel and glared down at Christina.

Feeling needy and itchy and oh-so-glad to see him, Chrissy reacted in her natural manner. She yanked back her foot, then kicked him in the shin.

"What do you think you're doing, sneaking up on me like that? And that was *my* fish. You had no right to throw it back."

"I beg to differ," Cole fired back. "You were torturing the poor thing with your inattention. You were asking to lose your lure."

"I was not. I still have my lure. I have plenty of lures."

"Then learn how to use them right."

"You don't think I can use my lures properly?"

"I sure haven't seen a sign of it so far."

"Keep talking and I'll lure you."

He snorted. "I'd like to see you try."

Chrissy had no other choice. Taking hold of the round neckline of her white linen blouse where it hung below her shoulders, she tugged downward and bared her breasts. "Come here, Cole."

"Oh, God," he said a third time, his blue eyes burning. "Every fish in the sea would be begging to climb on your hook."

Then he was down on the floor with her, kissing her. Touching her. Part of Chrissy was appalled by her actions. Part of her knew she should stop this reckless behavior. Part of her sensed that whatever business had taken him away for the past ten days wouldn't be business she liked.

But another part of her, the heart of her, reveled in being in Cole Morgan's arms once more.

When his mouth fastened around her nipple and sucked, she shivered. When his hands delved beneath her flowing skirt, sweeping up her thigh, she shuddered. When his fingers found her woman's flesh and worked her, fast and frenzied, driving her higher and higher and higher until she tumbled over the peak, she shattered.

While she lay trembling, boneless and sated, he entered her, claiming her in one long, hard stroke. Then he took her up again.

Cole. Cole. Cole. His lips on hers were hungry. His manner desperate. He had the way of a man fighting a tide, battling a demon. And the devil was his own desire.

Chrissy gave herself. Swept along on a flood of senses that surged and crested, then surged and crested again, she sank into the rolling, boiling heat. It was a magnificent hell.

Again and again he pounded into her, driving deep, gloriously deep. Her name tore from his lips, a cry, a groan, a prayer and the sound of it filled her with power.

Her hands swept over his sweat-dampened skin, her nails digging into his back as she arched her hips and met him stroke for stroke. Her mouth raced boldly across his body, licked him, nipped him, explored him until another climax ripped through her.

But still, he didn't stop. They rolled across the floor, thrashing, writhing. Violent. His mouth and his hands were merciless. It was torture now. He was killing her. She wanted it to end. She never wanted it to end. Pleasured pain. Painful pleasure. *Oh, Cole. I love you . . . love you . . . love you.*

"Mine, Lady Bug. You are mine."

This time when she fell, he plunged with her.

Chapter

12

❦

Cole tried to feel bad about falling on Christina like a man possessed, but he didn't succeed. He felt too good to feel bad.

Rolling onto his back, he lay with his eyes shut as he tried to catch his breath and took stock. He had intended to go about this a little more smoothly. Seduction was a significant part of the plan he'd put together to woo Christina to the altar, but it looked like he'd miscalculated his own response in the area of sexual intimacy. In hindsight he realized he should have known better. One taste of Christina Delaney was like one sip of water on a blazing summer day. It fell far short in quenching a man's thirst.

Beside him, he felt Christina stirring. He was just starting to reach for her when she asked, "Where have you been?"

Cole grimaced. "C'mon, honey. Can't we enjoy a little stretch of peace before the war starts in again? Couldn't we start with a hello or something?"

"Excuse me," she drawled in a dry, rueful tone, "but I do believe we just took care of the 'something'."

She did have a point there. "Yes," he said smugly. "Now that I think about it, that's about the nicest 'hello' I've ever had."

"Me, too," she replied, her lips stretching into a slow, satisfied smile.

He took her hand in his and gave it a squeeze. "You sure are something else, sweetheart. In addition to being delectable and delicious, you are always a surprise."

"Why do you say that?" she asked, her gaze warm and tender.

"Well, for one thing, I thought you'd be spittin' mad at me when I returned to Hartsworth."

"I am." She closed her eyes and gave her body a sinuous stretch. "If I ever get my energy back, I'll light into you for leaving without so much as a word to me."

Cole lifted her hand to his mouth and nipped at it gently. "Honey, if this is the way you react when you're angry, maybe I should go away more often."

She cocked open one eye. "Maybe you should go away—period."

"Ah, Lady Bug." He rolled toward her and nuzzled her neck. "That's not a very nice thing to say."

She bent her head, offering him more surface to kiss. "You make me cranky. I don't like being left behind. Where did you go, Cole?"

He sighed heavily, then debated how much to tell her for just a little too long.

Impatience brewed in Christina's eyes as she tugged her blouse back up over her shoulders, ruining the magnificent view. "You have no room to talk about being nice. Leaving like you did was downright mean." She punctuated her sentence by flipping down her skirt to finish covering herself.

Damn. Next time get her clothes off, Morgan, instead of just out of the way. Obviously the sex hadn't taken the bite out of her temper like it had his. Sitting up, he reached for his trousers. "What do you mean 'like I did'?"

"As soon as Grandfather announced Lana and Welby's betrothal you stormed out of the Great Hall and left Hartsworth without a word to me."

"Actually," Cole drawled in his driest tone as he stood and pulled on his pants, "I left the Marble Hall when he announced I was gonna marry a man."

That brought a flash of a smile to her lips, though he'd have missed it had he not been watching closely. No real surprise she found that amusing. When it had happened, even Cole had seen the humor in the moment. For a second, there, the entire Marble Hall had gone quiet, as if the guests had been transformed, joining the ranks of marble statues.

Christina sniffed with disdain, then stood and glided over to her chili pot where she gave the mixture a thorough stir. "So what was this mysterious errand of yours, Cole? Why did you leave so suddenly?"

He shrugged. "As it was I had business to take care of, and I wanted to get it done as soon as possible."

"What business?"

"We'll get to that later. First I want to know about these plans you've made with Bennet. What's this Anglo-Texan Society all about?"

"Well." Christina tossed a disgruntled look over her shoulder. "News does travel fast here in England.

What happened? Did Lana meet you at Hartsworth's front door to tell on me?"

"No. I haven't seen the lovely bride-to-be since my return. As a matter of fact, I was with Melton when Bennet's invitation to this barbecue you've cooked up arrived."

"Melton?" She jerked the spoon from the chili, sending red drops splattering against the white marble mantel. "You were with Melton? You went to London?"

"Yes." Cole couldn't help but grin when a blend of outrage and envy tracked across her face. "It's an amazing city. I've done my share of traveling, but I've never seen a city quite like that one. And old. Why, we think the missions of San Antonio are old because they were built in the last century. That was just yesterday when compared to someplace like Westminster Abbey."

"Never mind the travelogue. Tell me about Lord Melton. Why did you rush off to see him? Did you learn something at the ball before you left? Did he have the Declaration? Did you get it?"

"Slow down, Bug. Give me a chance to answer." Cole sauntered over to the fireplace where he lifted a poker and began stirring the fire. He considered her questions and chose his answers carefully. Only a fool would tell her he went to see Melton in order to wrap up this Declaration search as quickly as possible so they could head back to Texas as soon as the marriage vows were said. Cole was no fool. *At least, most of the time I'm not.*

He ignored her first couple of questions and addressed the last two. "Melton's grandfather somehow ended up with stacks of documents out of the Texas Embassy in London. While going through the papers following his grandfather's death, Melton developed an interest in the history linking Britain and the Republic of Texas."

"Cole," Chrissy warned, impatience glinting in her eyes. "What about the Declaration?"

"He doesn't have it."

"Oh." She frowned.

"But he knows who does."

"Oh?" Her brows winged upward.

Distracted by the way her blouse slipped off one shoulder, Cole didn't respond. She poked his bare chest with her index finger. "You are making me angry."

You're driving me insane. He gave his head a little shake and reined in his thoughts. "How is it that you always manage to stir things up? If it's not a pot of chili, it's a plot of one sort or another, or . . ." his gaze slid to the swell of her breast visible above her gaping blouse ". . . me. You stir me, Chrissy. In ways I've never been stirred before. You make me hungry."

For a long moment, she went still. Something flashed through her eyes, an emotion he couldn't put a name to, but one that made him glad he'd given voice to the words in his heart. Then she smiled a slow, womanly, gird-your-loins-fella-'cause-I'm-fixin'-to-make-you-pay lifting of lips, and he wondered just what he'd let himself in for.

"Shall I feed you?" she asked, her voice a breathy purr.

Cole blinked. "Oh, please. Yes, please." If he had a tail, he'd have wagged it.

She laughed. Placing a finger against her own mouth, she kissed it, then set it against his chest at the spot she'd poked moments before. Cole glanced down, fully expecting to see steam rising. Right along with the rest of him.

"Sit down then, sir, and I'll see to satisfying your appetite."

Christina had a glint of mischief in her eyes that warned Cole she had a trick tucked beneath that enticing black ribbon decorating her sleeve. However, she tempted him with a prize spectacular enough to risk the gamble, so he moved quickly to do as she bid. Grabbing a few pillows off a nearby settee he stretched out in front of the crackling fire, his eyes never leaving her as she removed a bowl from the plate warmer and lifted the lid off the Dutch oven.

The aroma of peppers and spice swirled around them as she filled the bowl with chili. Then, kneeling beside him, she dipped a spoon into the steaming bowl and lifted it toward his mouth. The soft laugh that escaped her made him reconsider the risk.

"Wait just one minute," Cole said, reaching out and grabbing her delicate wrist. "I recognize that look in your eyes."

Her tongue drew an enticing circle around her lips. "I don't understand."

Cole narrowed his eyes and stared deeply into hers. "It's the same look you wore when you liked to have killed me with that habeñero pepper. It's your Chili Queen look and I don't trust it."

She answered with an impish smile. "Now, Cole. This isn't a hot pepper, it's my chili."

"Well, I hear you've been fiddling with the recipe."

She wrinkled her nose. "Excuse me, but why would I 'fiddle' with the recipe that won me the title of Queen of the Chili Queens of San Antonio?"

Because her kneeling position placed his head at the perfect angle to peer down her blouse, Cole became momentarily distracted. "What's a scorched tongue mean in the big scheme of things, anyway?" he murmured.

"Oh, you big baby." Chrissy lifted the spoon to her own mouth, blew gently on it, then ate the spoonful of chili. "Mmm . . . just perfect, if I say so myself."

Again, she licked her lips, and Cole clenched his teeth to hold back the groan.

She dipped the spoon into the bowl a second time, then held it up to her mouth. As she blew a stream of air over the steaming chili, her gaze met and held Cole's. An aching need pulsed through him. She put such promise into her look that it was all he could do not to fling the spoon away and lay her flat. But Christina was a woman with a purpose, he knew, so he made a supreme effort to rein in his impatience.

"You said you were hungry, Cole?"

A low rumble of agreement grated from his throat.

"Here, then, have a bite."

As she directed the spoon toward him, Cole instinctively opened his mouth. The chili never made it there, however, because Chrissy deliberately fumbled the spoon and the warm red concoction spilled onto his chest. "Oh dear," she breathed. "I'm so sorry. Let me clean you up."

She pushed him down onto his back, then leaning over, she licked up the chili.

Cole sucked in a harsh, uneven breath. "Wicked. God, woman, you are such a tease."

She glanced up. "Oh, I'm not teasing. I'm always very, very serious about my chili." Lowering her head again, she took his nipple between her teeth and nipped at him, then used her tongue to lave away the slight twinge of pain. While doing that, she dipped her finger into the bowl. "See?" she said, holding her chili-slick finger up to his mouth. "Taste it."

The woman was a natural seductress, and the slender thread by which Cole held on to his patience stretched to its limit, but didn't break. *Two can play at this game, Lady Bug.* He sucked her finger into his mouth. Flavor exploded on his tongue and he watched her, making promises of his own, until he elicited a shudder she couldn't hide. *Ah, victory.* "Mmm . . ." he murmured, finally releasing her finger. "So good."

Christina, being Christina, fought back. She dipped her finger into the bowl of chili, then licked it, slowly, base to tip and all the way around before drawing it into her mouth and sucking it clean. "Of course. I am Queen of the Chili Queens, after all."

Cole thought he might expire on the spot. He rasped out, "The Chili Queen of England."

"And you are my subject."

"No, honey." He shook his head slowly. "I'm pretty sure I'm your slave."

She straddled him, then grabbed hold of his wrists and pinned him down. "Then tell me where the darned Declaration is."

Cole was well and truly trapped. Not that he couldn't free himself as easy as cutting warm butter, but her position had her breasts dangling right there within reach of his tongue. He didn't have the heart to move.

"You're a wicked woman, Chrissy Delaney." He sighed out a breath aimed right at a nipple. "Bennet has it."

Her tip puckered and hardened and Cole blew a second breath just for good measure. She trembled ever so slightly, and dragging his gaze up to her face, Cole watched her waver between conversation and surrender. *Got caught in your own trap, didn't you, darlin'? Guess you've learned the road to seduction runs both ways.*

Then she released his wrists and sat up.

Dammit, Morgan, you spoke too soon.

"Bennet," she repeated as she rolled off of him and sat at his side. "That's wonderful. It's perfect. I've made arrangements to—"

"I know all about your *arrangements*," Cole interrupted, disappointment in her choice adding a dry bite to his tone. "I know you meant well, Bug, but you've stirred up a recipe for trouble with this Anglo-Texan notion of yours."

"What do you mean trouble? Lord Bennet is excited about it. An event like this will provide the perfect opportunity for him to show us the missing Declaration."

"Then what?" He lifted his hand and started playing with the end of the black ribbon that dangled from her sleeve.

"What do you mean?"

"How do you plan to get from seeing the Declaration to taking it home?"

Her spine stiffened. "I'm not going home. I'm sending it back to Texas with you."

Cole opened his mouth to argue, then reconsidered. "Let's focus on the first problem, shall we? How do you plan to get Bennet to give you one of his most prized possessions?"

Cole could tell by the way Chrissy dipped her chin and turned her head away that she didn't like that dose of reality. "We don't know it is one of his most prized possessions. Maybe all we'll need to do is ask for it."

"And maybe when the sun rises in the west tomorrow morning I'll climb out of bed and put on a dress."

She scowled at him. "Grandfather is willing to provide me a substantial amount of money. Bennet might sell it to us."

"And your brother will don a bustle and take the stage name Paradise Devine while he tours the country in Dr. J. L. Lighthall's gilded chariot singing operatic arias."

The picture he painted coaxed a grin from her, which in turn lightened Cole's mood. He rolled onto his side, propped his elbow on the floor and rested his head in his hand. "Let's back up a bit, why don't we? Tell me what your plan was when you posed the idea for this club."

While she took a moment to organize her thoughts, he tried to squelch his desire to pull her against him and pose a few ideas of his own.

Chrissy smoothed a wrinkle from her skirt as she said, "My original thought was to lure Lord Melton to Harpur Priory so we could question him about the Declaration along with Bennet. Then when Lord Bennet mentioned a number of other Englishmen who have expressed interest in Texas, I thought it might save time to bring them all together in case our information was wrong and neither Bennet nor Melton had the document. Then we could question the likely suspects without having to travel all around the country. Since Bennet told me not all these men were the house party type, I thought we needed a different approach to entice the men to come. The Anglo-Texan Society just popped into my mind, and it felt right."

She explained to him how she'd proposed the idea to Bennet and his enthusiastic response, particularly to the notion of being president of the group. She finished by saying, "What do you have against it, Cole? Why do you say I've stirred up trouble?"

"Ah, honey. I have to admit it sounds like a darn good plan. Too bad you didn't hear what Melton had to say about Bennet and his obsession."

"Obsession?"

"Yes." Cole sat up and tugged around the pillows so they supported his back. Then, lifting the bowl of cooling chili from the floor, he raised a spoonful and took a bite. A delicious blend of flavor and spice exploded in his mouth. "You honestly do make a mighty fine bowl of Texas Red, Bug."

"Cole." She rolled her eyes with impatience. "Tell me what Melton said."

After taking two more quick bites of chili, Cole continued his tale. "Once I explained my reason for making the trip, Melton was happy to share what he knew about Bennet and his Texas collection. He confirmed that Harpur Priory boasts a so-called Texas Room where you'll see the type of items you'd expect to find in a museum exhibit. Old newspapers, battle-field memorabilia, everyday items like cook pots and tools brought to Texas by early settlers. And animals. Apparently ol' Bennet has a weakness for taxidermy. Sounds like he has ten times the number of trophies as your grandfather."

"Ugh." Chrissy shuddered.

"I tend to agree with you on that. Hunting is one thing, but setting a bunch of stuffed animals around the house isn't my idea of decorating. Anyway, Melton says the highlight of the collection is none other than a copy of the Republic of Texas's Declaration of Independence. However, he also said our chance of getting it away from Bennet is slim to none."

"Why?"

"Because Melton made a considerable effort to buy a number of different items in Bennet's possession—things like unpublished diaries, old maps." Cole paused significantly before adding, "The Declaration."

"Bennet refused?"

"Flat out and forever. Turned down every offer Melton made, and he put forth some fine ones. Seems that once Bennet gets hold of something, he never lets it go. Which, I must say, is one reason I'd like you to stay away from Harpur Priory."

As the mulish look he recognized so well spread across her face, she folded her arms and shook her head. "Cole, I have to go. I made plans . . ."

"I know. I know. I'd have to hog-tie you to keep you away, and even then I'm not certain it'd work." He ate another spoonful of chili, then added, "And I must confess that part of me considers your plan about this Anglo-Texan Society inspired."

She nodded, accepting her due. "It is a good idea and I don't see why you think I've 'stirred up trouble' with it."

"Melton said Lord Bennet is considered rough around the edges in social circles. He doesn't spend much time in London and he hasn't taken his seat in the House of Lords since inheriting the title. He's not married and has pretty much kept to himself up until now. As a result, few people have actually heard the fellow expound upon his knowledge of our state or visited Harpur Priory and seen the man's Texas Room."

Christina made the connection without his having to say it. "You think the Anglo-Texan Society will raise his stature."

"And make him less willing to part with anything, certainly not the prime item in his collection."

"I see your point," Christina conceded. "I'll agree it might be more difficult to convince Bennet to cooperate, but that doesn't mean it can't be done. I'm very good at convincing men to do what I want."

"Stop right there." To punctuate his point, Cole aimed his spoon at Christina, giving his wrist a flick as he did so. A small dollop of chili flew off the silver and landed on Chrissy's shoulder. He made a mental note to lick it off directly. "You get to batting your lashes in Bennet's direction, and I'll have to put my boot down."

Chrissy reached for Cole's shirt and used it to wipe her shoulder.

Ornery Lady Bug.

After another bite of chili, Cole said, "Melton thinks Bennet is a few fish short of a stringer. After listening to the man go on and on about the Alamo, I tend to agree."

Chrissy sighed and shifted, stretching her legs out in front of her and flexing her bare feet. "I'm not certain I agree. Lord Bennet strikes me as a very nice man."

Cole's gaze locked on her toes. He wanted to nibble on them. Clearing his throat, he said, "The earl didn't like him, though, did he? From what I've seen, Thornbury is a good judge of character."

Chrissy sniffed. "I don't know about that. He likes you."

"I rest my case."

"And people pay you to practice law?"

Now she wiggled her toes and Cole found it to be one of the most erotic acts he'd ever witnessed. The heat that had been thrumming through his loins could no longer be denied, and he decided that for now he was done talking about Lord Bennet.

"C'mere, Lady Bug," he rumbled, reaching out to play with one of those teasing toes. "I think it's time we finish what you started a little bit ago."

She went still, her gaze focused on her foot. "What I started?"

"You know what I mean." Her drew one finger up along her instep. "Most folks use napkins to clean up their chili spills, not their tongues."

She shivered and shut her eyes. "Cole Morgan. Haven't you figured out by now that I'm not like most folks?"

"You're not?"

"No, I'm not. And I've spent a good deal of time these past ten days thinking about it. You know what I realized?"

She surprised him when, graceful as a swan, she rose to her feet. She tugged at the ribbon encircling her left sleeve. As it floated to the ground, she continued. "I am fairly certain I was destined to be a Fallen Woman."

"You are not a Fallen Woman," he grumbled, his gaze on the ribbon.

She laughed. "Of course I am. I'm the very definition of the term. I am a woman of good birth who gave myself to a man without benefit of marriage. Twice."

Cole sat up. "Now you're making me angry."

Her fingers found the ribbon around her right sleeve. "What I've come to realize is that I truly need not feel guilty for it. It's my destiny. It's the reason why my behavior has been so . . . on edge . . . for half of my life. I never fit the box society builds around proper women. I tried, heaven knows I tried. Think about it, Cole," she said as the second ribbon drifted toward the ground. "When did I first start having trouble with my mother? About the time she decided I had outgrown the trappings of childhood and it was time to mold me into a lady. My mother—"

"I'm truly not comfortable bringing Elizabeth into the conversation right now," Cole rasped, his gaze hard upon her waist where her hands now worked to untie the knot in her sash.

"No, I suppose not." The tightness in her voice betrayed her, as did the fact her hands stilled. "Anyway, I realize now I was never meant to be a lady. The wildness, the recklessness, is in my blood, and I'm done trying to deny it." The sash fell to the floor. "You gave me a gift when you gave yourself to me, Cole. You gave me my freedom. Now I need no longer fight the useless battle to conform to rules that society has assigned me simply because I am female. Now I can indulge the fire in my blood without worry of ruination. I'm already ruined and I've discovered that's a wonderful thing, not the end of the world like girls are taught from the moment they get their monthlies."

She crossed her arms and grabbed handfuls of her blouse, then pulled it up and over her head, baring herself to his gaze. She stood boldly before him, defiant and proud. "So ruin me some more, Cole Morgan. I really like it."

Cole's blood was doing some firing of its own. Never in his life had he suffered such conflicting emotions. On one hand, lust had him firmly and literally by the jewels. On the other hand, he was as angry as he could remember ever being. As much as he wanted to surrender to the first—and God, did he want to surrender—he knew that addressing the latter was more important.

Standing, he braced his hands on his hips. "You have to be the most infuriating woman ever born. I swear, you have the body of that marble Diana over there, but your head is even harder than hers. Number one," he held up one finger, "you are not a Fallen Woman. You and I anticipated the wedding vows, is all."

"Now, Cole—"

"Number two," he said, raising his voice as he added a second finger to the first. "As far as destiny goes, I'm it. I'm your destiny, Chrissy Delaney. *Me.* For all this thinking you've been up to, why haven't you figured that out? I thought you were smarter than this. It's not recklessness riding your blood, it's me. You love me, Chrissy. You love me, and that's why your blood runs wild around me. Hell, you've probably loved me for years, and I was too young and stupid and blind to see it even though I know now that I've loved you for damn near forever, too. That's why we made love before, and that's why we made love this morning, and that's why we'll make love in a few more minutes once I get through hollering at you."

She sucked in a deep breath and her eyes narrowed and flashed. "I never said I love you."

"Tell me about it." Cole threw out both hands. "This is not something that has escaped my notice. I take comfort in the fact, however, that while you refuse to verbalize it, you do assure me of your love in alternative ways."

"Oh, really."

Her slow, snide drawl pricked his temper like a thorn. "Yes, really."

"Such as?"

His hands worked the fastening of his pants as he advanced on her. "You baited me in a horse race."

"Hah. I was ten years old back then."

"You loved me when you were ten years old. Just like you loved me when you were older and followed me to a bordello." He shoved down his britches, then kicked them off.

"I was curious," she replied, her gaze dropping.

"You were jealous. Just like you were when you found out I was seeing the Widow Larsen, so you got yourself engaged to the next man who asked." Naked, he stood close to her, felt her heat radiating from her body, caught her scent, a mixture of soap, spice, and innocence that beckoned him like Parisian perfume.

"You live in a fantasy world, Cole Morgan."

Slowly, he shook his head. "Not anymore. My fan-

tasy is standing here before me. You are my fantasy."
He gave her scarlet skirt and the petticoat beneath it
a tug until they slipped over her hips and floated to
the floor. "So the fantasy is the reality. We love each
other, Lady Bug. You've shown it. Now say it."

"Cole, I . . ."

He bent his head and licked at the spot on her
shoulder he'd promised himself earlier. He felt her
tremble. "Say it."

She shut her eyes. "I can't."

Frustration hammered him and he took her by the
shoulders and gave her a small shake. "Why, damn
you? Why?"

When she looked at him, tears swam in eyes that
pled for understanding. "I may be my mother's daughter, Cole, but I'm nothing like her."

"You're so much like her it's spooky."

They were the wrong words to say, and he knew it
the moment they left his mouth. Wrapping her in his
arms, he pulled her close and immediately tried to explain. "I love you for your loyalty. For your humor and
your wit and your spirit. For your compassion and
your passion for your beliefs."

"Ah, passion," she said, her voice cracking. "Now
that I can accept. I do believe you love my passion. So
indulge in it." She rubbed herself against him. "Indulge in me."

Desire, fierce and hot, ripped through him and he
held his control by a tenuous thread. "Believe me,
Chrissy. Believe in me. I love you. I know you love
me. Believe in us."

"I can't. I can't trust in your love, Cole."

"Why?"

She drew a deep breath, then said softly, "Would you have asked me to marry you had we not 'anticipated the vows'? Be honest with me, Cole."

He felt the trap, but saw no way to avoid it. Still, he tried. "Maybe. I know I wouldn't have let you betroth yourself to Welby. I probably would have proposed to you before that happened even if we hadn't made love."

"What about my mother? Would you have married me without asking her permission?"

Hell. No way out of this one. She knew him too well. "Of course I would have asked your mother for your hand. That's the proper thing to do."

"And if she'd said no?"

"That's a stupid question. She never would have said no. She wants us to be married."

"Answer my question, Cole."

He hesitated, just a second, before saying, "I'd have married you anyway."

She laughed softly, though her eyes remained sad. "Sorry, Cole, but I don't believe you. I know how much you love my mother."

"But I'm *in love* with you, dammit."

Chrissy wrapped her arms around him, and her hands slithered up his back to bury themselves in his hair as she guided his head down toward her uplifted face. "Let me give you what I can, Cole Morgan."

"What is it?" he asked, drowning in the jade pools of her eyes.

"I'm in love with you, Cole Morgan. You're right about that. I love you desperately."

Cole barely felt the first touch of her lips so lost was he in her words. The gift of her love sent him soaring, yet her denial of his own feelings added weight to his wings. Only when the sound of her low-throated moan reached his ears did he surrender, and then only to this moment's struggle. She loved him. She realized it, and for now, it would have to be enough. It was a start. In time she'd come to trust him. Given time, she'd accept his feelings for her.

And in the meantime, since her ears weren't willing to listen to the truth, he'd work on convincing her body. Cole slipped one hand beneath her knees and swept her up into his arms. "I assume the plunge bath is heated?" he inquired.

"Yes."

"In that case, let's see what we can do about washing up the mess we made. I think I see a spot of chili right about . . ." He flicked his tongue across the tip of her breast. ". . . here."

An hour later, they helped towel each other dry. Another hour after that, they finally reached for their clothing. Due to the sparseness of her attire, Chrissy took but a few moments to dress. Cole never thought twice about asking her to hand him his jacket. Even when the papers fell out onto the fishing pavilion's floor, he wasn't overly concerned. Not until Chrissy bent to pick them up did he experience a flash of unease.

Maybe it's best she doesn't see who else I visited while I was gone. Cole opened his mouth to speak as he took a step toward her, but by then it was too late.

Chrissy glanced down at the first of three folded sheets of paper and her jaw dropped, then shut with a snap.

Well, hell. Cole realized their blissful interlude was now officially over.

Chapter

13

Reading the contents of the first sheet of paper, Chrissy's heart pounded as fiercely as it had a short time ago when Cole mercilessly teased her body. "This is a license for marriage in the village church at Ticknall. For you and me."

"Uh, yes."

Chrissy read further. "It's dated the morning after my grandfather's cowboy ball."

Cole shrugged. "It was my first stop."

"I see," she murmured, trying to keep her emotions in check. A glance at the second piece of paper had her blinking her eyes and looking again. This document she read from beginning to end before making a comment. "A civil license?"

Scratching his head, Cole winced. "Just trying to be thorough. Laws are different over here and I thought it best to cover all the possibilities."

The third document came as no particular surprise at that point, because she had heard some of the young ladies talking about such things during her grandfather's house party. "A special license."

Pointing toward the paper in her hand, he said, "That's the best one. Got it straight from the Archbishop of Canterbury. It'll let us get married at any place, any time."

"You did quite a bit of traveling."

"It wasn't so bad. I like trains much better than steamers. The side to side swaying is better for me than the up and down."

Considering their recent behavior, Chrissy couldn't stop the suggestive thought that flashed into her mind. She did, however, keep her mouth shut against it. Clearing her throat, she said, "I suppose you're having the banns read, too?"

He nodded. "In the local village church for three weeks."

"Being thorough."

"Yep."

"I see."

Cole braced his hands on his hips and stared down at the floor for a full half minute before looking up and pinning her with a solemn-eyed stare. "Uh, Chrissy?"

"Yes."

"I really would like it if we could figure out a way to make this work for both of us."

"By *this* you mean . . . ?"

"Us getting married."

From out of the blue, tears collected in Chrissy's eyes. "Oh, Cole."

For a moment, he just stood there visibly willing her to say more. When she didn't—she couldn't—he closed the distance between them and lifted his jacket from where it lay draped over her arm. "I do love you, Christina Elizabeth Delaney, and I hope that before too much longer, you can bring yourself to believe it."

She blinked rapidly, willing the tears not to fall. Then, unwilling to end this interlude on such a note, she forced herself to speak. "Cole, about getting married."

He waited expectantly as Chrissy searched for the words she wanted to say. When a full minute passed in silence, his mouth twisted in a rueful grin. He shrugged into his jacket, then leaned down and lightly kissed her lips. "I reckon it'll keep for the time being, Lady Bug. As long as you know where I intend for us to head, I guess it won't hurt anything to wait a little while until you're ready."

In a small voice, she said, "I don't know if I'll ever be ready, Cole."

Honest amusement replaced the wry look in his eyes. "You'll be ready. Sometime, someplace." Repossessing the marriage licenses, he slapped them playfully against her forehead and added, "And, as I've certainly proved here today, my Lady Bug. You can always count on me to be primed and ready."

One week later Chrissy sat beside her grandfather and across from Lana and her viscount as the earl's carriage made the turn at the gate that marked the lane to Harpur Priory. Michael and his sister had deserted the roomy coach soon after departing Hartsworth, the boy to ride a well-mannered little gelding, Sophie to double up with Cole. The journey had taken just under two hours to complete and despite the pleasant traveling accommodations, Chrissy couldn't wait to disembark from the coach.

She wanted to be with Cole.

Since his return to Hartsworth, they had spent most of their days and many of their nights together. They had fussed and feuded over a plan to gain possession of the Declaration. They had laughed together and teased each other and offered glimpses into one another they'd always kept hidden in the past. And when night fell and Hartsworth slept, they loved one another, using their hands and mouths to convey words of admiration and tenderness, affection and desire.

As the days passed, Chrissy had slowly lowered her guard. The man had officially conquered her heart and now lay siege to her mind in an attempt to gain her trust. He was doing a right fine job of it. Twice already during the coach ride from Hartsworth she'd found herself imagining a world where she lived as Mrs. Cole Morgan.

Darned if it didn't feel like heaven.

Chrissy smothered a sigh, not wanting to cause her coach mates to believe they bored her with their discussion of Viscount Welby's extended family, including the Dowager Viscountess, whom Lana and the children were scheduled to visit later that month. Chrissy dreaded the thought of the Klebergs' departure. They were family now, and she would miss them desperately once they were no longer part of her daily life. But Lana was so wonderfully happy and watching her bloom beneath Welby's effusive regard was such a treat. They had scheduled their nuptials for six months hence, though after watching them together, Chrissy wouldn't be surprised to see the viscount produce a special license of his own much sooner.

As far as wedding plans for herself were concerned, Chrissy had reached a conclusion about that, too. She had given herself permission to put off that decision until the Declaration was in their hands. She needed both the time to think matters through and the deadline to force her to move forward. For the time being, she wouldn't worry whether she dared trust in his claim of love. She'd wait a little while longer to decide if she dared to give her hand in marriage to Cole Morgan.

Be honest, Chrissy. What you decide may not matter. Knowing Cole, he's liable to take it anyway.

"And he says I'm marble-headed," she muttered.

"What was that, my dear?" her grandfather asked.

"Oh. I didn't mean . . . never mind. Are we there yet?"

Lana laughed. "Why Chrissy, you sound just like my children."

Welby turned from the window and said, "You can see the house now. Its low-lying position deep in the park is a reminder of Harpur Priory's monastic origin. Members of medieval religious orders liked secluded sites for their buildings."

"They did?" Lana asked, encouraging him with a look to elaborate.

As Welby launched into a discussion of architectural accomplishments during the Middle Ages, Chrissy got her first look at Lord Bennet's ancestral home, her first thought being, *My, how ominous.*

The Greek Revival portico extended from a

Baroque front, obviously a later addition to the main structure, according to Welby. "I'll know better once I've seen the place up close, but I imagine Harpur Priory is a hodgepodge of fourteenth and fifteenth century walls."

The gray sandstone walls were forbidding, no matter how old they were, and Chrissy felt a trickling sense of unease as the coach descended the gentle slope toward the south front. "In Texas we'd never build in a gully like this," she observed. "Looks to me like it's asking to flood."

Welby continued, "Notice that the house is a rectangular block with projecting corner pavilions. This design for country houses was much favored in England around seventeen-hundred. Note how the pavilions are defined by fluted pilasters that support a classical cornice." He studied the structure silently for a moment, then added, "That cornice is magnificently bold and elaborately decorated. I suspect its design was derived from a plate in Philibert de l'Orme's treatise on architecture."

Chrissy felt her eyes starting to cross at the lecture as the earl observed, "You truly are well versed in the subject, Welby."

"Architecture is a particular interest of mine." He grasped Lana's hand and offered her an adoring smile.

Harrumph. The earl solicited Lana's gaze, then said, "See that the young pup builds his mother the most elaborate dower house in England. Your marriage will be the better for it."

Dryly, the viscount replied, "I've had the plans drawn for years now. I ordered building to commence two weeks ago."

They had no more time for discussion about Welby's mother because the coach rattled to a stop. They had arrived at Harpur Priory.

Cole was there to take the footman's job away from him, and he boldly placed his hands around Chrissy's waist and swung her to the ground. "Hey there, Lady Bug. How was the drive? I wish you'd ridden with us."

His hands lingered at her waist and he stood closer than was proper. Chrissy suspected he might kiss her then and there. "Marking your territory, Mr. Morgan?"

He frowned and made a stab at looking affronted. Then he did lean down and give her a quick buss on the lips. Chrissy pulled away, laughing and saying, "I guess I should be pleased you chose that method rather than lifting your leg."

"Now Miss Delaney, no need to be crude."

Then, because he'd timed it that way, he turned around to greet their host who had come out of his house to meet them, visually anxious to welcome a pair of honest-to-goodness Texans to Harpur Priory. The handshakes and backslapping were at odds to the greetings Chrissy had witnessed elsewhere in England. This was reminiscent of a true Texas howdy and gave her a sharp tweak of homesickness.

You'll never be happy making your home in Britain, her conscience whispered. *Texas is in your blood.*

It was a truth she could not deny. With Cole or without him, someday she'd go home. Right this moment, staring up at the imposing facade of Harpur Priory, she wished someday was today.

Well, let's lift the curtain on this play. The faster they found the Declaration, the quicker she could go home. Maybe that's what needed to happen. Maybe she needed to go home with Cole and see how he acted around her mother. Maybe that would show her if his claims of love were true or motivated by guilt and the fear of displeasing the almighty Elizabeth Delaney.

Chrissy wanted to think about that notion some more, but time ran out. Bennet approached and welcomed her to Harpur Priory. She pasted on a smile and said, "Thank you, Lord Bennet. I am so looking forward to the first meeting of the Anglo-Texan Society. Why, I've felt as if this day would never arrive."

"My feelings are the same. The days have dragged since my departure from Hartsworth despite my being terribly busy making meeting arrangements and preparing my speeches. Did you see my herd as you drove in? I had the longhorns moved from their usual pasture to the front park. My lawn will suffer for it, of course." He chuckled for a moment, then continued, "So what did you think of them, Miss Delaney?"

She hadn't noticed them. She'd been too busy looking at the stern lines of Harpur Priory. "A fine herd, Lord Bennet," she replied. "Nothing says Texas like a herd of longhorn cattle."

Beaming, Bennet nodded rapidly. Had the man a tail, Chrissy mused, it would be wagging fast enough to kick up a breeze.

"Come in, come in, come in. Allow me to offer you a refreshment while my servants deliver your luggage to your rooms." Bennet showed them into the drawing room where soon they quenched their thirst with, of all things, iced tea.

"What is this?" the earl demanded, holding his

glass up to the sunlight, his mouth fixed in a sour twist.

Chrissy smiled. "It's sweet tea, the official drink of the State of Texas, Grandfather."

"Now Chrissy," Cole said, "I thought whiskey occupied that slot." Glancing at the earl, he added, "Bad whiskey it is, too."

"I have harder spirits also, Thornbury, if you'd prefer that," Bennet said worriedly. "I have planned everything during this meeting to be authentic to Texas." Wringing his hands, he added, "Perhaps that was a mistake. Like you, Miss Delaney, some of my other guests are bringing family members along who do not share our interest in the Lone Star State. Perhaps I should revise the menu. Oh, dear. I simply don't know."

"I would be happy to assist in that area if that's agreeable to you," Lana said, stepping forward.

"Oh, yes. Thank you, my lady. That's such a relief."

Lana smiled graciously. "I'm happy to help, however, you're mistaken in designating me as a lady already. Lord Welby and I are only betrothed. I am still Mrs. Kleberg."

"Oh. Yes. Well, that's right. I apologize. It's just that you have the bearing of an aristocrat so I became confused."

"Easy to understand, Bennet," said Welby, walking up beside his wife-to-be. "I daresay my Lana could show scores of titled British women the true definition of the word 'lady'."

Chrissy sighed at the romance of it all. Cole nudged her in the side, winked, and rolled his eyes. She held her hand up to her face as if hiding a yawn and stuck her tongue out at the Texan.

He laughed, and said, "So, Bennet. Where is this Texas Room I've heard about? I'm anxious to see it."

"Now? You don't wish to retire to your bedroom for a rest?"

"It's just a short ride from Hartsworth to here. Why, I'd have to turn in my Texas Ranger badge if I needed to rest after a jaunt like that."

"You're a Texas Ranger?" Surprise and something else flickered in Bennet's eyes.

"Nope." Cole shot him a mischievous grin. "I won the badge from a Ranger in a poker game. It is a treasure though." He paused, then casually asked, "Do you have one of those in your collection?"

"No. No I don't. I would love to have one, however. Very much."

"Hmm . . ." Cole folded his arms and cocked his head to one side. "Well, I might be willing to give mine up. Maybe before this meeting is over, you and I can work a trade."

"I don't trade my things, but I am always willing to purchase what I want. Yes, I'm certain we will work something out. Come along, then, Mr. Morgan, and any of the rest of you who are interested. I'll show you Harpur Priory's Texas Room." Bennet all but skipped as he exited the drawing room.

Cole and Chrissy were the only people who accompanied him. The earl was content to occupy a seat beside the fire, and after asking Welby to go find her children who had not made it in from outdoors as of yet, Lana accompanied the majordomo to the kitchens in order to speak with the cook about the menus for the coming meeting days.

Welby led them down a hall and up a staircase, allowing little time for more than peeking into the rooms they passed. Chrissy was able to identify a Caricature Room, a room done entirely in yellow, and a library. When she quit looking side to side and glanced down the hallway in front of them, she spied the Texas Room right off. The pair of stuffed longhorn cattle standing guard on either side with miniature Texas flags hanging from each horn gave it away.

At the doorway, Bennet gestured for them to precede him. Cole walked into the room, then stopped so abruptly that Chrissy bumped into him. "Well," he said in a tone dry as a South Texas August. "Your taxidermist must be a happy man."

Peeking around Cole, Chrissy's eyes went round. The room was stacked wall to wall with stuffed animals. "Oh, my."

To the left a coyote appeared ready to spring. On the right, a mountain lion posed with his mouth opened in a snarl. Directly in front of Cole, a black bear stood on his hind legs with his right paw lifted in slashing position. Chrissy took a step back and said, "I didn't know we have bears in Texas."

"Used to out in the East Texas forests. I don't know if any live there still today."

Chrissy's gaze skimmed over the armadillo, a pair of prairie dogs, a particularly ugly javelina before halting in shock. She blinked, but the image didn't go away. "A camel?"

Bennet grinned. "A dromedary. Not native, of course, but imported to Texas in 1856 for use as pack animals. I thought I should have one in my Texas Room."

"Certainly," Cole observed, eyeing the ugly beast

with wonder. "No Texas Room would be complete without a camel."

Chrissy gouged his side with her elbow. "Quit being snotty," she murmured, moving toward the center of the room. It was quite a collection, no doubt about that. Along with the menagerie, paintings of Texas scenes hung over every available inch of the walls. Over a dozen display cases stood scattered across the floor, filled with various items of interest. Chrissy glanced in the one nearest to her and saw that it contained pen and ink sketches of prominent Texans such as Sam Houston and Ben McCulloch. Next to it sat a beautiful ebony case displaying paraphernalia relating to Texas railroads. She spied arrowhead collections, a barbed wire sampling, and branding irons by the dozen. Nowhere did she see anything that resembled a historical document, much less the highly valued Republic of Texas's Declaration of Independence.

Disappointment washed over her. Maybe Lord Melton's information was wrong. Maybe Bennet didn't have the Declaration after all.

Cole made a show of examining the display cases closely. Every so often he'd *hmm* or *ahh*. Bennet spent the time pointing out various items of interest to Chrissy.

Finally, Cole wandered back to the front of the room and said, "This is interesting," he observed. "I'm sure that someone unfamiliar with Texas would find this collection quite illuminating."

Bennet puffed up like a toad. "Certainly my collection must be interesting to Texans, too."

Chrissy shot Cole a chastising look. What good would it do to alienate the man? "Of course it is, Lord

Bennet," she assured him, favoring him with a smile. "Why, I've lived in Texas all my life, but I've never seen a javelina this closely."

Cole seemed determined to be a bore, however. He stuck his hands into his pockets, rolled back on his heels, and shrugged. "This is all nice, but I was hoping to see something unique, something that a fellow wouldn't see looking out the back door of the log cabin."

This time she moved close to him and used the width of her skirt to hide the fact she stepped on his foot. "You don't have a log cabin."

He flashed Bennet a grin. "She's telling me to be nice. Sorry, *mi amigo*, I didn't mean to cast aspersions on your Texas Room. It is a right fine collection, and it has certainly set off a wave of homesickness in me. I reckon I'm just disappointed. I had thought I'd try to talk you into doing some swapping, but I don't see anything here I'd consider trading my Ranger badge for. I have a special interest in old things, you see. Your collection here is mostly modern Texas. Except for the bear, maybe. And I don't think he'd fit in my pocket."

Bennet drew himself up straight as the branding iron beside him. "I have older items. I have a collection of items from the mission period."

Cole trailed his gaze across the cases. "Where? I don't see 'em."

"They are not currently on display."

"Oh." Cole's mouth pursed in a disappointed pout that had Chrissy blinking her eyes and giving him a second look. She'd never before in their lives seen that particular expression on his face.

"Well . . ." he continued with a heavy sigh. "That's not my favorite period, anyway. I have a real affinity for the days of the Republic. I oftentimes wish I'd been born fifty years earlier. Why, imagine what it would have been like to be alive during the War for Independence. I could have followed the army and fought at San Jacinto."

Chrissy felt obliged to point out, "You could have fought at the Alamo, too."

Cole looked at Chrissy, then his gaze skidded over to Bennet. "Maybe I did. Maybe I died at the Alamo and was reincarnated because my life was cut tragically short."

Chrissy started to laugh, but the look on Bennet's face kept the sound frozen in her throat.

His eyes glimmered with interest and excitement. "Do you believe in reincarnation, Mr. Morgan?" he asked.

"I don't know. I tend to wonder about it at times. Why else would I be attracted to certain periods of history so intensely while others barely scratch the surface of my interest?"

"I know exactly what you mean. Exactly! I, myself, am fascinated about the Republic of Texas. I have studied every piece of information I could find on that ten-year period. So many times I've asked myself why. Why do I crave knowledge concerning that place and that time? Why do I need to surround myself with items that were made and used by people in the Republic of Texas? Why have I been drawn to that short sliver of history?"

Because you are crazy, Chrissy thought. Perhaps as crazy as Cole was smart, drat his hide. The man was subtly goading their host, obviously hoping to get Bennet to show him those items not "currently on display."

This was pure Cole Morgan. He needed but a few minutes with a person in order to identify which strings required pulling to manipulate the fellow where Cole wanted him to go. The talent served Cole well both personally and professionally, though it was one Chrissy always considered her duty to resist.

"You have a collection from the Republic of Texas?" Cole asked, closing in on the kill.

Chrissy added, "I do recall your mentioning a knife from San Jacinto, I believe."

A wince betrayed Bennet's regret at having allowed the slip. "Well, yes. Yes, I do."

"Now that I want to see."

"It's my private collection. I normally don't show it to anyone."

Cole slapped him on the back. "Then it's a good thing Christina and I are Texans and not just 'anyone.' Shall we go see it now?"

Bennet backed away. "Oh, no. That's not possible. Not possible at all. My other guests will begin to arrive at any time, and I must be here to receive them. Then too I must prepare for the lecture I am scheduled to give tomorrow." He walked over to a bell pull and rang for a servant, who responded almost immediately. "My staff will show you to rooms now. Allow me to say once more, welcome to Harpur Priory."

As they were ushered from the Texas Room and down a carpeted hallway, Chrissy said, "You pushed him too hard, Cole. That's not like you."

"Well *I* don't like *him*. Mark my words, Christina. Something is wrong with that man."

Cole stood in front of the bedroom window staring out at the longhorns in Harpur Priory's park as the door snicked shut behind the footman. Idly, he reached toward the marble-topped table nearby and snagged an apple from the tray of fruit and cheeses provided for his comfort and took a bite. Flavor exploded on his tongue, juicy and sweet, and he'd just lifted the fruit to take a second bite when he heard the door behind him open. "Well, well, well" he said, glancing over his shoulder. "If it's not the apple of my eye."

"Oh, just eat your fruit," Chrissy said, stepping into Cole's bedroom and shutting the door behind her. "We need to talk."

"You know, Bug, as often as you sneak into my room, I have a difficult time understanding why you balk at moving in permanently."

She scooped up a small square pillow off the settee and chucked it at him before sitting down. "Bennet must have moved the Declaration to his private collection. We need to plan how we'll get him to show it to us. We must see it before we can make him an offer for it."

"Ah, don't worry. He just needs a little convincing. I'll take care of it."

She sat back and folded her arms. "Like you 'convinced' him earlier? What were you thinking of? What happened to your smooth, subtle approach?"

"I guess I used it all up on you last night," he replied, shooting her his wickedest grin.

That took some of the pepper out of her chili. Her lips lifted and her eyes softened, "This is the first bit of privacy we've had all day. I missed you when I woke up this morning."

"I missed you, too. Be glad you weren't in my bed, though, Lady Bug. I was still asleep when Michael decided he needed to show me the new puppy Welby gave him yesterday. I tell you what, as good morning kisses go, I'll take yours over that mutt's any day."

She sailed across the room, went up on her tiptoes and planted a quick kiss on his lips. Then she punched him in the gut. "You say the sweetest things."

He pasted on a pained expression when what he really wanted to do was grab her up and carry her to bed there and then. *My love*. The sound was as sweet as an entire bushel of apples. "Marry me, Chrissy."

"Don't, Cole," she said, wincing.

He felt a sudden rush of frustration at her response. "I'll just keep asking."

"Tell me something I don't know. That's thirty-seven times since we left the plunge bath."

"You've kept count?" The idea soothed away his frustration. Now he really wanted to take her to bed.

She shrugged. "Marriage proposals are something a woman tends to keep track of. But they are not what I came here to talk to you about."

He tugged at his tie. "You came to tell me the basket of fruit in your room didn't satisfy your hunger and only I can do that?"

"That is second on my list," she replied, smiling, though he could tell she didn't want to. "Don't take this personally, Cole, but I think your approach with Lord Bennet is all wrong."

Dammit, she *had* to talk business. "I almost had him," he said in a voice that had its share of pout in it.

"Perhaps. We can't be certain. I'll admit the reincarnation business was inspired."

"Do you ever think about that sort of thing, Christina?" Grabbing her hand, he pulled her back to the settee and sat her down beside him. "Every now and then, I do. Especially when I get a very intense sensation that I've lived that moment before."

"Yes, I know that feeling. I'm experiencing it right now. You're trying to change the subject because you know I'm right. Believe me, I've been in this place a thousand times before."

"Now wait just one minute—"

She reached up and brushed a lock of his hair off his forehead in a gesture more motherly than intimate. Cole scowled as she told him, "You rushed him, Cole, and now he'll retreat."

"Temporarily, maybe, but the man is anxious to please. I'll talk him into showing me the Declaration."

She shook her head. "I'll have more success working my wiles on him. Here's what I—"

Temper rolled inside him as Cole lurched to his feet. "No. I forbid it."

Christina visibly stiffened. "Careful there, Morgan," she said in a tight, brittle voice. "It's not your place to forbid me anything. We're here for only four days. We have no time to waste. I could tell at Hartsworth that Lord Bennet is not immune to my charms, so it makes more sense for me to approach him."

"Honey, only dead men are immune to your charms, and I'm not sure about all of them. But it doesn't matter because I won't have my wife playing the flirt with another man, period."

She stood and faced him. "I'm not your wife."

"You are in my heart."

"Oh, Cole." She sighed heavily. "And you dare to call me stubborn."

"So it's a character trait we share. Imagine how our children will be. Of course I reckon the girls will be more stubborn than the boys. Something about being female takes stubborn to new heights."

"As much as I'd like to lay into you about this, I won't be distracted, Cole."

Distraction was exactly what both of them needed, in Cole's opinion. He winked and said, "Oh c'mon, Lady Bug. Lay me."

She narrowed her eyes and glared at him. "I'll lay you out flat. My fist to your face."

"That's not what I meant."

"I know, but it's all you're going to get. For now at least." She approached him and grabbing his shirt front, tugged him down toward her and kissed his cheek. When she drew back, her eyes were solemn. "Cole, cooperate with me on this."

"I can't, honey. It would tie me into knots. Besides, it's not right. It's not honorable."

She flinched, then stepped away from him. Injury dulled her eyes and when she spoke, her voice was brittle. "Yes, of course. What was I thinking. Mother wouldn't approve of such behavior, would she?"

"Now, Christina. Don't—"

"Batting my eyelashes and sweet-talking a man in order gain his cooperation, why, it borders on prostitution, doesn't it?"

Whoa. Where did this come from? Cole frowned at her. "Don't be stupid. This has nothing to do with whoring."

"No, you're right. It doesn't. I exaggerated. What I didn't exaggerate, however, is what my mother would think of my methods."

"Elizabeth isn't here."

"Thank God for that particular favor," she exclaimed, throwing her arms wide. "All right. Fine. Let's hear your plan, Morgan. What are you going to do to ensure that you walk away from Harpur Priory with our Declaration in your hand?"

"Well, I'm not going to flirt with Bennet, for one thing."

The minx stuck out her tongue at him.

Cole folded his arms and glared. "We've been over this before. Nothing has changed. First, since Bennet apparently considers himself an expatriated Texan of sorts, I intend to appeal to his ego, to promise him a place in Texas history."

"And if that doesn't work?"

"I'll buy it from him."

"And if he's not willing to sell?"

"I'll steal it from him."

"Now that's honor, Cole Morgan," she said, shaking a finger in the air. "Heavens, I am continually amazed at how your mind works. A while back you mentioned having doctors in London study me. Well, I think they could create an entirely new level of psychiatric study with you as their subject.

"It's obvious we can't work together on this. But don't worry, Cole. As soon as I have the Declaration of Independence in my possession, I'll turn it over to you. I won't have any more time to waste on such trivialities. You see, I intend to go with Lana and the children to visit Lord Welby's castle. He tells me he has three brothers. He thinks I'd be the perfect match for one of them."

"That's an empty threat and you know it, Christina. You're not going anywhere but to the altar with me."

That shut her up. Finally. She stood there, her chest rising and falling with the force of her angered breaths, looking more beautiful, more alluring, than any woman had the right to look.

"Maybe that's true," she said, lifting her chin high. "Don't think I'm unaware of the risks we've taken of late, and I suspect you hope to force the issue by giving me a child."

Cole felt his eyes go wide. Damn, the woman had sand. "Now don't get snippy on me. I don't remember hearing the word 'no' come from your mouth. Except as a pout when you've wrung me dry and you're still wanting to play. Really, Christina, you need to be a little more understanding in that area. Seven times in one night is a lot for any man. You're not going to make me feel like all my starch is in my shirt just because I wanted to sleep for an hour or so before giving another go at it."

Her back went stiff as a fence post. "Embarrassing me won't win you any favors, Cole."

He approached her, took her by the shoulders. "I don't want favors, I want your word. Don't play the flirtatious Chili Queen with Bennet."

"Why? Why are you trying to change who I am?"

"This has nothing to do with who you are, honey. It's who Bennet is. There is something fishy about that man. I don't trust him, and I don't want him to focus on you. Do this for me, would you? Please?"

"Please?" She blinked theatrically. "Cole Morgan said please?"

"I know." He sighed as if the weight of the world was on his shoulders. "Mark it on your calendar."

She looked at him for a long moment, then a smile twitched at her lips. "All right, I have an idea. How about we compromise? I'll act more British cool than peppery Chili Queen while you make a run at convincing Lord Bennet to show us his private collection. Then, depending on your luck, we'll reassess how best to proceed."

"That's as good as I'm going to get from you, isn't it?"

"Yes."

"In that case, I agree to your compromise," he said with a scowl.

She laughed softly, then wrapped her arms around him and buried her head against him. "You can be such a pouty little boy."

Cole held her tight. "Thank you. I do try."

They stood there for a time simply holding one another. He closed his eyes, enjoying the moment and almost didn't hear her when she said, "I thought you were criticizing me, wanting to change me."

It was, Cole realized, a clue to the puzzle that was Christina Delaney.

"Change the Queen of the Chili Queens?" he murmured in response, nuzzling her hair. "I'm not about to fiddle with a perfect recipe."

He felt her smile against his chest.

Sometimes, Morgan, you actually get it right.

*　　　*　　　*

Lord Bennet donned knee-high boots with a stitched silver star on the heels to call the first Anglo-Texan Society meeting to order in the drawing room at Harpur Priory. Chrissy watched the proceedings from a seat in the front row within excellent eyelash-batting distance—if such action were needed.

Following a relatively short organizational meeting, the group of fifteen men and three women voted to begin the day's lectures immediately, so anxious were they to get on with the educational aspects of the gathering. It came as no surprise to Chrissy that Lord Bennet stood up to speak first. His topic, the first of a trio of presentations he apparently intended to give today, was "Siege at the Alamo."

Chrissy was shifting in her seat within the first five minutes. Though she wouldn't admit it aloud, Texas history didn't excite her. There simply wasn't enough of it yet to spark her imagination, especially since this trip to England where "old" had an entirely different implication. Still, she did believe in the necessity for a people to preserve their history, hence her dedication to the search for the Declaration.

*Which is why I'm sitting through this discourse on death pretending to listen when I'd rather be—*She glanced at Cole, who stood toward the back of the room, leaning against the wall, arms crossed, his gaze fastened upon the speaker with a look of captivated interest, and words she never expected popped into her mind. *—upstairs making babies.*

Chrissy Delaney, you are a certified mess.

That, and a woman in love.

Yesterday afternoon, while the steady trickle of arriving guests kept Lord Bennet occupied, she and

Cole had explored the manor house, examining as many nooks and crannies of the sizable structure as possible. It came as no real surprise that they found nothing to suggest a "private collection" of any kind. As peculiar as Bennet had acted when mentioning it, he undoubtedly kept it well hidden.

After searching the house, they had ridden the grounds of Harpur Priory. They'd had a fine time exploring every folly, pavilion, grotto, garden house and gatehouse they stumbled across. The excursion had been enjoyable but unproductive, and this morning when Chrissy awoke, she'd felt an urgency to accomplish something today. It had made breakfast excruciatingly difficult. She'd sat directly across from Lord Bennet and the urge to flirt her way past his defenses liked to have choked her. But she'd promised Cole his chance to do it his way, so she'd gritted her teeth and tamped down her natural inclination.

Recalling the missed opportunity, she let loose a sigh that came out louder than she had intended. She had to think fast when Lord Bennet looked at her and asked, "Do you have a comment to make about the drama of March 5, 1836, Miss Delaney?"

March fifth . . . March fifth . . . what happened then? The Alamo fell on the sixth, that much she did remember. She glanced at Cole who glared at her, then to his foot as he made an exaggerated drag across the floor with the toe of his boot.

"Moses Rose!" she exclaimed, making the connection. March fifth was when Colonel Travis was said to have drawn in the mission's dirt with his saber and invited all who wanted to stand and fight to the death to cross the line. One man chose to leave—Moses

Rose. "I've always felt sorry for Moses Rose. You know in Texas today one of the terms used to call a man a coward is to say he's a first-cousin of Moses Rose."

That set off a heated discussion about what makes a man a true hero. Chrissy did her best not to say anything more, but Cole happily chimed in. When Bennet finally regained control of the conversation, the majority of the audience appeared to view Cole with new respect and Bennet with unabashed approval.

Bennet continued his lecture through the Fall of the Alamo to the Mexican Army. Ardent applause accompanied the finish, followed by twenty minutes of questions. When Bennet frowned over one question and referred it to Cole, Chrissy knew he had fully recovered from his mistake of pushing Bennet too fast yesterday.

Cole rubbed his palm along his jaw line. "Actually, I do know something about that. Somewhere in the early 1840's the Republic of Texas decided the Church of the Alamo and any mission outbuildings belonged to the Catholic Church. Folks have bickered over ownership in years since, and the Church has sold a couple pieces of the property. Local citizens keep working on it and we have hopes that soon the remainder of the Alamo property, the part containing the church, will soon be offered to either the city or the State of Texas."

"So there is interest in preserving that important historical site?" asked a gray-bearded gentleman.

"Very much so. In fact, just a couple years ago a group calling itself the Alamo Monument Association formed to raise money for a monument to the defenders. They have the design developed, and I firmly

believe that someday the monument will get built."
He snapped his fingers and added, "You know, I just
might have one of the books they published with me.
It's called *The Alamo: America's Thermopylae*." He
paused just long enough to grab everyone's attention,
then asked, "Any of you fellows have one of those
books? Do you, Lord Bennet?"

"No. No, I do not." He gazed around the room.
"Does anyone's library contain this book?"

Chrissy saw a roomful of heads shake and an avari-
cious light enter Lord Bennet's eyes. *My my my. He's
done it.* She could tell by the look on the Englishman's face that Cole had just bought his way into the
private collection.

As long as he actually did have the booklet, that is,
and why he would have one with him, she didn't
know. She didn't believe he could have been far-
sighted enough to guess he might need one. She
could think of dozens of other things that would have
made the list of possibly useful items before a book
about the Alamo, especially since you could all but
paper your walls with them if you wanted. A fund-
raising effort by the Alamo Monument Association,
demand for the book had been greatly overestimated.
The Alamo: America's Thermopylae was on sale at
nearly every shop in the city.

That's where she'd seen Cole with a copy. It was a
couple of days before she'd been named Chili Queen.
He'd tossed a coin onto a counter and grabbed one off
a stack, rolling it up to use like a flyswatter against the
overly friendly teenage boy buzzing around her as
shopped. "That's how you deal with pests, Christina,"
he'd explained to her after embarrassing the young

Romeo with a slight pop to the head. Then he'd stuck the booklet in the inside pocket of his jacket. He must have brought that same piece of clothing with him to England.

Chrissy made sure to stand close enough to eavesdrop when during an intermission a short time later, Lord Bennet offered to show Cole his private Texas collection after luncheon. "If you would bring along the Alamo book, I will be in your debt."

"It will be my pleasure, Bennet." Cole slapped him on the back as though they were long-time pals. When Lord Bennet excused himself moments later in order to take his seat for a lecture entitled "How Texas Got Its Lone Star," Chrissy tugged Cole down the hallway and into the music room.

After glancing around to ensure their privacy, Cole yanked her into his arms and planted a quick, hard kiss upon her mouth. "Am I good?"

"You are very, very good, Mr. Morgan. As long as you are lucky enough to have one of those books with you."

"No luck about it," he returned. "I brought an entire trunk of stuff from home, anything I thought might help if the person in possession of the document wished to make a trade rather than sell the Declaration outright."

"Oh. That was smart."

"I've been known to have a spell of intelligence upon occasion."

"Rare occasions."

"Brat."

Chrissy shot him a grin, then said, "You will take me with you when you meet him, of course."

"As long as you promise not to flirt."

She rolled her eyes, but before she could chastise his lack of faith the Earl of Thornbury wandered into the music room. "Finally. I've been looking for you two. I cannot bear to sit through another one of those lectures. Chrissy, would you care to join your grandfather on a walk in the garden?"

"I'd love to."

"Excellent," the earl said before addressing Cole. "And Morgan, you'd best hurry back. The speaker specifically asked for your presence so you can comment on his talk."

Cole sighed. "I should have kept my mouth shut."

"Too late now, Morgan," Chrissy quipped, linking her arm through her grandfather's. "Go learn something. It won't hurt you. I'll walk with Grandfather, then put my chili on to cook. I'll meet you and Lord Bennet at the stable at one o'clock. Just think, come suppertime we might just have our hands on the Declaration."

"That's a nice thought." He leaned over and kissed her cheek, then whispered in her ear, "But not as nice as this. Come midnight, I intend to have my hands on you."

Cole paced the length of the stables, then turned around and did it again. Nervous energy fueled his steps. Funny how today's discussions had made him yearn for home. He wanted nothing more than to get the Declaration, scrape the damned British mud off his boots, and head for Texas. With Christina as his wife.

Moments later Bennet arrived and ordered a groom to hitch up a buggy. Chrissy hurried in a few minutes later. "Thank you so much for agreeing to show us your private Texas collection," she enthused, offering

Bennet a blinding smile and too many bats of her lashes. "I'm so very excited."

When she reached out and touched the Englishman's arm, Cole shot her a fearsome scowl. *You crossed the line,* he silently accused.

Just making sure I get to come along, she winked in return.

"You are coming with us?" Bennet said, frowning. "Hmm . . . very well. Except, I only brought one blindfold."

"Blindfold?" Cole repeated.

Bennet opened one side of his jacket, and reaching into an inner pocket, pulled out a length of black silk. "I realize this may seem rather overdone to you, Mr. Morgan, but once you see my treasures you'll understand why I keep their location secret. I find it simpler to conceal my collection's location than to post round-the-clock guards."

"I'm afraid I cannot allow Miss Delaney to be blindfolded."

Turning toward Christina, he said, "Perhaps we can arrange another time for you to see Lord Bennet's private collection."

"No need for that," she cheerily replied. "We can use Mr. Morgan's handkerchief for an extra blindfold."

"Very well," said Bennet.

Cole opened his mouth to protest, but recognized he'd be wasting his words. Instead, he said, "I insist you stay close to me, then, Miss Delaney." And to Bennet, he added, "See she doesn't fall or injure herself in any way."

Cole was tense as he assisted Christina up into the buggy for the ride to who-knew-where. He didn't trust Bennet as far as he could throw him, but he couldn't put his finger on just why.

The buggy rattled out of the stable yard and down a gravel road, the crunching of rock beneath the wheels an obvious clue as to their path. Luckily, the morning fog had burned away, so Cole used the warmth of the sunshine on his body to help determine the direction they traveled. He managed to draw a mental map of their route until Bennet headed into the forest and began a series of quick turns.

Having lost the sun, Cole paid close attention to the sounds and scents floating in the air around him. He smelled water, though he couldn't hear it. He tuned out Christina's friendly chatter with the Englishman, and listened to the sounds of horses' hooves and carriage wheels rattling over rock in addition to the quiet thud of travel upon a packed-earth path.

Cole suspected they'd traveled in circles for much of the time that passed before the Englishman pulled the buggy to a halt. Cole reached to untie the blindfold, but Bennet stopped him. "Not until we're inside, please."

"Inside what?"

Bennett avoided an answer. Instead, he said, "Watch your step as you leave the carriage, Mr. Morgan. Miss Delaney, allow me to assist you."

"Why, thank you, Lord Bennet," Chrissy said, her voice light and bright. "Isn't this fun. Why, being blindfolded just adds to the excitement, doesn't it?"

Cole seriously considered pulling the silk from around his eyes and tying it around her mouth.

Bennet continued, "You'll want to avoid the briar two steps behind you. Take five steps forward, then climb three steps. Duck your head approximately eighteen inches and take three more steps forward. At that point, I'll escort you the final short distance before removing the blindfold."

Cole did as instructed, using his hands more than necessary to feel his way. Holly, a briar, and a smooth marble column. A folly of some sort, he concluded.

"Ow," he muttered when he failed to stoop low enough during the duck-your-head part. Cool, musty air greeted him inside the structure, but he was unable to distinguish any particular odors, especially since Christina obviously had doused herself with a floral-scented perfume before joining them.

So much for her word not to work her feminine wiles.

"This way," said Bennet. "Fifteen steps down to a landing, around to your left, then twenty-two more. Stop immediately at the bottom or you will run into the door."

With every step they descended, Cole regretted allowing Christina to come along. The sense of foreboding weighted his boots like heels of lead.

"Here we are," said Bennet.

Cole felt a tug at the back of his neck and the blindfold fell free. They stood in a narrow, brick-lined tunnel in front of an arched, carved wooden door that appeared to have been standing for ages. Holding a lamp in one hand, a key in another, Bennet moved forward to unlock the door. Hinges squeaked as the door swung open. Cool, musty air greeted Cole's nostrils as his eyes rounded and he exclaimed, "What the hell?"

It was a crypt. A big one. Complete with dusty tombs, spider webs, and, Cole would wager, a rat or two.

"Oh, my," Christina said, the cheer gone from her voice.

Cole took her hand. "If this is a jest, Bennet, it's not funny."

"This way. This way," said the Englishman, leading them forward. "It's a burial place of holy men, Miss Delaney. Nothing to fear, I assure you. We're almost there. Now that you are here, I honestly can't wait to show you my treasures."

Cole really, really wished Christina had stayed behind.

Soon Bennet stopped before another door. "I know you'll be impressed. Wait here until I light the lamps, please." He opened a simple latch and pushed the door open. Moments later a flame flickered and golden light bloomed in the room. Beside him, Christina gasped.

The room before them appeared to be a windowless manor house drawing room, the furnishings, gilt and gilding surpassing even the splendor of Hartsworth. "How beautiful," she said as they walked inside.

Cole was shocked. After viewing Bennet's public Texas Room, he'd expected to find another taxidermist's dream including coyotes or mustangs or at least an armadillo. The only stuffed items in this room were the leather wing-back chairs in front of a fireplace and a trio of settees placed along the walls.

The other similarity between this place and the other Texas room, however, were the display cases. Made of rich mahogany and trimmed in shining brass, these pieces were even fancier than the ones back at Harpur Priory. Cole's heartbeat sped up as he approached the first case. He felt Christina's hand tremble in his.

"The theme of this room is Freedom," Bennet said. "And speaking of that, did you think to bring the Alamo book?"

Cole reached into his pocket, pulled out the booklet, and tossed it to Bennet even as he gazed upon the first case. It was filled with weapons: guns, bows and arrows, knives, bayonets, whips, bludgeons, steel traps, even a slingshot. "Looks to me like 'Death' might be a better choice."

Bennet replied without looking up from the book he was reading. "I have attempted to collect one of every conceivable weapon ever used in Texas. If you are aware of any I am missing, please let me know."

Cole moved to the second case. A collection of men's razors, with placards listing names familiar to all Texans. Jim Bowie, Stephen F. Austin, Sam Houston, Randolph Wilcox, Davy Crockett. Cole halted, his gaze shifting backward. Randolph Wilcox? *Never heard of the man.*

The third case was filled with eyeglasses. Again, mixed among the familiar he found the name R. Wilcox. "Strange," he murmured to Christina. "You ever heard of this Wilcox?"

"No."

Since eyeglasses and razors weren't what they'd traveled these thousands of miles to find, Cole guided them steadily toward the back of the room where a small case stood separate from the others. Walking up to it, his heart stood still. He read:

UNANIMOUS

DECLARATION OF INDEPENDENCE

Made by the Delegates of The People of Texas,

In General Convention,

At the town of Washington

On the second day of March, 1836.

Cole was captured by the words printed on the page, drawn into the story of the birth of a nation written down for all to witness. Silent and unmoving, his heart swelling with a national pride he hadn't known he possessed, he read the entire document. It wasn't until he reached the end and his gaze skimmed back up the page to reread the words "hereby resolve and declare, that our political connection with the Mexican nation has forever ended and that the people of Texas do now constitute a FREE, SOVEREIGN, and INDEPENDENT REPUBLIC," that he realized what was wrong.

The words FREE, SOVEREIGN, and INDEPENDENT REPUBLIC shot at his brain like a bullet.

They were all set in capital letters. They were typeset. Not handwritten.

He looked at Christina and said, "This is a fake."

Chapter

14

❦

Chrissy's gaze held Cole's as the truth sank in. She couldn't believe this. She simply couldn't believe it.

Bennet rushed up beside them, his eyebrows drawn together in a fierce scowl. "I beg your pardon?"

Cole gestured toward the case. "It's a fake. It's not the real Declaration of Independence."

"It most certainly is. It is one of the two hundred broadsides the editor of the *Telegraph and Texas Register* printed from an engrossed holograph copy of the Declaration. It has the typesetter's mistake that authenticates it." He pointed to the signatures. "See, he omitted two names."

"It's a copy of a copy," Cole said with a weary laugh.

Chrissy shook her head at Lord Bennet. "You're supposed to have a handwritten copy. That's why we came here."

"That's why you came here?" Bennet repeated, reaching out and grabbing Chrissy's wrist. "What is going on? What is the meaning of this?"

The moment Lord Bennet touched Chrissy, she

watched Cole's patience run out. He grabbed Bennet by the lapels and, lifting him off the ground, backed him against a wall. "I'm done with this. To hell with subtlety. To hell with all this sneaking around."

He gave Bennet a shake. "Melton said you have a handwritten copy of the Republic of Texas's Declaration of Independence. Now, first you're going to tell us where it is, then we're going to reach an agreement as to what remuneration you want for it. Miss Delaney and I are taking the document home where it belongs."

Bennet's eyes bugged and went wild looking. "But the copy is all I have."

Cole shifted one hand to grip Bennet around the throat and Chrissy got a bit worried. "Cole, be careful. You probably shouldn't hurt him too badly."

"Please," Bennet begged. "It's true. I had the other for a little while, but she came and took it back. That's why I'm so careful about this room. I don't want to be robbed again."

"Robbed?" Chrissy said.

Cole allowed Bennet to slide slowly down the wall until his feet once again touched the ground. "Are you trying to claim that someone stole the Declaration from you?"

A woman. Chrissy had distinctly heard him say *she* came and took it.

Bennet nodded. "Well, it was hers to begin with so she claims it wasn't stealing. However, the child did sell it to me so I consider myself the legal possessor. I met the price. It's not my fault the charge was only a bag of candy and a ham."

"Ham?"

"The child loves pork."

Cole closed his eyes and Chrissy watched him count silently to ten. "Lord Bennet, where is the Declaration of Independence?"

The Englishman squeaked out the word. "Scotland."

He might as well have shouted it, so loudly did it seem to resound through the room. Scotland. Chrissy didn't want to go to Scotland. She wanted to go home. "Oh, Cole. What are we going to do?"

"Scotland," he muttered in reply. "Well, don't that just twirl your kilt."

What they did next was follow an irate Lord Bennet back through the crypt. Chrissy worried Cole might hit him when he waved the blindfolds in their faces. The man was beside himself with righteous indignation at their behavior, and Chrissy attempted to soothe his ruffled feathers by appealing to his sense of history and obvious love of Texas. "We had hoped to purchase the document from you, Lord Bennet. We would not have used nefarious means to get it."

Cole's snort didn't help matters at that point. Asking just how the Declaration ended up in Scotland didn't improve Lord Bennet's mood much, either.

"I originally purchased the document from the family of a hero of San Jacinto."

"For a bag of candy and a hunk of ham," Cole clarified.

"It was the asking price," Bennet said, puffing up like a toad. "The Declaration was the centerpiece of my collection. I had owned it for two years the day that woman banged on my door. She wanted it back.

I, of course, refused and then two days later, it turned up missing. I knew she had stolen it."

"If it was so important to you, why didn't you attempt to retrieve it?"

"I did, but—" he broke off abruptly and shifted his gaze away. "I failed. Rowanclere Castle is an unconquerable fortress."

Chrissy realized there was more to the story, but by then they had reached the surface, exiting the entrance to the crypt through a door leading into a small building that appeared to be the inside of a . . . "It's a plunge pool, Cole. We missed this yesterday on our tour of the grounds."

He stopped, glanced around, then fired a grin her way. "We wouldn't have found the room on our own no matter what," he observed. "We'd have never looked farther than the pool."

When they exited the pool house and she spied the manor's roof through the trees, Chrissy realized the buggy ride had been a hoax. The main house was but a short distance from the plunge pool. As he drove the buggy toward the stable yard, the Englishman asked for and received Cole's impatient assurance that he would not reveal the private collection's location to a soul. Somewhat mollified, Bennet asked if they intended to stay for the evening's barbecue.

"If you want us there, we'll stay," Chrissy told him.

"But Christina—" Cole began.

She silenced him with a glare.

"Yes, it would be best for you to remain," Bennet said stiffly. "People would wonder, otherwise, and besides, you must oversee the serving of the chili."

"It's settled then," Chrissy said with a nod.

She couldn't have been more wrong. As Bennet pulled the buggy into the stable yard, Michael Kleberg came running up. "Miss Chrissy. Miss Chrissy. We've been looking everywhere for you. The earl wants to speak to you right away."

"Where is he?" she asked, concern sweeping over her.

"Pacing the front hall. You'd better hurry. I think he might leave without you."

Chrissy threw a worried glance Cole's way, then hurried toward the house, Cole right on her heels. Rushing inside the manor, she spied her grandfather speaking to a baggage-toting footman and immediately her apprehension evaporated. The man was beaming, a smile wreathing his face.

"Chrissy. Thank goodness you're back. Hurry, my dear. We're leaving for Hartsworth immediately. Word has arrived. I have the most wonderful news."

"What is it, Grandfather?"

He swept her into a fierce hug, then laughed. "Your mother has finally come home."

Cole thought it fair to say that over the course of their acquaintance, Christina had surprised him literally thousands of times. With that in mind, he shouldn't have been surprised by her reaction to Elizabeth's arrival in England, but he was.

Lady Bug flatly refused to return to Hartsworth.

"Christina, you have to go. She's your mother."

"I'm staying here and serving my chili at the barbecue tonight just as I promised."

Cole raked his fingers through his hair, then looked at Thornbury. "Why don't y'all go on. We'll borrow a horse for Christina and catch up with you."

The earl didn't take much convincing, so anxious was he to see his daughter for the first time in over twenty years. Within moments he had loaded up and departed, leaving Cole facing Christina alone in the entrance hall.

He might as well have been in the stable staring down a mule.

"Excuse me," she said, as if he were no more than a fly buzzing about her face. "I believe I'll join the Anglo-Texan Society for this hour's lecture."

Cole took hold of her arm and pulled her into the closest empty room—the library—and shut the door behind them.

"Don't you grab me like that," she protested, struggling.

He let her go. "I swear, woman, it's a good thing you weren't fightin' for Santa Anna. Texas never would have won the war. You're too damned stubborn to quit."

"Don't curse at me, either," she demanded, turning her back on him.

Cole shut his eyes and counted to ten, then did it three more times. Damn, but the afternoon had been hard on his temper. "Christina," he said when he could speak calmly. "Please explain to me why you don't want to see your mother and brother. They've traveled all this way to see you."

"Have they?" she asked, whirling around.

The tears that sparkled in her eyes baffled him and he said, "That's what Jake put in the note he sent with the servant, isn't it?"

"And you believe that?"

He scratched his jaw and made a wry grimace. "Actually, I suspect he's figured out what I've been doing with you, and he's come over here to kill me. Your mama must have come along to see I get a proper burial."

"No, my mama came along to make certain I didn't accidentally end up happy."

The bitterness in her voice stopped him cold. What in the world was she thinking? "I'm lost in the English fog here and you know how thick that is. Explain what you mean by that, would you please?"

"Don't you see?" She crossed to the desk and lifted a crystal paperweight. Staring blindly into it, she said, "She's come to make sure I do her bidding one more time. You thought she was a force to be reckoned with at home, imagine how she'll be here. Lady Elizabeth. An earl's daughter."

Christina set the paperweight down hard. "Well, I'm not going to cooperate. You can go on back to Hartsworth, Cole, and tell her she's wasted the trip. She won't force me to marry you. I'll go sell chili in the village square before she makes me do that. I'll eat a habeñero pepper while singing 'The Yellow Rose of Texas' in front of the church on Sunday morning before I'll marry you!"

"Godammit!" He wanted to throw something, but he settled on a glare. "What is it with you and your mother, and why the hell am I in the middle of it?"

"You've always been in the middle of it."

"Is that part of this?" He lifted his arms and stabbed the air with his hands, palms out. "You resent me? You resent that they brought me into your family?"

She grimaced and shook her head, dismissing the charge. "No, not at all. I've loved you since the day you moved into Delaney House. Maybe not the same way I love you now, but love nonetheless. It never occurred to me that my parents or Jake would or could feel any differently."

"Then what the hell is the problem? You tell me you are not going to marry me to spite your mother. Excuse me if that doesn't make a lot of sense to me."

"I'm sorry." She sighed and closed her eyes, then brought her fingers up to her head and massaged her temples. "I didn't mean it to sound that way. Cole, I know I don't always act logically or sensibly, especially where my mother is concerned. It's as if my emotions override everything else."

"Now *that* makes some sense." It also took some of the steam from his anger. She was hurting, he could see that, and he realized it was desperately important he understand why. He went to her, put his arms around her. "Christina, talk to me. Help me figure this out. Tell me what is wrong."

Long seconds ticked by before she spoke. "I think it's possible you could make me the happiest woman in the world. But I know you also have the power to destroy me."

"Destroy you?" Cole tilted up her chin and met her gaze. "Chrissy, what in the world do you mean by that?"

"You might think you love me now, but I know it can't last. You'd send me away, throw me away. Just like everybody else."

Cole glanced down at his chest, looking for the knife that surely must be stabbing his heart, so badly did he hurt. "Dammit, Lady Bug. How can you say that? I understand you might have some doubts about some things, but not that. Never that. Don't you trust me at all?"

Now the tears were spilling down her cheeks, but for once, they didn't touch Cole. He couldn't feel her pain past his own.

"Don't you see, Cole?" she asked, her voice trembling. "How can I trust you when you are part of them—the Delaneys? You're one of them and they said they loved me but they sent me to England. They sent me away to school."

Cole gaped at her. "For God's sake, woman, that happened years ago. What does it have to do with now? Besides, I had nothing to do with sending you away. Your father did that."

"Yes, and my mother let him do it."

Her eyes took on an agitated gleam that shook Cole to the core.

"She didn't stop him," she continued, "and she's my mother and supposed to protect me and she didn't. I loved her more than anyone else in the world and she betrayed me."

Emotions were a riot inside him. Had the woman lost her ever-lovin' mind? "Excuse me, Christina, but I don't see your mother standing here in this room with us. So why are you bringing her here? How does what she did or didn't do years ago have anything to do with why you don't trust me now? I'm not your mother, I'm your lover!"

"Are you?" She wiped furiously at her tears. "Or am I just handy?"

"Handy! Hell, Chrissy, you've never been handy a day in your life."

"And that's it," she said, shaking a finger at him. "That's exactly it. I'm an inconvenience, aren't I? I'm not the kind of woman you want for a wife. I'm not a social asset. I won't do your law career any good."

"That's the damned truth. I'd spend half my time bailing you out of trouble."

"See there, I'm right. You've never made a secret of the fact you think my mother hung the moon. You want a wife like her."

Her mother again! Chrissy wouldn't listen to him, wouldn't hear him. Wouldn't believe him. Cole felt the last of his control snap. Fueled by frustration and fury, he attacked. "Maybe I do. Maybe I do want a wife who dresses and acts like a lady. Maybe I do want a wife who considers a good reputation something to value. Think how nice it would be not to worry what sort of scandal my wife will bring to my doorstep next. Imagine the joy of walking into a room and *not* find my mate flirting with every man in sight. Picture my life with a woman who doesn't argue with everything I say. I guess you're right, Chrissy. I guess the attraction between us was just sex. I guess I do want a lady wife. I'm glad we got that settled."

Anguish furrowed across Chrissy's face as his conversational bullets hit their mark. She made tiny, grieving sounds as she sank into a chair. A part of Cole recognized he'd gone too far, but any remorse he might have felt was overwhelmed by his own gut-wrenching pain.

With one last, furious glare, he turned his back on her. "Enjoy your barbecue, Chili Queen. I'm off to Hartsworth. There's a *lady* there I'm anxious to see."

At the barbecue that night, Chrissy served up her chili with a smile. She accepted the accolades with graciousness and cheerfully answered the numerous questions about her recipe and the spices it contained. She took a turn along with a number of other guests at attempting to throw a lasso, chuckling at her pitiful effort, ignoring the concerned glances Lana and Lord Welby sent her way.

And then she danced. Dressed in her scarlet skirt and white blouse, barefoot, she whirled and twirled to the strum of a guitar and the keening of a fiddle. She laughed and she sang and she flirted with her partners.

The Chili Queen had come to England.

But inside, Chrissy cried.

Cole had left her. He'd saddled up his horse and ridden away from her. Because, of course, she'd finally made him admit the truth.

He wanted someone like her mother, not a Chili Queen. She'd known it all along.

Then why does it hurt so bad? Why does it break your heart in two?

Because she loved him, of course, she always had. She feared she always would.

She buried the thought as the rhythm of the music pulsed around her, sank into her bones. She moved with it, soothed herself with it, without conscious thought. And while she danced, while she smiled and twirled and winked at the man who partnered her, she fought back the tears that threatened.

The music ended and defiantly, she reached up and planted a quick Chili Queen kiss on her dance partner's lips. "Thank you, Lord Harcourt. It was a pleasure."

Chrissy refused the next dance claiming her feet needed to rest. As she started to leave the circular section of lawn serving as the ballroom floor, she sensed a change in the atmosphere. She glanced around and her smile died.

"Mother."

Elizabeth Delaney stood flanked by Cole on her left, Jake on her right, with the earl standing behind her. *My family*. Chrissy felt a fierce rush of love even as she spied the disapproval pasted across her mother's face. Elizabeth's horrified voice came to her as if through a water-logged tunnel. "Why Christina Delaney, just look at you. You are a scandal wherever you go."

Laughter bubbled up inside Chrissy. Maybe this wasn't real. Maybe she was asleep and having a nightmare. She looked at Cole, saw his grimace, and her heart sank to her toes.

Then, like she'd been doing all her life, Chrissy left her family.

"She's headed for the house. I've got to go after her," Cole said, starting forward.

Jake put a hand on his arm. "Let me. We're the ones she is running away from. You stay here with Mother."

Glancing at Elizabeth, Cole spied the tear rolling down her cheek, and he clamped his teeth together to prevent the curses from escaping. Bringing them here, like this, had been a very bad idea.

As Jake jogged after his sister, Thornbury chastised his daughter. "That was a poor greeting, Elizabeth."

"I didn't intend to sound so harsh."

Cole laid a comforting hand on Elizabeth's shoulder. "I know. Sometimes talking to Christina, words just come out that way." Earlier today was a good example. He'd said some cold, cruel things to the woman speaking out of anger and bruised feelings. Her lack of trust and her accusations had hurt and he'd left Harpur Priory in a lather.

The ride helped him calm down, and once that happened, he began to regret what he'd done. As soon as he had arrived at Hartsworth, he'd decided to turn around and go back. He'd greeted Jake, and chastised Elizabeth for having played such a mean trick on her family by claiming a serious illness as a method of matchmaking. Her apology was obviously heartfelt, and it had soothed Cole's simmering anger over the action. So when Elizabeth suggested they all accompany him back to Harpur Priory, saying she couldn't wait another day to see her daughter, he made only a half-hearted protest. He believed a talk between mother and daughter was long overdue.

He still believed that, but in hindsight, this reunion should have taken place in private. Of course, he hadn't known they'd find her dancing barefoot in her Chili Queen clothes when they arrived. Otherwise, he'd have done it all differently.

Oh really? asked his conscience. *You knew she was cooking chili. You knew there would be dancing at the barbecue. You knew she was upset.*

Hell, knowing Christina, he should have expected to find exactly what they found.

Shaking his head, he gazed toward the house. *Ah, Lady Bug, I'm sorry.*

He slipped his arm through Elizabeth's and led her toward a seat at a table. "Let me fix you a plate. I'm sure you must be hungry. I am."

It was true. The aroma of Christina's chili reminded him he hadn't eaten since breakfast. He was on his second helping when Lana and Welby stopped by the table. "Why, Cole. I'm surprised to see you here. Chrissy told me you left with her grandfather."

"Uh, we came back." He motioned toward the food line where Thornbury was loading up his plate for the third time. Then he nodded toward Elizabeth. "Lana, have you met Christina's mother?"

Her brows lifted in surprise, then she smiled at Elizabeth and said, "No, I have not had the pleasure."

After the introductions, they exchanged small talk about the Delaneys' trip from Texas, then Lana turned to Cole and asked, "Have you seen Michael and Sophie lately?"

"No, I haven't. We haven't been here very long, though."

"Oh. Well." She sighed a frustrated mother's sigh. "I put them to bed an hour ago, but when I checked on them a little while later they had decamped. I expected them to have sneaked back down to the barbecue, but we've seen no sign of them."

"Have you checked beneath all the tablecloths?" Cole asked.

"That's a good idea," said Welby. "Excuse me, and I'll see to that chore."

"Thank you, Bruce," said Lana. Glancing at Cole, she laughed uneasily. "I'm sure they'll turn up any minute and Lord Welby will be disgusted with all three of us. I've worried him, I'm afraid. I just had a strange feeling that something was wrong."

Cole didn't like that. He was a believer in a mother's intuition of trouble, having seen it so many times in Elizabeth where Chrissy was concerned.

"I'm sure they're fine, honey. Tell you what. Where haven't y'all looked yet? I'll track 'em down and give them a tongue lashing for causing their mother such worry."

"Thank you, Cole," she replied, her smile weak but appreciative. "My children are scamps of the first water, but it isn't like them to disappear this way."

"We'll find them, Lana," Cole said, giving her hand a comforting squeeze. "It's my guess they're with Christina and since she doesn't want to be found right now, it's making the search for your children a little more difficult. So instead of worrying about safety, worry about choosing what punishment to dole out. You know if they're with Christina, they're safe as a pair of possums in a hollow log."

After seeing Jake was on her trail and knowing a search through the basement rooms would keep him occupied for a while, Chrissy ducked into Harpur Priory's ironing room to hide. Her head was spinning, her emotions were a wreck, and she needed time to gather herself before facing the visitors from Texas.

Aware her brother would be methodical in his search now that he'd tracked her to the basement, she slipped up a servant's staircase and chose to lose herself among the manor's most elaborate and least visited rooms, the state apartments.

She wandered through the State Drawing Room to the State Music Room, and had settled down at the mahogany and satinwood harpsichord to peck out a tune and think when she heard Michael and Sophie Kleberg's telltale laughter.

"Lana put them to bed long ago," she murmured, rising to follow the sound. The children had no business being here in this part of the house. These grand rooms were designed for display, rather than living in. They certainly were not rooms in which to play.

The giggling came from the State Bedchamber. Chrissy walked inside and winced. "Michael! Sophie! Quit jumping on that bed this instant."

The laughter died abruptly. Slowly, two pairs of eyes peeked out from behind blue damask bed hangings. Michael assumed that sheepish, boyish expression guaranteed to melt a female heart while Sophie offered her innocent little cherub's smile. Chrissy could resist neither one.

"Oh, you two. This the last place you should be. Why aren't you in bed where you belong?"

Michael jumped down onto the floor. "We weren't tired and we started playing spies so when we saw Mr. Bennet come inside, we followed him here."

Sophie nodded, her eyes round and excited. "He went inside the wall, Miss Chrissy. We're waiting for him to come out again."

"Went inside the wall?"

"It's a secret door," Michael explained. He pointed toward the wall. "Right—"

He gasped, then dove for the concealment of the bed hangings as the door under discussion began to swing open. Chrissy thought it best to follow. They'd upset poor Lord Bennet enough today. Better he didn't know the children had invaded the State Bedchamber.

The man carried a leather-bound book in one

hand and murmured something beneath his breath as he approached the bed. Chrissy cringed back away from the curtains, certain they were about to be found.

Instead, he reached into the hangings, felt along the gilded bedpost, then grabbed a lever hidden ingeniously in the carved palm tree design. He pushed the lever and Chrissy heard the secret door swing shut. Sophie's wide eyes met hers, and she held a finger up to her lips until the sound of Lord Bennet's departing footsteps died away.

"You two will be the death of me," she grumbled as she crawled from the bed and headed for the door with Sophie at her heels. "Come along. I'll see y'all back to bed."

Michael didn't immediately follow. Chrissy turned back at the snick of a latch. The hidden door swung open once more. "I just want a quick peek," said Michael as he darted through the opening.

"Michael," Chrissy insisted. "Get back here."

"I'll get him," cried Sophie before she, too, darted through the door.

Chrissy sighed heavily, then went in after them.

Deep shadows concealed the passage and she stumbled, almost falling, when her foot found the first descending step. Of the Klebergs, she saw no sign. "Children," she called.

From below came the echoes of their voices.

"Troublesome pair," she murmured. Why, the Klebergs' shenanigans made her own childhood escapades look angelic.

Chrissy descended a spiraling staircase that seemed to go on forever. This was not a normal servants' staircase with its narrow width and dank, dusty steep steps. She spied no exits from the passageway.

Upon reaching a point where light from the room above no longer penetrated the gloom, she noticed a small ledge, upon which sat a matchbox. Gazing below, she saw the yellow glow of a lantern. "Intrepid explorers," she murmured as the shadows deepened to near dark. Weren't those two afraid of anything? By now she figured she must be below the lowest level of the house.

Chrissy continued to descend. Before long she noticed that the light, which earlier had been moving in a spiral like herself, now remained motionless. Seconds later, more light flared and she heard echoes, louder now, of the children's voices. Chrissy picked up her pace and soon she saw just what the children had exclaimed over.

The staircase ended behind a door that led into the crypt directly across from the room housing Lord Bennet's private collection. Chrissy paused long enough to do a quick mental geography comparison to where they'd gone yesterday and where she was now. Yes, she could see how it all fit together. The crypt was large, its tunnels running between the manor and the pool house. No telling how many other rooms and tunnels were hidden below the grounds of Harpur Priory.

No telling how many other secrets they contain, Chrissy thought, shuddering.

"Michael. Sophie. We are not supposed to be here," she said, walking into the lushly apportioned room. To her surprise, the children were nowhere to be seen. Hearing their voices, she glanced to the left and spied another opening, one she'd not noticed yesterday. Looking closer, she saw that it had been concealed by a tall display case now shifted out of the way.

Chrissy walked into the second, smaller chamber and found the Kleberg children standing in the center, gazing around them in wonder. Mud-chinked logs covered the rock walls and gave the appearance of the inside of a cabin.

Sophie looked up at Chrissy and said, "This is just like that old homestead cabin on that ranchland Mr. Cole bought."

Glancing quickly around the room, Chrissy saw that indeed, it was quite similar. A wedding-ring quilt adorned an iron bed and braided rugs softened the hard rock floor. A Dutch oven was nestled amongst coals spread in a false hearth, and an oil lamp sat on a rosewood table, an intricately carved piece that looked strangely out of place, but at the same time, perfectly at home. In log cabins all across the American frontier, families mixed heirloom pieces with those made on the spot from whatever resources were at hand.

A Bible lay opened on the table. Curious despite herself, Chrissy glanced down and read the names written on the record of marriage: Randolph Allen Wilcox and Maribeth Leigh Jones. "Randolph Wilcox," Chrissy murmured. The name seemed familiar, but she couldn't quite place it. The page opposite the marriages recorded births and only one was listed. "John Randolph Wilcox, born December 3, 1851, Houston, Texas."

"My mama had a rocker like that one at home," said Sophie, pointing toward the hearth.

As Chrissy looked toward the chair, her gaze snagged on the oil painting hanging above the mantel. It was a portrait of a man, woman, and child, and something about the painting bothered Chrissy. She walked closer and read the brass plate attached to the frame. "Randolph and Maribeth Wilcox, and their son John. Bluebonnet Ranch, Texas."

She frowned. Something about the painting bothered her, but she didn't want to take the time to figure it out. A sense of urgency plagued her. "Come along, you two. We don't belong down here. Proper house guests don't make themselves at home by snooping in their host's private rooms."

"Now that," came a voice from behind her, "is what they call in Texas a dead open fact."

Chrissy cringed. "Lord Bennet, I'm so very sorry," she said, turning around. "The children . . ." Her voice trailed off.

Lord Bennet held a Colt revolver pointed at her heart.

Chapter

15

❧

Lord Bennet's voice dripped menace as he finished her sentence for her. "The children made a very big mistake."

Immediately, Chrissy pulled the children behind her. "I don't understand."

"Perhaps not at this moment, but I fear soon you will. I am sorry for this, Miss Delaney. I truly am. But y'all have discovered my secret, and I'm afraid that is something I simply cannot allow."

"Your secret?" Chrissy's mind raced. "You mean this room? We won't tell anyone about it, Lord Bennet. You have my word."

He sighed. "If it were only the room, I might be convinced to let you go. But, of course, it's much more than that."

Sincerity rang in her voice as she insisted, "I don't know anything. I didn't learn anything."

"You will figure it out eventually. You are a smart girl. You found your way down here, didn't you?"

Michael poked his head out from around Chrissy.

"She's not really very smart. She just followed us. We're not that smart either 'cause we saw you open the secret door and then you left these others open. We'd have never found this place otherwise."

Bennet ignored the boy, his gaze drifting past Chrissy's shoulder toward the portrait hung above the mantel. "I realize to be safest I should shoot you all right now. However," he paused, his mouth dipping in a frown, "that would be terribly messy and quite permanent. Hmm . . . I wonder if there is another way."

"Oh, I'm certain there must be," Chrissy hastened to say, never taking her gaze off the gun.

"Maybe if we give this some time, one of us will think of something." Bennet frowned. "Of course, they'll look for you. I'll need to do something about that."

He thought for a moment, then crossed to the trunk that sat at the foot of the bed. Removing a coiled rope, he shot them a fierce look and said, "Don't move now."

He set down his gun, but even as Chrissy debated the intelligence of rushing him, he withdrew a knife from his boot and cut the rope in two places. Seconds later, he again held the gun pointed at Chrissy and she cursed herself for failing to act.

"No," he said, reading her correctly. "You made the right decision. I'm a strong man, Miss Delaney. You wouldn't get past me." He tossed the pieces of rope her way. "Now, I want you to tie the youngsters' hands behind their backs. Children, go sit on the bed."

"Tie the children? It's cruel. I won't do it."

"It is better that I shoot them?"

Chrissy and the Klebergs did as he demanded without further protest. Bennet observed her actions, saying, "Tie them well. I'll check your knots and the children will be the ones to pay if they are sloppy."

Once Sophie and Michael were secured, he tied Chrissy's hands and ordered her to sit on the horsehair sofa. Then returning to the trunk, he took a bed sheet and began to tear it into strips. Chrissy decided to try and reason with him one more time. "Don't do this, please. There's no need."

He smiled sadly, "You saw this room, the Bible, the painting. Come on, Miss Delaney, do you honestly expect me to believe you haven't figured out my true identity?"

Her gaze flew to the painting, then back to him. The truth hit her like a fist. He wasn't Lord Bennet at all. The baron was an imposter. "You're the boy."

"Like I said, you're a smart girl." He touched the brim of an imaginary hat with the barrel of the gun. "John Wilcox at your service."

"How . . . ?"

"Quite easily, actually. I was a third generation Texan, you see. My grandfather fought with Sam Houston at San Jacinto. Family had a nice farm down near Bastrop. Then my mama died in childbirth and my pa drank himself to death. I was seventeen when I lost the homeplace in a card game."

He paused for a moment, then shook his head. "I had three aces. Thought for certain I'd win that hand."

"You bet your home in a card game?" Michael asked incredulously.

"I should have cheated, although if I hadn't lost my home I wouldn't have been riding with a gang of horse thieves when the real Lord Bennet joined up. He looked so much like me everyone swore we were brothers."

Bennet approached her, and using a strip of bed-sheet for a rope, bound her ankles together. "He was a British remittance man. His allowance came twice a year and every single time it arrived he'd get liquored up and talk on and on about his hoity-toity family back in England. I used to wear my ears out listening to him."

He sauntered over to the bed where the children cowered, their eyes round and fearful. Chrissy wanted to kill the man at that moment.

He continued his story as he tied the children's ankles. "When the letter came telling him his brother was dead, and the title and family fortune had come to him, well, it just seemed the natural thing to do to take his place."

Chrissy didn't want to ask how, but he must have seen the question in her eyes because he shrugged and said, "I killed him, of course. He all but asked for it, being so loud-mouthed about his family, telling me everything but their boot sizes. At first I intended to take the money and return to Texas, but I discovered I like being a British lord. It has worked out well, although I do get homesick from time to time. That is why I started my collection, why I built this place. I wanted a tangible reminder of home where I could retreat to when I needed."

Chrissy's heart sank. Up until now she had found comfort in the fact he didn't appear anxious to harm them. But if he'd killed to gain this life he now led, she had to believe he'd kill again to protect it. "What are you going to do to us?"

"Well, that is a problem, isn't it?" Sophie started crying when he tied a gag around her mouth. Michael thrashed, to no avail. Bennet approached Chrissy with one last length of cloth and said, "Tell you what I'll do. I'll sleep on it, and we'll see if in the morning I have thought of a way I can risk letting you live."

She shuddered when, after tying her gag, he touched her arm. But rather than take further liberties, he settled for removing one of the black ribbons adorning her sleeve. Returning to the children, he removed one of Sophie's shoes and tore the cuff from Michael's sleeve. "Y'all go on to sleep now. Maybe luck will be with you." He extinguished the lamps adding light to the room and added, "Things could look brighter in the morning."

Then he left, shutting the door behind them, sealing Chrissy, Michael and Sophie in the pitch black darkness of the underground crypt.

The searchers found the overturned boat at midmorning.

Lana, having grown increasingly distraught throughout the long night, collapsed into her fiancé's arms when a man approached carrying a waterlogged shoe.

"Found it along the far bank, Lord Bennet," he said, pointing across the narrow lake.

Cole recognized it as Sophie's, and fear tore like talons at his gut.

Jake Delaney cleared his throat. "Any sign of my sister?"

"Maybe. Found a couple of rags." The man reached into a bag, then pulled out a damp and muddy scrap of flannel and a length of black ribbon. "Could she have been wearing this?"

Elizabeth Delaney gasped and clutched her son's arm. Cole pictured Chrissy as he last saw her wearing her Chili Queen outfit complete with black ribbons tied around the sleeves of her white blouse.

Cole's heart stopped. Welby said grimly, "That looks like the boy's pajamas."

Seconds or maybe hours ticked by as Cole stood frozen, staring at the ruined ribbon. Fear choked his throat while nausea churned in his stomach.

"They drowned?" cried Thornbury.

"No." Cole abruptly rejected the idea. "I don't believe it," he said, his jaw set like granite. He wouldn't believe it. He shoved the broken oarlock with the toe of his boot and declared, "Chrissy and those children did not drown. Why would they take a boat out after dark anyway? Chrissy wouldn't do that. She's smarter than that."

"But the children are something else," Welby replied, his grim gaze scanning the bank. "I could easily picture Michael conjuring up the idea to go fishing. If he and Sophie somehow fell into trouble, Chrissy might have put herself in jeopardy attempting to save them."

"She was upset when she saw us," Jake agreed, dragging a hand along his jaw. Despair etched his face. "She always did like walking by the water to do her thinking, and the way she took off when Mother and I arrived . . . well . . . she likely had some thinking she wanted to do."

"No." Cole shook his head, his hands making fists at his sides. His mouth was so dry he had to work up a spit to speak. "They didn't drown. We will keep looking. They are here somewhere, alive and healthy, and by God we will find them."

One of the men who discovered the overturned rowboat agreed. "You find 'em one way or another. If they're in this lake, their bodies won't stay down forever."

Cole shot him a furious glare as another man protested, "Not necessarily. The gates on the dam have been open. The bodies are likely well on down the river by now. We can call off this search."

When Lana let out a moan of anguish, then fainted dead away, Jake had to restrain Cole from letting a fist fly at the loudmouth bastard's face. He settled for whirling on Bennet. "You said you're magistrate here, correct?"

"I am."

"You will order these people to continue looking for Miss Delaney and the children until they have been found."

"But Mr. Morgan. The girl's shoe . . . the ribbon."

"Do it!" Thornbury demanded, shifting to stand by Cole.

Throughout the day and late into the evening search parties combed the grounds of Harpur Priory, including every nook and cranny of the manor house. They discovered nothing more than wrinkled coverings on the state bed. "This might be a clue," Lana said upon learning of the discovery. "They've always liked to jump on beds."

Cole climbed up on the bed himself to look at anything the Kleberg children might have seen. Through the window he spied the lake in the distance and the spot where the capsized boat had been discovered.

Dread socked him in the stomach like a fist and he jerked his gaze away from the distressing sight. *No, there must be something more. Where are you, sweetheart? Give me a clue, here.*

At dark Bennet suspended the search for the day and at Cole's insistence asked volunteers to meet back at the manor house the following morning to begin again. Most of the Anglo-Texan Society members, clearly believing Christina and the children had met their fate in the lake, expressed their intentions to depart Harpur Priory as planned the next day. Cole would be glad to see them leave. He needed all the naysayers gone. *So help me, I'll damn well deck the next person who dares to say they're dead.*

Cole made a third sweep through the house before acknowledging his own need for rest and retreating to his room. Forty hours without sleep and half of those spent in ceaseless worry had left his eyes gritty, his body weary. But when he fell onto his bed, slumber eluded him.

His mind was plagued by waking nightmares of "what ifs" and "should haves."

All day long he'd tried not to let the fear clawing at his gut gain control. Fear could cripple a man's thinking, and he'd be useless to her then. Chrissy needed him. He felt it. He felt her, alive and breathing and needing his help.

Please, God. Let her be safe. Let them all be safe.

Impatient to resume the search, Cole lay on the bed wishing the night away until his body's need for rest overpowered the demons in his mind and he fell into a light, restless sleep.

* * *

Fueled by both fear and fury, Chrissy worked all night attempting to free her ropes. She'd counted to ten after Bennet/Wilcox shut the door, then rolled to her feet and hopped toward the bed and the children. Halfway there, she'd lost her balance and fallen, but eventually, she managed to crawl in next to the crying children and offer what little comfort she could. When they finally drifted into an exhausted sleep, she went to work.

Her first thought was to knock over the lamp in hopes of breaking it, so she could use a shard of glass to slice her bindings. But when she rolled into the bedside table sending the lamp teetering, then falling, it was her bad luck that it landed without breaking.

Shortly after that, Chrissy thought she heard signs of a search in the outer room, and she had screamed against the gag, to no avail. It had been time for a new plan. She'd sat in the dark, mentally taking inventory of everything she remembered seeing inside the cabin. She needed something with a sharp edge, but what? The furniture was all wooden with smooth edges. No help there. Nothing on the walls. Then she'd recalled the trunk.

It took her what felt like forever to maneuver it open and then to her dismay, she'd found only bedding inside. While she'd mentally cursed that bad luck, the lid fell, smashing her fingers. But as pain radiated up her arms, her spirits had soared. The metal latch had scratched her on the way down. She had found her tool.

The motion was awkward, and it took hours of dogged determination, but eventually, her muscles screaming and her wrists bleeding, the ropes fell free.

Chrissy wanted to shout for joy, but all she could manage was a satisfied groan.

Moments later, both the gag and the binding around her ankles had been dealt with. The first thing she did was try the door, but it wouldn't budge. Next she debated whether to wake the children in order to untie them or allow them to continue to sleep. Guessing their fear would affect them worse than their discomfort, she decided to let them sleep at least until she managed to light a lamp.

Finding matches was no easy task in the pitch dark of an unfamiliar room. While she searched, she planned how to effect their escape.

Finally, she found a box of matches on the mantel. Soon, a soft oh-so-welcome yellow light chased away at least a portion of the gloom. Setting the lamp beside the bed, she saw to the children's bindings. Michael awoke when she freed him. Sophie remained asleep while Chrissy rigged the trap she'd planned during the long night.

"We must listen hard so we're ready when he opens the door," she told Michael. "Surprise is our best weapon."

Thirst drove them to search the room for something, anything to drink but they found nothing. Michael did find a deck of cards, so once Sophie awoke, Chrissy distracted the children with games.

Time dragged on, exactly how long, Chrissy couldn't tell. She tried to remember how long a person could survive without water. Three days? Four? What about the children? Two days, perhaps?

Tension and worry escalated each time Sophie asked for a drink. If Bennet, rather, if Wilcox walked through the door at that moment, she could have taken his life with little regret.

She was reading softly to the children from the Bible when they heard the sound of scraping. "Now," she whispered, blowing out the lamp, then rushing to get into position. "Be ready."

Slowly, the door opened, a hand holding a lantern leading the way. Light shone upon the children pretending to sleep in the bed, the strips of cloth back in their mouths, their hands and ankles crossed as though still tied.

Holding the heavy cast iron Dutch oven as her club, Chrissy waited . . . waited . . . waited . . .

"Are you still breathing down—" *Whoosh*.

"Run!" Chrissy cried as the pot connected with the villain's head and knocked him to the floor.

Michael and Sophie flew off the bed and hit the floor running, jumping over the groaning, cursing man and out of the hidden room. Chrissy followed on their heels, but darting out of the collection room in near pitch darkness, the children turned the wrong way.

"Where is it, Miss Chrissy? Where is it?" Michael ran along the wall, hitting it with his palms, searching for the opening that led to the staircase.

"Here, this way," she replied, guiding them to the left.

Finding the door, they pushed it open and dashed inside.

"Climb, fast as you can," Chrissy said, herding them ahead of her. But the way was dark and poor Sophie fell twice.

A roar of rage from below sent shivers up Chrissy's spine.

"Hurry!"

Chrissy scooped Sophie up into her arms and continued to climb. Her heart pounded. She struggled to breathe. Thirst was a vicious beast.

How much farther? Were they above ground level yet? Surely so, but the stairwell was so dark, it must be nighttime.

Below her, closer now, came the sound of Wilcox's footsteps. She wanted to sob with desperation. Instead, she yelled, "Scream, Michael. Wake the household!"

Then a hand brushed her skirt. "No."

Faster. Faster. Another tug. Chrissy knew what she must do. She set Sophie onto her feet, saying, "Go . . . go . . . go . . ."

Then she turned to meet her killer.

Unable to sleep more than a few hours, Cole wandered Harpur Priory's halls and waited for dawn. Old ghosts haunted his mind, memories of Christina and the wrongs he had done her throughout the years. *I'll make it up to you, Lady Bug. I promise I will.*

He refused to believe he wouldn't have the opportunity. He refused to believe the woman he loved was dead.

Intent upon his thoughts, upon first hearing the screams, he thought they were all in his mind. Even so, he started walking toward the sound.

"Help us! Mama!"

Everything inside of Cole froze. He turned his ear toward the noise.

"Mama . . . Mama . . . Mama . . ."

"Michael? Sophie?" he yelled, starting to run.

"Help!"

Then they were barreling toward one another down the long gilded hallway that paralleled the state rooms. The children were dirty and bedraggled, both shoeless, and more beautiful than all the contents of all the treasure houses in England. Yet even as the joy blossomed in his heart, his gaze swept past the little ones, searching for sight of Christina. Seeing only an empty doorway.

"Mr. Cole. Mr. Cole. Help us." Michael held his younger sister's hand, pulling her along. Then he added the words that made Cole's blood run cold. "He's got Miss Chrissy and I think he's gonna kill her."

They flew into Cole's arms, weeping and wailing, and it took him valuable seconds to calm them down enough to make sense of what they were saying. By the time they'd provided the pertinent facts, he heard Lana's cry from behind him.

Cole released the children, who immediately ran toward their mother. He called out to Welby. "It's Bennet. He has Chrissy down in the crypt. There's a staircase in the state bedchamber. Get her brother and some light and follow me down."

Then he was off, flying down the hallway and into the bedroom. The hidden door hung open like a black wound in the wall and he dashed inside. "Chrissy!" he yelled as he started down the staircase.

From far below him, he thought he heard her scream. *Sonofabitch, I'll kill you.* Cole flew down the staircase, descending into the darkness. "Chrissy!"

He heard a pop. A shot? *Oh, God.*

Around and around he raced down the staircase wondering if he'd ever reach the bottom. Then finally, abruptly, the staircase ended and he found himself in what amounted to an underground graveyard without a source of light. "Chrissy?" he called again, then stopped and listened hard.

His voice echoed, then died away. Then silence. Cold, total silence. Dead silence.

Chrissy fought, twisting and hitting and biting, but her opponent was bigger than she, stronger than she. And he was furious.

Blood ran from a wound in his head behind his ear. She felt it when she swung at him, smelled its metallic scent. She had hoped to hit his temple and knock him unconscious. Now the bad aim might cost her her life.

At least the children had gotten away and for that she was thankful.

"You've made me lose everything, you bitch. Those children will tell. I tried to be nice. I tried not to kill you, and you repay my kindness this way. To hell with you. Literally. You are going to die now, although it won't be quick or easy. In fact, you may well go insane first."

At the foot of the staircase, he had paused long enough to light a lantern, and for a few sweet seconds Chrissy had yanked herself free. When he caught her again, he backhanded her so hard that it scrambled her brains. By the time she gathered herself enough to resume the struggle, he was dragging her through the crypt, his arm locked around her neck, his voice a demented murmur against her ear.

". . . since that braggart told me all the family secrets, I have just the place. An appropriate place. Lucky for you that the canons needed somewhere to hide their treasures when the king's men came around."

Chrissy forced herself to think. The man was physically her superior, but she refused to let him outsmart her. She needed a weapon, something to balance the scales. She'd tried for his gun half a dozen times already, but he guarded it well. Her sash, perhaps? Maybe she could get it around his throat. It would be awkward, but she had to do something. Was there anything else? What was in her pockets? A handkerchief, one of Sophie's hair clips, a small bag of her special spice blend she'd added to her chili at the barbecue. That's all.

Maybe I could gouge his eyes with the hair clip. Maybe I could . . . his eyes. The spices. Of course.

Timing would need to be perfect.

"Do small, enclosed places bother you, Miss Delaney?" Wilcox asked, his tone dripping menace. "I hope so."

He stopped before one of the numerous stone tombs in the crypt. This particular one was a rectangular marble box probably three feet wide, six feet long, and four feet deep. An effigy of a woman with an Elizabethan ruff around her neck adorned the lid.

Wilcox threw Chrissy against the tomb, then pulled his gun. "Down. Sit down."

Keeping the weapon aimed at Chrissy, he bent and removed a block of stone along the base of the tomb revealing a lever. He pushed the lever, and Chrissy heard a scraping sound as the tomb's lid swung open. At that point, Wilcox's threat became clear.

He intended to enclose her in the tomb.

When he reached into the stone box and removed

three small bags, her own hand slipped into her pocket. As unobtrusively as possible, she scooped chili spice into her fist, then rested her hand in her lap.

"The jewels and gold will have to do me for now," said Wilcox as he slipped the small bags into his jacket. With a low, maniacal laugh, he added, "I'll leave your body to guard the bigger items. As long as I don't return for them too soon, it shouldn't be a problem."

He stepped away from the tomb and motioned with the gun. "Inside now, Miss Delaney."

Slowly, she rose to her feet. *Do it right this time, Chrissy.* "I won't climb into that coffin."

"I'd rather not shoot you, but I will."

At that moment, she heard the far off echo of her name. "Chrissy," came Cole's voice. "Chrissy!"

The sound distracted Wilcox and gave her the opportunity she'd waited for. Lunging forward, she screamed and threw the spices right into his eyes, then grabbed for the gun, wrenching it from his hand.

He yelled a curse, one hand clawing at his eyes while the other struck out at Chrissy. She dodged the fist, shaking, quaking, as she fumbled to grip the pistol.

There. In her hand. The guard. The trigger.

He hit her as she fired.

"Bitch!" He hit her again and the world went black.

Cole couldn't see a damned thing. How stupid of him not to stop long enough to grab a candle. He'd been so damned scared he'd acted without thinking.

He yelled her name at the top of his lungs, then listened again. Nothing, again.

Think, Morgan.

She could be right next to him and he wouldn't know it. He had to have light. It was either wait for Jake to bring it, or find some on his own. Surely, if Bennet used this place for a lair, he'd keep lamps placed around. Cole just had to find them.

He felt his way forward and found a door. Opening it, he breathed a sigh of relief. A yellow glow filtered from the doorway to a room across from him.

Reminding himself he'd already used up his share of recklessness by coming down here without a light, Cole approached the room cautiously and quietly. Edging up to the door, he peeked inside.

It was the collection room Bennet had shown him yesterday. No one appeared to be inside. Then a voice floated from off to the side. "Come in, Mr. Morgan. Please."

Cole turned his head to see a second room revealed. *This was where he held them*. "Chrissy, are you in there?"

Bennet said, "Come see for yourself."

Cole wasn't about to walk into that room unarmed. Mentally picturing the display cases scattered throughout the room, he quietly moved to the one that contained the knives. He dumped over the case, broke the glass, and chose a Bowie knife and a smaller one better for throwing.

"I do prefer you leave my treasures alone," said Bennet.

"Chrissy, answer me," said Cole.

"I'm afraid that's not possible."

Approaching the door to the hidden room, Cole mentally slammed a door on the cold fear that threatened to overwhelm him at Bennet's claim.

Taking a deep breath, he looked inside. *It's a damned log cabin.*

Bennet was sitting in a rocking chair staring up at a painting on the wall. He held a Colt revolver in his right hand. Chrissy wasn't anywhere in sight. "Where is she?"

"Well, well, well, Mr. Morgan. Come in. Come in." Lamplight flickered, casting dancing shadows across the floor. Cole picked up the faint scent of the Kleberg children on the air. And Chrissy. She'd been here, but she wasn't here now. He knew that.

Keeping a wary eye on Bennet's gun, he advanced farther into the room. "What have you done with Chrissy?"

The evil in Bennet's smile sent a chill chasing up Cole's spine. "No more than she's done to me." He held up his left hand then, a hand covered in blood. "She's killed me, you see. Gut shot. I thought it was only a scratch at first. Hardly hurt. Hardly bled. Then I moved her and it was like something inside me ripped apart."

"No, dammit!" Cole advanced on him. "She's not dead. What have you done with her? Where is she?"

Bennet laughed weakly, his gaze returning to the portrait hanging on the wall. "Where is she?" he repeated. "Why, she's on her way to hell. Just like me."

Cole grabbed him around the throat, determined to force the truth from him. But it was too late. Lord Bennet's eyes had gone to glass.

Chrissy's whereabouts died with him.

Chapter

16

Chrissy awoke slowly to a savage headache, a raging thirst, and a nauseated stomach. The gag in her mouth muffled her groan and the total darkness surrounding her caused her a long moment of confusion. Then like nightmares, scenes of recent events replayed themselves through her mind. Finally, she realized where she was. The tomb. He'd shut her in the marble box in the crypt below Harpur Priory.

Chrissy tried to scream, but little sound emerged. She tried to lift her arms and push against the lid above her, but she had no room to maneuver. She lay atop a lumpy bed of canvas bags filled with hard-edged objects that gouged into her skin. The tomb's stone slab rested only inches above her, and had she been a little broader in the shoulders, she wouldn't have fit from side to side.

Yet, she fought to free herself, pushing against the lid until her muscles gave out. Heedless of the gag, she screamed for help until her voice dried to a rasp.

Time drifted by and she was fairly certain she swam

in and out of consciousness. Each time she came to, her aches and pains bothered her a little less. A peaceful numbness crept over her and she sank into the freedom of her thoughts.

Idly, she wondered if the tomb was airtight and if she'd suffocate. No, she'd be dead already if that were the case. Maybe she'd die of thirst instead. She wondered which type of death would be easier.

The worst thing about dying, she decided, was the thought of leaving Cole. What would he do when he couldn't find her? How long would he continue to look for her?

Forever.

In the darkness, Chrissy closed her eyes. It was true. Cole would look for her until he found her, if it took him the rest of his life. She knew it. She'd been a fool to deny him her trust.

So trust me now, his voice whispered through her mind. *Trust me to find you in time. Fight for your sanity, Christina. Fight for your life.*

As the mist took her once more, she silently answered, *I'll try.*

They lit up the catacombs like a ballroom, stripping Harpur Priory's lamp room bare and robbing half the rooms in the house of theirs. Cole and Jake located four hidden exits out of the tunnels that stretched in all directions from the main crypt beneath the manor.

It was a lot of area to search, and Cole was well aware that more exits and hidden rooms were likely to exist. The church on this property dated back seven hundred years and a lot of hiding, spying, building, and destroying had taken place during that time. They found a new nook or cranny every time they turned around.

At first light, they began searching the areas around each of the exits. Both capable trackers, Cole and Jake quickly established that neither Bennet nor Chrissy had left the crypt by those paths during the night. It wasn't necessarily what Cole had hoped to find, but at this point, every piece of information was valuable. "She's down here somewhere," he told her brother. "And she's alive. I can feel it. I know it as well as I know my own name."

Jake wearily rubbed the back of his neck. "God, I hope you're right. I'm getting scared, Cole. Real scared."

At that point Elizabeth Delaney led a half dozen servants down the circular staircase into the crypt carrying trays of sandwiches and drink. "Boys?" she asked hopefully. "Any news?"

Cole smiled for the first time all day. He could be fifty years old and she'd still call him a boy. "Not yet, Elizabeth. But we'll find her. He didn't have time to take her very far."

Unsaid was the reality that Bennet had managed plenty of time to hurt her.

Tears sparkled in Elizabeth's eyes. "What have I done to her? Why did she run? I love her, boys. I love her so very much."

"I know, Mama," Jake said, wrapping his mother in his arms. Over her head, his anguished gaze met Cole's. "We all love her."

Cole couldn't bear to see Elizabeth's tears, and he wished for some way to ease her burden. Producing

Chrissy would be the best solution, of course, but he felt compelled to offer her what he could. "I love Christina. She owns my heart. I've asked her to marry me." When she turned to look at him, her expression filled with anxious joy, his mouth twisted in a rueful smile and he added, "She hasn't accepted me yet, but I'm working on it."

Then she was in his arms, hugging him hard. "You've been my son for a long time now, but this . . . Cole . . . it's a dream come true for me."

"Mama's plan worked," murmured Jake, shaking his head. "I'll be damned."

They resumed their search and half an hour later, his fine brocade vest smeared with dirt, Lord Welby emerged from one of the tunnels and said, "Cole, you might want to see this. We've found another burial room."

"Chrissy?"

"Not yet, but—"

Cole took off at a run.

They searched the path thoroughly to no avail. Nor did the next two hidden chambers they discovered yield any sign of Chrissy. The longer they worked, the more disheartened the searchers became. Cole began to see doubt and sympathy in the looks they shot his way, but he patently ignored them. When a footman approached him about calling a halt for the day, he damn near swung on him. "She's down here somewhere, and she's alive. We won't stop until we find her."

By late afternoon, desperation had begun to claw at Cole. He prowled into the collection room, lifted one of the small glass display cases, and heaved it against the wall with a loud, frustrated shout. Glass crashed and fractured. Jake came running. "What happened?"

"Nothing happened, dammit!" Cole whirled on his friend, his fists clenched at his side, his heart threatening to shatter like the glass. "We're missing something, Jake. We have to be." His gaze shot toward the hidden room where Bennet died. "A little quicker. If I'd just been a little quicker."

Chrissy's brother raked his fingers through his hair. "Look, let's go over it all again. Maybe you'll think of something new. We'll figure our distances again. Maybe he had time to take her farther than we think."

"Or maybe he didn't take her anywhere at all." Cole exited the collection room and walked to the base of the staircase. "I'll hear that scream in my dreams for the rest of my life." He moved back out into the main passageway stalking down its length. "It had to come from close to here, Jake. I'm certain of it. The sound wasn't muffled enough. . . ." His voice trailed off as he calculated the amount of time it had taken him to descend the long staircase. "Why the hell couldn't I have been just a little quicker?"

He braced both hands on one of the tombs, leaned over, and hung his head. Never in his life had he felt this tired. "Hell," he murmured. "I know she's down here. I swear I can even smell her."

Jake clapped Cole's shoulder in comfort. "I think you're right, brother. We will find her. Don't you give up on her now."

"I'm not giving up. I'm not . . . I do." He snapped up straight. "I *do* smell her. I smell the chili. Here, bring me a light."

Jake rushed to grab a lantern as Cole hunkered down beside the tomb. "There. Look." He brushed his finger across a spot of red dust, then brought it up to his nose and sniffed. Then sneezed. "Ground chili peppers."

He looked at Jake. "Get help. We're opening this grave."

"What?" Jake said, his chin dropping. "But that lid has to weigh a couple hundred pounds. One man couldn't move it by himself."

Cole walked all around the tomb, carefully studying every carving and crease. "He could if it had an opening mechanism. We saw one in that last tunnel Welby discovered."

"Sonofabitch," Jake said, catching Cole's enthusiasm. "That might be it. A latch and lever contraption."

"But I don't have the patience to solve hidden puzzles right now," Cole stated.

Moments later, five strong men surrounded the tomb as Cole wedged a crowbar into the seam between box and lid and pushed with all his might to give them fingerholds. That done, he dropped the tool and added his strength to theirs. Stone grated against stone as slowly, the heavy stone lid moved.

First a corner. Then more. Then . . .

"Oh, God," Jake croaked.

Chrissy! Cole's mind screamed.

The woman he loved more than life itself lay in the tomb, still and pale as a corpse.

Cool, sweet water slid down her parched and swollen throat. A soft, gentle mattress caressed her bruised limbs, and a fluffy blanket warmed her. *Ah,* thought Chrissy, *this must be heaven.*

Then her mother said, "This cut on her head will scar. She's lucky it's on the back of her head rather than her face. It will look ugly, I'm afraid."

A hand reached for hers, cradled it tenderly. "None of that matters," said Cole. "What matters is that she wakes up healthy."

I'm trying, she silently told him. *I knew you'd find me.* Then she drifted back into the mist.

The next time awareness bloomed, a gentle, soothing tug on her scalp told her someone was brushing her hair. She sighed into the sensation, too weak to open her eyes, but craving the comfort of human touch. When Cole spoke, she tried to work up a smile.

"I think her color is better, don't you, Elizabeth?"

Chrissy's mother replied, "Yes, I do. Her skin looks better, not so . . . sluggish. Maybe you've finally dribbled enough water down her throat."

Ah, it is Mama's hands manning the hairbrush. How many years since she last brushed my hair?

Peaceful now, Chrissy allowed herself to sleep.

Cole sat in a chair beside Chrissy's bed, his hands clasping one of hers. Periodically, he'd bring it to his mouth and press a kiss against her palm. Despite the doctor's cautious optimism, he worried she wouldn't wake up.

Elizabeth Delaney shared his concern, and she didn't mind voicing it. "What if the blow to her head damaged her brain? What if she never wakes up? What will I do then?"

."Chrissy will wake up," Cole said.

"But what if he damaged her mind? Not by the blow, necessarily, but by shutting her up in that big stone coffin. You know how she hates being confined in any way. I can see where it might drive her insane."

"Elizabeth, please," Cole protested, his patience thin. "She'll be all right. Your daughter is a very strong woman."

"Yes, I guess she is at that. Otherwise, she'd never have given her father and me so much grief over the years. She has always been so independent, so headstrong, even as a child. Remember that time not long after you came to live with us when she decided I had dismissed a housemaid unfairly? For an entire month, every time the girl opened her mouth she complained about it."

The memory managed to bring a smile to Cole's face. He quoted. " 'I protest the dismissal of Miss Maria Montoya, pass the butter, please.' She convinced her father to rehire the maid, if I remember correctly."

"Yes. She always did wrap her father around her little finger. Until it came time to send her to boarding school." Smugness colored Elizabeth's tone as she said, "I won that one."

"Won?" Cole brows winged up. "I didn't realize it was a contest."

"Yes, well. Not a contest, more a war. You probably never noticed how much a distraction her behavior was for her father. At times it threatened to compromise his position as a federal judge. Of course I missed her desperately once she was gone, but I was comforted by the fact that the school we chose for her would deal with those unladylike tendencies she exhibited." She paused for a moment before adding sadly, "But she came home a flirt and a jilt."

Elizabeth sighed. "It's enough to break a mother's heart. But now, thank God, she has you. You are just who my Christina needs. You'll steer her right. You'll change her. Being your wife will change Christina into the woman I've always wanted her to be."

"No," Chrissy's voice croaked.

Cole went stiff. He jerked his head around toward the bed and joy filled his heart. "You're awake," he breathed. "You're awake! Thank God." Immediately he was there with a glass of cool water which Chrissy downed thirstily. His voice shook a little as he asked, "How are you feeling, honey?"

"I'm . . ." she shuddered. "I'm fine, I think. It's like a nightmare." Then she looked up at him, those beautiful green eyes searching his. "You saved me, didn't you?"

"I found you in the tomb."

"I knew you would. I just knew it. It made me feel . . . safe."

He had a lump in his throat the size of a watermelon. "I'm glad, honey."

Her smile warmed him like summer sunshine, chasing away the last of the cold that had gripped him since her disappearance. "Thank you, Cole. Thank you for saving my life."

"Oh, my baby," cried Elizabeth. She edged Cole aside and sat on the bed next to Chrissy, then slipped her arms around her and gave her a hug. "You're so lucky to have a man who loves you as much as he does. He never quit searching, never. Everything will be just fine now. A little more rest and you'll be well and we can plan your wedding."

Chrissy blinked. Her smile died. "No," she said again, her voice weary. "No we won't."

Elizabeth patted her hand. "Now, Christina, I realize you probably want to do things your way, but believe me when I say you'll need help planning a wedding here in England. Weddings are much bigger productions here than they are at home."

Her skin was as pale as the sheet she lay upon, and Cole could tell her strength was waning. She looked up at him, an unreadable message in her eyes. "We're not getting married," she said softly. "Cole and I agreed."

"Chrissy . . . ," he began.

"Oh, poppycock," Elizabeth said with a sniff. "Of course you are getting married. Cole told us he loves you, and I know you've loved him for quite some time. Quit being difficult, Christina."

Chrissy sank back onto her bed and turned her head toward the wall. Cole's heart ached. How could he be filled with such relief and such sorrow at the same time? For a long moment, the only sound in the room was the ticking of the clock on the mantel.

Then Cole shoved his hands into his pockets and scowled at Elizabeth. "Why do you do that?"

"Do what?"

"Attack her like that."

Elizabeth's shoulders squared. "What do you mean?" she questioned, her tone bristling with defensiveness. "I don't attack her."

"Yes, sometimes you do. Sadly, this is one of those instances. Chrissy isn't being difficult. Nor does she have to change." He paused and looked at her, willing her to meet his gaze. She did, and he smiled at her. "She's wonderful just as she is."

"Of course she is wonderful," Elizabeth said, scowling. "She is my daughter and I love her."

Chrissy pushed up onto her arms. "Do you, Mother?"

Elizabeth gasped and slapped a hand against her breast. "Why, Christina Delaney. Of course I love you."

"You never say it. All you ever do is berate me. Usually in a kind manner, I'll admit. After all, we must keep up appearances."

"I don't—"

"You do," Cole said, jumping back into the conversation. "I don't know why I never noticed it before, but you do. What's worse, you do it in such an agreeable way that those around you never think to question the truth of what you are saying."

He laughed without amusement, then said, "I've long wondered how the boldest woman I know could be so insecure inside, but now, finally, it is crystal clear to me. You do that to her. You're a mother hen who pecks at her chick until she's bleeding inside."

The hairbrush clattered to the floor as Elizabeth made a little wounded moan. Chrissy gazed from Cole to her mother, her mouth gaping open in shock. A mixture of anger and anguish rushed through Cole as he turned away from the woman who for so long now had been his mother.

He'd never intentionally hurt her before in his life.

Then Jake stepped forward from a corner of the room. "Now, wait just one minute, Morgan. There's no call for you to talk that way. My mother loves her daughter."

"I know she does," Cole replied, capturing Chrissy's stare. "I know she does and that's the saddest part of all." He looked at Elizabeth and asked, "How can you love her, but constantly undermine her? Why do you do it?"

"I don't undermine her." Elizabeth's voice trembled. She glanced at Chrissy. "Do I? Am I a terrible person? I only want what is best for you. That's why I chose Cole for you. He'll make you a fine husband, Christina. He's so very much like your father. He'll help you curb your . . . inappropriate enthusiasm."

"But what if I don't want to be curbed?" Chrissy asked. "Why can't anyone love me the way I am?"

Ah, this was the heart of the matter, and the pain in her voice damn near sliced Cole in two. He sat on the edge of her bed and stared at her intently. "I do, Lady Bug. I love you exactly as you are."

He could see in her expression that she wanted to believe. Rather desperately, he thought.

"That's not what you said, Cole. You said you wanted a lady who dresses right and acts right."

Elizabeth interjected. "But you can be that lady for him, Christina. You can be the wife he deserves."

Cole muttered a curse beneath his breath, before looking at Chrissy's mother and saying, "I love you, too, Elizabeth. You are a mother to me. I love you and I respect you and I'd lay down my life for yours. But I feel those things for your daughter, also. Those and more. I think you need to hear why."

He shifted his gaze back to Chrissy and brushed her cheek with his thumb. "Your daughter is like you in very many ways, Elizabeth. She is generous and loyal and strong. She is fervent in her beliefs and she is outspoken in her opinions. She'll fight against injustice. She'll protect the innocent with her life. We saw her do that with the Klebergs. Those are all qualities I see in you."

Elizabeth sniffed. "I know Christina is all those things. I'm very proud of her for that."

"I hope you are. But you should be proud of her differences, too, because they help make her the vibrant woman she is."

"You mean like her reckless behavior?"

"I mean her courage, her willingness to live life to the fullest. I mean her wit and her energy and the joy she brings other people."

He saw what he thought might be hope kindle in Chrissy's eyes. Silently, she implored him. *Do you truly mean it, Cole?*

Her mother sniffed with disdain. "All that is easy for you to say, Cole, but you are not her mother. You haven't needed to worry about the consequences of her behavior. Understand this. A mother's primary duty is to ensure that her daughter is marriageable. Thank God you have been brave enough to see past the weaknesses in Christina's character, otherwise she'd never find an acceptable husband."

Chrissy's brow dipped at that. "Wait a minute," she protested weakly. "I found lots of appropriate men. I've been engaged, what, seven times?"

"Eight if you count Welby," Cole corrected.

Elizabeth dismissed the argument with the wave of a hand. "I never believed you'd marry a one of them, and I was right. You love Cole. He's the only man for you." She shot him a smile and added, "He's strong enough to subdue the outrageous side of your character."

"I don't want to subdue her," Cole snapped. "I thank God she's a Chili Queen. If not for those chili spices she'd still be down in that tomb. It shames me that it took me so long to see Chrissy for who she is. It shames me that I, too, thought she should conform more than is right for her nature. It shames me that I ever thought, even for a moment, that I might be better off with a more socially compliant woman for a wife."

He glanced at Elizabeth and said, "I love you dearly, Elizabeth, but you've been wrong about Chrissy, too. So has Jake. We haven't loved her for who she is. We wanted to love her for who we wanted her to be. Chrissy deserves better than that from us. She deserves love without strings placed upon that love, and that's what I intend to give her."

He slipped off the bed and knelt on one knee. Taking one of her hands in his, he said, "I love you, Chrissy. You. Just like you are. Chili Queen, flirt, and all. I don't want to change you or control you or do anything but love you. Can you accept that, finally? Can you accept me? Will you marry me, Christina Delaney?"

Chrissy cleared her throat. "It's my choice?"

"Yes, *yours*. Not your brother's or your mother's or mine. Your choice, Lady Bug. As long as there is no baby, I'll abide by it."

"Baby!" Jake exclaimed.

Chrissy pursed her lips and thought for a moment. "What is today?"

"Wednesday," growled her brother, glaring at Cole.

"I won't know about a baby for at least another week." Chrissy lay back on her bed and closed her eyes. "Sunday, Cole. I'll give you my answer this coming Sunday."

Well, hell.

I'm gonna kill Christina Delaney.

Cole swung the ax, cleaving a log cleanly in two. The hardheaded, mule-stubborn, muscle-minded woman. She wouldn't see him. Wouldn't speak to him. Wouldn't respond to the damned letter he'd slipped under her door.

"Give me your answer on Sunday," he grumbled, setting up another log. "Just because I said I wouldn't try to change you didn't mean I'd let you walk all over me."

He split the log with two solid strokes. "Backed off because you looked pale," he muttered. "Weak." He'd thought to give her a day of rest, then hash the rest of their relationship out in private.

"What you get for thinking, Morgan," he mumbled.

He cut three more logs before heaving the ax blade into the ground. Leaning on the handle, he gingerly touched the cut below his eye he'd received Wednesday afternoon. Damned Jake had a wicked right hook.

Cole hadn't defended himself at first. He knew he deserved the beating for touching Christina. Hell, he deserved it for being so stupid as to mention the possibility of a baby in front of her mother and brother. But when Jake proved unwilling to allow a couple punches to settle the matter, Cole had thrown a few jabs of his own. All in all, it had been a satisfactory fight.

He wished like hell he could find the same satisfaction with Christina.

What really chapped him about her behavior was that the ban didn't extend to anyone else. All day long folks were in and out of her bedroom. Her mother, her brother, Thornbury, Lana and the children, even Welby. Yet, every time he tried to gain entrance, a footman was there to bar the way. Cole about blew his top yesterday when Christina refused to see him for the third time that afternoon.

Feeling better for the exercise, but still muttering beneath his breath, Cole stacked the wood on the woodpile, grabbed his shirt to use as a towel, then slipped it on for the trek to the manor house and the bath that awaited him.

He was taking a shortcut through the statue garden when he came upon an exceedingly glum Jake Delaney sitting on a bench throwing pebbles at Adonis's private parts. "What has you down in the mouth?" Cole asked.

Jake scowled and threw another stone. "Scotland. Rowanclere Castle."

Cole didn't even try to smother his laugh. "Gonna take a trip, Jake?"

"You're an ass, Morgan."

Still grinning, Cole took a seat beside him. Jake sighed heavily, threw another rock, then said, "Chrissy gets every bit of her stubbornness from Mama."

"She's sending you after the Declaration?"

"Yeah. Even though we've already located one of them."

"Really? When? Where? No one told me about it."

"The fellow who owns Castaway Bait Company had one. Apparently it had been passed down through Drew Coryell's family. Remember Roger Mayfield's daughter Hannah?"

"The pretty one? Didn't he bring her to the Historical Society meetings a few times when he was president of the group?"

"That's her. Anyway, a few years back she was briefly—very briefly—married to Coryell. He'd shown her the document. So once she found out the Historical Society was searching for missing copies of the Declaration, she looked up her old flame and convinced him to give it to her."

"That's good news," Cole observed. "As long as we have one copy, finding the others aren't as important."

"Not according to my mother," Jake replied, giving the grass beneath his feet a vicious kick. "She's bound and determined for me to track down the one that woman supposedly stole from Bennet, or Wilcox, I should say."

It was all Cole could do not to chortle aloud at the gloomy note in Jake's voice. "You'll enjoy Scotland. I hear the lassies are lovely up there. And when you find the woman who bested Wilcox, give her my regards, will you? I tell you what, Jake, that man was downright crazy. It shames me to think Texas produced a fellow like that."

Jake nodded glumly. "He certainly had more than a few spokes missing from his wheel. Makes you wonder what sort of home he grew up in to make him want to create a copy of it in a crypt."

"Maybe he was born bad," Cole replied thoughtfully. "Or, could be losing both his folks so young made him that way. Doesn't really matter, though. One way or another, this world is well rid of him."

"Can't argue with you there."

The two men sat quietly for a moment as Cole pondered the events of recent days. Details yielded by the scrapbook uncovered during a search of Harpur Priory following the imposter's death had shocked them all. The man's evil hadn't begun with murdering the real Lord Bennet and taking his place. Newspaper clippings told of crimes committed by a young John Wilcox while handwritten notations kept up a running tally of killings he carried out in the process. According to the articles, the Texas Rangers had been hot on Wilcox's trail, so the decision to take the real Lord Bennet's place had likely been an easy one. What was one more murder in a long list? Especially when it brought the killer significant wealth and a life of ease at the price of a little homesickness.

Cole cleared his throat, then voiced a nagging concern. "I just hope Chrissy doesn't suffer too much knowing she fired the shot that ended up killing him."

Jake winced. "Uh, I um . . . you see . . . Hell, I told her you killed him."

Cole considered the lie for a moment, then nodded. "Good. Let's keep to that story. Chrissy doesn't need to shoulder that burden, and besides, I wish I had done him in myself. It's one of the bigger disappointments in my life that he died before I could finish the job for him. And now that I've heard the whole story of what he did to Chrissy and to the children in order to protect his true identity, I wish he'd died a much harder death."

"Me, too," observed Jake. "Although, I understand being gut shot is particularly painful."

"Yes."

The two men's gazes met and they shared a satisfied

smile. After that, the conversation turned to Jake's travel plans. "Have you been able to discover exactly where in Scotland you'll find this Rowanclere Castle?"

"Yes," Jake said with a groan. "My grandfather thinks he's heard of it. He thinks it's up north. Up in the mountains."

"The Scottish Highlands." Cole winced. "That's too bad."

"Why do you say that?"

Cole clapped him on the back, biting back a laugh as he stood. "I heard it can get awfully cold in the Highlands. I know how much you like ice, snow, and bitter wind."

Jake sneered and made a rude hand gesture. "Go chop some more wood, why don't you."

Cole walked away grinning, feeling better than he had in days. "And no wonder," he murmured, glancing toward the western sky where the sun was beginning to set. "Tomorrow is Sunday."

Chrissy stared at the gown hanging on the wardrobe door and smiled wistfully. It was a beautiful dress. Made of satin and silk, beaded and bustled, it was the height of fashion for any well-born lady.

It was a gift from her grandfather, and how he'd obtained such a fine piece of work in such a short amount of time left her marveling at his influence. In fact, he'd managed all the arrangements she'd requested with seemingly minor effort. Chrissy appreciated his efforts more than she could say. Anything to make this day easier was a great help.

Chrissy was nervous. As she sat at her dressing table fixing her hair, her foot beneath her robe tapped a mile a minute. Even her hand trembled as she poked another pin into the hairstyle she was attempting. "You're a mess, Chrissy Delaney," she said to her reflection. "You know you're doing the right thing, so why be scared?"

The knock at her door became a welcome distraction. "Yes?"

The door cracked open and her mother stuck her head inside. "May I come in?"

Chrissy's spine straightened in an automatic defensive response, but she forced a smile. "Certainly. Please." Then in a conciliatory gesture, she added, "I could use some help with my hair."

Elizabeth brought a dress bag in with her, and she hung it in the wardrobe before approaching Chrissy. "I'd love to assist you in styling your hair."

Chrissy wanted to ask her what was in the bag, but she didn't feel comfortable doing it. She and her mother had been tiptoeing around one another since the conversation last Wednesday.

The desire to make things right with her mother was a physical ache inside Chrissy. Now, as Elizabeth pulled the pins from Chrissy's hair and picked up the hairbrush, she searched to find the right words to say.

Elizabeth spoke first. "You have such beautiful hair." She paused for a moment, then added, "I think you should wear it down today."

"What?" Chrissy's eyes rounded in shock. How many times had her mother fussed at her for leaving the house without putting up her hair? "But Mother, that's not . . ."

"It is you, sweetheart. It's right for you. I understand that now. Let's brush it till it shines, shall we?"

Chrissy didn't know how to respond, so she sat quietly until Elizabeth put down the brush and reached into her pocket, removing a white satin ribbon. "Is this all right with you? We can add a flower or two to make it more festive."

"Um, yes. That's fine."

Chrissy watched in the mirror as her mother threaded the ribbon through her hair. "So very beautiful," Elizabeth repeated. "It's the same color as your father's was when he was younger. Same texture, too. I always envied you your hair."

"You did?"

"I envied many things about you, Christina. That's a terrible thing for a mother to admit, isn't it? I watched you bloom from a girl into a young woman and I began to feel old. That's a pitiful, poor excuse for my behavior, isn't it?"

Chrissy had to consciously stop her mouth from gaping open. Elizabeth smiled sadly, then met her daughter's gaze in the mirror. "I was jealous. You were so close to your father. Much closer to him than to me, and I was jealous of both of you. I just wanted to be your moon and stars, but you looked to your father for that."

"Mama, I never knew . . . I didn't mean to hurt you."

"Oh, I know that." Elizabeth tied the ribbon in a bow, then fluffed the loops. Placing her hands on Chrissy's shoulders, she said, "I've done quite a bit of thinking since Wednesday. Cole opened my eyes to many things. I want to apologize to you, my daughter, and I want to try to explain."

Emotion welled in Chrissy's eyes and she blinked back tears. "Mama, I've done a lot of things wrong, too. I know I've been a trial for you. I'm sorry that I—"

Elizabeth gave her shoulders a squeeze. "Hush now. This is my apology, my explanation. You see, Christina, I wanted to protect you. I've heard it said that what bothers a parent most is seeing her own faults repeated in her children. With you, it was like looking at myself twenty years younger, making the same mistakes I made. I ran away with a man, remember. I was a Scandal. It brought me the happiness of this family, but it also brought me much loneliness and pain. I didn't want you to have to go through what I did." She paused for a moment, then added, "I sound defensive, don't I?"

"You sound honest," Chrissy said.

Elizabeth reached for her daughter's hand and tugged her to her feet, then led her toward the bed where she sat down beside her. "I've always tried to be a perfect mother, so the challenges you gave me made me feel like a failure."

"Challenges?" Chrissy said ruefully. "Don't you mean trouble?"

Her mother laughed. "Semantics, but I won't argue that one. My dear, what I've come to realize these past few days is that maybe instead of trying to be a perfect mother, I should be happy being a good one. Maybe then you and I could be friends."

"Friends?" Chrissy's smile was tremulous. "I like the sound of that."

"I love you, Christina Elizabeth Delaney, and I'm sorry I haven't told you so often enough. I'm sorry my actions have caused you to doubt my love. I'm sorry my words have sometimes been cruel and have given you reason to doubt yourself when you should've had no doubts. Cole said it well the other day. You are like me, true, but it is our differences that make you so special. I was wrong to think you needed to change, honey. You're fine just the way you are. You're wonderful just the way you are."

The tears spilled despite Chrissy's best efforts. "Do you mean that, Mother?"

Elizabeth gave her hand a squeeze, then rose from the bed and walked to the wardrobe where she removed the dress bag. "I know your grandfather went to a lot of trouble to provide you this gown, honey, and it is an extremely beautiful dress. However, I thought this design might suit you better and your grandfather agrees. I made it myself. If you'd like to wear it today, I'd be honored."

She removed the cloth cover, revealing her gift. Chrissy's breath caught. "Oh, Mama. I can't believe you . . . oh, I love it. I love you. This is gorgeous. It's perfect. It's . . ."

"You, honey." Elizabeth's smile beamed as she added, "It's the perfect bridal gown for Chrissy Delaney."

"This had better be good," Cole grumbled as he followed Jake and Welby out of Hartsworth's front door. "What does the earl want with me this morning anyway? Why couldn't it wait? I'm trying to track down Christina. She wasn't in her room when I knocked, and today is the day she promised to talk. She and I have a few things to settle, you know."

"Quit your whining, Morgan," Jake said. "This is important, and it won't take long."

"What's it about?"

Welby said, "You Texans aren't blessed with an abundant amount of patience, are you?"

"You think not? Hell, I've waited since Wednesday on Christina, haven't I? That took some patience, I'm telling you. That took the patience of an entire church full of saints. And I'm no saint."

Jake snorted. "That's obvious, considering you bedded my sister before the wedding."

Cole stopped short. "Are we going to fight about this again, or are you going to quit bringing it up every time I see you? Which is it, Delaney? One or the other."

Jake rolled his eyes and kept on walking. Welby said, "Please, Morgan, we're almost there."

"Where?"

The viscount pointed, "Just over the hill."

Cole scowled, impatience tugging at his gut. He sensed a conspiracy of one sort or another afoot here. "Jake better not be trying to dump the Declaration hunt back on me. I am not going to Scotland."

They topped the rise and Cole gazed down upon the bucolic picture of English countryside. Sheep dotted the rolling hillside like cotton puffs and fluffy clouds dappled an amazingly sunny sky. Birds soared and swooped, their songs a source of music on the gentle breeze. A small church sat nestled among a grove of oaks and in the distance, Cole could see the slate roofs of the village.

Jake was already halfway down the hill headed for the church. Cole wasn't too surprised by the apparent destination. After all, it was Sunday morning and the household at Hartsworth often attended services at the church rather than the manor's chapel.

When Jake disappeared around the front of the church, Welby motioned to Cole. "Follow him, if you would. I'll be along in a minute. I believe I have a stone in my shoe."

Cole shrugged, then walked the rest of the distance toward the church. Rounding a corner, he glanced toward the front steps and stopped dead still. "Christina?"

"Hello, Cole."

She stood on the front church steps dressed all in white, and could have been an angel but for the fire glistening in her hair. She looked healthy again and so beautiful she stole his breath.

He cleared his throat. "New Chili Queen clothes, Christina?"

"Mama made them." She twirled in a slow spin that sent the gauzy white skirt swirling about her ankles and the sleeve of the snowy peasant blouse slipping off one shoulder. "Do you like it?"

"You're exquisite."

She dipped into a curtsy that caused her blouse to gape and offered him a glimpse of her breasts. He damned near chewed his tongue. Searching desperately for a distraction, he said, "I went by your room earlier. You weren't there."

"I may have been out walking. I have some things I need to say to you, and I wanted to get the words just right."

"Oh." Cole blew out a breath. Well, he'd been wanting to settle their situation. Why, then, now that the moment had arrived, was his stomach tied in enough knots to moor a sailing ship? What if she rejected his offer of marriage? Would he be able to let her go?

Hell, no. He wasn't letting her go. He didn't care what she said or how long it took. Chrissy Delaney was going to marry him.

She smiled at him and said, "First I want to thank you for standing up for me to my mother. You made us both think about what has been wrong between us and how we might fix it."

A thank you. Well, damn. So much for hoping for a declaration of everlasting love.

"Second," she said, lacing her fingers together. "I want to apologize for doubting you. I allowed my fears to rule my heart, and as a result I treated you in a way you didn't deserve. When Wilcox put me in that tomb and told me I would die, I trusted you to find me, to save my life. I realized then how foolish I had been. If I trusted you with my life, I should certainly trust you with my heart."

"I didn't lie about loving you, Chrissy."

"I know. You are an honorable man, Cole Morgan. I know that you are true to your word. It was wrong of me to question it."

Cole found himself relaxing. Maybe this wouldn't be a fight after all.

She tucked a stray curl back behind her ear and said, "Third, I want to tell you that I love you, now and for always."

He exhaled a breath in a whoosh. "Thank God, Lady Bug. You had me worried there. I—"

"Hush. I'm not through yet."

"Oh, all right."

"Lastly . . ." she paused, grimaced, drew a deep breath, and started to sing,

There's a Yellow Rose of Texas,

That I am going to see

No other fellow knows her

No other, only me.

She cried so when I left her

It like to break my heart

And if I ever find her

We never more will part.

Before the last note died, she reached into her pocket and pulled out a walnut-sized, apricot-colored habeñero pepper. As she brought it to her lips, Cole recalled her claim: *I'll sing "The Yellow Rose of Texas" while eating a habeñero pepper in front of the church on Sunday morning before I'd marry you, Cole Morgan.*

His mouth was just starting to lift into a grin when he remembered the pain one of those peppers had given him the night she'd been crowned Queen of the Chili Queens. "Chrissy, no!"

"I'm good for my word, too, Cole Morgan." Then she popped the pepper into her mouth. Immediately, her eyes began to water and she gasped for breath. Little squeaking sounds of pain emerged from her throat.

At that point, the church doors flew open, and Michael and Sophie Kleberg came bounding down the steps. He held a pitcher and a goblet, she a basket of rolls. "Here's your water, Miss Chrissy," the boy said, filling the glass.

Water sloshed over the goblet's sides as Sophie

added, "We put a little holy water in there, too. We figured it's the perfect thing to douse the hellfire of that pepper. Here's Mama's bread. Do you need more than one roll?"

As Chrissy drank thirstily, then took a bite of bread, her brother walked up and withdrew three folded pieces of paper from his coat pocket. "Here, you'll need these. I wasn't sure which one was right, so I brought 'em all. As soon as Chrissy catches her breath, we can get started. Everyone is waiting inside."

The marriage licenses. Cole gazed at his teary-eyed bride and chuckled. "Aren't you just full of surprises, my Lady Bug."

"Will you marry me, Cole Morgan?" she croaked.

He grinned and cocked an eyebrow. Enjoying the moment, he twisted his lips into a thoughtful frown, and scratched behind his ear. "Hmm . . ." he said finally when he spied impatience glowing through the tears in her eyes. "Will I marry you? Well, Christina, does the Queen of the Chili Queens put hot peppers in her Texas Red?"

Yes was the obvious answer.

The bloom of her brilliant smile made him ache to hold her. Taking her hand, he yanked her against him and took her mouth in a deep, thorough kiss.

It took a minute for his lips to start burning, but when he began to wonder if they'd actually caught fire, he released her and grabbed the water from Michael. He emptied the pitcher in a series of gulps while Christina laughed in a raspy voice. "What's the matter, Morgan? My kiss too hot for you?"

He took her arm, and led her up the steps toward

the church's front doors. There, he paused, and waited for the others to enter the sanctuary and take their seats. When he and Christina were alone, he finally answered her question. "Honey, let's just say I hope it's a very short service because I can't wait to get going on the honeymoon. You not only scorched my mouth with that kiss . . ."—he glanced meaningfully down at his pants—". . . you put a jalapeño in my pocket, too."

Mischief kindled in her eyes as she stood on her tiptoes and pressed a kiss against his cheek. "Don't worry, Morgan. If it gets too hot, I'll blow on it."

Available from

GERALYN DAWSON

Simmer All Night

The Kissing Stars

The Bad Luck Wedding Cake

The Wedding Ransom

The Wedding Raffle

PUBLISHED BY

SONNET BOOKS

Return to
a time of romance...

**SONNET
BOOKS**

*Where today's
hottest romance authors
bring you vibrant
and vivid love stories
with a dash of history.*

2353

Visit the
Simon & Schuster Web site:

www.SimonSays.com

and sign up for our
romance e-mail updates!

Keep up on the latest new releases,
author appearances, news,
chats, special offers, and more!
We'll deliver the information right
to your inbox — if it's new,
you'll know about it.

SIMON & SCHUSTER
A VIACOM COMPANY
www.SimonSays.com

POCKET BOOKS

SONNET
BOOKS

**SONNET BOOKS
PROUDLY PRESENTS**

Sizzle All Day
Geralyn Dawson

**Coming soon in paperback
from Sonnet Books**

**The following is a preview of
Sizzle All Day. . . .**

Scottish Highlands,
1884

Jake Delaney was a man on the run.

From his mother.

"It's damned embarrassing," he told the small dog sharing the saddle with him. "I'm thirty-four years old. I'm my own man. I've driven cattle from San Antonio to Wichita. I've fought a gun battle with stage robbers and won a knife fight with a murderer. I truly believed I had my share of sand."

The dog snorted.

So did Jake. Sand, hell. He'd taken one look at that matchmaking light in his mother's eyes and run for the hills. The hills of Scotland, that is.

The dog gazed up at him with liquid brown eyes, her long ears flopping in the cadence of the horse's gait. She'd been a good, if unexpected, companion on this trip north. Jake liked females who listened well and didn't wear out a man's ears with talk of hairstyles and fabrics and fashion.

That's all he'd been hearing of late. He'd spent the past few months escorting his mother around London. Elizabeth Delaney had returned to England after more than twenty years in Texas and thrown herself into the welcoming arms of blue-blood society. It was Jake's bad luck that the marriage of her daughter to a longtime family friend had whetted Lady Elizabeth's appetite for family weddings. No sooner had Chrissy and Cole Morgan left on their honeymoon than Elizabeth turned her speculative gaze on him.

"I'll be damned if I'll marry one of those simpering English misses," he told the dachshund he'd christened Scooter. "If I did want a wife—which I don't—I'd want a woman with some pepper in her. I like heat in my women."

And in the weather, too, he silently added as the dog whined and burrowed her way inside his coat. Springtime was too damned cold in these mountains. Think of how miserable he'd feel had he made the trip during the winter months like his mother had first suggested.

Jake might have been born in Britain, but he was South Texas bred. He thrived in the sizzling heat of a Texas summer, and he wasn't cut out for cold. He was more than ready to reach his destination, which, according to the map drawn on the advertising flier he carried in his coat pocket, should be just up ahead.

Five minutes later, his horse rounded a bend, and

Jake spied the end of his current trail. "Rowanclere Castle," he murmured, reining his mount to a halt so he could study the place.

He scratched Scooter behind the ears as he blew a soundless whistle of appreciation at the sight of a fairy tale come to life. Turrets and towers and thick walls of gray stone rose high above the deep blue waters of a small lake—or loch, to use the vernacular. Colorful flags fluttered from poles atop each of the four semicircular turrets of the small rectangular keep.

Jake had visited larger castles since arriving in Britain, but certainly this was the most beautiful. Rowanclere possessed an air of welcome, whereas most of the others he'd seen stood in stark relief as forbidding hunks of stone and mortar.

The dog nuzzled her way through the placket of his shirt and pressed a cold, wet nose against his stomach. When he felt a drop of drool slide across his belly, he lifted her up and glared into her eyes. "You are a forward bitch, aren't you?"

She licked his face in response, and he grinned. Then, tucking Scooter safely into his arms, he gave his horse a kick and headed for the castle on the hill.

Gillian Ross stood at a turret window and watched the horseman approach. The timing was perfect. She was dressed and ready. "I canna do this," she said with a groan.

"Certainly you can," replied Flora Ross Dunbar.

She studied her twin sister's face for a long minute before she frowned, licked her thumb, then reached out and smudged the black actor's paint that covered Gillian's face from the line of golden blond hair to the base of her neck. "Wasn't it your idea, after all?"

"Yes, but . . . quit spitting on me," Gillian replied, pulling away from her sister. "I didn't intend to take it quite this far. I don't want to be cruel, Flora. What if I truly frighten someone?"

Her sister scoffed. "Have you forgotten what you told me when you proposed this plan? Our guests are coming to Rowanclere in order to look for ghosts. They won't be frightened to find one. They'll be thrilled."

Gillian sighed heavily as she brushed a streak of dirt off the filmy white gown she wore. "Aye, you are right."

"Of course I am right. I'm always right."

Gillian shot her twin a droll look, then pointedly focused on Flora's hugely pregnant belly. "Of course. That is why you await the delivery of your child here at Rowanclere, rather than at home with your husband."

"My child will be born at Craighellachie Manor. I've two months yet, Gilly." Shrugging, Flora added, "You need me right now."

Her attention returned to the approaching visitor, Gillian said glumly, "Robert will kill us both for this."

"He might." An impish grin flashed across Flora's face as she quipped, "then you could haunt Rowanclere in truth."

"Just don't let me die with this paint on my face, please? It itches."

"I promise." Flora continued to smile as she re-arranged a long golden curl of the wig glued to the top of a mannequin's head that sat on a nearby table along with the other accoutrements of the plan. "Gilly, believe me when I tell you Robert won't object to my coming to Rowanclere while he was away. Not too much, anyway. He loves you, too. He knows that without you, he and I wouldn't have . . ." She patted her protruding belly. ". . . *him* to look forward to."

"Her," Gillian said automatically. She and Flora had a wager on the baby's gender, which Gillian felt certain she would win. Ever since she'd rescued the baby's mother from a certain and nasty fall down the stairs at Craigellachie Manor, she'd sensed an extra-special closeness with the child. Gillian couldn't wait to be an aunt to her niece. These days her arms ached to hold a baby, and since her own prospects of marriage appeared dismal, she'd have to settle for loving her twin's little girl. For now, anyway. "At least until my prince comes."

"What was that?"

"Nothing. Hadn't you best hurry downstairs?"

Flora glanced out the window. "Yes. And you'd best get in position. Our guest is almost to the gate.

What is his name again? This man who takes spirit photographs?"

"Delaney. Jake Delaney." Gillian rubbed her itchy nose, careful not to disturb the paint, then sighed once more. The photographer was to be the test. If she could fool him, she might stand a chance of deceiving the other members of the College of Psychic Studies scheduled to arrive from London later this month. Following the path of her sister's gaze, she again voiced the question that had been running through her mind since her father's death three months ago. "I wish I could have thought of another way to save Rowanclere."

On her way out the door, Flora stopped and looked back at Gillian. "You mean like marrying that disgusting Earl of Tain for money? Pardon me, sister, but I think turning Rowanclere into a tourist hotel is a much better option."

"Yes, if I hadn't opened my big mouth, that is."

Flora wrinkled her nose. "They caught you off-guard with all their questions."

"That they did." Six weeks ago, during Gillian's visit to London to solicit business for the new venture, she'd had a conversation with members of a hunt club about the amenities Rowanclere offered. After answering numerous questions about local fishing, hunting, and golf, she'd been surprised when the Earl of Harrington had asked an unexpected question.

The memory of her answer was burned into her

brain. *Is Rowanclere haunted? Why yes, yes it is. We have two ghosts, in fact.*

"I opened my mouth to say no, Flora. I promise I did. I don't know what came over me to tell such a lie."

"It's all that reading you've been doing," her sister replied, motioning toward Gillian's bedside table. "*Spiritual Magazine*."

"That is for research purposes. I sent for it after the earl arranged to have his conference at Rowanclere."

"I am glad to hear that. You know Uncle Angus is worried these Spiritualists will try to convert you to their cause."

"If it pays enough I'll consider it," Gillian said grimly. "I can pretend to be a clairvoyant or a medium easier than a ghost. We'll see how the conference goes. Perhaps that will be an easier way to save our home from the tax man."

It wasn't an entirely far-fetched idea. The Spiritualist movement had swept through society from America to Europe. Seances were the rage in London these days. Clairvoyants provided entertainment at parties, and spirit photographers held showings in galleries. It had been Gillian's bad luck that interest in the supernatural had even invaded the membership of the St. Giles Hunt Club.

The Earl of Harrington had listened politely to her description of game in Rowanclere's forests, but it was Gillian's positive response to his question about hauntings that truly captured his interest.

Thus, one week following her return from London, Gillian had received bookings for every guest room in the castle. The College of Psychic Studies, of which the earl was a member, wished to hold its annual conference at Rowanclere.

Gillian couldn't afford to refuse them. With the Earl of Harrington, Viscount Randolph, and the Marquess of Bothridge listed as guests, she knew positive reports upon their return to London would ensure a steady stream of visitors throughout the summer months. She desperately needed cash in the coffers to pay the taxes due in the fall.

Gillian groaned, then met her sister's gaze. "Go show our guest to his room, Flora." She lifted the black kerchief from the table beside the mannequin head and tied it around her head, concealing her golden curls. Picking up the voice trumpet, she said, "Let's hope Mr. Jake Delaney is ready to meet the Headless White Lady of Rowanclere."

Jake carried Scooter in one arm, his saddlebags over his shoulder, and a small satchel in the other hand as he followed his beautiful landlady up the twisting staircase to his tower bedroom. As Mrs. Dunbar turned with the spiral, he warily eyed the bulge beneath her gown and said, "I'm sure I can find my way myself, ma'am. No need for you to make this climb in your condition."

She flashed him an amused smile. "Worried, sir?"

"Terrified, ma'am."

She laughed. "Ah, Mr. Delaney, you remind me of my husband. Don't fash yourself. I'm fit as can be, and the baby will not be arriving for months yet. Now, tell me what is wrong with the poor wee pup."

"She hurt her back and can't move her hindquarters," Jake replied as Mrs. Dunbar paused outside an arched wooden door. "Her owner was a friend I made in London, and she couldn't bear to put her pet down so she asked me see to it. When the moment arrived, those big brown eyes got to me and I couldn't do it. But Scooter here has adjusted to her problem, so I decided to keep her."

"Aren't you the kind one?"

"No, I wouldn't say that. I'm a . . ." Jake's voice trailed off as the door swung open to reveal a view through the window opposite the door spectacular enough to rival his landlady's face. "Well, twirl my spurs if that isn't the prettiest sight I've seen since leaving Texas."

"Texas?" Mrs. Dunbar repeated. "I wondered at the accent in your speech. I thought you were from London, Mr. Delaney."

"London by way of San Antonio," he said, striding into the guest room.

Thankfully, she dropped the subject and after pointing out the features of the well-appointed room, departed.

Jake's first action was to set about building a fire, and soon he had a nice-sized flame crackling in the fireplace. "I don't know about you, but I'm cold clear through to the bone," he said to the dog as he warmed his hands. He'd have loved to take a hot bath, but settled for a change of clothes. To that end, he removed pants, a shirt, and clean underwear from his satchel and hung them near the fire to warm. Then, pulling a rocking chair close to the fireplace, he sat, tugged off his boots and socks, and stuck his feet toward the fire. Heat soaked into his skin and he groaned aloud. It felt so damned good. A few minutes later, greedy for more of that delicious warmth, he stood and shucked off the rest of his clothes, toasting his front side first.

From behind him, he heard Scooter start to whine. "What's the matter, girl? Come over here by the fire if you're cold, too."

Ordinarily, the dachshund would tug her way toward the sound of his voice, but this time Scooter ignored him. Curious and with his front side finally warm, Jake turned his back toward the heat as he peered through the deepening shadows toward the dog.

But found a ghost, instead.

A portion of the room's rock wall appeared to have dissolved, and in its place floated a filmy white figure. Jake's heart climbed into his throat as he stared at the apparition that held a lantern at its side in one hand and its . . . oh, God . . .

It held its head in the other.

"Sonofabitch!" Jake whispered, taking an inadvertent step backward.

At the same instant, the ghost let out a squeal. "Eeeek! Where are your clothes?"

Jake froze in shock at the very human voice, and a number of things happened at once. The fire hissed, then popped and spat out an ember that landed on his rear. He jumped as pain leached into his skin, then grabbed the nearby water pitcher, intending to cool the burn.

While Jake tended his posterior, Scooter darted forward and began nipping at the ghost. In addition to the dog's barks, Jake heard a tearing sound from the direction of the wall as he doused his left buttock.

Then the figure literally lost her head.

It rolled toward him, its long tresses twisting like a golden rope. The pitcher slipped from Jake's grip and shattered against the stone floor. Repulsion swept over him, even as he recognized the object as nothing more than a painted wooden model. When it rumbled to a halt at his feet, he stared at it in frozen surprise until a distinctly feminine gasp evoked his attention.

His gaze trailed the length of white cloth that now stretched from Scooter's teeth up to the prettiest set of plump, rosy-tipped breasts he'd seen this side of the Atlantic.

"Sonofabitch," he repeated, breathing hard. He took a step forward even as the lamp flickered off, the opening in the wall closed, and the figure disappeared.

Damn. That was no ghost, but a flesh-and-blood woman. *And fine flesh it was.*

Bending down, he lifted the head by the hair and held it out in front of him, studying the grotesquely painted face in the firelight. What sort of trick was this? What had she been trying to accomplish?

He stood there, naked, pulse finally beginning to slow as he stared at the object dangling from his hand. Then a voice seemed to come from the mouth, mere inches from his manhood.

"Finally," said the snickering ghost. "I finally get my first glimpse of glory."

Jake yelped and the head hit the floor with a thud.

Look for
SIZZLE ALL DAY
Wherever Books Are Sold

**Coming Soon in Paperback
from Sonnet Books**